Twilight

Twilight

Kim Pritekel

P.D. Publishing, Inc.
Clayton, North Carolina

ISBN-13: 978-1-933720-30-2
ISBN-10: 1-933720-30-1

9 8 7 6 5 4 3 2 1

Cover design by Stephanie Solomon-Lopez
Edited by: Kay Porter/Medora MacDougall

Published by:

P.D. Publishing, Inc.
P.O. Box 70
Clayton, NC 27528

http://www.pdpublishing.com

Dedication

For Bodhi.
May all your dreams come true, and never stop following your
passions, whatever they may be.

Prologue

The world was one big swirl, mixing with the cool breezy night. Christine stepped out of the rental car she had parked smack in the middle of the rickety old bridge. She had no idea that bridges like this even existed anymore. They certainly didn't in L.A.

The boards creaked under her booted feet, her unsteady body reeling as the chemicals raced through her bloodstream, slamming every nerve ending alive as they passed. Her vision blurred, and the rail she was heading for seemed to recede. She reached out a hand, trying to catch it and bring it back.

The brunette nearly fell as the rail hit her midsection, knocking her off balance. She giggled to herself, thinking of those warning signs on rear-view mirrors: *Warning: Objects may be closer than they appear.*

Grabbing onto the rail, she steadied herself, looking over it, down into the murky depths of the river. Which river? Hell, she couldn't remember. All she knew was it was some river in the podunk town she had found herself in.

Raising a leather-clad leg, Christine rested her boot against a rung of the railing, grunting slightly as she pushed with her thigh, her other boot finding the top of the railing. She cursed at the splinter that lodged in her hand as she grabbed the nearest support pole, the dangling light attached to it swinging back and forth as she disturbed it with her head.

"Fucker!" Christine slurred, bringing a hand to her head, then grabbing the pole with both hands as she began to lose her balance again.

Steadying herself, she once again looked down into the water, midnight black in the near moonless night. The swinging lantern cast eerie shadows on everything, shadows dancing across the wood planks of the bridge, shadows dancing across Christine's features.

She felt a sting behind her eyes and shook her head to try and get rid of it. She was also trying to shake the memories that were beginning to flood back, her high wearing off, the numbness wearing off. She was starting to be able to think, and she didn't want to think, feel, remember.

The crowd in front of her, huge and loud, demanding, wanting every part of her that they could get or could take. The band behind her, playing, exchanging glances with each other as Christine stood there, microphone between her hands, forehead resting against the silver head. She had missed her cue twice already, and she didn't care. She couldn't remember the words; her mind and focus had been stolen by the good hit she'd taken in her dressing room.

"What the fuck is the problem?" the lead guitarist, Joey, had asked, after he'd made a stroll up to her, playing the entire time.

The question snapped Christine out of her stupor for a moment. She grinned at him, telling him it was all good, and then turned back to her audience, not seeing any of them, not one single face.

A disaster. A total, fucking disaster. Christine felt the sting in her eyes worsen and then wetness on her cheek, chilled by the breeze.

Her eyes refocused on the water below, so inviting, so calming in its chaos. She felt the weightlessness as one boot left the security of the railing. She leaned further over, seeing her leg dangling above the churning river. Leaning further, further, further. She got another splinter in her palm as she let go, she realized. It was her last thought.

Frizzy synthetic red hair brushed across the ceiling of the Dodge Ram. A pale hand slammed against the steering wheel in time with the music on the radio, and a ridiculously pale face, streaked with color, bobbed to the beat of the gloved hand, flopping that frizzy red hair around like a huge bush.

"Yeah, sing it, Britney!" Willow sang out, her painted green eyes closing for just a moment before opening to squint with raucous laughter. She wasn't exceptionally keen on Britney Spear's attitudes or public persona, but the girl could sing.

Willow loved the buzz she got after doing her gigs on the side. All the energy from the little rascals at the birthday party seemed to flow into her, giving her a natural high like nothing else. Even her main job as a nurse on the children's ward didn't affect her the way the parties did.

She reached down to the volume knob and cranked the sucker, laughing at herself as she sang along, quite horribly, with the next song that came on. The loudness made it worse, because she had absolutely no idea what the words were.

Life was good for Willow Bowman as she drove out of the small town of Williamsburg, Oklahoma, a short distance from Oklahoma City, and headed toward her small ranch.

Her voice gave out finally, probably God's way of telling Willow to shut it, but she continued to bob her head and beat the steering wheel along with the music.

Heading around Dittman's Curve, she approached the bridge, named after some old guy who had done something or other for the town a hundred years ago. *What Dittman really needed to do was fix his bridge,* she thought.

As she neared the bridge, she noticed a car parked smack dab in the middle of it, lights off, looking abandoned.

"Shoot," she muttered. The one-lane bridge was the only way to get to the ranch. Eyes still on the bridge, Willow blindly reached across the console until she felt the passenger seat, then her phone.

Movement caught Willow's eye, and she looked to the rail of the bridge.

"Oh my God!" Pulling the truck to a stop, she dropped the phone, leaving the engine running and door swinging, and ran to the rail. There was a huge splash in the dark depths. Without another thought, Willow climbed up where she had seen the dark figure before it had jumped and followed suit.

The water was freezing, chilling every part of her, stabbing at her like thousands of tiny knives. It took her a moment to get her bearings, then she began to thrash around in the near complete darkness, using her hands to feel around frantically.

It was cold, but Christine had figured it would be. She allowed the cold to embrace her, swallow her. She was angry for a moment as her body's natural survival instincts made her hold her breath, her body far more interested in surviving than her heart.

As she sank further into the dark water, her brain was still hazed enough to feel it as a comforting cocoon, engulfing her body, vanquishing the demons that lurked above the surface of the water.

She felt the numbness begin to overcome her again, that lack of feeling or even ability to feel, inside or out. She welcomed it, prayed for it, *wanted* it.

Something grabbed her wrist, bringing her out of her reverie. She began to thrash, horrid images swarming her mind, scenes from a child's nightmare. She tried to escape the demon that had followed her into the depths, but it refused to let go.

She took in a lungful of water as she tried to scream, then began to thrash anew as she tried to expel it, only to take in more water.

Floating, floating, blackness, sinking, sinking...

Willow broke the surface, synthetic hair now covering one eye, and dragged her find out of the water and to the banks of the river. It was heavy, but Willow was determined. The body was that of a woman, she saw, one whose own face was half covered by long, dark hair. Not bothering to move it away, Willow jutted the woman's jaw back, plugging her nose, and leaned down to blow hot, life-giving air into the open, chilled lips.

Sitting back up, she pressed on the woman's tank-top clad torso, feeling the woman's chances of survival speeding away with each second.

"Come on," she panted as she went back to giving air. After several more tries, Willow threw herself back, startled at the feel of water hitting her lips. She looked down, relief filling her as the woman coughed, the movement racking her entire body and throwing her halfway to her side as she spewed a stream of water to the sand beneath her, following it with more coughing and spasms.

Willow sat back on her heels, waiting, watching, in deep concern. The woman calmed after a few moments, still coughing, but alive. She slowly rolled onto her back, head turning, then she jumped violently.

"Fuck!" Christine exclaimed, as she saw a monster sitting next to her — a mass of smashed red hair covered part of the face, which was streaked with white, black and blue. A slash of red extended from the lips down the chin and splotched the neck.

"Shh, it's okay," Willow said, realizing she must look a sight. She yanked off the wig to reveal short, wet blonde hair, turned a strange gray-green in the night. "Are you okay?" she asked, her voice soft as she put a hand to the woman's arm.

Christine calmed again, finding it funny that she'd been dragged out of the river by a clown. She hated clowns. As a kid they used to creep her out. She nodded, trying to sit up, but the hand that had been on her arm moved to her shoulder.

"Just lie there. Can you breathe?" the woman asked, and Christine nodded, taking several deep breaths just to make sure. "Okay. Stay here." The clown jumped up and ran, though Christine couldn't work out how she was able to do so, given the massive red shoes she had on.

They must have made great flippers to swim in. This thought sent a giggle through Christine's still fuzzy brain. Within moments she heard rocks crunching under foot and the low, soft voice of her savior, coming back, having a one-sided conversation.

"Okay. Thanks, John. We'll be here." Willow flipped her phone shut and knelt down next to the woman again. She lay there, staring up at the sky, then closed her eyes, resting an arm across them. Sighing, Willow couldn't stop the questions from parading across her mind. Why had the woman done this? Was it suicide or an accident? Who was she? From the woman's dress, a black tank top with black leather pants and heavy boots, she doubted she was from the area. Also, the car had a Hertz sticker on the back window.

She sat next to the woman, waiting for the ambulance to arrive. It wouldn't take long for the ambulance to get there; the hub wasn't far. But the drive to the hospital in Oklahoma City, that would take much longer. She began to shiver, the chill night breeze seeping into the completely saturated material of her once baggy clown suit, which now clung to her like a second skin.

"Do you have a name, honey?" she asked quietly, reaching out to brush some of the hair from the woman's face.

"It doesn't matter." The arm came down, and blue eyes looked into Willow's briefly before turning away. Finally the woman sighed. "Christine," she said quietly.

"Nice to meet you, Christine, though I'm sorry it has to be under these kinds of circumstances." Christine could see worry in the other woman's eyes, and that surprised her. They were total strangers to each other; why should she care? Shit, those in Christine's life who knew her better than anyone on the planet didn't care about her or show the kind of concern this woman did.

"Yeah. And you, Bozo?"

Willow stared at her for a moment, about to protest when she remembered her current get-up. She chuckled lightly. "Willow Bowman."

Christine nodded in acknowledgment, then turned to look back up into the heavens as the sound of a siren not far away broke the quiet of the night.

The lights of Mercy Medical's ER nearly blinded Willow as she parked her truck and hurried in after Toby and Allen, the two EMTs.

The sound of chaotic activity surrounded her as she pushed through the ER doors, hurrying alongside the gurney on which Christine had been strapped down.

"Why am I here?" Christine asked, her head lolling from side to side, her face pale with heavy, dark shadows beneath her closed eyes.

"Just to make sure everything checks out okay," Willow said, holding the woman's hand.

"I don't need to be here," she muttered, then began to cough violently, bringing up more water. She had had similar fits the entire way in the ambulance. As doctors and ER nurses emerged onto the scene, Willow knew it was her cue to back off; Christine was no longer her patient.

She grabbed a cup of coffee and headed out into the waiting room, wanting to get out of the way. She told one of the nurses to notify her the moment they were done with Christine.

"Hey, girl, what are you doing here?" Rachel Smith asked, lightly touching Willow's arm as she sat in one of the black, plastic chairs against a wall.

"Hey," she smiled, then sighed. "Guess I decided to go fishing at," she looked at her watch, noting that the hands weren't moving and a very menacing bubble was floating around the face. "Shoot," she turned to her friend, "some late hour." She leaned against the wall behind her, exhaustion finally taking root.

"What? What happened?" Rachel sat in the next chair, hands clasped between her spread knees.

"Oh, you wouldn't believe it." Willow opened her mouth to speak, then she noticed two men walking through the automatic doors of the lobby. One wore a smart black suit and had a large, black leather satchel in his hand. The other was also dressed in finery, though more understated — a white button-up shirt, its sleeves rolled to the mid-forearm, tucked into expensive-looking gray slacks. He wore more rings on one hand than Willow even owned. His slicked-back salt and pepper hair gleamed as brightly as they did.

The men immediately began to look around; one spotted Rachel in her scrubs. Walking over to her, the man with graying hair, yet young skin, smiled.

"Excuse me, nurse, but I need to find someone." He looked from one to the other of the women, frowning slightly when he saw the clown makeup smeared over Willow's face. The expression made her extremely self-conscious. In all the hubbub, she had forgotten completely about her appearance.

"Who?" Rachel asked, standing.

"Uh," the man turned to the suit behind him, who handed him a piece of paper. "Willow Bowman? We were told by one of your fine physicians she was here," the man said. "I understand she's a nurse at this hospital?"

"I'm Willow Bowman," Willow said, also standing. The man looked at her, doubt evident in his eyes. "It's a long story," she said softly. "What can I do for you, mister?"

"Robert Knowles." He extended a hand, which she took, after removing her ruined white glove. "I need to speak with you concerning tonight's events. I assume it's why you look like a drowned rat?" His smile was tight-lipped, and Willow wasn't so sure she liked this guy.

"Ah, yeah." She looked down at herself, then back up at him. He held out a white handkerchief to her.

He turned back to Rachel. "Is there somewhere we can speak with Ms. Bowman?"

"Sure. Follow me to the conference room." Rachel looked at her friend, who only shrugged.

"Ms. Bowman will join us once she's cleaned up a bit," Knowles said. Yeah, Willow didn't like him.

She splashed water all along the white sink, rinsing off the last vestiges of makeup, then looked at herself in the mirror. Her face was clean, though there wasn't much she could do about her attire. She had unbuttoned the coverall-type clown suit, letting the top hang down, arms flapping around her legs. She was glad she'd worn a tank top underneath it.

Pushing open the doors of the conference room, Willow saw the two men, the suit standing over a laptop, a tiny printer buzzing away next to it, spitting out a sheet of paper. Robert Knowles was sitting at the head of the table, his fingers steepled under his chin, an expensive gold watch glittering against a tanned wrist, and a large, gold pinky ring on his right hand.

"Ah, Ms. Bowman. Please, have a seat." He indicated the chair to his left, and Willow took it, glancing at the suit across the table from her, who had yet to speak.

"What's going on?" she asked, looking back to Knowles, who sighed and sat forward in his chair.

"Have you spoken with anyone about what happened tonight? Other than emergency personnel, of course."

"No. Listen, Mr. Knowles..."

"*Ms.* Bowman," he interrupted, stunning Willow into silence. She started as something was put before her by the suit. Looking at it, she realized it was a check. Her eyes flew up to meet his hard gaze.

"This is a check for twenty-five thousand dollars," she said, her voice breathless and even more confused.

"And all yours if," he held up a well-manicured finger, "you do one simple thing for us."

"Us? What, you and the suit?" she thumbed at the other man who was busy typing on the laptop. Robert Knowles chuckled, making Willow's skin crawl.

"No. Jack is simply Ms. Gray's attorney. What you'll be doing will be for her, me, and Ms. Gray's reputation."

Willow stared at him, utterly baffled for a moment, his words flowing through her head, trying to make sense of what he was telling her. Ms. Gray, Christine.

"Holy shit!" Her eyes widened, and her hand flew to her mouth. The men exchanged a glance, then Robert looked at her again. "I pulled Christine Gray out of Chandler River?" she breathed. He nodded. "Christine Gray as in won six Grammys last year?" He nodded once more.

"Perhaps now you see just how important it is that we get your full cooperation with this." The paper from the printer was slid in front of her. She looked down at it, realizing it looked like a contract of sorts.

"What is this?"

"It's your promise that you'll keep what happened tonight to yourself," Robert said simply. She picked it up and began to scan over it.

"So," Willow drawled, her eyes still sweeping over the document, "you're saying I get the money if I keep my trap shut?"

"Ms. Bowman, Christine has a great many fans who are young girls, girls in their teens, early twenties. These fans look up to her, emulate her. In her music they find inspiration for their own lives, as well as words they can relate to. These girls would be devastated to find out their heroine, their role model, has fallen from grace."

Willow looked up at the man, the corner of her mouth quirking at his spew of crap. "You play a good game, Mr. Knowles," she chuckled. His brows drew together in irritation.

"Then let me put it to you this way. If this got out, Christine would be finished. Better?" He sighed, flopping back in the chair, his hand going to his forehead. "Cleaning up this mess is going to cost her enough as it is."

"How did you know where to find her?" Willow asked, dying of curiosity. It was a hoot seeing these "citified" boys in the boonies. Knowles glanced up at her.

"Christine's tour manager knew the circumstances under which Ms. Gray left tonight. He was concerned." The man wiped at a smudge on the polished table with a fingertip. "Luckily there aren't all that many hospitals in this area."

Willow turned back to the contract under her hand, then glanced over at the check. Instantly, as if the lawyer were reading her thoughts, a gold pen appeared before her. She picked it up, tapping it against her chin as she read over the document.

"I'll sign your contract here, Mr. Knowles, but I don't want your money."

"The check stays here, Ms. Bowman. Whether you chose to cash it or not is entirely up to you." She nodded, scribbling her signature across the dotted line.

"This is a legal document, Ms. Bowman," the lawyer said, taking the pen and contract from her before the ink had a chance to dry. "If you were to breach it, Christine Gray can and will take legal action against you. Do you understand this?"

Willow nodded, sighing warily. "Yes."

"Thank you," Robert Knowles said, standing. "Good evening to you." With amazing efficiency, the attorney packed up the laptop and printer, and both men were on their way.

Willow glanced at the check, taking it in her fingers. "Holy crap," she whispered. "I just saved the life of the woman who won the Grammy for best female vocalist last year."

Chapter 1

After her meeting with Robert Knowles, Willow went out to her truck, tucking the check into the glove compartment, not wanting to chance it getting ruined in her saturated pockets.

Shivering and soul-tired, as the nurses called it when one of them had been drastically affected by something at work, she then headed to the female employees' locker room. Glad to find a pair of scrubs in her locker that were not too smelly, she hurried into the shower room, stripping out of her pasted-on clothing and stepping under the warm, calming spray.

She felt her skin thawing, but her heart was still like ice. She kept seeing Christine's face as she lay there on the river bank, so vulnerable, death hovering in the air.

Willow could not reconcile in her own mind the face of the woman she had rescued that night with the woman she had seen on television and on CDs and magazine covers. What had caused someone like that, who had the world at her feet and money and fame in abundance, to do something so drastic?

She wondered if the toxicology reports would tell them anything. The look in the woman's eyes had been dazed and fuzzy and the pupils very dilated, which the near-drowning could only partially explain. Willow had a hunch there was more to it.

She stepped out of the small stall, pushing the curtain aside. Grabbing a towel, she quickly dried herself and slipped into the scrubs. She had no shoes and eyed the big red ones.

Opting to not look like Patch Adams, she stuck some surgical booties on her feet and headed out to get some information.

The air in the ER was cool and sterilized, as it was in every ER that Willow had been or worked in. She saw Dr. Samms making some notes on a chart and hurried over to him.

"How is she, Brad?"

The large man looked down at Willow, seeing the worry in her beautiful green eyes. *If only she wasn't married.* He closed the chart, tucking it into a plastic chart box mounted on the wall above the nurses' station.

"She's okay. Nothing major sustained, though her bloodstream was hosting one hell of a party." He sighed, crossing his muscular arms over his broad chest. He and Willow often worked out together in the hospital gym. It was a great way to stay in shape and ease the tensions of their respective jobs.

Willow nodded, biting her lip. "I was afraid of that. Can I see her?"

"Sure. She's in Three resting."

"Thanks, bud." Squeezing his bicep, she hurried down the hall past the other cubicles, some with closed curtains, some empty and ready to be used. At Three, the curtain was pulled and the beeping of machinery behind it could be heard.

Gently pushing the curtain aside, she slipped around it, looking into the dim space. The lights above Christine's gurney had been turned off, only a circle of light breaching the top of the curtain. Red, green, and blue lights shone in the dimness.

Willow's eyes quickly adjusted, and she focused on the form of the woman tucked under a thin, white blanket, arms out, a hospital band wrapped around one wrist, an IV taped to the back of her hand.

Willow looked down at the closed eyes, long, dark lashes, and face at peace in slumber. She studied the face, with its high, sharp cheekbones and prominent jaw. The skin was very pale, and blue veins were visible beneath the surface.

Christine's hair looked dark black against the paleness of her skin and the white bedding beneath her. A few wisps rested against her face. Gently, Willow tucked the strands behind an ear.

Reaching behind her, she found the chair she knew was there and scooted it forward until she was able to sit. Taking Christine's hand in her own, she felt warm skin, relieved beyond belief not to find it as cold and stiff as it had been at the river.

Sighing softly, Willow lowered her head, her exhaustion making her eyes burn and feel heavy.

Christine could sense someone was with her. As the haze lessened, she realized that someone was holding her hand. Eyes slowly fluttering open, she turned her pounding head, closing her eyes for a moment before opening them to focus on the figure slouched over in sleep in a chair next to her bed.

Short blonde hair, light blue scrubs. Who was this? A nurse from the ER? A doctor, maybe? Her gaze fell to their joined hands, the hand in hers tanned against her own pale skin, the nails trimmed neatly, well taken care of. A small hand, no, petite. Looked like all of her was petite — narrow shoulders and fine features.

The face.

Christine concentrated on the face, much of it hidden by the angle at which the woman slouched. Dark blonde brows, a slight crease between the closed eyes. The woman looked as though even in slumber she was worrying about something.

A very gentle face, lips lightly brushing against one another, the blonde hair slightly covering the tops of her small ears.

As Christine drifted off to sleep again, she wondered who her visitor was.

Willow woke with a start, her eyes popping open to see Rachel smiling down at her. Easing into reality, she sat up, looking around. Her gaze moved to the woman in the bed, and she realized that their hands were still linked. She was, however, surprised to see that the position of their hands had changed and that Christine's fingers now curled around her own.

Rachel said nothing, turning away to give her friend some privacy. She knew how compassionate Willow was, all too often taking the pain and fear of her patients onto her own shoulders. It always worried Rachel. Willow was one of the best nurses at Mercy, and she didn't want to see her burn out. Their jobs could be incredibly stressful.

Willow gently pulled her hand free of Christine's, laying the larger hand on the bed. Pulling the sheet up to tuck in her patient, Willow turned to Rachel, nodding toward the partially open curtain.

Once out of the cubicle, she led her friend away so they could talk without disturbing Christine.

"You should go home, Willow. It's late, and Kevin's going to be worried."

"Oh, crap." Willow ran a hand through her hair, her eyes even more heavy than before. "I need to get home. Call me if anything changes, okay?" she asked her friend, who nodded and patted her shoulder.

"I will. Now get to bed."

The drive home was long. As Willow drove across the Dittman Bridge, a shiver passed through her and her eyes were drawn to the spot where Christine had jumped. A wave of sadness washed over her.

Taking several deep breaths, she forced her eyes straight ahead as she drove the last ten miles to her ranch.

"Mmm, must have been some party." Kevin rolled over still half asleep, pulling his wife against his naked body.

"Had an emergency at the hospital," Willow murmured, settling her tired body against the soft mattress.

"Everything okay?" Willow's husband sounded a bit more awake, though his eyes were still closed.

"Mm hmm. Talk tomorrow," she slurred, already asleep. It had been a long day.

The day outside was gray, the rain having stopped only an hour earlier. Christine gazed out, noting that the sky didn't look quite as pregnant as it had earlier.

She brought her knees up in the chair, pressing them against her chest and wrapping her arms around them. As she rested her chin on her knees, she sighed deeply. She felt strange, somehow changed beyond recognition from the person she had been this time the day before.

A soul-altering choice, said the lady from the psych ward, who had administered a mental evaluation that morning. Christine guessed they wanted to see if she was crazy or just really fucked up. She voted for both. She craved a cigarette like nothing else.

So — she'd finally tried it, finally gone over the edge that she had always been able to step back from before. Christine shivered, realizing how close she'd come to succeeding in ending it all. She also realized how close she was to not caring.

She flinched slightly at the sound of the key in the door to her room, but she didn't turn around. Her gaze was still fixed on the gray world outside her window, glass with little metal crisscross bars embedded into it.

There was quiet murmuring just outside the room, then footfalls, followed by the heavy sound of her door being closed and locked.

"Hello, Christine."

"Bob."

Her manager was silent as he took a seat on the bed behind her chair. The room was sparsely furnished. Simple bed, no rails, no bars, and bolted down, the chair she sat in. A bathroom off to the side with a pedestal sink and toilet. Everything nice and snug, nothing she could harm herself with.

"Quite a mess you've gotten yourself into here," he said, his voice quiet, tired.

"So it would seem." She didn't look at him, in truth not wanting to see the disdain she knew she'd find in his face.

"Everything's been taken care of — hospital staff, doctors, ambulance drivers, the police, and the crazy little clown who fished you out." He snickered. "Apparently she's a nurse of some sort here."

He looked at his client, studying the back of her head, her dark hair hanging free. He knew it hung wildly around her face, giving her the feral look that her fans loved. It took some willpower not to reach out and touch it.

The silence grew heavy. Christine changed position slightly, letting one foot slip to the floor, still holding the other leg tightly.

"Why'd you do it?" he finally asked, breaking the silence with the effect of a sledgehammer through glass.

"I don't want to talk about it with you, Bob." Christine's voice was low, tacitly suggesting a change of topic. He didn't bite.

"Christine, I'm your friend."

"Friend?" She turned on him then, blue eyes blazing brilliantly, expensive white teeth bared. "No, I don't think so. I'm no friend to you. I'm your meal ticket. Always have been."

"Christine..."

"No!" she hissed. "If I meant anything to you, you never would have scheduled this tour. I told you I needed a break, that I was struggling. You knew." She turned back to the window, hugging herself as she walked over to it, jaw muscles clenching.

"But the album..."

"Fuck the album. What about me?" she almost whispered. "Not like what I thought or wanted has ever mattered. Should have fired your ass years ago."

"You'd be nothing without me and you know it," he spat. She looked at him over her shoulder.

"Maybe not. But I'd still have me." Turning back to the window, her shoulders falling, she said sourly, "Do something useful, Bob. Get me the fuck out of here."

Chapter 2

Willow turned up the volume on her stereo, continuing to fold laundry as she listened to the impassioned lyrics of "Swan Song," the latest release by Christine Gray. The song was much slower than most of Gray's intense, upbeat pieces. This had just a piano and a cello, in the background, and Christine's strong, but velvety voice.

With a pair of unfolded socks still in hand, Willow sat on the edge of the couch, closing her eyes as she listened to the words. Such sadness, emptiness. The song was filled with a longing for love and acceptance. It talked about how the world expected the singer's very soul, yet gave nothing real in return, as money, after all, couldn't buy happiness.

Willow was surprised to find that she had tears streaming down her cheeks, as images of the night more than a month earlier flashed before her mind's eye.

She had been a nurse in the children's ward for six years and had experienced babies dying in her arms, but nothing she had seen before had prepared her for the profound way she was affected by the soul-shattering sadness she had seen in that woman's blue eyes. Or the loneliness and desperation.

That was why she had stayed with Christine in the hospital for as long as she was allowed. She wanted her to know that she wasn't alone. That she had someone there who cared and would hold her hand through her pain.

Blue eyes closed, body swaying with the music she was creating, Christine ran knowing fingers across the piano keys.

She had written more music in the past two months than she had in two years. As the emotion passed through her, it filled her with a peace that only music could give her, the creation and execution of it giving her a sense of control that she didn't have anywhere else in her life.

During her stay at Promises, she'd started having the dreams again and remembering things she had thought long dead. Demons of her past, some self-invoked, others thrust upon her, haunted her and dogged her nocturnal steps.

Her therapist at the exclusive rehab center told her that now that her body and mind were free of the poisons she had been feeding them, the gates were wide open for her to face whatever had caused her to run in the first place.

And therein lay the problem; she didn't want to face the ghosts.

Christine stroked the ivories with a lover's caress. Music was the only thing she'd ever had that hadn't betrayed her or demanded something from her. Music gave itself willingly to her, allowing her to bring it forth into the world freely and willingly, never asking questions or wanting answers. It just *was*. Through music Christine could tell a story, share a part of herself without the vulnerability that talking about it would have.

No one knew the real her, and that was how she wanted it. She had always been so grateful that when Bob had found her in that shit-hole bar in Queens, she'd been doing her own stuff. She had been smart enough at four-teen to make sure he knew she would *only* do her own stuff and that any cov-ers he wanted her to do he could shove up his ass.

That was basically where her creative freedom had stopped.

If she were to play for Bob the piece she was playing now, he would laugh, then tell her to burn it; it had no place in *his* show.

Christine did not want to think about all of that. Those thoughts dogged her days as it was. Right now, all she wanted to do was lose herself in her music and forget about all the things that were wrong in her life. That was part of the problem. She'd started to allow everything to weigh so heavily upon her shoulders, not dealing with any of it, that it had started to overwhelm and then finally control her.

Her counselor said that was why she had turned to drugs. She wanted to numb the internal turmoil and pain.

Christine snorted softly at the truth of those words. Music was becoming her new drug. One addiction for another. Her creative juices had started to churn within her soul, demanding to be let out. She was happy to oblige.

Her fingers came to a halt as a knock sounded on the door to her suite.

"Come in!" she called, pushing the bench back and standing, carefully closing the lid of the baby grand as the door opened, then swiftly closed. "Good afternoon, Margaret."

"Hello, Christine. Were you practicing?" Margaret asked, arranging her bulk on the couch that faced its twin, where Christine seated herself.

"Composing, actually." Christine ran her arm along the length of the back of the couch, her head slightly tilted as she studied the woman sitting across from her.

Margaret Olson looked at the white Baldwin, then to her patient. "I see no music." Christine tapped her temple.

"All up here." She smiled.

"Ah. If only I had one-tenth of your talent," Margaret said with a sigh. Christine chuckled. "Alright." Getting down to business, the older woman opened a manila folder, searching through some papers as she spoke. "Last time you talked about dreams that were coming back." She glanced up at Christine, then gazed back down at her notes from their previous session. "Have you had any more since last week?"

Christine blew out a breath, glancing out the french doors, which over-looked the beautifully manicured grounds of the exclusive rehab center. "Yes."

"When was this?" Margaret clicked her pen, which was poised over a clean sheet of legal pad paper.

"Sunday night," Christine said, her voice quiet, almost fearful. The coun-selor waited for her patient to continue, as she had learned she would in time. Her *own* time. As Christine began to speak, her voice remained quiet, almost haunted. "The alley again."

"Tell me about that alley, Christine."

It was dark, the best time to be up and about. That's when it was easiest to score a little extra money. She hated to do it, but if she had learned anything from those bastards who fucked and gave birth to her, it was that everyone did what they had to do.

With a sigh, Christine headed down the dark streets of Queens, New York. It amazed her what a shit place it was considering it was named after royalty or some such shit. Whatever. Well, royal pain in the ass, maybe. Speaking of which, hers sure hurt.

Guy from the night before... What the fuck had she been thinking, letting him shove his dick up there? Jesus, and people get off on that shit? Oh well. He'd given Christine dinner for the next week from that. Backdoor men, that's what Adam called those guys.

She really needed to get a gig and soon. This street shit was for the birds. Damn, it was cold. She wrapped her arms around herself, then quickly dropped them. Dude needed to see what he was buying.

The streets were slow, a few cars passing now and then, and she was beginning to get impatient. The boots she wore, fake leather and extremely shiny, reached to her knees, thighs bare to just below her ass, where the mini she wore ended. God, she hated skirts. Her legs felt like they were about to get frostbite. Luckily this piece-of-shit outfit came with a little jacket. Her tits may have been cold, nipples like rocks, but her arms were relatively warm.

Ohhhh, a car! Dark in color, its headlights nearly blinded Christine as it pulled to the curb, squeaking to a stop next to her. The window rolled down with a mechanized buzz.

Walking over to the small sedan, she leaned down, making sure plenty of her size Ds could be seen in the low-cut shirt.

"Hey, sugar." Looking in, she saw a man, big surprise. His hair was short, kind of choppy, like his barber had gone a little nuts with the scissors. The thing that really caught her eye was his left cheek, all pockmarked. It kind of reminded her of that actor guy from that movie, Stand and Deliver.

"How much, sweetheart?" he asked, his voice surprisingly high-pitched.

"Well, that's all up to you. What's on your mind?" Christine grinned, cocking an eyebrow. God, he made her skin crawl.

"Stand back a little, honey, so I can get a look at you," he said, leaning slightly over the passenger seat. Standing upright, she held her arms out, turning in a small circle. She turned back to face the car, hand on her hip. His face was buried in shadow, but she thought she could hear a small moan coming from the car. It took everything in her to not vomit on his front tire. "Get in," he said, his voice taking on an unmistakably aroused tone.

Stepping to the car again, Christine noticed the tenting action going on in his trousers. Rolling her eyes, she took a deep breath, putting her hand on the cool metal of the handle.

"Christine!"

She jumped, startled almost out of her skin, and glared at her friend, Adam, telling him with her eyes that he better have a very good fucking reason for interrupting.

Adam reached Christine, grabbing her hand and yanking her away.

"What the fuck are you doing?" she hissed.

"I don't trust this, Chris," he whispered, keeping an eye on the guy Christine had turned her back on. "This car looks like the one that Chantal drove off in when she disappeared." His dark eyes met hers, pleading. Christine sighed, not happy. Not that she was looking forward to her time spent with tent boy, but she needed the damn money. Even so, she knew her best friend would never steer her wrong.

"Fine." Turning back to the guy who had to be blue ballin' by now, Christine grinned sexily. "Sorry, but there's been a change in plans."

To her shock, he nearly drove over her foot, as he slammed the car in gear and screeched into the night.

"I'm so sorry, Chris, but I just had a really bad feeling about that guy," Adam said, his hand resting on her shoulder. Shrugging it off, she turned and started walking away. "Chris! Come on." She could hear him running up behind her, but being the stubborn ass that she was she didn't stop. All she could think about was that she had been going to use the money to add to her savings for a guitar.

It wasn't two days later when Christine was back on the street and a familiar silver car pulled up to the curb. This time, though, it was the light of day, and she was wearing her one pair of jeans. Man, it felt so good not to have her ass or tits hanging out.

"Hey, kid," a deep voice called out as the car drove slowly along with Christine's steps. She looked over at the man behind the wheel and the familiar gesture of his fingers caressing the hair that connected his mustache to his goatee.

"Wanna date, stud?" she called out, winking and walking over to him. He pulled the car to a stop and rolled his eyes.

"Dream on, Christine."

"I'm dreaming, sugar." Leaning down to his window, she lifted her sunglasses and put them on her head. "What's up?"

"Working on a case. You seen this guy?" Detective Harmon handed her a picture. The guy in the picture had dark eyes, dead, dark eyes. He wasn't smiling, like in a mug shot photo or something. He was a white guy, dark hair, long and messy, bits of gray in his eyebrows, thick and heavy over those dead, dark eyes.

"Nah, haven't seen 'im." She was about to hand the picture back when she looked at it again. "Shit," Christine whistled between her teeth. The left side of his face was all scarred up, just like that guy the other night.

"What's up, Christine? You've seen him, haven't you?" She nodded, suddenly feeling sick to her stomach. Her eyes met the detective's.

"He killed Chantal, didn't he?"

"Who says he killed anybody?" The detective's blue eyes looked into Christine's, like he was looking through her.

"Come on, Mike. You're homicide." She waved the picture around. He smiled, nodding as he tapped the steering wheel with his thumb.

"You know I can't tell you anything, kid. You seen him or not?"

"Yeah, I seen 'im. Just a few nights ago."

"You telling me the truth, Christine? This is serious shit. Don't play with me." He leaned his arm out the car, letting it dangle over the edge, hand lightly tapping the driver's side door.

"Don't worry, Mikey." She handed the picture back with a smirk. "You're too cheap for me to play with." He threw his head back and laughed, waggling his finger at her.

"Careful, kid, or I'll send vice after you."

She held her hand up, palm to the ground. "See this, detective?" He glanced at her steady hand. "Controlled fear."

He chuckled. "Alright, alright. What'cha got for me?"

"Well..." She looked out at the street, almost like she thought that bastard was going to pull up at the curb or something. "He tried to pick me up. I almost went with him. My buddy recognized his car from the one Chantal got into the night she went missing."

"Why don't you come downtown and tell me this, Christine?" he asked, hitching his thumb at the backseat of his car. She shook her head.

"Not happening, Mike. I got things to do today."

He sighed, also looking out over the streets. "Okay." Grabbing a pad of paper, he wrote down what she told him, then looked at her expectantly.

"What? What more you want?"

"What type of car was it? What was he wearing? Did you notice anything new about him? Hair style? Color? Eye color? Tattoos?"

"Whoa, dude. I didn't blow him right there, ya know. I never got into his car." For some reason she felt the need to tell him she hadn't gone through with it. Mike Harmon was the only guy with a good job Christine knew who didn't treat her like the trash she felt she was.

"Alright. Start slow. Kind of car? Color and make." His pen was poised over the pad.

"I don't know what kind of car, but it was a sedan, a small one. It was a dark color, blue or black, I think."

"Okay." He scribbled in absolutely unreadable writing. "Hair? Color and style?"

"Dark and really short. The dude looked like someone had taken to his head with pruning shears or something." She laughed at the memory. "He looked like a dumb ass." Mike chuckled. Christine closed her eyes for a second, trying to think of anything else that had caught her eye about the guy or his car. "He had on dark clothes, but I noticed he wore a Chicago Bears shirt."

"Okay, good, good. Why didn't you go with him?" He was eyeing her and she shrugged.

"I was going to. Like I said, my buddy recognized his car and stopped me. He owes me big, too."

"He probably saved your life, kid."

"Maybe." She shrugged, not figuring that was a huge save.

"Well, if you or your friend remembers anything else, give me a call."
He handed the girl a business card. Not bothering to look at it, she tucked it
into the back pocket of her jeans. "Here, kid. Get yourself some lunch."

Stunned, Christine took the five-dollar bill, also tucking it into her
pocket.

"Take care of yourself, Christine." He started his car and, with a final
wave, drove off. She watched him go, then hurried toward the McDonald's on
the corner, mouth already watering.

"These dreams are pretty vivid," Margaret said, her voice quiet. Christine
nodded.

"Yes, they are." She sighed, running her hands through her hair, leaving
it in disarray. The counselor was quiet for a moment, studying her patient,
who hadn't looked at her during the entire telling of her story.

"How did you feel about that? The fact that you might have been his next
victim?" Christine looked at the woman for a moment, not sure what to say to
the kind, knowing smile she saw. She turned away again.

"I don't know that I would have cared. There wasn't much to save, you
know?" Christine leaned back into the soft cushions, her hands tucked behind
her head and her eyes on the older woman.

"Did they catch him?"

"Yeah," she snorted. "But not before the bastard nabbed three more
girls."

"Did you know them?"

Christine was quiet for a moment, her mind reeling back, then slowly she
nodded.

"And what about your friend? Adam, was it?"

Christine couldn't keep the smile off her face. "He's fine."

"Present tense? You keep in contact with him, then?"

"Oh, yeah." She turned her brilliant smile to Margaret. "He's my boy, *my*
kind of people."

"And what kind of people is that?" Margaret asked, putting her pad of
paper aside and crossing her legs. She studied the woman in front of her. *Such*
a lovely girl.

Christine smiled, looking down at her lap. "I'd rather not talk about
that."

"Alright. You look good, Christine. You've put on some weight. I must
say, a woman of your height — what, five-ten? — should *not* weigh one hundred and thirteen pounds." The mother in Margaret came out. Watching her
own daughter go through a terrible struggle with anorexia was a difficult
thing.

"Yes, well it's hard to keep the weight on when dinner for three days and
nights at a time is four lines of coke."

Margaret smiled sadly. "How do you feel?"

"How do I feel? Good question." Bringing her hands out from behind her
head, Christine stood, walking over to the french doors and looking out. A few

fellow residents were strolling around the grounds, some talking with each other, some alone. Sitting on a stone bench was a fellow musician she was stunned to see at Promises. "Interesting," she muttered.

"What was that?"

"Huh?" Realizing she'd been asked a question, Christine turned from the doors and walked back to the couch. "I feel okay, I guess. Very worn out."

"What are your plans once you leave here? You're to be released in what, three weeks?"

"So they tell me."

"Do you feel you're ready?"

Christine studied the older woman, taking in her caring features, concerned eyes, and motherly bulk and felt something she hadn't felt in many, many years — she wanted a hug.

Shaking that thought out of her mind, she shrugged. "To be honest, Margaret, I don't know a damn thing anymore. I'm void of all thought and understanding of myself."

"What does that make you want to do? How do you want to deal with that?" Margaret's soft voice made Christine smile. She knew what she was getting at.

"Don't worry, Margaret," she said quietly, smiling at the counselor. "I think I've learned my lesson."

"In what way?" Margaret uncrossed her legs, straightening the skirt of her dress, then re-crossing them.

"I could have hurt another person this time," Christine whispered.

"The nurse?"

"The nurse." Christine dropped her head, shame filling her.

"What about your fans? How do you feel about them? The last concert..." Margaret's voice trailed off, seeing the hurt and uncertainty in the piercing blue eyes, made electric by unshed emotion. *If only Christine would allow herself to cry, to release her pain.*

"They'll come back," she said, her voice so low Margaret almost missed it. "They always do. Bob will make sure of that."

"You about done with my air compressor, there, Kevin?"

Willow's head shot up from the fence she was working on. Her husband, wiping his forehead with his hat, headed over to greet Richard Dean, their closest neighbor at three miles.

"Hey there, Dick. Yeah, sorry about that. Come on into the garage. I'll get it for you," he said, patting the old man's back.

Willow smiled as she turned back to her work. She had been telling Kevin for months to get the thing back to Dick, but he hadn't listened. Stubborn male. She had no idea what he'd been using the thing for in the first place.

"Ouch, dang it!" She snatched her finger away from the wire cutters that had pinched the skin on her index finger, making it bleed. She stuck the wound into her mouth, a mumbled curse aimed around the finger at the fence. Examining her hand, she saw that it was just a small cut.

Once her work had been interrupted, Willow realized just how hot it was. She looked up into the May sky, blue as a robin's egg. Snatching the doo-rag from her short hair, she wiped her face down with it, then beat the kerchief against her thigh, and decided to go in for some iced tea.

The walk back to the house was a long one, but beautiful and peaceful. The soft whinnies and snorts of the horses could be heard, as well as the squawk of chickens in their pen. The dogs were out running, making those chickens squawk, but it was okay. Life over the past six days had been good.

Willow and Kevin had taken some well-deserved vacation time, using it to try to get to repairs and improvements on the ranch they'd been wanting to do for a couple years but had never seemed to find the time for. It was Saturday, and she'd be going back to work Monday night.

"Hey, honey?" Kevin called, pulling Willow from her thoughts.

"Yeah?" she called back, stopping just shy of the square plot of grass that was the "backyard" on the two hundred and sixty-five acres of land they owned. Kevin came out from the shade of the garage, his hand shielding his eyes from the sun.

"Have you seen the attachments to the air compressor?"

She shook her head. "Nope. Did you look in your work bench?"

"Why would they be in there?" He rolled his eyes and headed back into the garage.

Willow headed toward the house again. "Five, four, three, two..."

"Here they are!"

She sighed, pushing the back door open, knowing damn well that he'd never admit to finding the attachments in the Bermuda Triangle of Oklahoma known as his work bench. Heading over to the fridge, she pulled it open and surveyed the contents, looking for the jug of iced tea she had brewed the night before. Moving aside Kevin's gallon of Gatorade, she spotted the green top of the pitcher.

Sighing with contentment, she pulled the jug free and poured dark gold liquid into a glass, drinking half of it down before she could even get to the freezer for ice. Breathing heavily as she wiped her mouth with the back of her hand, she filled the glass once more, adding a few cubes of ice.

Kicking her hiking boots off — she hated shoes and ditched them at every possible opportunity — she padded around the cool Mexican tile of the kitchen with pleasure and hauled herself up onto one of the tall bar stools that sat before their breakfast bar. The newspaper had been tossed there earlier that morning, neither she nor Kevin having had a chance to read it.

"He's a cool old guy," her husband said, almost bouncing into the house, tugging his Gatorade out of the fridge and drinking straight from the plastic jug.

"Yeah, he is," Willow said absently, shaking out the pages of the *Williamsburg Gazette*. Kevin walked over to the bar, Gatorade in hand.

"Give me the sports, will ya, honey?" He sat next to her, seeing his wife glance at him and do a double take, a grin spreading across her lips. "What?"

Without a word, Willow reached up with her thumb to wipe the red smudge from Kevin's upper lip. He looked away sheepishly.

"What can I say, I like my fruit punch Gatorade."

"Obviously. Here." Handing him his section of the paper, she went back to the leading stories of their small area of the world. She grazed the local stuff, not caring much about the local pig competitions or how large a squash Meridath Graham had grown this year, and made her way to national news.

A familiar picture caught her eye, and she zoomed in on the short blurb beside it.

> *Singer/songwriter Christine Gray, who mysteriously dropped from public view last winter, has announced that the concert tour for her latest album, Swan Song, which was canceled after she was hospitalized for exhaustion in February, has been rescheduled.*
>
> *"All tickets to the cancelled performances, including an encore appearance in Oklahoma City, will be honored for Ms. Gray's re-scheduled concerts in those cities," said Gray's agent Mark Hutch-ins, who added that Christine was feeling great and in good spirits and was looking forward to seeing her fans.*

Willow smiled, resting her chin on her palm. She had thought about Christine often, wondering what had happened to her, where she'd ended up. The news had been no help, nor E! nor Entertainment Tonight.

Robert Knowles had done his best to keep things under wraps in the rest of the world as well as inside the hospital, she figured. She couldn't help but wonder how much that silence and privacy had cost Christine.

"Who's that? She's pretty," Kevin said, resting his chin on his wife's shoulder.

"Christine Gray," Willow said absently, reading over the article again.

"Who?"

"She's not country, honey, you wouldn't know her." Willow grinned, gently patting her husband's stubbled cheek.

"Hey, I'll have you know I once shook the hand of George Jones!" he said, looking at her with narrowed brows. She loved it when he looked at her like that. In that moment she knew *exactly* what he had looked like as a young boy. She was filled with love, but she wasn't through torturing him just yet.

"Who?"

"God, what kind of country girl are you? You do your state shame, woman," he muttered, turning back to his sports page. She snickered, taking up her own section again.

Willow stepped out onto the wrap-around porch of the smoky blue two-story with the white trim. The trim was something else she and Kevin had accomplished during their working vacation. It had taken thirty years off the old farmhouse.

She smiled, closing her eyes as she inhaled the early Sunday morning air, hands wrapped firmly around her mug of mint tea. She loved the way two worlds were merging as the sun peeked over the flat plains of her beloved Sooner state — the songs of male crickets frantically rubbing their back legs together, desperate for a mate, saluting the night, melding with the songs of the birds in the dozens of trees around the house, helping to birth a new day.

This was her time, a time of peace and tranquility where she could regroup and gather strength from the dawning of new life.

She was usually just getting home around this time, getting her tea and watching the day reborn as Kevin got up and prepared for work.

She looked out over the pastures, hearing the horses start to wake, snorting, their hooves stomping lightly on the ground. In the distance she saw the headlights of Macy Allen's car as she delivered the Sunday morning paper to all the outlying farms and ranches. Willow usually passed the small blue car on her way in from the hospital.

Sipping from her mug, she made her way slowly down the stairs of the porch to the flagstone path that led to the edge of the landscaped part of their yard and ended in the dirt road that led to the gates of their property.

She noted the colors that spread across the sky, pinks and oranges, stretching fingers through the clouds, with rays falling through the cracks to spotlight scenes on the plains.

Memories of an earlier time began to flood Willow's mind. Her grandfather had been born in the farmhouse in 1918, his parents adding another story to the tiny, one-room house as their family began to grow. Eight children later, everyone began to disperse and find their own place in life.

Willow's grandfather, Earnest, had stayed on, loving the land far too much to leave it. His brothers had gone off to fight in World War II, while he'd remained, the sole son left to run the ranch. His father, aged and weathered by that time, was far too weak to run things.

Earnest Wahl had lost three of his four brothers in the war, as well as one sister, Rose, who had gone over as a WASP. The other sister, Lucille, had married and moved off to New Jersey. Earnest's remaining brother, Carl, had no interest in the life of a farmer/rancher; he made his way west to explore the world of real estate, making his fortune in San Francisco.

Deep in these memories, Willow walked to the fence, which she needed to finish fixing today. She pushed the gate open and headed across the road to the mailbox, standing tall before a ditch filled with water for irrigation. Grabbing the paper from the paper box mounted on the mailbox pole, she tucked it under her arm and headed back across the road.

Willow had spent hours and hours and hours with her grandmother on this land. Myra Wahl — now she was an interesting woman.

Born in Rifle, Colorado, in 1932, at the height of the Great Depression, she was the third of six children, born to poor farm hands. Having no interest in the farm life, she ran away from home at the age of sixteen, going off with the strong man at a carnival that passed through town.

By that time, WWII was over and the population was desperate to have its spirits raised, so many of their young men having not come home. The carnival was a great success, and Myra traveled all around the US and Canada with Dale, working as a weight guesser and dancer in one of the carnival's many shows.

Eventually tiring of the carnival life, Myra decided to find her own way. She began hitching rides along Route 66, where a lonely driver named Earnest Wahl picked her up. That had been in 1951. They'd been together until the day Earnest had died, October 2, 2000. Myra and Earnest had only one child, a bouncing baby boy, who eventually became Willow's father.

When Willow's grandfather had died, Myra had decided the ranch was too much to take care of. Since her granddaughter had always loved the place so much and her son had his own life and home and no interest in taking on another residence, Myra had passed the ranch in its entirety, repairs and all, to Willow. Willow recalled visiting as a child.

Everything in her grandma's house had intrigued her. It was filled with big, sturdy furniture, every bit an antique. It amazed Willow how she had a set of pans, the silver kind with the copper bottoms, and after fifty years of use, the copper was as clear and unblemished as it had been the day the pans were made.

Willow would sit on a stool in the kitchen, next to the counter, watching as her grandma washed dishes, her heavily corded hands lovingly scrubbing every bit of food, baked on or otherwise, from the pans, then dipping them in the hot rinse water, her skin beet red from the heat, and setting the pan on the spread-out towel. Willow would grab the newly washed pan, drying it just as lovingly.

"How have you kept these so nice, Grandma?" She glanced over at her grandmother, setting the pan aside to grab for the bouquet of flatware she had just washed.

"Time and patience, my love," she smiled, winking a light blue eye at Willow, who rolled her own eyes. She knew that was her way of telling her it was her secret. She would always sprinkle something into the dishwater from a corked bottle filled with mysterious white and blue granules.

They were silent for a while, the only sound the quiet, soothing splashing of water as Grandma continued to wash the supper dishes. Willow never understood why she called it supper when it was only two-thirty in the afternoon! See, with Grandma there was supper, then there was dinner. Dinner was served at five-thirty sharp. Willow was never hungry when dinner came along because she was still so full from supper three hours before!

Her logic was dizzying.

"Grandma?" she asked, setting aside the glass casserole dish she had just dried.

"Yes, love?" The older woman pulled the plug from the large, stainless steel sink, using the sprayer to get rid of all the suds.

"I was out with the horses earlier and it looks like Wanda is about to pop any minute." She glanced up at her grandmother, seeing wrinkles of concentration marring her otherwise smooth forehead. Though she was a year from sixty, she was aging very well, which was surprising considering she spent most of her life outside in the harsh sun. Grandma had a permanent tan that Willow was grossly jealous of. Grandpa had one, too, though it

always made her laugh when he took off his almost ever-present baseball cap. He had a perfect line of white across his forehead just under his hairline. Grandma called it a farmer's tan.

"You think so, do you?" Grandma asked, wiping down the counter and sink with a dry towel. Willow nodded.

"She started to really stomp her feet when I was over there earlier. I don't know," she shrugged, "I just feel it." Hopping from the stool, the child put it away, against the wall by the door to the kitchen, where Grandpa always sat when he took his boots off. Grandma would fillet him for supper if he got mud in her immaculate house.

"Let's go have a look." Grandma kissed Willow on the temple as she neatly hung the towels on the magnetic hooks attached to the side of the fridge, then led the way toward the door.

Willow's father had inherited his mother's youthful wandering spirit. Throughout Willow's youth, he had moved them from this house to the next, one town to the next, and even spreading across state lines. She had no real childhood home to speak of, never living anywhere longer than a few years.

Willow had figured it out once and been stunned to realize she had attended nine schools and lived in more than a dozen houses or apartments.

The ranch had become her sanctuary, something that she knew she always could return to, something that would be in the same place, look the same, feel the same, *be* the same. Willow spent nearly all of her summers there and, when her parents lived close enough, her weekends, too. Her grandmother once had even called Willow's mother, Helen, to see if there was a problem at home because the girl wanted to spend so much time at the ranch.

Helen had been hurt by the question, but Willow hadn't the heart to tell her mother that it was because she felt she had no security with her own parents, and so she sought what she craved with her grandparents.

It had been even worse when Willow's parents had divorced during her sophomore year of high school. She had felt lost and adrift. Once again the ranch had provided the emotional nourishment she had needed. She had even gone so far as to consider moving in with her grandparents indefinitely. But by that time, Earnest was getting sick and Myra had enough to deal with, so Willow had stayed with her mother and Helen's new boyfriend, Shawn, who eventually became Willow's stepfather.

"Wow, look at that," Willow breathed, eyes huge with what she was seeing. The new mother and her colt lay together in the hay, the baby trying her very best to stand, without much success. Her thin, bony legs weren't cooperating.

"You were right, my love. You've got a good instinct," Myra whispered, her arm slung around her granddaughter's waist. "Maybe you should be a vet instead of a nurse."

The girl shook her head adamantly. "I want to be a nurse. I can do far more for people than animals."

"A noble stance, Willow." *She smiled at the girl, and Willow smiled back, feeling the warmth of love and pride fill her. Grandma made her feel that she could do anything and she'd still be proud of her. It was a good feeling.* "What should we name her, my love?"

"Hmm." *Willow chewed her lip as she studied the brown colt. As she looked at her, she noticed a splotch of white on her nose. It was small, but Willow knew it would get bigger. It looked like a lopsided star.* "Star," *she said, looking over at Grandma, who she was proud to say was a wee bit shorter than she was even then.* "See her nose?"

Blue eyes twinkled, and Grandma nodded. "Star it is."

Willow strolled to the pasture. The horses, seeing her coming, walked over to the wooden rail fence.

"Hey, guys," she murmured, reaching a hand out to pet them. "How's my girl, huh?" The big, brown horse snorted, nuzzling her with a hairy nose and tickling Willow's face. She smiled, running her thumb over the bright, white marking that gave the horse her name. Star had three babies of her own now, all grown and busy making her a grandmother many times over.

"Hey, you," Kevin's soft voice said from behind her. She leaned back into him, smiling as his warm arms snaked around her to clasp under her breasts. "I missed you this morning," he said into her ear, kissing the tip.

"Mm, sorry," she sighed in contentment. "I need to get myself back into a routine. Staying up all night Monday night will not be so fun if I don't."

"Hmm, true." Together they watched the horses, absorbing the warmth of the dawning day and of each other.

Kevin hated how often he awoke alone, even when his wife was not working, but he understood her need for the alone time. He did his best to not complain too often, though he had hoped they could have at least spent their last morning together in bed, before the real world of work encroached upon them. He decided to try.

"So I was thinking," he said, leaning down to nibble lightly at his wife's neck. "This is our last day together," he moved up to her lobe, encouraged as she tilted her head a bit, "and maybe we could spend it in bed." Willow closed her eyes as her head tilted even more, feeling the soft lips and tongue spread to her jaw. A soft moan escaped her as a large, warm hand cupped one of her breasts.

Kevin knew he had her. Her breasts were so sensitive; the nipple was already pressing against his palm. Willow turned in his arms, her mouth finding his. Yeah, he had her.

Christine set the silver tray of empty dishes in the hall outside the door to her suite.

Belching loudly, she put her hand to her stomach, feeling full and content. She walked over to the french doors; she'd miss the view when she left. It was amazing how vibrant and beautiful things were to her again. Through the haze of the past ten years, the world around her had started to lose its color, flavor, and beauty. How had she allowed herself to become numb to the sounds of life? Weren't they music of a sort?

Wrapping her arms around herself, she leaned against the open doors, not quite stepping out onto the balcony. She had done that one night and nearly fainted. Looking down had reminded her entirely too much of that lost night in Oklahoma three months earlier.

It was almost time to go home, and Christine was glad of it. She wanted her own house, her own bed. Plus she missed Millie. That surprised her. The housekeeper had been with her for just over two years and had quickly become a cherished friend, as well as one hell of an employee. Millie had no family in California to speak of, and her son was clear across the country in Nashville trying to become the next Kenny Chesney.

Christine shivered. Who on earth listened to that country babble? The stuff gave her ulcers. How could anyone have that many problems in one song?

Glancing over her shoulder at the unexpected sound of a knock, she headed back across the room and pulled the door open.

Her eyes widened at the smiling face that waited on the other side.

"Adam!" Finding herself almost picked up in his thin arms, Christine hugged her old friend for all she was worth, thrilled beyond words to see him there. Finally pushing him away, she held him at arms' length, looking him up and down, finally gazing at his face, its skin slightly darker than her own, white teeth blinding in contrast.

"Hey, gorgeous," he said, his deep voice resonating through her.

"My God, come in, come in." Ushering him inside, she closed the door behind him, turning to look at him again. His dark brown hair was long, pulled back into a ponytail. "What are you doing here?" She walked over to him, pulling him into another hug, this one warm, soft, and comforting to them both. He held her, chin resting on top of her dark head, breathing in his past.

"I heard you might need a friend. So here I am, friend."

"I've missed you, buddy," she whispered, her head resting against his narrow chest. After a long, contented moment, Adam slowly pulled away, taking Christine by the hand and leading her to the couch. He looked around the opulent room as he did so, amazed and awed by where she had ended up.

"Robert Downey, Jr. really stayed here, huh?" He grinned broadly at his friend, who rolled her eyes, smacking him lightly in the stomach. He became serious, his intense hazel eyes boring into Christine's. "What's going on, Chris? Why are you here?"

Sighing, she looked away, ashamed to face him. "I almost did it, Adam," she finally said, her voice quiet and alone.

"How?" he asked, his voice almost choking over the single word. Christine chuckled ruefully, unable to look at him.

"I jumped off this old, rickety bridge into a river."

Adam closed his eyes, swallowing heavily as he tried to keep his emotions at bay. He couldn't keep the image of a pale, bloated Christine from his tortured mind.

"Why didn't you call me?" he whispered. "I would have been there in a heartbeat."

"I know." She turned to her friend now, seeing the pain on his face. She hated knowing that she'd put it there. "I know." Cupping his prominent jaw in her hand, she made him look at her, brows furrowed. "I lost control, Adam." She shook her head to emphasize her point. "I lost it."

"What were you on?" His voice was low and serious.

"Everything. Anything." She sighed, glancing at the hand that grabbed hers, holding it tight. "I was taking anything I could get my hands on, Adam. I totally fucked up, bud. I may have ruined my career."

"I heard about the concert in Oklahoma City," he said quietly. She met his gaze, her face filled with terror.

"How?"

"It was all over the news, in the papers. They said it was because you had worn yourself to exhaustion, but I knew something was wrong. I'm only sorry I couldn't get here sooner."

Christine closed her eyes, taking several deep breaths, her stomach in knots. She wasn't so sure she should have eaten as much as she had for breakfast.

"I'm just glad you're here," she finally said.

"And don't worry, Chris. There's no way you could ruin your career. They love you. Don't you know that?"

"I don't know, Adam. I just don't know anymore."

"How did you get out of the river?"

Christine grinned, feeling foolish. "A clown saved me."

"What?" Her friend looked at her as though she were crazy. "Jesus, you really were on some bad shit."

She laughed, letting it roll out of her throat with abandon. He grinned, confused.

"No, really. It was this woman, a nurse or something, who was dressed as a clown. Scared the shit out of me, too. I hate clowns."

"Oh man," Adam laughed. "Why was she dressed as a clown?"

Christine shrugged. "I have no idea. But I do know she saved my life. In a lot of ways." She blew out a breath.

Chapter 3

"Hey, girl!" Rachel jogged across the hospital parking lot to her friend and one-time college companion.

"Hey." Willow smiled, stopping her trek to the building. Rachel grinned, out of breath from her short run. "What's up?" Willow shifted her bag from one shoulder to the other, already in her scrubs for the night's shift.

"Did you see that article in the newspaper?" Rachel asked, digging through her own large bag and bringing out Sunday's paper, folded so that Christine Gray's picture smiled up at them. Willow nodded but took the paper from her friend anyway. She wondered how long ago the picture had been taken; the singer had looked nothing like the black and white, grainy image when she rescued her.

"I'm so glad she's doing better," she said quietly, glancing up at her friend, who also nodded.

"I know. Did you tell Kevin about it?"

"No." Willow sighed. "I know he won't say anything, but...I don't know." She shrugged, a sheepish grin tugging at her lips. "He didn't even really know who she was when I pointed it out to him yesterday. I think the specialness of it would be lost on him, you know?"

"Yeah."

"Did you tell Connor?"

"Yeah. And don't worry, he won't say anything, either," Rachel said, taking the paper back and stuffing it back into the bag. "Sometimes it still amazes me that she was here."

"I know." Willow was silent for a moment. She and her friend hadn't talked about that night since it had happened; they were both afraid to. What if someone else heard them? Was it breaking the rules of the contracts they had signed? "It was so scary that night, Rach. I couldn't believe my eyes when I saw someone plunge off the bridge."

"You're brave, Wills. I don't know that I would have jumped in after them."

"Sure you would have. You're a nurse, it's instinct."

"Not to risk my life, it isn't." She smiled as Willow chuckled lightly. "I give total props to you, my friend. That was really an incredible thing."

"Thank you." Willow glanced shyly at her friend before smiling down at the asphalt of the parking lot they were crossing.

"I'll be so glad to get rid of these damn nights." Rachel sighed. "It's just a good thing that Connor works from home and can work any ol' crazy schedule. How is it working with you and Kevin?"

Willow shrugged, holding open the tinted glass door for her friend.

"Thanks," Rachel said.

"It's okay, I guess. We manage. Don't have much choice. To be honest, the hardest thing is taking care of the animals almost by myself."

"Kevin doesn't help?" Rachel pushed the button on the elevator that would take them to the floor where the nurses' lounge and locker room were.

"He does, but I'm the one there during the day. I mean, shoot, he doesn't even get home until after dark half the time." Willow leaned back against the stainless steel walls of the large elevator, hands tucked behind her butt, palms against the cool steel.

"Well, if they'd hire someone else down at the lumber yard, I doubt he'd have to work so damn much."

"I agree." Willow looked up at the illuminated dial above the doors, watching as their floor came nearer. The car jolted to a stop, and the doors slid open.

"Hey, are we all still on to go see that new action flick this week? I hear it's getting great reviews." Rachel pushed open the locker room door, and her friend followed close behind.

"Uh, I think so." Willow turned the dial on her lock, the numbers whizzing by until it clicked and the lock slid down, allowing her to remove it. Every time she released the lock she couldn't help but think of high school and fumbling with the lock the first day of classes.

"I can't wait! And Connor! My God, you'd think the world had come to an end."

As Rachel went on and on about the movie, Willow noticed something. At the bottom of her locker lay a white business-size envelope. It must have been slipped in through the vents in the door. She bent down to pick it up.

"What's that?" Rachel asked, noticing her friend's preoccupation.

"I don't know," Willow said absently, turning the envelope around in her fingers. Written across the front were her name and the hospital's address. There was only a P.O. box for a return address.

"Maybe it's anthrax." Rachel grinned. "I'm just kidding, Wills, jeez."

"Funny." Now curious, the nurse shook the envelope, holding it up to the light.

"Oh, jeez, come on. Just open the damn thing."

Slipping her finger under the flap, Willow ripped across, the paper slicing easily. Inside was a piece of paper, folded in thirds. Opening it, she saw it was a hand-written letter. Something else slid out of the folds of the paper. She caught it, realizing it was tickets. Eyes trailing back to the letter, she read:

Dear Ms. Bowman,

I feel strange writing a letter, not having done it in a very long time. I can't thank you enough for what you did, risking your life to save that of a complete stranger. I've never seen such heroics, and I can't believe people like you truly exist.

I wanted to say thank you. Because of you I have another shot, and that is something I won't take likely, nor will I soon forget it. Not in this lifetime, anyway.

Please accept the tickets enclosed. You and a guest are invited to my show in Oklahoma City, June 13. I hope to see you there and thank you in person.

Yours, Christine Gray

Willow looked up at her friend, stunned, then looked back at the letter, quickly reading it again.

"What is it?" Rachel asked, trying to read over her friend's shoulder.

"It's from Christine Gray," Willow breathed, handing the letter to her with a trembling hand. Rachel read over the letter, her eyes getting wider and wider with each passing line.

"Oh my God," she said, a smile spreading across her full lips. "That's incredible."

"Yeah." Willow swallowed, still unable to believe that Christine Gray had taken the time to write her a personal missive, as well as send concert tickets! As she studied the tickets, she noted they were good for backstage entrance, too. She looked up at Rachel. "Guess what?"

"What?"

"You're going to a Twilight concert with me." Willow showed her the tickets, and both women erupted into cheers and whoops. A fellow nurse walked in, eyeing the pair as if they were nuts. Quieting down, they quickly stowed their bags, then hurried off to their respective floors.

Willow leaned against the restroom sink, her blonde bangs falling into her eyes, the hairs sticking to the moist skin under them. Taking several deep breaths, she pushed off the sink, looking up into the mirror above it. She looked so worn down. Her eyes glowed green from the upset, and there were bags below the lower lids.

"Honey, are you okay?" Dr. Maureen Halston asked, her hand on the nurse's back. She looked with concern at one of the most compassionate women she'd ever been blessed to know. She worried continually that Willow would give too much of herself to her patients and not have anything left for herself.

Willow sniffled, running her hands through her hair and nodding.

"Yeah. I'll be okay." She laughed nervously, feeling foolish. "You know, after all the years I've been doing this, you'd think I'd get used to losing them." She looked up at the doctor with pleading eyes. "Does it ever stop, Maureen?"

The twenty-year veteran sighed, shaking her head. "No, honey. You're always affected by God's special babies, but you learn how to deal with it. You *have* to, Willow."

"I know." She sniffled again, running the back of her hand across her nose. The doctor smiled, heading into a stall to grab a wad of toilet paper.

"Here, honey."

"Thanks." Willow blew her nose, then sighed, trying to make her heart release a bit of its sorrow, just enough to allow her to get back to work. "I'll be okay, Maureen, thank you." She smiled up at her friend.

"Okay. I'd best get back to it." With a quick one-armed hug, Dr. Halston was gone, leaving Willow with her thoughts.

The grounds of Mercy were impeccably kept, the grass beautifully green and the flowerbeds arrayed in a riot of colors and smells tucked into brick planters.

Willow sat on the edge of one of those planters with her arms wrapped around herself as she stared out into the hot summer afternoon. It may have been in the upper nineties on her skin, but inside her skin it felt like the dead of winter.

It was almost three in the afternoon. She'd been at Mercy for just over eighteen hours, and she was feeling the strain. She'd worked long shifts before, and she was usually able to push the fatigue away and turn that stress into determination.

But this time...

Willow folded her legs up, wrapped her arms around her knees, and rested her chin upon them. She thought back to the events of the past day.

"Hey, sweetie. How are you today?" she pulled up a chair, taking Melissa's hand in her own. She noticed the girl's fingers wrapping around her own, so small and thin. Very pale. How could she not be pale? In and out of Mercy for long stints over the past six months.

"Okay," Melissa said, her voice very quiet, whispery. Blue eyes, made huge from all the weight the girl had lost, embraced by dark circles and dark lashes, which fluttered as she blinked. "'M so tired, Willow."

"I know, honey." The nurse smiled at her and caressed the back of the girl's hand with her thumb. She couldn't help but feel her heart swell at the sight of the lovely twelve-year-old girl. Her hair had long been gone — chemo. Her doctors and all the nurses were doing everything possible to save her from the leukemia that was ravaging her body.

Willow's heart was breaking, knowing that Melissa's time was short, but she still prayed with everything in her that she'd be okay, that a miracle of the sort that Maureen talked about so often would happen, saving this poor, innocent kid.

Still, she held strong.

"Can I get you anything, sweetie?" Willow asked, glancing up as someone walked into the room. She smiled at Melissa's mom, Ellen, then turned back to the girl.

"No," she said, looking over at her mother. "Hi, Mom."

"Hi, sweet pea." Ellen took the chair across the bed, reaching out to Willow, who took her hand and squeezed it. As she looked into her eyes, she could see Ellen knew what Willow did — time was running out. They both turned their eyes back to the beautiful young girl in the bed between them. "Your dad is picking up Brian. They'll be here soon."

"'Kay." Melissa was fighting to stay awake, her eyes getting heavier and heavier.

"Sleep, honey," Willow said, squeezing the girl's fingers. "We'll be here when you wake up." The girl mumbled incoherently, then nodded off. Willow looked back to Ellen, nodding toward the hall with her head. She nodded, standing. Leaning over her daughter, she kissed the girl's naked head, then followed the nurse out.

Willow closed the door to Room 212 as they stepped out into the hall. Turning to Ellen, she saw that she was beginning to cry, her dark eyes liquid. It broke Willow's heart.

"Come here." She opened her arms. Melissa's mother fell into her embrace, crying into her shoulder. Squeezing her eyes shut, Willow tried to keep it all inside. The last thing Ellen needed was for her to fall apart, too. "I know," the nurse cooed, feeling the woman's pain and anguish.

It took several minutes for her to calm, but finally she did; even so, Willow didn't break physical contact with her. With her arm around Ellen's shoulders, the nurse led her toward a small area down the hall where a couple of sofas were set up, as well as vending machines.

"Want some coffee, Ellen?" Willow asked, kneeling before her. The dark head nodded, and the nurse quickly made herself busy making the coffee that she knew so well — two packets of Splenda and a dollop of cream. "Here you go." Helping her to keep the coffee from spilling in her trembling hands, she sat next to the devastated mother, rubbing gentle circles over her back.

"She's going to leave us soon, isn't she?" Ellen asked, her voice trembling as badly as her hands. Willow sighed, not sure how to answer that. She had yet to lie to the family and sure didn't want to start now, but at the same time, she didn't want to cause Ellen any more pain than she was already in.

"She's put up such a good fight, Ellen," Willow said quietly. Ellen turned to look at her, dark eyes pleading.

"Please just be straight with me, Willow. I need to know." The last came out in a whisper, and Ellen started to cry again. Afraid the coffee would spill over the woman's hands and lap, Willow took it from her, resting the cup on the table next to her chair. Taking her into her arms again, Willow let her actions speak for her.

Out of the corner of her eye, she saw Tammy Wistoff, another nurse, running down the hall and sliding almost comically to a stop, then waving her hand frantically. Willow gently pulled away from Ellen to go to Tammy.

"Willow, Melissa is asking for you and her mother," the young nurse said. Just one look at her eyes and Willow felt a stab of dread in her heart. Glancing over her shoulder, she met Ellen's eyes, looking pleadingly at her.

With a sigh and a heavy heart, Willow went over to the woman and held a hand out for her.

"What?" Ellen asked. "You're scaring me, Willow."

"She's asking for us, Ellen."

Making their way down the hall, Ellen clutched at Willow with one hand while using the other to try to get hold of her husband and son on her cell phone.

Comforted with the knowledge that they were close, the two women hurried into Melissa's room.

"Hey, baby," Ellen whispered, standing next to her daughter's bed and taking her hand. Blue eyes, faded and so tired, turned to Willow, and she, too, went to the side of the girl's bed. Slowly, as though she had a twenty-pound weight in her small hand, Melissa held her hand out to her, which she took.

Melissa blinked, though it was almost as if in slow motion. In the past few days she'd gotten so weak.

"I love you, Mamma," she said suddenly, looking at her mother, whose eyes were filled with tears.

"I love you, too, my baby," Ellen responded, clutching her daughter's hand in both of her own, bringing it to her lips. Willow could feel her own eyes stinging. Then Melissa's gaze was on her.

"Hi, sweetheart," she whispered, smiling down at her.

"You're so cool," the girl said, the softest smile on her lips. Willow's own smile widened, her vision becoming even more blurry.

"I think you're pretty cool, too, Melissa."

She smiled, eyes closing before her head turned and once again she looked at Ellen.

"Mamma," she whispered, almost like she was caressing the endearment with her lips. "Don't cry, Mamma." Melissa reached up with deliberation, the tip of her finger touching a tear that slid gracefully down Ellen's cheek. "I'm not scared."

With those few words Willow lost her battle against emotion. She tried to hold in the sob that was struggling to get free. Luckily only tears come out, quiet, unobtrusive. Part of her felt like she should leave, giving mother and daughter these last moments alone.

There was a commotion in the hall, then Ellen's husband, Jack, and their son Brian hurried into the room.

"Baby, Daddy's here," Ellen whispered, making room for him. Willow smiled at the fourteen-year-old boy, standing to give him her spot next to his sister. Slowly she backed away and out of the room.

New tears fell as Willow heard Ellen's voice echo in her head, "No!" That was the moment that Melissa had lost her battle and her young body had finally been able to find peace.

She buried her face in her hands, tears slipping between her fingers, making her shiver as the cool breeze caught the wetness, cooling her skin.

After a while, Ellen had found Willow and had clung to her, thanking the nurse over and over again for everything she'd done for Melissa and the family. Willow accepted her thanks but felt she did not deserve them. No, she wasn't a doctor or a miracle worker, but she should have been able to do more, just a little extra.

She felt like she'd failed the girl, and it ate at her.

Sniffling several times, Willow swiped at her eyes and pulled her cell phone out of her pocket, flipping it open and staring at the keypad. All she had to do was press the button with the number one on it, then send, and she'd be connected to Kevin.

With a sigh, she flipped the phone shut, gently setting it on the planter beside her. She'd have to do as Maureen said and deal with it, find a way to let it go on her own.

Eyes closed, Christine inhaled deeply, just the barest touch of a smile curling the corner of her lips. Opening her eyes, she looked around. Everything was just as she'd left it before starting her tour — scattered sheets of blank paper feathered out on the wood floor in the shadow of her beloved grand. Finished work was still resting on top of the piano; the lid was down.

Walking over to the instrument, she fingered some of the pages, her mind automatically conjuring up the music, following the notes with her eyes for a brief moment before memory finished the song.

Striding past the piano, she walked over to the bar at the far end of the spacious, nearly empty, room. The late morning sunlight filtered in, coloring everything bright and clean.

She opened one of the cabinets next to the small bar fridge and was surprised to see it empty.

"Millie," she murmured, a pleased smile quickly spreading over her face. As Christine expected, the trashcan under one of the cabinets was filled with empty bottles of varying shapes and sizes. Christine knew if she bent over the small, stainless steel sink she would smell the distinct odor of alcohol.

Walking back across the room, her bare feet padding over the cool, oak boards, she seated herself at the Baldwin and lovingly lifted the lid. Reaching out a finger, she tapped middle C, listening to that one beautiful note resonating in the room, which stood two-stories tall, an outer wall of glass providing a view into the Japanese gardens.

Closing her eyes, she sat straight, hands poised above the keys, and began to play, her fingers racing over the ivories, the music flowing like water, her ears drinking it in. She needed to feel the music.

Her body swayed with her emotions, rising and falling, cresting only to slam down again upon the rocky shores of melancholy. Though the music was sad, Christine could not have been happier.

"Okay, here's the plan." Bob clicked a button on the small remote that rested unseen in his hand. "We follow basically the same route as last time." A list of cities in various states all around the country popped up on the large, white screen. Another click and bullets appeared next to certain cities. "In these places you'll be meeting with camera crews for pre-arranged conferences, in which," he looked sharply at Christine, "you will continue with the story of fatigue and over-doing it, got it?"

She nodded dumbly, her eyes on the screen but her mind in outer space. She tugged at her bottom lip with her fingers as she slowly propelled the chair back and forth, using her feet for leverage.

"Good deal." He clicked again and went through a quick slide show of the various venues she'd be playing at, including Coors Field in Denver. "The good thing about doing this now instead of February is that in Colorado you'll be in the stadium this time as opposed to the Pepsi Center, where we were before. More seats, more people, bigger pay check."

"For who?" she muttered, eyes reaching the ceiling. Bob looked at her, clicker at the ready.

He ignored the comments and moved on to the next slide. It showed Christine at an earlier show, hair wild around her face, makeup dark and smoky. She recognized the pants she wore — black leather, slung low on her hips, and black boots. Very similar to what she wore at every show. The top, however, was new.

"What is this? I don't own a top like that. Hell, it's not a top, Bob, it's a friggin' bra!"

"I know," he grinned, obviously proud of himself. "I had Wayne play a bit with a picture of you during the Toronto tour, cut and paste with his computer, and voila!" He indicated the picture. "This is our new look."

"No way." Christine sat forward in her chair, her hands clutching the edge of the conference table, ready to rise. "I am thirty-one years old, Bob, and the skanky fifteen-year-old look is out. You have me looking like a goddamn prostitute!"

"Old habits die hard, eh, Christine?" She looked at him, stunned and deeply wounded. As she opened her mouth to say something, he quickly continued. "You need to do something to get back on the map, Christine. You've been out of the game for six whole months! *And* you fucked up during a goddamn tour! We've got to get you back in the spotlight."

"And dressing me like a whore is the way to go?" she growled, her nails digging into the wood.

"Careful, Christine," Bob warned, his own voice lowered.

She looked at him with her face like stone, hatred running through her veins. Biting her tongue, she decided to change the subject.

"By the way, I'm doing much better. Thanks for asking."

"I know you are." He tossed the clicker across the smooth wood table. "I've spoken with your doctors."

"And?"

"And what?" He rested his temple against his fist, studying his client with hooded eyes.

"Forget it." She shoved out of the chair, heading toward the door.

"Christine."

She stopped, her hand on the door. She glared at him over her shoulder.

"Why should I give you my pity or congratulations? You did it to yourself."

She stared him down, neither of their gazes wavering. He was pushing her more and more, and she wasn't sure how much longer she could take it. His threats were beginning to wear thin, and her priorities were shifting.

Without another word, Christine walked out, leaving the door open behind her. Bob called out after her, "Fittings are set up for Wednesday!"

Christine slammed through the double glass doors of Bob's offices, nearly running over a passing woman as she headed toward the elevator. She hastily pulled her long hair into a ponytail and tugged a baseball cap on low. She would put on mirrored sunglasses once outside to hide her famed blue eyes from the view of fans and paparazzi.

She got about ten feet from the building before she heard the first rush of camera clicks.

"Fuck," she mumbled under her breath, not in the mood to deal with the photogs. Fans she could handle. After all, it was because of them she was allowed to do what she did and make a living from it. But the photogs, or hounds as she thought of them, were a whole different story. They sniffed around the city all day and night for a high-profile celebrity to snap unsolicited pictures of to sell later to high-paying magazines, newspapers, collectors, and magazine shows.

She increased her pace when she heard her name being called by a chorus of photog hopefuls.

"Christine! Over here! Look this way, Gray!"

This, of course, drew the attention of fans and autograph dealers. It still astounded her that an autograph dealer had made fifteen thousand bucks off a 'graph from her last year. The more elusive the celeb, the more their 'graph went for, it seemed.

It made her sad, never knowing if someone wanted her autograph because he was truly a fan or because he was trying to make a quick buck off her.

Up ahead she spotted a little girl, probably about eleven or twelve, standing in front of a shop window with an older version of herself. Dark brown eyes peered at her shyly from under black bangs, white teeth appearing as they clamped down on a lower lip.

Christine pushed her way through the growing crowd of photogs, grinning when she saw the girl talking excitedly to the woman at her side, pointing at the singer and looking as though she were about to bounce right out of her shoes.

The older woman glanced at Christine, her own dark eyes widening in shock, and nodded vigorously at the little girl — who then took off at a dead run at Christine.

The girl stopped just short of Christine, suddenly turning very shy and uncertain. Christine smiled down at the girl, bending slightly so she was more on her level.

"Hi," she said, as all the paparazzi clicked away at the exchange. Christine stood upright, annoyed, and turned to the rude intruders. "Come on, guys. Give us a moment, huh? I promise to give you a few when I'm done, okay?"

"Cool! Thanks, Christine!" Jerry Mitchell, whom she had seen many times, grinned at her.

Turning back to the star-struck girl, Christine smiled. The girl smiled back.

"Can I have your autograph?" the girl managed to say around the finger that had found its nervous way between her teeth. Christine smiled.

"Sure. What's your name, hon?" She smiled up at the older woman who stood behind the girl and handed Christine a pen and a deposit slip she'd torn from her checkbook.

"Juanita," the shy girl said.

"Juanita. That's a very pretty name." She gave the girl her famous smile, beautiful white teeth, blinding. This made the girl even more shy; she seemed to grow younger before Christine's eyes. The girl leaned back into the body of the woman behind her, as a reassuring hand came to rest on the girl's shoulder.

Using her knee for a solid surface, Christine quickly scribbled out a message to the young Juanita, then handed the page to the girl.

"Here you go, hon."

"Thank you."

"You're welcome. Oomph!" Christine was taken by surprise when the girl launched herself at her, wrapping her thin arms around her neck. Grinning, she hugged the girl, giving her a squeeze before letting her go. The older woman said something to the girl in Spanish as Christine stood and shook her hand.

"Thank you again," Juanita said. The pair smiled at Christine and headed back toward the store they'd been about to enter. Christine was filled with a sense of pride that a sweet kid like that would want *her* autograph and think *she* was something special. Yeah, it made all the paparazzi in the world worth it.

Turning, she put on her game face, ready to pose.

"Alright, boys. Who's first?"

They both flinched at the sound of breaking glass. Adam looked around frantically for the sound. His dark eyes finally met Christine's in the darkness of the alley.

"Are you sure you wanna go in there?" he whispered. Looking up and down the trash-filled alley, she sighed, nodding as she met his gaze.

"I have to, man."

"No, you don't. Chris, we'll find another way. You can stay with us again for a few days. You know Mom won't mind..."

"It's not about finding a place to stay, Adam, or having money for a place. Man, this is my chance!" her voice was filled with passion, as were her eyes. Imagine, the guy was giving her a chance to sing!

"But this place is a dive, Chris. You're not even old enough to get in this place, let alone sing here." He grabbed her by the shirt, dragging her into the shadows as two men started to fight in the mouth of the alley, one thrown out into the street, the other following.

The truth of the matter was, Christine was scared to death. The Diamond Back was not exactly top of the line entertainment in Manhattan, but it was the only gig she could get, so she was taking it. She wanted to explain that to her friend, but she knew he wouldn't understand. He didn't get how much she wanted to sing and play her guitar. Adam didn't have a passion of his own, other than finding trouble, so he could never understand.

"Listen, Adam, I'm gonna do this, so either you can sneak in with me to listen or you can grab the next train home. Your choice." She turned and headed toward the back door to the bar, showing far more confidence and bravado than she actually felt.

"Wait." Adam snagged her arm, nearly pulling her off her feet. She glared at him. "I just worry, okay?"

"Yeah, I know." Christine grinned at him, tapping him playfully on the cheek. *"I love you, too, bud. Now I have to go."*

This time he didn't stop her, and she made her way into the dark, smoky bar. The stage was tiny and behind a screen of chain-link. The Diamond Back was known for its fights and rowdy patrons, so she was glad it was there.

It was Christine's first appearance there, though she'd played at any number of other cheesy joints. It was quick money, usually in the neighborhood of about seventy-five to a hundred bucks. It meant she didn't have to swing a trick for a couple of weeks. She was thrilled.

Grabbing her guitar, Christine stepped on stage. There was no house band that night, and she certainly didn't have a band of her own, so it was just her. Oh, and Pluck, her guitar.

She had on the best pair of jeans she owned, only a couple holes instead of connect-the-dots holes, topped by a black t-shirt. She was stylin'.

Adjusting the microphone, she looked out at the crowd, which was mostly men in very dangerous looking chains and leather, looking at her rather expectantly. So, she was supposed to entertain the gorillas, eh? Standing on that five-foot by five-foot stage, just her, a microphone, and a stool...

"Hi," Christine said, the microphone screeching shrilly and earning her boos from the crowd.

"Hey, honey, ain't I seen you somewhere?" someone yelled out. She felt the hair on the back of her neck stiffen. Fuck, all she needed was to run into a client. Thinking fast, unable to see the guy's face as the lights were in hers, Christine quirked a grin.

"I don't know — you been to Hef's mansion lately?" To her surprise and relief that got a round of laughter. Before any more questions or comments could be shot her way, Christine lowered the guitar strap over her shoulder and placed her fingers on the instrument's neck. *"Here we go, boys."*

Looking down at her fingers as they strummed the strings, she got herself in the right frame of mind, head beginning to bob with the acoustic beat she was creating. She decided to ease this crowd into her own stuff, first warming up with a few classics. Bob Seger, Bonnie Raitt, then really get them excited with "Holding Out For A Hero" by Bonnie Tyler. Those boys were whooping and cheering. Shit, she'd never had so many offers in one night in her entire life!

They were nice and ready for her, so Christine launched into a song she'd written last year.

"Okay, this next song is called 'Clutch', and it was written by yours truly."

Damn, she was having fun! She couldn't remember ever having such a responsive audience before. She would definitely be coming back to the Diamond Back.

With more drinks shoved in front of her than she could remember, she popped the top off a Corona and took a swig from the golden liquid, a very satisfied smile spreading across her face.

"Are you even old enough to drink that?"

"Excuse me?" She turned around, ready to grab some nuts until she saw who was sitting on the stool next to hers, one manicured hand casually dangling off the edge of the scarred bar. He was dressed in a gray suit, tie perfectly tied, dark gray. His hair was dark and immaculately slicked back from a tanned face. "Who the fuck are you?"

"My name is Robert Knowles, and I'm wondering if you're old enough to drink that." He indicated the cold one dangling by the neck from her calloused fingers.

"Fuck off, Bob." Christine turned her stool, her back to him.

"How old are you, kid?"

"Old enough to know where the sun don't shine and to stick my bottle there." She glared at him over her shoulder, and he laughed. Real funny.

"Look, kid, I'm not here to cause problems for you or bust you. I was walking by this...bar," he said grudgingly, looking around with distaste, "when I heard you singing," the contempt in his voice obvious.

Christine turned her stool, glancing over at him. Looking him up and down, her nose wrinkled. "Great. So I got me an old guy for a fan. Lucky me."

"No, but perhaps you'll have an old guy as a manager."

She looked at him, trying to read his eyes. This dude's serious! Turning to fully face him, she tilted her head, eyeing him as she sipped her beer.

"Here's my card. I'll be in town for another few days." He reached into the inside breast pocket of his suit jacket, bringing out a very thick wallet. Opening it up, he dug for a moment, then withdrew a black card, handing it to her tucked between two of those manicured fingers. "I hope to hear from you, Christine. You've got quite a talent."

She took the card, looking at it. In silver, textured letters she read: ROBERT T. KNOWLES, MUSIC ENTERPRISES LTD. Looking back up to him, she saw he was already getting off his stool. Tucking the wallet away, he looked around once more, then without so much as another glance at Christine, he left.

The last of the bags were loaded into the belly of the black and silver bus. There were two identical vehicles idling behind it.

"Are we all good?" Stone Lee, road manager extraordinaire, asked into the small cell phone/walkie talkie in his hand.

"All loaded and ready to roll," answered a tinny, disembodied voice.

"Okay. Let's roll 'em!" he called out, waving his arm high in the air for the other drivers to see. All the buses went from idle to roaring life as the large man climbed the stairs of the first bus. The doors closed behind him, and with the whoosh of released air brakes, they were moving.

The early morning air was crisp, but there was already every indication that it would be a hot day in L.A.

Stone made himself comfortable on the five-seater couch toward the front of the bus, the television unwatched as he typed away on his laptop, making sure everything was still good to go for the first two concerts. They would hit all of California, move up through the Northwest, then over and down, zigzagging their way across the country.

Christine was in her private quarters, which took up the entire back half of the bus. She lay on the queen-sized bed, knees drawn up, bare toes tapping to the beat on the comforter as the music played through the headphones of her iPod.

She much preferred headphones to the larger speakers of a stereo. Somehow they brought the music closer, made it more personal and intimate. Three Doors Down sang to her as she lay with her fingers clasped over her stomach and her eyes closed.

Christine was filled with the mixture of fear, anticipation, and excitement that nothing but being on the road could bring her. She had been told that ticket sales were outstanding, with most of the concerts sold out. But still, would her fans forgive her for abandoning them last winter?

Sighing, she threw those thoughts out of her mind, instead concentrating on the music. She had to get herself clear in the head for the performance that night. It would be the first concert she'd given sober in more than two years. Part of her was excited at the thought of actually being able to be present for the concert, rather than going through it in a numb haze. Oh, but what she wouldn't do for a calming hit of weed.

This thought startled her, making guilt course through her. Margaret had warned that this could and probably would happen. "You can't expect a habit of over a decade to just fade and go away overnight," the counselor had warned.

That wasn't good enough for Christine. She was stubborn and impatient, and she wanted it to happen *now*. She had worked so hard to give up the want and need for the numbness that drugs had provided for her. Life was so much easier when you didn't have to feel.

"Check, check, check. Check one, check one, check one."

As the sound engineers and set builders did their thing, Christine met up with the boys in the band to discuss how the show was to go that night.

Afterwards she walked the large auditorium, big enough to hold twenty-thousand pulsing, cheering, screaming fans. She smiled at the thought, closing her eyes to imagine their voices, all mingling into one beast of excitement.

"Okay," she breathed, "maybe this won't be so bad."

"Why didn't you tell me, Willow? Damn it, I'm your husband. I know how attached you were..."

"I'm fine, Kevin." Willow looked at her husband's reflection in the mirror, telling him with her eyes that she didn't want to talk about it. He didn't take the hint.

"When did she die?" he persisted, sitting on the closed toilet seat, watching as his wife applied a touch of makeup to the eyes that had first caught his attention six years ago. Intense eyes that looked at you, *into* you. It made lying hard.

Willow sighed as she twisted the cap off her mascara, looking at herself, and then opening her eyes wide as she lined her lashes. "Two weeks ago."

"Two weeks." He did the math, brows knit. He shook his head, not remembering any change in Willow's demeanor. He sighed, picking at a stringy wedge of toilet paper that had been left after some of the tissue had been ripped from the roll.

He hated how much Willow kept to herself, wishing that she'd let him help her. He knew that the death of the girl with leukemia must have been devastating to her. She had been with the family since the kid got sick. That much she had told him.

"Do you trust me, Will?" he finally asked, watching as she brushed something across her cheeks and forehead. He didn't understand all that makeup stuff, and since she didn't wear it much, he had no idea what was what. She stopped what she was doing and looked at him.

"Of course. What kind of question is that?" Willow felt slightly hurt at such a question.

Kevin shrugged. "I don't know. It doesn't matter." He stood, kissing the back of her neck. "I hope you guys have fun at the concert. That was really nice of Rachel to get you guys tickets like that." He appraised the beautiful woman in the mirror, wrapping his arms around her waist.

"Yeah, it was." Willow couldn't meet his eyes. She felt guilty as hell lying to him about where the tickets came from, but if she told the truth, she'd have to tell him about that night in February.

"I'll see you when you get home." One final kiss to her cheek, and he left her alone in the bathroom.

Willow sighed, understanding why Kevin was upset with her but not knowing what to do about it. They had dinner with Rachel and Connor two nights ago, and Rachel had brought up Melissa's passing. Kevin had been stunned, looking at his wife with questioning eyes. Willow had expected a discussion that night when they'd got home, but instead he had waited until that morning.

"So, since when do you keep stuff from me?" he asked, putting away the laundry Willow had washed the day before. Confused, she glanced up at him, making the bed.

"What?"

"That girl who was sick. The one we took to the movie that time." He closed the closet door, perhaps a little harder than necessary.

She sighed, realizing he was ready to rumble now. "I wasn't aware that I had to keep you updated on everything at work." Tossing the folded socks from the dresser to the bed, she opened the sock drawer and began to move things around, making room for the freshly washed items.

"Oh, come on, Willow. It's not about that and you know it. I'm not your keeper, but Jesus, you really cared for that kid, and from what Rachel said at dinner, you were pretty devastated when she died."

"Look, Kevin, it's my job, okay? I took on the responsibility of becoming a nurse, so now I have to deal with it. And I certainly don't need you to

babysit me, alright?" As soon as the words were out of her mouth, she felt like a real bitch. Sighing, Willow ran a hand through her hair. "I'm sorry."

"No. No worries. You'll deal. Fine." Kevin rushed by her, out of the bedroom. Willow didn't follow, knowing how he was when he was upset. She decided to leave him be.

Putting the rest of her clothes away, she headed to the bathroom for a shower.

"Honey?" Willow pulled her wallet out of the purse that sat on the kitchen table. Not hearing anything, she looked over her shoulder, trying to spot her husband. She could hear the faint sound of the television and walked into the living room.

Kevin sat on the couch, arm resting along the back. Willow leaned down, hugging him from behind.

"I'm sorry, honey," she said into his neck.

"It's okay," he said quietly, turning his head to give her a solid kiss on the lips. "You two have a great time, okay?" Willow nodded.

"Okay." She hugged him tightly, then let him go, grabbing her keys from the table and tucking her wallet into the back pocket of her jeans, then heading out.

"I have never seen so many women in all my life," Rachel muttered, leaning over to her friend, who chuckled.

"I guess that's what happens when you're a lesbian icon," Willow muttered back, eyeing all the excited women around them.

"You're kidding? What, is she, like Melissa Etheridge or something?"

"Of the alternative music world, yes."

Rachel looked at her, surprised. "How do you know?"

"I read about it," Willow whispered, smiling at the look of confusion on her friend's face.

"Huh. Guess I didn't know you were such a fan," Rachel whispered back. The lights began to lower.

"I'm not."

The lights were nearly completely dimmed now, the front of the auditorium and darkened stage filling with gray smoke. A pulsing beat began, low, almost too quiet to be heard, but it could certainly be felt. Willow's bones pulsed with it.

"Mm, you feel that?" a smoky, deep voice riding on velvet said, sensuous as it spread throughout the auditorium. The audience started to go nuts.

Willow and Rachel looked at each other, matching grins spreading across their faces. The excitement was palpable.

The beat was getting louder, and blue lights were slowly rising, pushing their way through the smoke. All around the stage were sparkling lights, creating the effect of a night filled with fog. The coolness from the dry ice machines reached the front row, where Willow and Rachel sat, making the effect that much more real.

"You feel it. Like a heartbeat," the voice said, followed by a long sigh.

"She's got a really sexy voice," Rachel whispered. Willow nodded in agreement, her eyes searching the stage. "I wish I sounded like that when I talked dirty." Dark figures began to be outlined as more lights rose — members of the band. A low guitar joined in with the beat.

"Feel it, want it, taste it," the voice whispered, as if in the throes of passion. The audience was on its feet now, eyes desperately scanning for the first glimpse of Christine Gray.

Willow gasped as a small burst of light illuminated the drummer from below, casting his features in freakish shadows, his sticks in continuous motion.

"That's right. Let's get a little light on the subject," breathed the voice over the audience. Willow was surprised to feel a little shiver down her spine, her excitement building with everyone else's.

Another burst of light and the guitarist was revealed, followed by the bass and keyboard players in swift succession. There was now a ring of smoky figures around the outer edges of the stage; the center was still in impenetrable darkness.

The drumbeat was at a feverish pitch now, resonating in the bones of the excited, anxious fans, nearly out of their minds with anticipation.

Suddenly all music stopped, and a heavy silence filled the large space and everyone in it. Willow was almost holding her breath, hearing her own heartbeat fill her ears.

A sensuous sigh, then blinding light. Thousands of pairs of eyes squinted at the burst. Mad cheering erupted once vision had cleared and they saw — Christine, standing center stage, head arched back, eyes closed, the silver light above her shining down like the very touch of God.

She wore fitted, yet comfortable, blue jeans, ripped in all the right places, and a ribbed, white tee molded to her torso, its capped sleeves hugging her firm biceps. Her dark hair was wild, spread across her shoulders and down her back. She was the picture of sensuous strength.

A heartbeat passed with the cheers at a deafening pitch, then the music began in earnest. There was a blast of fire and smoke, and Christine Gray was visible in all her glory, the light full-on, blue eyes gazing out upon her sea of fans, microphone held to her mouth as she began to sing.

Willow, caught up in the rush of adrenaline, was on her feet with twenty thousand other people, dancing in the aisles. The front row was close enough to the stage that they could take a few steps and touch the apron.

Standing on that stage, singing her heart out, Christine felt her blood roaring through her veins. The audience was a black blur to her, save for the first six rows or so. She scanned those, seeing a mass of faces looking up at her in absolute adoration, some singing along with her. She played to them, walking to the very edge of the stage, feeling hands grabbing at her legs. She touched some of those hands, kneeling down and singing directly to certain women.

As she moved her way down, seducing them with her voice and words and what had been described by more than one journalist as "unearthly beauty and sexiness", she reached the seats that had been reserved for Willow Bowman and her guest.

She recognized one of the women as one of the nurses from the ER that night. She studied the people flanking the redhead. To her right was a man, so she figured the woman sitting on her left must be Willow. She looked so much different without the creepy clown makeup. When Christine looked into those green eyes, though, she knew it was the same woman.

She smiled at the nurse, bowing slightly and looking up at her through her bangs.

Willow looked at the singer, not four feet from her, and her excitement level rose. She blushed, having the sole attention of Christine Gray. She almost fainted when the woman bowed to her, giving her a playful wink before standing and moving on.

"Oh my God!" Rachel yelled above the music, tugging excitedly at her friend's hand. Willow grinned.

Chapter 4

Willow and Rachel stood in a dimly lit hallway lined with large, black instrument and equipment cases.

"What are we supposed to do?" Rachel whispered, looking around, seeing the door behind them that she knew led to the now empty auditorium.

"I haven't a clue," Willow said, resting against the cool, cinderblock wall. The security guard had told them to wait there, so that's what they were doing and had been doing for about five minutes.

"Ladies." Both nurses turned, startled by the sudden appearance of a very large man, bald and dressed in black, an I.D. hanging from his neck. He beckoned to them. "Follow me."

As he led them down the hall, they stuck together nervously. Closed doors began to appear in the wall to their right, various signs marking their purpose — Electrical Room, Storage, Props, and then Private.

The Mr. Clean look-a-like stopped at that door, holding it open for them. "Go on in," he said. The door closed behind them, and the large man was gone.

They were in another hallway, this one well lit. Noise could be heard further down where the light from various open doors could be seen. There was laughter and whooping before conversation. People, all dressed like Mr. Clean, swarmed from room to room, talking amongst themselves, some barking out orders for the removal of equipment or the breaking down of the stage flats. None paid a lick of attention to the women.

Willow felt uncertain in a strange world that she didn't understand. She had no idea where they were supposed to go or what they were supposed to do. She felt like an intruder.

Finally a familiar face appeared out of the closest of the rooms, which they were beginning to realize were dressing rooms. He'd been playing guitar; his long, blond hair, down and free during the show, was now pulled back into a ponytail. "Hey. Are you the nurse?" he asked, walking over to them, a half-drunk bottle of water in his hand.

"Yes. Willow Bowman," she said, holding out her hand.

"Hey. Nice to finally meet you. I'm Joey Manning." He grinned at both women, charm oozing from him. "Come on, I'll take you to Chris." He turned to head back down the hall, and Willow and Rachel followed. Rachel's eyes were fixed firmly to his leather-clad butt, and she fanned herself.

Christine held her hands in tight fists, willing them to stay put. She watched as Bob went through her makeup kit, tossing tubes and compacts to the floor.

"These colors don't work for you," he muttered, opening a tube of lipstick, grimacing at the color.

"Be glad I wear the shit at all, Bob," she growled. She hadn't expected him anywhere on the tour. He usually stayed back in California, making more deals on her behalf.

"And what the hell is this shit?" He walked over to her, leaving the mess on the vanity counter and floor. He snapped the white tank top she'd changed into mid-show. "This isn't what you were fitted for." He looked into her eyes, level with his, dark and dangerous.

"It's called a shirt, Bob." Christine stared back with just as much intensity. "And I told you back in L.A. that I wasn't going to dress like a whore."

He moved in closer, nose to nose with her. "And *I* told *you* to wear it." It was a battle of wills as they stared each other down. Robert Knowles could tell it was going to be tough this time. Seems his ingénue had turned into a downright diva.

Fine. He knew how to deal with her and nip the problem in the bud.

"Don't fuck with me, Christine," he murmured. "What would the world say if they knew their hero was a two-bit whore with a drug problem?"

Christine was trembling, hatred seething through her at an alarming pace. Her nostrils flared, and her pulse raced in her temples and neck.

The clearing of a throat broke the spell — and thoughts of homicide. Christine tore her gaze from Bob and saw Joey standing in the doorway.

"Chris, you've got some visitors," the guitarist said quietly, moving aside to reveal Willow and Rachel.

"You enjoy your little nurse," Bob said, bringing her attention back to him. He took a step back, bringing his hands up to brush non-existent lint from Christine's shoulders. "We'll continue this later." Turning, about to leave, he stopped. "Oh, and if you ever again play that sappy, Liberace bullshit you did during your encore, I'll pull your song-writing rights." With that, he was gone.

The manager eyed the two women as he passed them in the doorway, stopping for a brief moment.

"Ms. Bowman, nice to see you again." He gave her a toothy grin, his skin as smooth and tanned as she remembered.

"Mr. Knowles." Willow smiled, but by the time he'd oozed by she felt nauseous. Something about the well-dressed man made her feel as if she were covered in slime.

Christine took several deep breaths, knowing she had to calm herself. She really wanted to meet and speak with Willow Bowman, but she didn't want to be completely keyed up when she did.

She'd have to give Joey a hug and kiss later on — he was keeping the women occupied, showing them around Christine's dressing room, explaining things to them, and making them laugh with various stories of being on the road.

Finally getting herself under control, Christine put a smile on her face and turned to the trio.

"Oh, don't lie, Joey. You set that fire in the Ritz, not Wade." The guitarist looked at her, relieved. He was running out of stories. Christine turned her winning smile on the two nurses. "Welcome, ladies."

"I'll leave you three be now." Joey grinned once more at the nurses, winking at Rachel and making her swoon.

Christine looked at the woman who had saved her life, able to really see her for the first time. She was a small woman, petite but not at all frail-looking. After all, she'd been able to drag her sorry ass out of the water. Her gaze was strong and steady, though from the flushed skin of her face, Christine could tell the nurse was nervous. She wore jeans that hugged her narrow hips and showed off her muscular thighs. A fitted baby doll tee set off the outfit.

"I must say," she said quietly, a soft smile grazing her lips, "you look a lot different minus the creepy clown makeup."

Willow smiled shyly, looking down for a moment before pinning her with those beautiful eyes.

"It's really nice to see you, Ms. Gray, to know that you're alright," Willow said softly, meaning every word.

"Please call me Christine." She turned to the Rachel. "I don't think we've met. Hi, I'm Christine Gray, midnight scuba diver."

Rachel was surprised at the way the singer poked fun at herself. She smiled, taking the hand extended to her. "Rachel Dodge. I'm a nurse in the Mercy ER."

"I thought you looked familiar. Thank you ladies so much for coming. I hope you had a good time?" She looked questioningly from one to the other.

"You were wonderful," Willow said with reverence. "I've never been to such an amazing show."

"It was fantastic," Rachel agreed, all smiles.

"I'm so pleased." Christine was surprised to feel the heat of embarrassment ride up her neck and the urge to say, "Aw, garsh, thanks." Instead, she turned to Willow and said, "I hope you don't mind, but there's something I've been wanting to do for months."

"Sure." Willow looked expectant then stunned when the tall, beautiful singer opened her arms and grabbed her in a tight embrace.

At first Willow was stiff at the unexpected physical contact, but she soon found herself leaning into the warm embrace, tentatively wrapping her arms around the singer's back. The hug was brief but ended with a firm squeeze.

Christine pulled away but kept her hands on Willow's shoulders as she looked down into her eyes.

"Thank you, Willow. Those words seem so puny for the depth of my gratitude, but I can't quite think of anything else to say."

Willow was stunned again. Christine didn't have to say a thing — she could see it in those bright, clear blue eyes. She nodded, hoping that Christine could see her acceptance of the gratitude.

"I'd do it again in a heartbeat," she finally managed.

"I have no doubt." They shared a smile, then Christine broke the spell. "So, did you ladies meet the band?"

"Just Joey," Rachel said quickly, then blushed furiously. Both Willow and Christine grinned.

"Well, come on. I'll introduce you to the rest of the boys."

As they followed her out of the room, Willow was lost in thought. She was amazed at how warm and generous Christine Gray was, as well as being drop-dead gorgeous. None of the singer's pictures or commercials did her justice. She was by far the most beautiful woman Willow had ever seen.

She thought back to that cold, frightening night six months earlier. Christine had been ghostly pale, her eyes sunken in, her body so thin she looked as though she could be snapped in half if not handled with care. In short, she had looked sick.

Now, she was tanned and vivacious, filled with life. It was a rare thing for Willow to see patients once they'd left the hospital. Seeing this magnificent turnaround filled her with an unending gratitude that she had been able to do what she did and have had the knowledge she needed to help Christine that night. It made it all worthwhile.

"What are you grinning at?" Rachel asked, brow raised.

"I don't know. I guess it's just an amazing thing for me to be able to see her, you know? After that night. I don't know." Willow shivered at the memory.

"That really got to you, didn't it?" Rachel whispered, eyeing Christine to make sure she couldn't hear them. Willow nodded.

"Yeah."

"Guys, I'd like you to meet two very special women." Christine walked into Eli's dressing room, where the band had gathered, beers already cracked open. The three men turned to look at Willow and Rachel. Christine brought the women to either side of her, a hand on each of their outer shoulders. "This is Rachel, one of the nurses who helped to bring my sorry ass back to the world of the living, and this is Willow Bowman. She saved my life."

Willow blushed, unsure what to do with the round of applause she got from the band. Finally able to meet their eyes, she whispered a thank you.

"Ladies, the guy standing over there, as you know, is Joey, known to his mother as Joseph Howard Dillon. Joey's up there with his idol and mentor Eddie Van Halen. Greatest guitarist in the world. Sitting with beer in hand, Eli Stein, drummer extraordinaire, and finally Davies Washington. Keyboards and bass."

"Nice to meet you two fine-looking ladies." Davies grinned, teeth blinding against his dark skin.

"Hello," Willow said shyly with a small wave.

"You guys were fantastic." Rachel's eyes were huge as she took in the guitars lying around, the drumsticks on the vanity counter, and the atmosphere that radiated from those guys. They were rockers, musicians. That was something she'd always been drawn to. When she was a teenager, she'd told her mother she wanted to be a groupie for Bon Jovi when she got older.

If only she weren't with Connor. She sighed at the lost opportunity. She'd certainly love to be a groupie for Joey Dillon. His long, blond hair, bright blue eyes...

Rachel shook herself out of her less than pure thoughts, seeing Willow smilingly studying her. She glared at her friend, feeling embarrassed.

"Hey, Chris, we were all about to grab something to eat. You comin'?" Joey asked, standing next to the singer, eyeing Rachel with an appreciative gaze.

Christine turned to her guests with questioning eyes. "You guys want to come?"

"Oh, we can't," Rachel said, true regret coloring her words. "I have to work tonight and get this one back home." She put her arm around Willow's waist.

"Do you work tonight, Willow?" Christine asked, leaning her shoulder against the doorframe, arms crossed over her chest.

"No," Willow said slowly, noting the smile that spread across the singer's face.

"Then how about this — Rachel, you go on to work, and I'll personally make sure Willow gets home before curfew." Christine grinned.

"Your bandmates are pretty crazy." Willow glanced over at the woman sitting next to her in the very back of the stretch limo. Christine chuckled.

"You have no idea." She met the smiling green eyes. "Thanks for coming to dinner with us. I hope we didn't scare you too badly."

"No. Not *too* bad." They shared a shy smile. "No, in all honesty, it was fun. You guys are so fun to watch together."

"Well, most of us have been together for many years. Eli is our newest member."

"When did he join?"

"Three years ago," Christine said quietly. Willow studied the singer's profile, feeling the sadness that roiled off her. Then she remembered.

"After the accident."

Christine nodded. "Yeah."

"I'm sorry." Willow recalled reading about it when she'd done research on Christine Gray. Three years ago original band member Frances Ray, or Frankie, had been killed in a horrible motorcycle accident.

They were both silent, as the long car turned and drove under the wrought iron arches onto the private road that led to Willow's ranch. Glad for the reprieve, Christine leaned toward the window, watching the dark scenery pass by. Unfortunately she wasn't able to see much, but she had the feeling the ranch was something to see come daylight.

"You live here, huh?" she said, her voice wistful.

"Yeah." Willow couldn't keep the pride from her voice. "My grandparents made this place special."

Christine looked at her, moved by the reverence she heard in her voice and saw in her posture.

The limo came to a stop in front of the farmhouse, and Willow turned to Christine. "Want a midnight tour?"

Christine was poised to happily accept but then realized the time crunch she was in. Smiling apologetically at Willow, she said, "I really would love to, Willow, but I can't. We need to get moving."

"Oh, of course." Willow smiled, feeling silly for even offering. Why on earth would this woman, famous, rich, talented beyond all belief, want to see how the simple people live? She wanted to melt into the car mat.

The door was suddenly opened, the driver extending a hand to help her out. She took it, surprised to find Christine following her out. She looked up at the singer uncertainly.

"Thank you for coming, Willow," Christine said. "It meant a lot."

"Oh." Willow was stunned by how genuine those words were. "It was truly my pleasure, Ms. Gray."

"Christine."

"Christine." Willow smiled sheepishly.

"Good. Here." Willow found something placed in her hand and realized it was a small slip of paper. "If you ever need anything, please don't hesitate to call." From the stunned look on Willow's face, Christine knew she could trust this woman with the personal information she'd just given her. It wasn't just anyone she gave a path of contact to.

"Thank you," Willow said with awe, having noticed a phone number on the paper she pocketed. She then found herself wrapped up in a warm hug.

"It was nice to see you, Willow," Christine said, releasing her.

"You, too. Please, please take care of yourself." Willow looked up into Christine's eyes, her own pleading. The singer smiled with a nod.

"I promise."

With that she was gone.

Willow watched as the red taillights of the limo disappeared into the darkness, a buzzing soaring through her body. She was filled with adrenaline as she fully realized how amazing her evening had been.

She felt like jumping up and down and howling at the moon. A natural high coursed through her; she had no doubt it was what being on drugs was like. She grinned from ear to ear, a little chuckle-growl erupting from her throat.

"Hey, babe," Kevin called out from the living room as Willow headed toward the stairs.

"Hey," she answered, voice in a daze. Kevin leaned back in the couch, trying to get a glimpse of his wife. "Did you have fun?"

"Amazing."

"Long concert."

"We went to dinner after." Willow tossed her keys and wallet onto the small table at the foot of the stairs.

"But I thought Rachel had to work tonight?" Kevin said, standing in the archway between the living room and the small foyer where his wife already had her foot on the bottom step.

"She did." With that quiet response, Willow headed up to bed. She was exhausted from all the excitement of the night. Kevin watched her go, shaking his head as he turned back to the living room and ESPN.

Willow headed out of the bathroom, the sound of soft flushing behind her, and grabbed her shirt from the hem, pulling it off in one fluid movement. Tossing it to the laundry basket at the foot of the bed, she emptied her pockets, pulling out change, ChapStick, and the folded piece of paper. Looking at it, she shook her head in disbelief.

"I can't believe she gave me her number," she muttered, tucking the paper into her jewelry box for safekeeping.

Christine sat back against the soft leather seat of the limo. She sighed happily, thinking over the evening. Willow was everything she expected someone so generous to be. She could sense a level of compassion in the nurse that she'd never seen before.

Such a beautiful woman. She hoped to see her again.

The ride back to the hotel was quiet. Christine was so lost in her thoughts that before she knew it, they were pulling into the circular drive and her door was being opened.

"Have a nice night, miss," the chauffeur said, tipping his hat.

"Thank you." He bowed slightly at the tip she gave him.

"Good evening, Ms. Gray," the doorman said, opening the tinted glass door at the front of the hotel.

"Good evening to you, too. Thank you." She passed through with a smile, hurrying to the elevator banks. She had a lot to do tonight, and she didn't want to be sidetracked by fans or the press. Truth be told, she was exhausted and just wanted to rest in a real bed. Not to be.

As the light flashed green, Christine removed her keycard and pushed open the door to her suite. She groaned when she saw a lone figure sitting in a chair, legs gracefully crossed, casually holding a tumbler filled with amber fluid in his well-manicured hand.

"What are you doing in here?" she sighed, headed toward her bedroom. She'd changed clothes after the show, but she was craving a hot shower.

"I told you we weren't finished with our conversation." He downed the rest of his drink, setting the tumbler on the table next to him.

"What's to talk about?" Christine called from the bedroom, digging through her suitcase until she found a comfortable pair of jeans and tank top to change into after her shower.

"Plenty."

She turned, seeing her manager standing in the doorway of the room, noting his perfectly tailored slacks with a white button-up shirt tucked into them, sleeves rolled up to mid-forearm. That was his "sloppy" look.

"Such as?" Tired of this, Christine turned to him, hand on hip.

"Such as what was that garbage you pulled out of your ass during the encore? That was *not* on the roster, Christine." Folding his arms across his chest, he took an aggressive stance.

"I wrote that song, Bob. I wanted to try it out on a live audience, and it worked. They loved it." She turned back to her mission, tossing a thong and pair of socks onto the bed next to the jeans and tank.

"You sitting at a piano, spotlight on you, singing some bullshit song about love, is *not* you, and it will *never* be you. Got me?"

Christine gasped, hearing Bob's voice suddenly directly behind her. She quickly moved away from him, putting the bed between them.

"Are you threatening me?" she asked, anger building.

"I'm simply telling you how it is. I've not steered you wrong in almost twenty years, and I'm not about to start now." Bob leaned against the dresser behind him.

"I'm a big girl now, Bob. I'm not some naïve kid off the streets," she pointed out.

"You think you can take care of yourself?" he asked, his voice rising, though still under careful control. "Then why the fuck were you in rehab not six months ago?"

Her jaw muscles frantically spasming, she made her way back around the bed in seconds, to stand mere inches from Knowles.

"Don't kid yourself, Bob," she growled. "My problems are my own, but know this: You're at the root of many of them. You're only going to push me so far, and then that'll be it. Got me?"

Bob stared at her, willpower alone keeping his jaw from dropping. In all his years as Christine Gray's manager, she'd never spoken back to him or outright threatened him. He was at loss for words. The singer used that to her advantage.

"Now get out of here so I can get ready to go." She grabbed her clothes, then headed into the bathroom, slamming the door behind her.

Robert Knowles stood there in the empty room, blinking rapidly. Swallowing his anger, he glanced down at the bed. Reaching out, his fingers made contact with the soft, silky material of one of Christine's shirts. Sighing sadly, he gently tucked the shirt back into the suitcase and left the suite.

"So this is California." Before this joker showed up she had never flown. She didn't like it. There was just something unnatural about being thirty-five thousand feet in the air when God hadn't given you wings.

"This is Christine Gray. Christine, Dr. Pollani." The two men left her by the door as they consulted. "Wayne, I want every part of her checked. I want to know anything she has, sexual diseases, birth defects, everything, and anything. If she has lice, I need to know."

"You've got it, Bobby," the doctor said, slapping the manager on the shoulder.

The door to the large office opened, almost knocking her on her ass. Christine growled. "Oh, sorry, hon." A young woman wearing scrubs entered, followed by a man and a woman pushing a table of equipment and covered tools. She held out a gown. "I need you to go across the hall and put this on, okay? I need everything gone, panties, bra, and all jewelry. Alright?"

With a smile, Robert Knowles left. Christine nodded dumbly, then went to change. Not sure what to do with her only pair of jeans and her shirt, one of the three she had to her name, she folded them and left them in the curtained cubicle.

In bare feet and trying to not let her ass show, she went back across the hall to the office where the doctor and nurse were waiting. Christine swallowed, uncertainty flowing through her in very unwelcome waves.

"Come over here, Christine, honey." The nurse grabbed her by the arm and led her to the scale where her weight and height were written down, Dr. Pollani and the nurse muttering amongst themselves. God damn, she felt so exposed! And that was before the doc told her to lie on the table and put her legs in the cold, metal stirrups! Christine had never in her life been so humiliated as when he sat on a stool between her legs looking into her twat, the nurse standing behind him scribbling onto the chart whatever he said.

She stared up at the ceiling, trying to forget what was happening to her. She could go out and fuck ten guys and not feel nearly as...bare. She cringed as something cold and metallic was inserted in her, making her feel as if she was being fucked by the Terminator or something. Vaginal and anal rape, at least it felt like it, finished at last, and she was sat up and asked a ton of questions. Then finally the doc got around to looking into her eyes, her nose, and her ears.

Like a day later, okay, so about two hours later, the doc was done. She was allowed to get dressed, then whisked off in a town car with tinted windows, up into the hills of Beverly Hills, through locked gates and on up to a mansion, the likes of which she had only seen in People magazine and reruns of Dynasty.

She was so tired; she just wanted a bed. Her body hurt from being almost ripped apart by that damn doctor.

The house was in chaos as she was ushered in, people flying around everywhere, barking orders, following orders, all of them ignoring her.

"Tonya, take her." Knowles shoved Christine toward a young Hispanic woman who took hold of her hand, wordlessly leading her toward the massive staircase.

"Where am I?" she asked, looking frantically around as they hurried past a hall of closed doors, the one at the very end being opened by a key Tonya slid in the lock.

"You're at Mr. Bob's house, and this will be your room while you're here." The door opened to a large room with a bed, two dressers, and two huge windows. A closed door off to the left led to what she assumed was a bathroom.

"How long—" The door closed and Tonya was gone. "Great fucking hospitality," she muttered, heading over to the closed door. Yep, bathroom, claw-footed tub, toilet, and oval mirror. Very basic. "Jesus. Feel like I'm in a fucking hospital."

The room was just as basic, though nice. Certainly nicer than where she had been in Queens. Looking out one of the windows she saw the sun was high, the grass green, and flowers in bloom.

Sleep came quickly. It wasn't anything new for her to sleep in a strange place, but this time it was nice for it to actually be clean. Man, some of those motels got nasty!

She didn't remember the last time she'd had sheets that felt or smelled so good. She stretched out her body, luxuriating in the feel of the cotton against her naked skin. Maybe this wouldn't be such a bad deal after all.

"Whoa, baby. Thatta girl." The horse pulled up to the fence, and Willow swung off her back. "That's my Star. Good girl." The horse snorted, nudging Willow with her nose. "How about an apple, huh?" Heading over to the bucket on the porch, she grabbed a nice, juicy Granny Smith and headed back to the rail fence that Star leaned her head over. "Here, baby."

The horse took the treat, the hairs on her nose tickling Willow's palm. She smiled, running her hand down the mare's nose, fingering the white star pattern.

"Hey, babe?" Kevin called out from the garage.

"Yeah?"

"Have you seen my fishing gear?"

Willow glanced toward the large structure, hearing things being moved around, then a crash.

"I'm fine!" Kevin called out, making Willow dread what she'd find. As she got to the garage, Kevin came out, fishing pole and tackle box in hand. Showing her the rod with a victorious grin, he loaded them into the back of his truck.

"Do you have everything?" she asked, peeking over the side of the large truck, seeing the tent in its bag, his sleeping bag, the cooler filled with food they'd bought four days before, and now the rod and tackle box.

"I think so." He grinned, settling his fishing vest in place. Willow knew that it soon would be accompanied by that horrible fishing hat he loved so much.

"You guys have fun, and no falling into the river this time." She poked him.

"Yeah, yeah." Leaning down, he kissed his wife, savoring her feel and flavor. "See you Tuesday night."

"Okay." Giving him one last squeeze, Willow let him go, watching as he climbed into the truck cab. With a last wave, he started up the engine and headed out.

Willow took care of Star, then headed toward the house. Kevin and his three brothers were going fishing for the next four days, leaving her by herself. She relished the time, almost skipping to the porch.

Walking into the quiet house, Willow trailed her fingers over the walls of the entry hall. She had been meaning to change the wallpaper, yet was hesitant. The paper had been her grandma's favorite, and for that reason she was loath to lose it, even though she hated it.

Peeking into the kitchen, she saw the dishes drying in the rack by the sink and the newspaper folded neatly at the edge of the table in the breakfast nook. All was quiet.

Not sure what she wanted to do, she hurried up the stairs, which squeaked all the way. On reaching the bedroom she shared with Kevin, she decided to take a long, hot bath in their jacuzzi. She stripped down, walking around nude to get a little "friend" from the top drawer of her bedside table. Tucking the small toy in her palm, she noticed her jewelry box out of the corner of her eye.

The paper was cool between her fingers.

Her eyes closed, Christine's fingers raced over the keys. Beethoven's "Moonlight" Sonata filled the large room and her soul. She loved the smooth feel of the ivory, the slickness of the black keys.

Eyes closed, head swaying, she found peace.

The music ended, the final note sounded with such love, such care, slowly dying out in the space.

Christine's head turned at the soft knock on her music room door.

"Yeah, Millie?"

"You've got a call, Christine." Millie walked into the room, cell phone in hand.

"Who is it?" She turned on the slick wood bench to give her housekeeper her full attention.

"Willow Bowman," Millie said, a twinkle in her dark eyes.

"Oh. Thank you." Christine smiled, taking the phone. The older woman nodded, then hurried out, softly closing the door behind her. "Willow?" There was a slight pause.

"Um, hi." Willow sounded so nervous.

"Are you okay? Do you need anything?" Christine sat forward on the piano bench, worry suddenly filling her. She heard a soft laugh on the other end of the line.

"I'm fine, Christine. I just, I don't know, just wanted to say hi, I guess." Willow leaned back against the headboard, tucking the phone beneath her cheek and shoulder. She felt nervous chills race up and down her spine; her palms were sweating, and her voice was almost quivering.

"Oh." Christine covered her eyes with her hand, feeling silly. "Hi. Sorry, just got worried for a second."

"It's no problem. I guess you did say call if I needed anything." Willow chuckled nervously, feeling like a dork. "How are you doing? I hear your tour was an all-around success. Working on anything new?"

"Yeah, I was pleased with the tour. Glad it's over for now, though." Christine smiled, her finger tracing one of the piano keys. "No, I'm taking a break right now, writing some new songs. Oh, and I'm fine."

Willow smiled, then took a deep breath to gather her courage. "Listen, Christine, um, I'm glad to hear that you're taking some time off because uh, well, to be honest I do have a *slightly* ulterior motive for calling."

"Oh?" Truly intrigued, the singer leaned back, bracing her weight on her hand.

"Yes. Um, well, see Kevin is out fishing with his brothers over the weekend, and I have some time off, and I was wondering if maybe, well, if perhaps, you might want that tour of the ranch now." She squeezed her eyes shut, grimacing as she waited for the answer.

"Yes," Christine said, not even thinking. She surprised herself with such a spontaneous reaction, but didn't regret it.

Willow shot up. "Yes?"

"Yes. I'll come."

"Oh." Willow let out her held breath, a smile spreading. "Oh. Great!"

"When would you like me to come?" Christine stood, heading out of the room to write a note for Millie to start on the arrangements.

"Well, uh, whenever it's feasible for you."

"Well, let's see." The singer glanced over at the wall clock. "It's ten-thirty a.m. here in L.A., about a four-hour flight, give or take, how about I get there around five?"

Willow blinked. "Yeah, okay!"

"Great!" Christine grinned. "See you then."

"'Kay." Willow hit the off button on her phone, a grin plastered to her face. Then, "Oh my God!"

Jumping up from the bed, she began to run around the house, cleaning like she'd never cleaned before, changing sheets on every single bed in the house, not knowing if Christine Gray would be staying for the weekend or if she'd don her cape and fly back home that night.

She quickly took a shower, making sure her little buddy was safely put back in the bedside table. There was no way she could do that, then face Christine Gray. She'd melt from embarrassment, thinking that perhaps the singer would somehow be able to look into her immediate past and see what she'd been up to that afternoon.

Pushing those thoughts from her mind, she quickly took care of the animals, then waited. Impatiently. Her eyes strayed to the clock above the kitchen sink for the fifth time in fifteen minutes.

"A watched pot will not boil. A watched pot will not boil." Willow gasped as the sound of gravel crunching under tires hit her ears. Taking a deep breath and wiping sweaty palms on her denim-clad thighs, Willow ran a hand through her hair and headed to the front door. Through the screen she saw the flicker of red as a car came up the drive, then the whole thing. A red Jeep Wrangler.

The Jeep pulled to a stop in front of the small yard. The woman behind the wheel was wind-blown and wild looking. She glanced over at Willow and smiled with a wave. Willow waved back.

Chapter 5

Willow glanced over her shoulder, stunned all over again to see Christine Gray following her up the squeaky staircase, overnight bag slung over her shoulder. Christine grinned knowingly up at her, making her almost trip over the top step as she reached the second floor landing.

She led her guest through the first door into a large, sun-filled room. Christine looked around, finding the rustic, country feel of the place almost comforting. She could feel the warmth and love that radiated from the old walls.

"Is this okay? I know it's not much. Probably not what you're used to." Willow smiled, leaning against the wall by the open door.

"No, this is beautiful." Christine smiled back, taking in the antique four-poster bed with its handmade quilt, the matching dresser and vanity. An antique water basin stood atop the small table under the window. "I love it."

Willow watched as she walked around the room, booted heels knocking on the old, wooden floor, which squeaked in a few places.

"How old is this house?" Christine set her bag down on the bed, smiling as the bag bounced a bit.

"Well over a hundred years."

"Show me." At Willow's look of confusion, Christine grabbed her hand, pulling her out of the room. "You promised me a tour, so come on."

Willow grinned, nearly tugged off her feet. "Okay, okay!"

"And, last but certainly not least, my babies." Willow hung her arms over the rail fence, nodding toward the pasturing family of horses.

"How many do you have?" Christine also leaned on the fence. She backed off a bit when Jack, a huge black gelding, snorted in her general direction.

"They won't hurt you. I have six. That big guy there eyeing you is Jack. He's seven and as gentle as a bear, aren't you, big guy?" Snorting again and tossing his head, Jack walked over to Willow's outstretched hand, sniffing it.

"Well, they're a bit too tall for my taste."

Willow eyed the tall singer, a brow raised. Christine smiled sheepishly, looking down. "Yes, well, the secret's out. I'm a big ol' wuss."

"I won't tell." Willow glanced at her companion, chewing on her lip for a moment, thinking. "Want to see the rest of the property?"

Christine's gaze left the horse, turning to the nurse. "Yeah," she said, a bit of challenge in her voice.

"Follow me."

"Okay, pull in the clutch here and give her gas at the same time. Easy, easy, now." Willow grinned, holding Christine back as she gunned the engine, almost sending her flying off God knew where. "Your brake is here." She squeezed the brake on the left side of the handle bar.

"Okay. I think I got it." Christine looked down at the red bike, which Willow had called a 1994 Yamaha WR 250. Her friend sat astride a matching yellow one.

"Ready?"

Christine nodded, revving her engine, as did Willow. With that, they were off in a spray of dust and gravel.

It was strange getting used to the feel of the bike between her legs and balancing it. She'd never been on a motorcycle before, not even a small dirt bike like this one.

Willow led them through pastures, down dirt trails, and through the small cherry orchard that took up the southern corner of the property.

"Oh, you have *got* to be kidding!" Christine exclaimed, pulling her bike to an unsteady stop. Seeing her companion still back in the orchard, Willow turned her own bike around and rode back to the red Yamaha. "I love cherries!" Christine grinned at Willow, then turned back to the trees before her. Rich, dark red and purple cherries covered the branches, hanging tantalizingly close to her reach. "May I?"

"Please. Help yourself." Willow sat back on her seat, amused and charmed, as her new friend jumped up to snag a handful of the fruit, humming as sweet juices filled her mouth.

"This place is amazing, Willow," Christine said, her hand filled with cherries, as she walked back to her bike and sat sideways on the seat. She looked out over the acreage, the trees, sun, flatlands, the beautiful, clear stream. All of it.

"Thank you. I love it here," Willow said quietly, a smile of pride and love on her lips. "It's very special to me."

"I can see why. You know, if this were my place, I'd grab my guitar and sit right out here." She hitched her thumb back at the tree where she'd just picked her snack.

"You know," Willow looked at Christine, her head tilted shyly, "Kevin's guitar is in the attic."

"He plays?" Christine perked up.

"He used to. That's how he got me to go out with him." Willow chuckled.

"Oh yeah?" All the cherries were gone.

"Yeah. He made up this *horrible* song and wouldn't stop playing it until I said yes."

"And so you said yes."

"And so I said yes."

"How long have you been together?"

"Seven years." Willow killed the engine on her bike, dismounting and plopping down in the shade of the huge trees. It felt good, just a lazy, late Saturday afternoon. She was amazed at how comfortable she felt with her visitor. Willow realized that Christine Gray was just a woman. A wonderfully talented and famous one, but a woman all the same. Human, flesh and bone.

"What are you thinking about?" Christine asked, her voice quiet, not wanting to break the peace that filled her.

"Hmm? Oh." Willow looked away, hiding her smile. "I was just thinking that I'm surprised about you."

Christine frowned slightly. "Why? In what way?" She stood from the bike and sat next to Willow.

"I don't know." Willow shrugged. "I've never met a celebrity before, and I guess I thought—"

"Okay, hold that thought." Christine held up a hand, a gentle smile pulling at her lips. "This weekend, here on your beautiful ranch, what say we're just Willow and Christine? Please?" They looked at each other for long minutes, and finally Willow nodded.

"Okay."

"Thank you."

"Well," Willow put her hands on her knees, ready to push up and stand, "you hungry?"

"Starved." Christine grinned.

"Come on. Let's get you fed." Willow stood up and held out her hand, which was taken in a larger, calloused one.

She was sleeping soundly, her body able to stretch out and relax for far too long when she bolted awake, nearly pissing herself as the door to the room she'd been dragged to the night before was flung open.

"Time to get up, Christine," a woman's voice rang out, managing to cut through her muddled haze. The woman walked across the room with purpose, grabbing the closed curtains and pulling them open, so that sunlight sprayed into Christine's eyes.

"Jesus Christ, lady!" Bringing her hands up, she covered her face. "Who the hell are you?"

"My name is Sandra, and I'll be your stylist." She walked back to the door from whence she'd so rudely come, and Christine finally got a look at her. Blonde hair piled on top of her head in some pompous do, pristine suit in a vomitous color of greenish brown. Dangly gold earrings and very high heels that made the muscles in her bare calves stand at attention. "You have three minutes." With that, she was gone.

"Fuck me." Scrubbing at her face, Christine pulled the covers back and groaned. This is crap. All I want is a good night's sleep and to be left alone! That thought was no sooner in her head than the door opened again. "What the fuck!" Snatching a pillow, she tried to hide her naked ass.

"I need you to shower as quickly as possible," the woman said. She was a creepy-looking chick, very dark hair, like bottle black, cut into a pageboy, eyebrows plucked to near nothing and extremely long lashes that had to be fake.

"What happened to three minutes?" Christine growled, not happy in the least.

"Deal. Besides, that was Sandra's rule, not mine." The woman went out into the hall, returning moments later with a large, pink case. She set it on the dresser top, opening it to reveal row upon row of various makeups in every shade Christine could imagine and even some she couldn't.

Stopping, she looked at Christine through the mirror. "Is there a problem?" she asked, her voice decidedly nasal. Glaring, Christine shook her head and padded into the bathroom.

She stood in the shower, letting the hot water run over her chilled skin. She didn't know how long she'd been there before she even touched a single bottle of soap. She was confused, yes, even scared, and felt utterly helpless. About to grab a bottle of shampoo, she nearly jumped out of her skin when someone banged on the shower doors.

"Scrub your face really well with this." A pale hand reached inside the damn shower stall! Christine couldn't believe this. She snagged the little jar from those clawed fingers, looking at it. It was clear glass, the goop inside looking sandy and rather disgusting.

"Ack!" she screamed out. That shit burns! Scrubbing her face as quickly as she could, she jerked the knob to cold, the cool water easing her burning skin.

Wrapped in a robe, she went back into the bedroom, the skin on her face still red and angry. There was quiet murmuring as she entered. Sandra and the goth bitch were talking amongst themselves, and a very queer-looking man was mixing chemicals of some sort, holding up his results to look at them in the bright sunlight.

"Oh good. You gave her the crème." Her head jerked when she heard Sandra's voice. She and the goth chick, who in her mind Christine referred to as GC, were looking at her. Sandra came over to her, walking around her in a slow circle. At first Christine tried to follow her progress, until, with an irritated sigh, Sandra put a stern hand on her shoulder to stay her and continued her journey.

"See anything you like?" Christine asked, feeling beyond exposed as her robe was opened.

"Hmm, not yet." Sandra grabbed a small tape recorder from the dresser, speaking closely into the mic. "Gray is too thin; call George this afternoon. Hold off on true fit until gain." Clicking the recorder off, she looked at Christine, head slightly tilted to the side.

She felt so completely out of her league here; she had no idea what to do or what to say. She didn't think she'd ever felt totally scared until that instant.

Within moments, she stood naked, three pairs of eyes on her and a cloth measuring tape on her skin. Standing straight, arms held out. Christ on a cross, she thought.

As measurements were called out, she closed her eyes, trying to pretend this wasn't happening. Suddenly she found herself ignored, the three heads bent over the page of measurements.

"How's it going, ladies?" Robert Knowles said, clapping his hands together as he stood in the doorway to the room. Christine's eyes bulged, and she grabbed the robe to cover myself. "Don't worry, honey. Nothing I haven't seen before." He actually winked at her!

"Her body is awful, Robert. I don't know what you were thinking," Sandra lamented.

"So fix it! What the hell am I paying you for?" Bob glanced over at Christine, taking in an eyeful, then turning back to the swarm of stylists. *And why the fuck didn't the hair guy, no matter how queer he was, bitch slap him for calling him a woman?*

"Does God make enough duct tape?" Sandra muttered, turning back to her notes.

"So how are you this morning? Did you sleep well?" Knowles asked, absently twisting his gold pinky ring around the hairy-knuckled finger.

"It was okay," Christine shrugged, trying to come off as nonchalant as possible, considering she was standing there with a terry cloth robe held in front of her naked body. *Man, he was giving her the chills.*

"Here." Large hands rested on her shoulders, and she found herself being turned around, her bare ass open to his gaze. Two arms reached around her, almost in some creepy fatherly hug. The robe was taken from her trembling hands, then spread over her shoulders. Quickly her arms found the sleeves, and she wrapped that puppy around her quicker than you could bat an eye.

"Robert, we need to talk," said GC.

"Alright. See you later, okay?" he said in Christine's ear, making her shiver. She nodded, turning to face him, backing away a step or two, just glad to get away from him. "Enjoy your day, ladies." And with that, he was gone.

It had been an amazing day. Willow stripped down, a cool summer breeze blowing in to cool her heated skin. Pulling back the cool, cotton sheets on the king-sized bed, she slid inside, sighing softly. She had very sensitive skin, and the feel of something sliding against it was often pure bliss. Tactile bliss.

Her head met the softness of the pillow, and her eyes closed. Only to pop open a few seconds later.

Willow's mind was abuzz with the events of the day, so unexpected and so much fun. Christine Gray, beautiful, talented, famous, and at *her* ranch!

After finally getting back to the house, Willow had dug Kevin's guitar out of the attic, as promised, embarrassed at the layer of dust and spider webs that covered the hard, black case. Cleaning it off, she'd handed it over to Christine who gladly took it.

Willow insisted Christine relax as she made them dinner — a wonderful pasta salad with vegetables grown in her own garden.

Christine sat on one of the stools at the breakfast bar, tuning the acoustic.

"Is that your favorite instrument?" Willow asked, chopping veggies.

"No." Christine smiled, strumming a simple tune. "I love the guitar, and it's pretty easy to lug around, but it can never match the beauty of the piano."

"Ah, the piano." Willow wiped her hands on a dishtowel, indicating with the flick of her head that Christine should follow. The singer gently set the guitar on the bar before her and obeyed.

She was led into a small room off the main hall. A fireplace was tucked into its corner, a couch in front of it, and an upright piano stood against the opposite wall.

"Ohh," Christine breathed, taking in the beautiful and very old instrument. "Wow. This must be your pride and joy." She looked at its dark cherry wood and two curvy front legs and brushed long, experienced fingers over the smooth, curved cover.

"Well, to be honest, my grandparents had it all my life. It's one of the few furniture pieces that I've kept in the house."

"Well, they had this piano all their lives, too, I'd say." She knelt down, looking under the keyboard, bringing a finger up to trace an inscription in the wood. "As I thought." Getting to her feet, she told Willow of her find. "This, dear Willow, is a Pleyel, I'd guess from sometime around the mid-nineteenth century." She lovingly caressed the wood. "You're sitting on a small gold mine with this baby."

"You're kidding?" Willow looked at the piano she'd seen almost every day of her life, stunned. "What's a Pleyel?"

"A French piano maker. May I?" Christine tapped the rounded cover.

"Please."

Willow quietly stepped up to the side of the instrument, leaning against the high top, and watched Christine's long fingers run across the aged keys, testing its tune. Within moments, the notes began to make sense and come together to form a wonderful song that Willow had never heard.

Not wanting to interrupt, she slowly made her way back to the kitchen, humming softly to herself as she finished dinner.

Willow turned over to her side, watching the tree branch sway in front of the window and the moonlight peeking through the leaves, creating strange shapes of shadow on the bedroom walls.

She thought about the way Christine had wolfed her food down, little moans of appreciation slipping out now and then, making Willow smile.

She had never seen someone eat so much, but she was glad to able to offer what she had. She encouraged a slightly shy-to-ask Christine to take as many helpings as she wished.

The highlight of the night, however, had been when they'd gone back into the piano room, Willow taking a seat on the couch, bare feet curled under her, and a glass of iced tea in her hands. Christine had taken her place on the piano bench, her back straight, her form perfect. The music she'd produced had brought tears to Willow's eyes. So fluid and heartfelt, bringing a round of enthusiastic applause when the song was done.

Christine had taken the gratitude with a shy smile, bowing to her audience of one, then moved on to one of her own pieces.

"That was amazing," Willow whispered, having made her way over to the piano during the song.

"Thank you."

"What is it called? Who composed it?"

"Well," Christine said, sipping quickly from her own glass of tea, resting on a TV tray next to the instrument, "it's called 'Twilight', and I wrote it."

"You wrote that?" Willow pointed at the piano, incredulous. Christine nodded with a chuckle. "Wow. Why that name? Is your group named after it, or is the song named after your band?"

"Yes." She grinned. "I love twilight, and I think it's one of the most important times of the day. Well, along with dawn, that is. But I think twilight is more important." She turned on the bench to face her friend. "See, for me twilight is kind of like the path for a new beginning. Everything that happened that day, good, bad or anywhere between, is gone, but not forgotten. Almost as if the next day you can try again, new slate, but with the memories of the past. You know?" She grinned at the memories. "Back home I used to climb up on my friend Adam's building and watch the sun go down before I, well..."

The singer stopped. *Before you what, Christine? Went out to be a whore?*

Shaking her head to clear the memory, she looked down at her hands, still resting on the keyboard. *Would her conscience always torment her?*

Willow stared at her for a moment, absorbing the softly spoken words. Finally she nodded. "Yes. I understand perfectly. The amazing thing is I got that from your song. The way the song...please forgive me; I'll probably butcher all of it as I know nothing about music or its terminology. Anyway, the way the song just kind of went along on its merry way, some high notes, some low and melancholy. But," she paused, chewing on her bottom lip as she tried to find the right words, "but the entire time, there is this kind of underlying build, like its all leading to something and something big, making my heart beat just a little faster and my body fill with anticipation. Then all of a sudden," she clapped her hands loudly, "it all comes together like the crest of a huge wave, falling over you in a sensation that I still feel as a shiver down my spine."

Christine looked at Willow's face as she expressed her thoughts. How bright her eyes got, the excitement flushing her features. White teeth gleamed briefly before pulling that full, lower lip inside her mouth.

She was truly touched by Willow's words, no matter how simple. She was beyond pleased that the music had filled her so completely and that she had been moved. Realizing Willow was no longer speaking, but was simply looking at her, she cleared her thoughts and smiled.

"Thank you, Willow. You explained it beautifully."

"Oh, I don't know about that." Willow nervously ran her fingers across the top of the upright, feeling suddenly very stupid for her little monologue.

"No, really. I understand perfectly what you mean and how it made you feel. It means a lot to me that you were touched so deeply."

"I was," Willow said softly. "Why don't you play more of this sort of thing? Like that song you played during your last encore at the concert. Just you and that beautiful grand piano. It was wonderful."

"Well," Christine cleared her throat, wanting to change the subject, "that was a rarity, and it probably won't happen again. Unfortunately it doesn't fit too well with Twilight's style."

Willow could tell there was more to it than that, but she decided not to push or ask.

Christine pulled her t-shirt on, lifting her hair to free it from the cotton confines. In t-shirt, shorts, and bare feet, she slowly opened her door, trying to stay quiet. Hearing nothing, she figured Willow was probably sound asleep, so she continued.

She crept down the stairs, wincing with the squeak that punctuated every step. Finally making the ground floor, she proceeded slowly, not knowing the house well enough to not run into something and lose a toe.

Heading down the hall that led to the kitchen, she fumbled around until she found the glasses. Spotting the little light on the fridge icemaker, she stuck the glass under the cubed ice slot, wincing again as the ice clinked into the glass, and the fridge motor groaned at the activity. As she filled the glass with water, the ice popped to life as the little air bubbles were broken by the water.

Listening, she heard nothing. Coast clear. She brought the glass to her lips.

"Christine?"

"Shit!"

Both women jumped and yelped as the glass slipped through Christine's fingers, falling to the floor with a crash. Christine gasped as cold water and ice covered her bare feet and splashed up onto her legs.

"Oh my God, I'm so sorry!" Willow exclaimed, her voice muffled by the hand which had flown to her mouth. "Are you okay?" Flicking on the light above the stove, she gasped. "Oh, Christine, I'm so sorry." She fell to her knees, picking at the pieces of broken glass that littered the floor, sucking in a breath as she saw a sliver sticking out of the top of Christine's right foot.

"It's okay. I'm sorry," Christine said, trying her best to not react to the sting in her foot and the blood coloring Willow's fingers red.

"No, no, hang on." Willow stood and hurried across the kitchen, careful to avoid the incredibly sharp little glass daggers spread across the tiled floor. Quickly grabbing the first aid kit from the downstairs bathroom, she ran back to find Christine on her knees, gathering pieces of glass into the palm of her hand. "No, no! Don't you dare clean that up."

Christine looked up, watching as her frantic hostess got the first aid kit set up on the counter by the sink. "I'm okay, Willow," she said quietly.

"No, you're cut." Willow grabbed Christine's hand, pulling her to her feet. "Can you walk? Or do you need to lean on me?"

Christine winced as she tried to put weight on her foot. Before she knew it, a strong arm was around her waist, and she was being led the short distance to the counter by the sink.

"Hop up." Between them they got Christine up onto the counter and her foot into the sink, where they could run warm water over it. "I know it stings.

I'm really sorry." Willow gently ran her fingers over the soft skin of the top of Christine's foot, making sure there was no glass remaining.

"Oh, I don't know." Christine grinned. "I'm thinking it's your very own personal way of dealing with burglars. You scare them so badly that they hurt themselves by dropping their weapons. You know, maybe they'd shoot off their own foot or something."

"Oh, stop." Willow glared playfully up at her patient, who was smirking at her.

Carefully drying the skin around the surprisingly deep cut, Willow looked at it carefully, trying to determine if it needed stitches.

"I think butterfly sutures will do." Looking at Christine, Willow saw the slight nod and turned back to the wound. Realizing Christine had in fact not been asleep, a worry line creased between Willow's eyes. "Are you okay, Christine? Was the bed uncomfortable?"

"No, it's great. I'm fine, just couldn't sleep," she explained softly. "My mind just doesn't always shut off, you know?"

"Yeah. I understand." Willow unwrapped the sterile butterfly strip.

"What about you? Why are you up? Did I wake you?" Christine leaned back on her hands, watching the nurse's gentle, yet very skillful fingers work on her foot.

"No." Willow smiled, placing a piece of gauze over the wound and taping it into place. "I was craving Oreos." She risked a glance up into Christine's face. "And I couldn't sleep."

Christine looked down at the neat dressing and gave a lopsided grin. "Will I walk again, doc?"

"In time." Willow patted the foot, then began to clean up.

"Oh, good. You know, it just won't do to have to run around stage with a walker or crutches."

"No, but if you're not careful, you'll be rolling around the stage in a wheelchair." Willow raised a brow at her empty threat, smiling when the other woman threw her head back and laughed.

"Come on, doc. Bring out the Oreos."

The strong, tanned fingers of Willow's hand held one side of the small, brown cookie, while the fingers of the other hand twisted, bringing the two halves apart, slowly and deliberately. Finally, in one solid piece, the white cream was revealed.

Christine forgot about her own cookie as she watched Willow's tongue snake out, the pointed tip catching the edge where the cream met the cookie, lifting it just enough to slide her tongue further under the thick layer and slowly lift it further and further, until just a dry residue powdered the dark lower layer of the cookie.

She wondered how Willow made such an innocent, child-like activity so erotic.

Turning back to her own cookie, she popped it into her mouth and sipped from her glass of cold milk.

Willow swallowed thoughtfully, totally unaware of the scrutiny she had been under moments before.

"So," she took a small sip of milk, "you're originally from New York, right?"

Christine glanced at her, taking another bite from the Oreo held gingerly between her fingers. She chewed slowly, mind churning. She dreaded having to lie, but she had no desire to answer the questions she knew were coming. Wiping the milk mustache away, she nodded.

"Yes. Born in Queens."

"Are your parents still there? They must be so proud of you." Willow smiled broadly, grabbing another cookie from the blue, white, and black package.

Christine smiled back, though her smile was very sad. She thought for all of three seconds how easily she could just say yep, they're so proud and they tell me all the time. But somehow she couldn't lie to the woman sitting across from her. It amazed her how much she felt she could trust Willow. She decided to tell the truth about her family for the first time in more than twenty years.

"I don't know," she said quietly.

"You don't know?" Willow cocked her head to the side slightly.

"I haven't seen my parents since I was nine years old."

Willow looked at her friend's face, seeing the pain in her eyes. The voice was so soft, almost as though Christine couldn't quite get the words out. Willow said nothing, waiting for more. She had the strangest feeling that Christine wanted to get some things out in the open.

"My father was a thug basically. Always in and out of trouble." Christine played with her milk glass, unable to meet the steady gaze from across the table. "My mother was a drug addict, also in and out of jail." She sighed. "One day they just didn't come home."

"Did they..."

"No." Christine shook her head, sitting back in her chair. "I think Gary got caught up in something over his head, and she got involved, too."

"Gary is your father?" Willow asked quietly.

"Yes. His common-law wife, Caren, gave birth to me. Anyway, in the long run, one day they packed up all their shit and were gone."

"They left you!" Willow's voice squeaked with the outraged surprise. Christine smiled softly. She'd had twenty-two years for it to sink in.

"It all turned out okay, Willow," she said softly, that same smile on her lips. Willow stared at her for a long moment, absorbing everything she'd been told, as well as adding little details of her own fiction. Sensing the discussion was now closed, she lowered her eyes and nodded.

"I'll just say one thing." She glanced up through her bangs. Christine looked at her expectantly. "I'm very sorry."

"Thank you."

"And," swallowing the sorrow that filled her for her friend, Willow smiled brightly, then yawned, "I don't know about you, but I think I'll be able to sleep now. Oh, excuse me." She covered her mouth as her yawn got bigger.

"Me, too." Christine lied, knowing that she was probably done with sleep for the night. She stood, closing up the cookie package and stowing it in the cabinet she'd seen Willow take it from. Willow rinsed out their glasses and turned to her friend. Squeezing Christine's shoulder, she wished her a good night, then headed upstairs.

Christine watched her go, then sighed and ran a hand through her hair. Trying to decide what to do, she saw the guitar standing in the corner of the room.

The apartment was empty, and she could just see a half-drunk carton of orange juice sitting on the dust-covered floor. She went over to it, dropping her pink backpack on the floor as she went. The juice wasn't cold any more.

Christine got a bad feeling.

Going to the only other room she saw that the bed was gone. Even that big ol' crucifix that was above it had gone.

She jumped as the front door opened, its many locks banging against the wall behind it. Voices, and they didn't belong to Gary or Caren.

"We gotta get this shit cleaned up. Got another tenant," a man's voice said, deep and gruff.

"I'll get right on it." Somebody left, but there were heavy footfalls across the wood floors. She looked at the doorway, waiting for whoever, feeling sweat starting to break out under her hair. She didn't have to wait long.

The man's gut appeared before he did. He looked like he was pregnant, and Christine had to stop herself from giggling at the thought. He was wearing one of those shirts Gary called a wife beater and dirty black pants that hung down under his gut.

"What are you doing here, kid? This ain't no goddamn playground! Get outta here!" He lunged at her, but she was faster. Running around him, she didn't even grab her backpack. Suddenly she was out of the smelly old building and out on the streets, traffic whizzing all around her and people on the sidewalks pushing past her.

It was hot, and Christine was scared. She wandered down the street, looking at every person who passed, desperate for a friendly face.

She made it the three blocks down to the almost non-existent park that was not far from her school. She heard laughter, kid laughter. Lacing her fingers in the chain link that surrounded the small, grassed area with a bench and a basketball hoop, she watched the kids play. There were about six or seven of them, and they all looked a little older than her, like around eleven or twelve. Boys.

There was one boy in glasses, smaller than the others. He was being teased and pushed.

"Come on, you little half-breed. Come get the ball!" one boy yelled out, holding the basketball high up. The kid with the glasses was trying to grab it from him. Christine was impressed that he was not giving up.

"Give it to me, Victor," he growled, taking a running jump, but the tall boy called Victor shot the ball over to one of his pals.

Then she got real mad. The kid with the ball threw it at the little guy, hitting him right in the face and knocking his glasses off. She heard them crack as they hit the small, cement court.

Fists clenched, Christine made her way over to the partially opened gate and ran up to the boys, pushing the one who threw the ball.

"What the..."

"You're an asshole!" she yelled out, pushing him again. She felt the anger of finding Gary and Caren gone again rising in her, like lava under her skin boiling to the surface. These jerks picked the wrong day to mess with someone. Christine took the kid to the ground with double grunts and started to whale on him.

His eyes squeezed shut and his head flapped back and forth as he tried to avoid the blows from her fists. "Get her off me! Get her the fuck off me!" the kid cried.

She growled as hands were anchored under her arms and she was pulled off, kicking and flailing. She landed hard on her shoulder, then jumped up, really mad now, thrashing out at anyone close to her.

"Jesus! You crazy, bitch!" Victor said, jumping back away from her. She glared at him, chest heaving with unvented anger and frustration. "Let's get the fuck outta here," he said, turning and walking away.

The other boys looked at her as they passed, one by one, including the kid she just beat the shit out of. He swiped the back of his hand across his bloodied nose, his broken lip trembling. It satisfied her to see how shook up he was. She smirked at him, just as she had seen Gary smirk at Caren after he beat her real good.

Once they all left, Christine turned and saw the kid with the broken glasses sitting on the cement, head hanging.

She saw the glasses all twisted and messed up, lying near the bench.

"Here." The kid looked up at her with a tear-streaked face and took the glasses from her fingers.

"Thanks," he said quietly. Plopping down next to him, she brought her knees up and wrapped her arms around them. "What's your name?" he asked, turning the broken glasses this way and that, his dark, curly hair flopping in his face.

"Christine."

"I'm Adam." He looked at her, a small smile on his face. "You really kicked some butt."

She grinned, looking down at the stained cement.

"You like basketball?" Adam asked. She glanced at him.

"Yeah. I like basketball."

Christine wiped the wetness from her cheek and stared up at the stars. Willow's ranch had brought her so much peace in the short time she'd been there. She wished she could stay there longer.

She set the guitar aside and scooted down, resting her head at the bottom of the tree, a hand behind her head.

It had been a long time since she'd thought about Gary and Caren. It seemed like a lifetime ago, and in many ways it was. These were things she didn't like to think about. Unfortunately her conversation with Willow over the Oreos hours before had brought everything back. Now she was being haunted by specters she had thought long dead or at least forgotten.

The sun would be rising soon, and she felt chilled. The emotions of the night made her cold inside, the kind of cold that a blanket or cup of coffee could not warm up. She'd yet to find anything that *could* warm her up.

Scrubbing at her eyes, she stood up with a groan, grabbed the neck of the guitar, and headed back toward the house.

"Thank you, Willow. This has been one of the most wonderful weekends I've had in a very long time."

Willow smiled into the hug, squeezing a bit before being let go.

"Even with your battle scar?" she asked, nodding toward Christine's foot. The singer chuckled.

"Yes. Even with my battle scar." She heaved her bag into the back of the Jeep.

"You're welcome here any time, Christine. If you need a break from all the glitz and glamour and adoring fans." They both laughed, but then Willow sobered. "Or if you just need a break," she finished softly.

"Thank you. And if you ever need a little glitz and glamour that the horses just can't provide..." Christine winked, making Willow grin.

"Will do. Have a safe flight." Willow watched as Christine climbed into the Jeep and drove away in a cloud of dust.

Chapter 6

Kevin grunted one more time, then slowly lowered his body, sweat making his skin stick to his wife's. Willow wrapped her arms around his neck, kissing the side of his head as her heart rate began to slow, her body relaxing.

"I love you," he whispered, laying a gentle kiss on Willow's lips. She smiled.

"I love you, too." She gave him a squeeze as he moved off her and rolled over. Within moments, he was asleep.

Feeling warm and content, but also rather sticky and not completely satisfied, Willow made her way to the bathroom to clean up. Looking at herself in the mirror, she wet her fingers, trying to flatten her wild hair.

After using the toilet, she headed back to bed, climbing in to find herself curled up in strong arms, with warm breath on her neck. She fell into a deep, peaceful sleep.

"Here you go, honey." Willow handed the little birthday girl a big, red balloon.

"Can I squeak your nose?" another gap-toothed kid asked. Willow bent over, and small fingers squeaked the red, bulbous prop. The kid gasped when Willow made a loud horn noise between her closed lips. He looked up at the nose and reached up again. But before he could touch the spongy nose, Willow reached out and tickled his sides, making him giggle.

"Okay, kids! Cake time!" little Amanda's mom called out from the back porch. A dozen screaming, laughing five- and six-year-olds ran to where a large cake with Care Bears on it was being settled.

Willow quietly eased her way from the kids' attention and headed inside the house to where Amanda's dad was waiting to pay her.

"Hey," he whispered, so as not to grab the attention of the kids. He opened his wallet. "Great job."

"Thanks, Ted." Willow grinned, stuffing the payment into the pocket of her baggy costume. "See you at work."

"Have a good one, Willow."

She turned to leave when she spotted the leftover burgers and hotdogs from the kids' lunch.

"Oh, jeez." She made a very hasty retreat to her car, where she leaned on the door, her hand to her stomach and her eyes closed. She willed her stomach to settle, taking deep breaths of fresh air and letting it fill her lungs.

Feeling the nausea beginning to pass, she fumbled with her keys, her hands shaky. Inserting the silver key into the lock, she slid behind the wheel, tearing the frizzy red wig from her head. It was almost as if the slightest bit of extra clothing made her blood boil and body heat rise.

She heard her mother's words echo in her head:

"You're fine, Willow. Now get up off the floor and finish vacuuming."

"But Mom, I don't feel good," Willow cried, wiping the back of her hand over her mouth, grimacing at the taste of fresh vomit.

"I said you're fine." Her mother loomed over her, her hands on her hips. "Everyone gets sick. You've gotten it out of your system, now don't be a baby. You're fine." With that, she left Willow alone on the bathroom floor.

She tried not to cry, knowing her mother was right and that she was making a big deal out of nothing. Everyone threw up. Why should she be any different? Special?

"I'm fine," she whispered, taking several more deep breaths.

"So you had to assure him he'd like it, huh?" Rachel grinned, closing the oven door and taking off the oven mitt.

"Yeah. I promised him there would be no...oh what does he call them? Right...weird vegetables." She chuckled, struggling to pop the cork on the wine bottle.

"What the hell are weird vegetables?" Rachel asked, stacking freshly baked rolls into a basket, then covering them with a towel to keep in their heat and freshness.

"Broccoli, spinach, mushrooms, or *shrooms,* as he calls them."

"Oh my God. So are there normal veggies?"

"Yes, there are, actually. They consist of peas, corn, carrots, and beets. It's a bitch to cook for him."

"No doubt!"

"Is Connor that difficult?" Willow glanced over at her friend, as she poured four glasses of wine.

"Not hardly. The guy will eat anything." She caught Willow's eye. "And I do mean *anything.*"

"Ew, gross! Far too much information, Rachel."

"Yes, well, that's easy for someone to say who has never had that done." Turning off the oven, Rachel got the salad together and tossed it with a set of tongs.

"I don't know. It's only fair, Rach. If I'm not going to go down on him, why should he have to on me?" Having gagged once when a boyfriend had roughly shoved himself down her throat, she was done with that nonsense. She had thought it one of the most disgusting things anyway. Luckily Kevin didn't seem to care much.

"I don't get it."

"Apparently you *do.*" They both laughed.

"So have you heard from Christine again? I cannot believe you didn't call me when she was there."

"I know, and I'm sorry. No, I haven't."

"But it's been what, a month or so? Here, take this."

"Yeah, about that." Willow took the salad in its large, wooden bowl and hugged the various bottles of dressing to her body.

"Are you going to call her?" Rachel carefully removed the casserole from the confines of the cooling oven, setting it on the stovetop.

"Why would I do that?" Willow pressed her back to the swinging door of the kitchen.

"Don't want to seem like some silly, obsessed fan, huh?" Rachel grinned, making Willow roll her eyes.

"It's not like that, Rachel. I don't know." She sighed as she thought of what she was trying to say. "She's not like that. She's fun, has a great sense of humor." She shrugged. "She's a normal person."

"And one, I guess, who isn't into suing for damages." Rachel's eyes twinkled with mischief. Willow blushed, looking down.

"Yeah. That was extremely embarrassing." With that, she butted the door open, and dinner was served.

"You guys are going to really like this," Connor informed his dinner guests, forkful halfway to his mouth. Kevin looked doubtful, but he was at least willing to try it, for his wife's sake. He'd never been a huge fan of Rachel, seeing her as a gossip and a somewhat overpowering personality. They'd always clashed, but had kept it to themselves, both loving Willow too much to hurt her.

"Thanks, honey. It's just a little something I threw together once," Rachel said as she buttered a roll.

Willow smiled at the exchange, looking down at her own meal. The casserole looked good and smelled even better. At first.

She suddenly felt a bubbling in her stomach. Turning her head, she pushed her plate away.

"Honey?" Kevin said quietly, noticing his wife had suddenly become very pale.

"I'm sorry. I don't feel so hot." Willow almost knocked her chair over in an attempt to get away from the smells and sights that were making her want to throw up.

Closing the bathroom door behind her, she squeezed her eyes shut as she tried to get herself under control.

"I'm okay, I'm okay," she whispered over and over again. "I'm not going to throw up, not going to throw up. Shit, gonna throw up—" Rushing over to the toilet, she flung the lid open and everything she had consumed that day reappeared, including the wine she'd just drunk, which burned her throat. The taste made her gag all over again.

There was a soft tapping on the bathroom door as Willow rinsed her mouth out.

"Honey? Willow, are you okay?"

"Yeah," she opened the door to a very concerned Kevin.

"Are you sick?"

"I don't know." Clicking off the light, she stepped out into the hall. Her husband rested his hand on her back. "Guess I have a touch of the stomach flu."

"Or maybe you got the plate Rachel intended for me," he whispered, nipping at her earlobe with his teeth. Willow giggled, playfully pushing him away.

"Stop. You two are like children, I swear." She gave him a one-armed hug before heading toward the dining room. "Besides, I haven't eaten a thing, yet."

"You okay, sweetie?" Rachel asked, meeting the couple in the hall. Her eyes were narrowed in concern, as she glanced at Kevin for answers. He shrugged, and her gaze turned back to her friend.

"I'll live," Willow muttered, not wanting to talk to anyone. She felt self-conscious about what her breath must smell like.

"Come on, Wills. Let's see what I've got for your tummy," Rachel said, grabbing her friend's hand.

"Rachel, I'm not four," Willow grumbled, feeling less than playful.

"Okay, hmm." Rachel put her fingers to her lips, looking through the medicine cabinet. Willow sat heavily on the closed toilet lid.

"I feel like a truck just rolled over me."

"Well, try this." Rachel passed the pale woman a bottle of Milk of Magnesia.

"Thanks." She unscrewed the cap and filled the little cup she was handed. Downing the thick liquid with a grimace, she handed it all back to her friend. "Yuck!"

"Give it a minute. It should help settle..." Rachel winced, looking away. "Or not." Rubbing small circles on her friend's back, Rachel was very concerned. "Honey, are you..."

"Pregnant!?" Willow's eyes were huge as she looked at the stick in her hand, a plus in the little window. "This can't be." She looked at it again. She was on the pill.

"It happens, Willow. In fact, it's not as uncommon as you might think." Dr. Adele Stride removed her latex gloves, tossing them into the wastebasket. "I bet Kevin's excited, huh?" the doctor, a long-time friend, smiled.

"He doesn't know yet." Willow stood, smoothing her gown in place. She sighed. "I wanted to make absolute sure first."

Adele studied Willow for a moment. She saw the slight frown on her face, but she chose to say nothing.

After leaving the doctor's office, Willow sat in her car, the keys dangling from the ignition unturned. She stared out of the windshield at the small, one-story building before her.

Without warning, she started sobbing, her face buried in her hands. The uncontrollable upset racked her entire body; tears of joy, tears of sorrow, and tears of fear.

Looking up through tear-blurred vision, she saw a woman, probably about her age, if not younger, carrying a toddler dressed in pants and little white tennis shoes. The child's thumb was in her mouth, and her black hair ran down her back in a shiny wave.

Willow's tears stopped, as she focused on the mother and child. The woman balanced the girl on her hip, holding her steady with one arm while the other hand unlocked the back passenger side door of the Jeep Cherokee. She said something to the child, making her nod with a smile, her dark eyes glimmering with the innocent happiness of youth.

The child was placed in a black and gray car seat and buckled into safety. Then with a small kiss to the child's cheek, the mother closed the door and moved to her place behind the wheel. As she got herself settled, Willow turned her gaze to the little girl who looked back at her through the window, dark eyes squinting against the harsh glare of the day.

Willow smiled, and the child smiled back, raising her colorful cup to her in an unintentional salute. Then the Cherokee pulled out of the space and out of Willow's sight.

She took another deep breath, running her hands through her hair, her eyes slowly following a path down her own body.

"A baby," she whispered, sudden giddiness making her laugh almost manically.

She drove home in a daze. She knew Kevin wouldn't be there when she arrived, and that nagged at her. She wanted so badly to tell him. Seeing the turnoff that would lead her toward the ranch, she had a sudden burst of inspiration. Doing a quick U-turn, she headed the other direction, back toward town, then through it, and into the neighboring town of Gail.

She smiled when she saw the orange diamond-shaped signs — MEN AT WORK. Driving past them, she pulled off onto the dirt shoulder, spotting Kevin's truck and pulling in behind it.

Checking herself in the rearview mirror, she spit on a Kleenex and rubbed the tear streaks from her cheeks and from under her eyes. They were still red, but what the hell.

Slamming the car door shut, she walked onto the building site, carefully avoiding random stacks of wood and plywood, as well as a wheelbarrow with remnants of dried cement crusting the edges.

"Excuse me, ma'am. Can I help you?" asked the first man she came to, his bare chest darkly tanned, a white t-shirt tucked into a belt loop.

"Yeah, I'm looking for Kevin Bowman."

The man turned to a group of men who were pounding away on the four-by-fours that would ultimately be part of the roof of the house.

"Hey, Johnny! You seen Kevin?" he yelled up. One of the men hitched his thumb back toward the other side of the house.

"He's talking to Norman."

"Thanks. Follow me." The man led Willow around the rubble, reminding her to watch her step until they reached a small group of men standing and talking in the shadow of a huge, green dumpster. Kevin was one of them.

He glanced over, sensing someone watching, and a huge grin spread across his handsome face at the sight of his wife.

"Hang on a sec, Norman," he said to one of the men, then walked over to his wife, pushing his sunglasses to the top of his head. "Hey, you." He kissed her quickly, looking down at her. "What's up?" His expression was a mixture of happiness at the unexpected visit and slight concern about its cause. Willow generally didn't come to a site unless there was good reason.

"I went to the doctor today," Willow began, her voice quiet, her eyes hidden by sunglasses. She studied her husband closely.

"Right. The stomach thing. Are you okay?" He tucked his thumbs in the back pockets of his jeans.

"Well, yes. And no." She smiled, but she felt her heart began to hammer against her ribcage.

"What? I don't get it." He watched as his wife shifted her weight from one leg to the other, sucking her bottom lip. Suddenly he felt a wave of unease wash through him.

"Honey, Kevin, we're going to have a baby." There, she'd said it.

Kevin stared at her, his face devoid of expression. "What?"

"I'm pregnant!" she said, her voice filled with joy.

"I don't understand."

"Oh, come on, Kevin. I know for a fact that you know about the birds and the bees," Willow joked, though she felt her joy beginning to ebb.

"But you're on the pill," he said. Yes, her happy balloon was definitely starting to deflate.

"Yes, I am on the pill, Kevin, which tells me that this baby is supposed to be here."

"So you're going to have it?" The words were out of his mouth before he could even think, and he knew immediately that it was the very last thing he should have said.

Willow stared at him for a moment, feeling her heart break and her eyes fill with tears. Without another word, she turned and stormed off. She heard her name called and heavy footfalls behind her. They only made her move even faster, until eventually she was running.

"Willow! Wait!"

She kept going until she reached her car. Her trembling hands dropped the keys before she finally got the large key in the lock. A hand rested on her shoulder, but she pulled away from it, opening the door and hearing Kevin's grunt as it smacked him in the midsection.

"Damn it, Willow, wait."

"Go to hell, Kevin." She slammed the door, barely missing her husband's fingers. She locked the doors when she saw him reach for the handle and revved the engine to life. She put the car into reverse, not daring to look at him, knowing full well that if she did she would stop and listen to what he had to say. She didn't want to hear him, didn't want to see him. She just wanted to be angry.

Nearly running over the MEN AT WORK sign, she headed away with the squeal of tires and a rubber trail on the street.

"Fuck!" Kevin yelled, hating himself for what he'd just done and praying to God that Willow could forgive him.

Willow wiped angrily at her eyes, the newest wash of upset blurring her vision and making her cheeks feel tight and sticky.

She drove around for a long time, not sure where to go at first. She didn't want to go home; she knew Kevin was probably calling there every few minutes. She knew he hadn't meant what he'd said, but still...

Driving through the gated community, Willow passed strangely shaped lots filled with beautiful townhouses. Fancy town cars were parked in many of the driveways, young kids in shorts and t-shirts working in the yards, watering, mowing, and pruning.

Finding number 216, a smart house with a Lincoln in the drive, Willow pulled up to the curb and cut the engine. Wiping her eyes and nose, she sniffled again, then headed out into the hot day.

The lawn was immaculate, of course, with darker patches where it had recently been watered. The flowers that lined the driveway were just as perfect.

The white sandstone townhouse seemed to glow in the afternoon sun, and soft music could be heard coming from inside, the screened door doing nothing for sound insulation.

Willow rang the bell, waiting as she heard movement inside, then the music being switched off.

"Willow!" An older woman hurried to the door, pushing it open with her hip and pulling her granddaughter in with her arms. Willow smiled, almost pulled off her feet as she was roughly hugged. The old woman still had some serious strength.

"Hey, Grandma." She closed her eyes, reveling in the warm security of the embrace. Grandma could always make her feel like everything would be okay.

Pulling away, Myra Wahl studied her favorite person in the world, a barrage of wrinkles forming around her mouth and eyes. She could see that something was terribly wrong.

"Come in, my love, and I'll make some tea." Willow followed her through the airy townhouse to the kitchen at the back. Within moments the two women were seated at the table, tall glasses of iced tea in hand. Myra studied her downcast granddaughter.

"You know, Willow, I could begin by telling you a bunch of gossip that you won't care about anyway, or we can just get to it." She squeezed a bit of lemon into her glass, watching her granddaughter as she lazily stirred the juice into the drink.

Willow studied a bead of condensation as it slid its way down the smooth glass, trying to get her thoughts and emotions in order.

"I'm going to have a baby, Grandma," she said quietly.

"Oh, honey! That's wonderful news!" Myra reached across the table, taking Willow's hand in her own. She was overjoyed.

"I just got back from Kevin's construction site." She took a deep breath, fighting the tears that were trying to break through again. "He's not thrilled."

"What? And he'll make such a wonderful father, too."

"I know." Willow sniffled back the threatening tears. "I don't know. We've talked about it, about kids, and we decided to wait." The tears began to fall. "I didn't do this on purpose, Grandma," she looked up at the older woman with pain-filled eyes.

"I know that, love. Kevin knows that, too."

"He actually asked me if I planned to keep it." She buried her face in her hands. "*It!* As if this baby is some sort of growth inside me instead of a human life that he helped to create."

"Oh, my love." Myra sighed, glancing out at the lovely birds bathing and drinking from the stone birdbath set up in the small backyard. She watched them flap their wings to shake off the excess water and then preen. "He's young, honey. You both are, and he's afraid. Your grandpa was the exact same way."

"Really?" Willow looked at her grandma, desperation in her eyes. "I love him, but I love this baby, too. It's crazy — it's no more than a tiny blob right now, but I love it as if it were sitting right here," she patted the table, and Myra nodded.

"Of course you do, love. It's a part of you, created of your own flesh and blood. This is a time of rejoicing, Willow, not tears." Myra reached over and gathered some of Willow's tears on a fingertip.

"I can't seem to stop," Willow sobbed.

"Get used to it, my love. Your hormones are going to be out of whack for some time." Myra stood, pulling her granddaughter to her feet and giving her a gentle hug. Willow accepted willingly, resting her head on the sturdy shoulder. "Give him time, honey. This is all new to him. We women are far stronger creatures than our male counterparts, I'm afraid." She smiled when she heard Willow laugh softly.

"Isn't that the truth!"

They parted and sat again. "Have you told your father?"

"No. Only you and Kevin know." She blew her nose, then sipped her tea.

"Well, I think you should stay here with me for a bit and make him sweat." Myra winked, making her granddaughter smile. That was truly one of the most beautiful pictures in the older woman's mind. Her granddaughter was an unusually beautiful girl with an equally beautiful personality. Kevin had no idea just what he was jeopardizing.

"Well, it's about time you showed."

"I'm sorry, Sandra. I had a photo shoot this morning." Christine tossed her coat on the arm of one of the many plush couches the designer had scattered around her studio. "What have you got for me today?" she asked, eyeing Sandra, who was impeccable as usual. Her hair was pinned up into some intricate style on top of her head, and her clothes were wrinkle free and fit as though she had been born with them on.

"Well," she said from behind her drawing board, "you could have at least called." She glanced teasingly at Christine. "Now," she said, tossing down her pencil and walking over to her favorite client. "Robert has sent over some rather," she paused, looking for the right word, "...interesting ideas."

"God. What now?" Christine sighed, running a hand through her wind-blown hair.

"Well, sometimes I think it would be easier, and far cheaper for you, if you just went out naked."

Christine glared. "What did he do?" she almost growled through clenched teeth.

"Come," Sandra led the way back to her drawing board, flipping back a few pages in the giant sketchpad. A drawing showed little more than strips of cloth, arranged in strategic patterns to hide Christine's more intimate spots; otherwise, all was revealed.

"No fucking way," she said. They looked at each other, then Sandra smirked and flipped to another page. "Jesus! I'd look like Cher!" Storming away, Christine stood before a floor-to-ceiling window, looking out over L.A. "This is getting out of control," she murmured.

"Christine, come back here. It's no secret how Robert is. Everyone in the business knows that. Especially with you."

Christine looked over at her long-time designer and reluctant friend. With a sigh, she walked back over to her.

"I already told him no. I told him I wasn't about to turn my creations into something you'd find on the Strip at two a.m. Here." She flipped to one last page and showed Christine what she intended to create instead. "You have a wonderful body, Christine, that's also no secret, and I think Robert's smart in showing that off. You have an army of lesbian fans who'd love nothing more than to see some great skin. The men, too, obviously."

Christine took in the designs, most of which were stunning.

"I figure this dress could be worn for the MTV Awards later on, and this one for the Grammys."

"Grammys? Sandra, I haven't even been nominated..."

"Yet. You and I both know you will be. Now, mouth shut, eyes open."

Soon Christine stood in the center of the room in a thong and matching bra, with her arms stretched out as Sandra took her measurements.

Christine had learned to disappear into her own little world while this was going on. She disliked the process; it still, after all this time, felt like an invasion of her personal space.

"When are you going to get rid of that man, anyway?" Sandra asked around the pencil she held between her teeth.

Christine snorted. "God only knows."

"You know, you're big enough now that you could easily drop him like a bad habit and be fine." Sandra scribbled down some notes.

"I know, Sandra." Christine sighed. "I know." It had been a long day, and she was sick of everything and everyone. She wanted to go home and rest, chill out, write some music and be alone. It was not to be.

After Sandra was finished with her, she would be headed to the valley for some interviews and then off to LAX to catch a plane to promote the new album.

Whoever came up with "no rest for the wicked" certainly had had her in mind.

"Are we finished here, Sandra?" she asked, getting antsy. Sandra, who had been working on some measurements of Christine's hips, glanced up at her irritated face.

"That time of the month is it?" She raised a perfectly plucked brow.

"No. That time of year. New album."

"Ah. Say no more, and yes, we're finished." Standing, Sandra draped the tape around her neck and tossed her notebook to a table. She looked at Christine. "You have changed since you came to us, Christine," she said quietly, looking deeply into a pair of the most beautiful eyes she'd ever seen. And in her business, with her clientele, that was saying a lot. She was around the most beautiful people in the world, with the most beautiful bodies created. Christine Gray, though. Ah, Christine Gray. She stood above the best of the best, her beauty not from a knife and nip tuck, but from the grace of DNA. She was a lucky one.

Christine stared back, not sure where this was going.

"You were so timid and sad." Sandra smiled a troubled smile. "You're still sad. Aren't you?" She reached out, uncharacteristically touching her. She brushed her fingers over a soft, tanned cheek. "Break free, Christine," she whispered. "Before it's too late."

Christine stared at her, this woman whom she'd known for seventeen years and with whom she had a love/hate relationship even though she respected her talent and vision. The unusually caring voice and personal touch brought a tightness to the singer's throat that she struggled to control.

"I need to go." She stepped away from Sandra and quickly dressed, grabbing her bag and heading toward the door. "Give me a call when you're reading for the fittings." And she was gone.

Sandra sighed, shaking her head.

"Christine! Over here, please! Look this way, Ms. Gray!"

Christine kept the smirk on her face, her trademark professional disinterested look. She'd used it at fifteen just because she had felt unbelievably uncomfortable with a swarm of photographers snapping at her, the new girl, and that discomfort had shown itself as a cocky smirk. It had stuck and was now expected.

What the paparazzi wanted, the paparazzi got. God forbid she actually be herself.

She hooked her thumbs in the pockets of her tight-fitting jeans, holes in all the right places, and turned this way and that, nearly blinded by a veritable sea of flashes. She recognized all the regulars — reporters from ET, E!, *People* and *US Weekly*, local news stations, and of course the piranha of that sea, the freelance photogs. They were the most dangerous and most bold, probably because they were certainly the most hard up.

"Hey, there's Lindsay Lohan!" someone yelled, making Christine grateful that the heat was off her. Keeping her façade in place until she was tucked safely into the back of the limousine, she sighed, and grabbed herself an ice-cold bottle of water from the small fridge.

Snagging her cell phone from the console, she saw she had six missed messages. Rolling her eyes, she tossed the phone down again. She had no interest in dealing with Bob.

With a small sigh, Willow tucked her cell back into her purse, then studied herself in the rearview mirror again. She looked like hell and felt about as grand.

Sniffling once more, she gathered up all her stuff and locked up the car, juggling her key ring to find the house key. Kevin's truck wasn't in the drive yet, so she'd have a few minutes to get herself together.

Patting her face dry with the washcloth, Willow stared again at her reflection in the bathroom mirror. She felt tired, and her eyes were burning from all the crying. As she stared at herself, she wondered if she'd overreacted about Kevin.

She looked down at herself. She could see absolutely no physical difference, but she *felt* different. It was all psychological, but there was a being growing inside of her body, feeding off the nourishment she was providing. That little being would form into a child; it was up to her and the baby's daddy to raise, mold, and teach that child.

Willow burst into tears again, plopping down hard on the closed toilet lid. What if she were a horrible mother? What if she were unsuitable and the kid turned into a raving lunatic serial killer?

In her misery she failed to hear the front door open then close, a pause, and heavy footfalls coming up the stairs, two at a time.

"Baby? Honey." Kevin set the bouquet of roses on the bathroom counter and knelt down next to his hysterically crying wife.

Willow looked up, seeing the hazy image of her very concerned husband through her tears. She tried to pull away from him as he wrapped his arms around her, pulling her into him.

"Shh," he cooed, mentally kicking himself over and over again for doing this to her. He was stunned when she spoke.

"I'm going to be a horrible mother!"

"What?" For a brief moment Kevin was relieved that maybe he wasn't the cause of such intense upset after all. That quickly ended when Willow pushed him away, swiping at her continuously leaking eyes.

"Why am I telling you that? You don't care." She stood, blowing her nose, then angrily throwing the spent tissue into the bathroom trash.

"Hey, that's not true or fair." Kevin also stood, trying to keep his temper and be understanding. That's what his mother had told him to do — be understanding and caring. He went over to her and hugged her from behind. She was stiff, but she didn't pull away. "I'm sorry about earlier, Willow," he said in her ear. "It was a knee-jerk reaction and, I admit, not a very good one. I was surprised."

"It's your baby, too, Kevin." She turned in her arms, looking up at him with beseeching eyes.

"I know," he said, his head lowering in shame. "I thought we were going to discuss when to have children." He looked at her shyly.

"We did talk about this, Kevin." She moved out of his arms, glancing at the roses, but making herself not react to the gift of her favorite flowers. "Do you really think I planned this behind your back? I said, okay, tonight's the night, God, knock me up?" Her anger was returning.

"Come on, Willow. Don't be ridiculous. I know it's not your fault—"

"Why does it have to be a fault at all, Kevin?" she whirled on him. "This is our *child*," she clutched her stomach, yet to show any signs of the life growing within, "and I *refuse* to see this miracle as a mistake. So with you or without you, I'm having this baby."

He looked at her, stunned and struck dumb. Blinking several times, he let out a breath.

"Are you threatening me?" he asked, his voice soft, all his anger drained by the shock of her words and the meaning behind them. She said nothing, but just looked him square in the eye, jaw as firm as her resolve.

The hotel suite was like any other Christine had been in — beautiful, opulent, and disgustingly expensive. This time, however, the promoters were paying the bill, so it was all clear and free.

She went to the huge bedroom. Her bags had already been unloaded and were waiting for her to unpack them. There was also a vase on the dresser filled with beautiful flowers of varying colors, shapes, and types.

Snatching the card with two fingers, she took it out of the small envelope:

Welcome, and I look forward to sharing stage space with you.

We expect you at dinner tonight, too.

Love,

Melissa & Tammy Lynn

Smiling, she tossed the card to the dresser and leaned down to take a deep whiff of the flowers, humming contentedly at the overwhelming fragrance.

She was glad to be in Colorado to do the benefit concert at Red Rocks. She loved performing there; the city lights behind the stage, the way the cool night air enveloped the performers and audience, bringing them together in a sort of outside bond.

Sliding off the light leather jacket she wore, she tossed it to the king-sized bed and walked over to french doors that led to a balcony that overlooked Denver proper. She didn't come this way often, but she always enjoyed her time in the Mile High City. Though how on earth these people lived at such an altitude amazed her to no end.

Turning back to the suite, she got herself a bottle of water to clear her throat so she could start her singing exercises. She always had to do more of them when in Colorado, getting her lungs ready to work harder.

She cleared her mind, taking deep breaths to cleanse herself from the inside out, almost putting herself in a momentary meditative state, releasing the breaths in slow, measured movements, eyes closed, body relaxed. She was about to open her mouth when her cell phone rang.

Growling as her concentration was shot, she walked over to the bed, fishing her phone out of her jacket. Looking at the digital display, she rolled her eyes. "Yes?"

"Jesus, Christine! Where have you been? I've been trying to get hold of you since you left Sandra's yesterday."

"I've been a little busy, Bob. Maybe if you wouldn't jam pack my days so full I'd have the time and sanity to answer your calls."

"Well, either way, how's it going? Are you there, yet?"

"Yes," she sighed, sitting on the end of the bed. "I was about to start my breathing exercises, so make this quick. I have to be downstairs in two hours." She ran a hand through her hair, feeling exhaustion already seeping in.

"Alright. Well, listen to the messages I left you, they have more information. But a quick rundown is you're not going to Philly anymore, but instead are hitting Baltimore. Also, the Kodak people want you in New York by Monday night."

"Jesus, Bob! I'm not seventeen anymore, trying to get noticed. Why am I doing all this shit?" She stood, pinning a hand to her forehead.

"To make up for your fuck up earlier this year," he said, his voice dangerously low. "If that gets out, you're ruined. The public has to think you're still with it and capable and willing."

"You make me sound like a cripple, Bob. Any particular reason?" Her voice was dangerously calm, belying her temper which was now on the boil.

"In some ways you are, Christine," he answered, his own calmness coming across the line. "You let yourself go and let yourself be taken over by that poison. I have to look out for you more than ever now."

"I have to go." She sighed, knowing that if she didn't hang up, she'd scream.

"Have a good show, and give my love to Sting." The wall of silence made her grit her teeth as she snapped the phone shut. Holding it in her hand, she squeezed hard, all too tempted to throw the thing against the wall.

Instead she set it down on the bedside table, hooked it up to its charger, and returned to her bottle of water and vocal exercises.

Willow stared up at the dying day, the twilight upon the land. The trees began to look like giant, black monsters against the purple sky, their arms reaching up for their salvation as another day was ending and night encroaching.

She ran a hand over Star's neck, the coarse hair of the mare's mane tickling her palm.

"Not sure how much longer I'll be able to do this, girl," she said quietly. The horse snorted in response.

The evening breeze blew warm air over her, displacing her short hair. She inhaled the smells only found on a ranch — animals, earth, feed, and nature. She loved it; it spoke to her of security and peace. It always amused her how the smells she loved so much made newcomers wrinkle their noses up in distaste.

Eh, what do they know?

Urging Star into a light trot, she headed back toward the stables.

In a Colorado hotel room a cell phone rang before the voice mail cut in. When finished, the lit up green display blinked MISSED CALL.

Chapter 7

"What? Stop that!" Willow swatted Rachel's hand away from her stomach. "Move on. There's nothing to see here." She quickly pulled her scrubs shirt over her head.

"I just can't believe there's a baby in there!" Rachel gushed, giving her friend a hug for the umpteenth time.

"Me, either." Willow grinned.

"Have things gotten any better with Daddy Dumbass?" Rachel slammed her locker shut, clipping her name badge to her shirt.

"Yeah. He's trying. I don't know." She closed her own locker. "I think it'll just take time for him to get used to the idea. He only found out a week ago."

"Are you guys talking yet?"

"We never really stopped. Things are just...I don't know." Willow plopped down on the bench. "I just feel very distant from him right now. I'm sure I'll get over it, and he'll grow up, and everything will be fine."

"Hmm." Rachel didn't sound so convinced. She opened her mouth to say something when there was a knock on the frosted glass window of the door. It squeaked open and Lindsey Huff stuck her head in.

"Um, sorry to bother you guys, but Willow, you have a visitor," the young volunteer said, her cheeks flushed.

"Thanks, Lindsey. I'll be there in a..." She stopped, seeing her visitor standing in the doorway of the locker room, where the volunteer had been.

"Holy shit," Rachel muttered.

"Hi." Willow walked over to the woman, a smile lighting up her face. Christine smiled in return.

"I was in the neighborhood." She held up two big brown teddy bears, one with a pink bow around its neck, the other with a blue one. "You never know."

"Oh!" Instantly emotion welled up in Willow's chest, and she flung her arms around Christine's neck, overwhelmed by such a sweet gesture. God only knew how busy the singer was, and she'd actually listened to her message and had come from God only knew where, just for her!

"Whoa!" Christine had to balance herself against the doorframe in order not to be totally bowled over by the crying nurse.

Mid-hug, Willow realized how obnoxious she was being. Feeling very self-conscious, she stepped back from the woman, who grinned down at her.

"Sorry." She stepped back to a polite distance.

"It's okay. I'm happy to see you, too." Christine gave Willow the most winning smile she had, wanting her to know her exuberance was very okay. "Here." She held out the bears again, and Willow hugged them to her.

"This is so sweet, Christine, thank you."

"Well, it's a very special occasion. Congratulations." She leaned down a bit, studying her with concerned eyes. "Are you okay, Willow?" The message had been harried and Willow had sounded very upset, causing Christine immediately to cancel her last shoot and catch a flight down to Oklahoma.

"Oh." Willow looked away, realizing suddenly that two very interested pairs of ears were still with them. She looked around, seeing Rachel sitting on the bench and Lindsey hanging out in the hall. "Want to get some coffee? I have about thirty minutes before my shift starts."

"Absolutely."

Teddy bears in arms, Willow led them toward the cafeteria. "Will this be okay?" she asked quietly, seeing people already beginning to stare. She had no doubt that Lindsey was telling as many people as possible who was in their hospital.

"We should be fine. And, if things start to get too bad you can beat them off with Anne and Andy there." Christine tugged on the ear of one of the bears.

They found a seat at a table toward the back of the cafeteria. Willow wanted to attract as little attention as possible. But if anyone bugged them, she was dragging Christine out of there.

"What are you doing here?" Willow asked, her voice hushed as she removed the lid from her hot cider and blew across the surface of the amber liquid.

"I got your message. I'm so sorry I couldn't be there for you." Christine looked so genuine, Willow wanted to cry again. "I just...well, I've been so busy, and everything has been beyond crazy, I kind of went on Ignore mode." She smiled sheepishly. "I was trying to avoid Bob."

"Bob?"

"Knowles. My manager."

"Oh. Can't say I blame you," Willow muttered, then looked up at her friend shyly. "Sorry."

"It's okay. So anyway, what's going on?" Christine wrapped her hands around her cup of coffee, which she'd already noticed Willow giving an envious look to twice.

"Oh gosh, you're so busy and yet you're here? I'm so sorry. Please, Christine, don't mess up your schedule or make it worse on my account, please—"

"Willow," Christine gently interrupted. "I'm here because I want to be. Okay?" Willow nodded. "Okay."

"Well, what's happening? Why is your schedule so busy? You must be exhausted."

"Yes. However," she placed a warm hand over Willow's, "we're not here to talk about me. I came here to talk about this wonderful news. Don't change the subject."

"I'm fine, Christine. Really." The sadness in Willow's expressive green eyes told a very different story. Christine decided to try a different tactic.

"Willow," she said, lowering her voice, "you live your life to help other people. You have one of the kindest hearts I've ever seen in another human being. Hell, your life and your job are spent helping." She paused, looking across the table to be sure that her words were sinking in. "Please let me be there for you. Let me help. Okay?"

Willow studied the beautiful singer, finally looking away, unable to meet that intense gaze.

"I found out about this the day I called you. I was five weeks pregnant and very thrilled about the baby..."

"But?"

"But." She sighed. "Kevin..."

"Isn't."

"No. He's not." Willow looked down, staring into her cup, wishing to God she could see her future in it. She felt the hot sting of unshed tears.

"I'm sorry." Christine squeezed the hand that her own still covered. Willow shrugged, taking several deep breaths.

"He just needs some time to get used to the idea." She smiled, though it was completely forced and very obviously so. "I have no doubt that I'll be so busy getting ready for the baby and throwing up that I won't even notice."

Christine studied her for a moment, then smiled gently. "I'm sure you will."

"Well, I need to start my shift, so..."

"Of course." Christine pushed her chair back and stood up. Willow did the same, smiling shyly up at her friend.

"It means a lot to me that you came. Thank you."

"Any time." Christine took Willow into a warm hug, tight but brief. "Take care of you and little you." She glanced down at what would soon be a little basketball.

"I will." Willow chuckled. "Take care of you, too. Okay?"

"I will. See you later, Willow."

"Bye, Christine." She watched as her visitor tugged on a baseball cap, pulling her ponytail through the back. Christine headed toward the sliding glass doors of the hospital entrance and was swallowed up by the night beyond.

The crinkle of the crisp newspaper filled the breakfast nook as pages were turned and straightened, then coffee sipped as a new morning dawned.

"Hmm. That big car show is coming back this year," Kevin murmured, absently sipping from his big mug, handmade by a local potter.

"You and Joe going to go?" Willow asked, running her finger down the page as she scanned for her horoscope.

"We might." There was more paper rustling, then the screech of Kevin's chair on the Mexican tile. "Wait," he said, brows furrowed. Willow ignored him, figuring if it was that big a deal he'd tell her about it. "Isn't this that singer you like?"

Willow glanced over at her husband, who was holding the paper up, his finger tapping a short story in the entertainment section.

GRAY VISITS HOMETOWN HOSPITAL

"Holy shit!" he exclaimed. Willow grimaced, knowing what was coming next. "She talked to you? It says here you guys were chatting at a table in the cafeteria." There was no accusation in his voice, just wonder and confusion.

"Yes, we were."

"Why didn't you tell me? What was she doing here?" He looked at her with furrowed brows.

Willow sighed, deciding to tell Kevin about Christine and their past. She just hoped he'd understand.

"Christine and I kind of know each other, honey."

Brows shot up. "How?"

"I saved her life." She looked at him, seeing a slow grin of disbelief spreading across his features. The seriousness of her gaze stopped the grin in its tracks.

"You're serious."

"Yes. She has come here before. She even stayed in our house once."

He threw the paper onto the table with a crisp slap. "What? Why didn't you say anything? How long ago did this happen? Where the hell was I?"

"Which?" She was beginning to feel the first strains of panicked guilt.

"Any of it. *All* of it!" He looked at her with hard eyes, unconsciously leaning forward in his seat.

"I saved her last winter." Willow sighed, looking down. "The concert Rachel and I went to was a thank you from her. She took us backstage after the show, then took me to dinner."

"Christine Gray took you to dinner?" There was doubt in his voice.

"Yes. I went to dinner with her and her band, and before I came in the house she gave me her phone number. I called her out of curiosity and invited her out here."

"Where the hell was I?"

"Fishing with your brothers."

"I see." He sighed, glancing out the window. "This would be the weekend your friend, *Marion* came to stay, right?" He glanced at her again, his eyes blazing. "Marion who is in the middle of a divorce and needed to get away. That Marion?" Willow opened her mouth to speak but was interrupted by the screech of his chair. It nearly fell over backwards as Kevin shoved away from it and stormed out of the house.

Willow ran a hand through her hair, then stood, pushing both her and Kevin's chair under the table.

It wasn't hard to find the man, who had retreated to his cave and play land — the garage. She could hear him sawing away at something and wondered just how good an idea it was to talk to him when he was not only angry at her, but also had a weapon in his hand. Deciding to take the risk, she entered his domain.

"Kevin," she said quietly as she took in the mass of materials spread out over the concrete floor of his workshop — wood, metal scraps, tools, and buckets of various types and sizes of screws and nails. He did not answer, nor did his sawing slow. "I'm sorry."

"Why did you lie to me?" he asked, his voice breaking her heart. He sounded like a little boy.

"When everything happened that night with Christine, her manger and lawyer made me sign a contract that I wouldn't tell anyone."

"I'm your husband, Willow!" He looked at her, face red from the exertion of his sawing mixed with his anger. "You should have trusted me."

"You're right."

"And the rest of it. I mean, this woman was at the house! It doesn't get any more personal than that." He sighed again, giving up on the sawing. He set the tool on his workstation, one hand on his hip, the other fingering some wood shavings. He did not look at his wife. "You've always been a private person, and I've really tried to do my best to understand that, to try and respect that." He looked at her.

"Yes, you have," Willow said quietly.

"Why do you keep stuff from me?" His voice was pleading now. "Respecting your privacy and you keeping stuff from me are two very different things. This isn't the first time, either, Willow. Why was Rachel good enough to go to the concert?"

"She was there that night, Kevin. She was working the ER."

"What happened? Why was Christine Gray, first off, here, and secondly, why was she in the hospital?"

"It's personal to her, I can't..."

"Jesus!" He stormed past her, yanking open the door on his truck and climbing behind the wheel. Glaring at her through the windshield, he started the truck, which roared into life, and backed out of the large garage with a squeal of tires.

"Crap." Willow plopped down on his stool, her head cradled in her hands. She knew she was wrong, that she should have told Kevin about all this long ago. She should have trusted him, knowing damn well he wouldn't go and yell it out on the rooftops. Truth be told, he would have said something akin to, "Neat." All this, Christine, meant far more to her than "neat," though. Somehow she had wanted to keep it her own little secret, to be able to take out late at night and look at. Like a little kid with a flashlight and a book under the covers.

Standing, she brushed off her shorts; there was dirt and dust everywhere in Kevin's shop. She walked out into the early morning sun, letting it warm the cold that filled her. She was tired of fighting. It had been happening a lot. And over the stupidest things.

Ever since she had told him about the baby they'd both been edgy, and Kevin seemed constantly on the defense. She thought back to a few nights ago.

She crawled up his body, kissing a trail as she went. She felt hands in her hair, caressing her scalp, sometimes tugging on the strands. She winced but said nothing. He still tasted like sweat.

"Mm," she moaned as she reached Kevin's neck, the little hairs of his day's worth of growth tickling her skin. "You know what's a good thing?" she breathed into his ear.

"That you're going to let me finally rest and recuperate?" he grinned. Willow chuckled against his temple.

"No, the fact that I can do this all the way to the end, just before I give birth," she purred. He stiffened and not in the good way. Feeling the change

in him, she sat up, straddling his body just in front of his erect penis. She looked down at him, brows drawn. His face was turned to the side, a hand resting behind his head. "What is it?"

"Guess I am just really tired," he said, a cold smile covering his lips.

"Bull." Anger began to fill her. "Does mention of our baby make you go soft?" Willow smirked at her little joke, noting that was exactly what was happening.

"Can we just have some time for us, Willow?" He looked at her, eyes blazing. "Can we just have some fucking peace before this kid comes? Jesus! I don't give a shit! I just want to fuck, okay?"

She was stunned and frozen with disgust. It only took her a moment to gain herself and push away from him. Sitting on the bed, looking at him, she pulled her legs up, knees against her naked breasts. He stayed where he was.

"What?" he asked, voice defensive.

"Where did you learn to be so cold?" she whispered. He sighed, then sat up, turning so his feet were on the floor and his back was to her. He said nothing, making her that much angrier. "Kevin?" He sighed again.

"Don't you like our life as it is?" he asked, standing and facing her.

"Yes, of course I do," she said, unsure where this was leading.

"Then why change it, Willow? Why bring a stress in that we don't need? Or want." He looked at her, eyes boring into hers, demanding an answer.

Willow stared at him, trying to keep her temper under control, as well as understand why this baby bothered him so much. She found her voice, though it was low and dangerously calm.

"Why do you hate your baby so much, Kevin?"

"I don't, but I don't feel we need it. We have such a good life, honey. We can go wherever we want at will, and we are finally doing really great financially," his voice trailed off, seeing the look of disgust on her face.

"You selfish bastard." He blinked in surprise but said nothing. "We're both almost thirty, and it's time to be grown-ups. We've had seven wonderful years together, and now I'm ready for a family. No, it may not have been planned in your perfect little world, but it happened, and I'm ready for this."

His jaw and lips tightened. "Well, I'm not."

Willow felt something tickling her neck, and she raised her tear-streaked face from her arms, which rested on the top rail of the fence. Star snorted, nudging her with her nose again.

"Hey, baby," she whispered, kissing the mare's nose. "What are we going to do, girl? Huh?" Snorting again, the horse bobbed her head, making her owner smile. "Yeah, I know we're screwed."

"Jesus!"

"What?" Sandra ran into the room, hot espresso sloshing onto her hand. "Fuck," she muttered, setting the tiny cup down.

"Oklahoma! She was in fucking Oklahoma!" Bob Knowles cried out, backhanding the newspaper in his hand.

"I ran in here for that?" Sandra untied the belt of her silk robe, letting the garment slide to the floor and reclaimed her place in the bed, a hazelnut breve in hand. "And here I thought it was something important," she muttered.

"Did she tell you she was going to Oklahoma?" Bob asked, turning to Sandra, his dark brows drawn to form a perfectly arched line above his dark eyes.

"By *she* I assume you mean Christine, and no, I wasn't on guard duty that day." She looked at the man next to her, as naked as she.

"Don't be smart, Sandra. This could be disastrous." He studied the story once again, scanning it for any minute detail he might have missed.

"For whom, love?" She sipped the rich drink, closing her eyes in satisfaction.

"What if someone finds out," he murmured. "My career would be over."

"Robert, you are absolutely obsessed. What say you loosen the reins a bit, hmm?" He gave her a questioning look. "Methinks the natives are getting restless," she finished quietly.

"What do you mean?"

"I mean, Christine is not the stupid, naïve fourteen-year-old girl you brought here almost two decades ago. She has learned well from you, Robert, and I fear she may very well turn those lessons back onto you."

"I have never steered her wrong, Sandra. Anything I have ever told her to do was in her best interest," he said, low and defensive.

"Hmm. I'm sure. But you must know she is chomping at the bit?" She sipped her coffee. "She's a grown woman now, and no longer needs daddy to guide her every move and shadow her every step. Or to question her. Robert, you've done everything you can do for her, so now just sit back and reap the rewards of twenty years of hard work."

Bob turned in the bed, his mood darkening significantly. "What are you saying? What has she told you?"

"Nothing. Nothing at all." Sandra smiled sweetly as she sipped her breve, her eyes never leaving her lover of more than ten years. She might fuck him, but she would never understand him. Hell, she didn't even like him half the time.

Knowles studied her, his eyes narrowing as he watched every muscle in her face, every nuance of her eyes. He was good at reading people, and Sandra was no exception.

"There's something you're not telling me," he said quietly.

"What's to be told?" Sandra grabbed the entertainment section from the paper that lay in a neat pile on Robert's lap. He snatched the page from her hands, tossing it aside.

"Tell me," he demanded, leaning forward, face inches from hers. She met the challenge, loathing to be intimidated.

"Look into her eyes, Robert. She's miserable, and I don't blame her."

"Is that so?" His eyes narrowed even more, becoming mere slits. "If you dislike the way I handle my business so much then why don't you go? Remember, Sandra, I made you and I can *unmake* you."

Oh, no. He did not just make a threat! "As I recall, *Bob*, Christine made me. And she made you, too."

With that, she threw the sheets aside and stormed into the huge, adjoining bathroom. In furious haste, she threw on her clothes from the night before and went back to the bedroom. Finger-combing her hair, she looked at the man who still sat in the massive bed.

Stopping at the door, she turned to him. "Don't forget, Christine is the one with the power now. In fifty years who are people going to remember? Christine Gray or Robert Knowles?" With that she was gone.

Willow chewed lightly on the arm of her reading glasses, looking down at her most recent work. The words and letters stretched out across the page, in the slightly crooked angle that she could never straighten on unlined paper. The last line caught her attention and made her eyes feel like they were on fire:

My heart bleeds.

Indeed it did. It made her sad that she was writing again after so many years; she only wrote when in the deepest pain or confusion. Both now applied.

Setting the glasses down, she sighed and closed the notebook, holding it against her chest as she stared out the bay window of the living room, watching as the sun began to settle over the landscape. The tips of the trees were beautifully golden. Off toward the main road leading to the ranch, she saw a pair of headlights, bouncing on the uneven dirt road.

Willow sat back in the large rocking chair her grandfather had built from scratch more than thirty years ago. She waited, a touch of nervousness gnawing at her spine as Kevin's truck pulled around to stop in front of the walk that led to the front porch, where she sat and watched.

He rolled the window down, arm leaning out. "Get in," he called out. When his wife didn't move, he continued, "Come on, honey, get in. Let's get some dinner."

Willow stared at him, undecided for a moment, then decided to try and salvage what was left of her day off.

Pushing out of the chair, she trotted down the few stairs to the path, then around the truck and slid in next to her husband. She wondered what was going through his head.

"Where did you go?" she asked quietly, snapping her seatbelt into place. "Joe's."

"I'm sure he hates me, huh?" She was only half kidding.

"No more than Rachel hates me." He pulled the truck around to the dirt road, pushing the gas before slowing once he got to the gate. He flicked the turn signal, they both looked both ways, then Kevin turned onto the main road that led toward town.

Christine laughed as she watched the boy attempting to play an old Hendrix tune. His concentration was so complete as to make him forget he was supposed to be tough — his tongue was sticking out of the corner of his mouth.

"Are you going to stop the agony?" Adam whispered. She smirked and elbowed him in the ribs. "Thank you so much for doing this, Chris. It was amazing, and I love to hear you sing. I don't get to much anymore."

"You're very welcome, bud." She smiled at her oldest friend, elbowing him again, but this time out of affection.

"They really loved you. I wasn't sure how it would go over, I mean, you're not 50 Cent or even Usher."

"Hey, I can rap with the best of 'em, word." Christine flashed a rapper sign at her friend, making him chuckle. "I'm glad they enjoyed themselves. And if you think those guys would be well received..." she let her thought drift off into his imagination. He paused for a moment, thinking, then turned to her.

"No way! You could get those people to do something like this?" He held his hand out to indicate the small, shabby building where his "boys" met every week or just hung out, keeping out of trouble.

"Sure, why not? I know people." Adam laughed, making Michael look up from his attempts on Christine's guitar.

"I'm sure you do. Come on." He led his old friend to the small office which he shared with the little fireball coming through the front doors.

"Maika'i!"

Christine turned at the familiar nickname. "Alice!" She grabbed the tiny woman in a massive hug, almost lifting her off the ground. Once parted, the small Hawaiian woman looked up at the best friend of her long-time partner. "You get more and more beautiful every time I see you," she said, her beautiful dark eyes twinkling.

"Well, I think you're full of shit, but as long as you don't call me *pupuka*, I'll believe you." She grinned while Alice let out a full-bodied laugh, which shook her entire four foot-eleven, ninety-seven pound frame.

"Come on, you crazy gal. I have dinner ready."

Adam handed over the reins of the club to one of the employees, and the three headed upstairs to their apartment.

"That was wonderful, Alice, thank you." Christine sat back in her chair, chewing the last bit of the lasagna, hand covering her stomach.

"You're very welcome, Maika'i." Alice smiled. Christine had always thought that Alice was one of the most beautiful women she'd ever seen. Though she was physically attractive, most of her beauty came from within. The woman's dark eyes spoke volumes about how she was feeling and glowed with a life Christine had never seen before.

"Come on, Christine. Let's go have a smoke." Adam stood, tossing his napkin onto his empty plate. He walked over to the small kitchen and opened a cabinet, pulling out two cigars. Wiggling his brows at his old friend, he headed out to the window that led to the fire escape.

"Do you want any help, Alice?" Christine asked as her hostess began to clear the table. Alice looked up at her, her eyes amazingly dark and filled with unshed tears.

"No, Christine. Go spend time with him." She smiled, a weak smile. Christine got the distinct feeling she wasn't to ask questions, but just to obey. Trying to shake the feeling of foreboding that was creeping around her heart, Christine followed Adam out to the rickety old landing.

"It's a beautiful night out," he said, clicking his Zippo.

"Sure is." Christine sat with her legs dangling off the landing, arms resting along the rail. "It's funny, I have no desire to live here again, but whenever I *am* here, I miss it, you know?"

Adam nodded, handing his friend a cigar. "I do know. Place gets into your blood. You'll never lose that, bud." He looked at her, his dark eyes shining in the darkness of the night, reflecting some of the light from the tenements around them.

"I wish I could convince you and Alice to come west. You wouldn't believe the space out there. I mean, yeah, L.A. is like this," she spread her hand out, indicating the humanity packed tightly into the area, "but there are other places in California that aren't like that."

He covered the stogie with his hand as he lit it, puffing to get the cigar to light properly, then held the flame out to Christine. She ducked her head down, puffing her own Cuban, then sat back, sighing as she exhaled the sweet smoke, closing her eyes in contentment.

"Honey, Maika'i, you want some coffee?" Alice asked, kneeling in front of the floor-to-ceiling window, hands resting on her knees.

"No, thanks, sweetie." Adam smiled, then leaned over and gently kissed her on the cheek. Christine watched the pair, loving to see them together, but ever envious of their obvious love and devotion to each other.

"Thank you, no, Alice. I'm still stuffed."

"Your loss," she muttered as she disappeared back into the tiny apartment.

"Crazy woman," Christine murmured, then took another long, satisfying drag.

"She's right. You are beautiful," Adam said, a soft smile curling his lips. Christine gave him a side-glance.

"Alright, what do you want?"

He laughed. "Nothing. Just agreeing with Alice."

"Yeah, well you look like shit, my man." She looked him up and down. His body was stick-thin, and his clothes hung off him.

"Yes, well, I've discovered the ultimate diet," he said, his voice somewhat bitter. Christine was surprised.

"What's that?"

"How are things going, Chris?" Adam asked, tipping some ash over the side of the fire escape landing. Again, she was surprised by the sudden change in topic, but went with it.

She sighed, knowing damn well what he was referring to. She ran her hand down the length of her long hair, feeling the cool strands across her skin.

"I'm taking it day by day, Adam. Trying not to make demands of myself that I know I can't fulfill, you know? Like this," she held up the cigar, "this is basically a no-no for what I'm trying to do, so I'm seeing it as a reward for what I've done."

"Makes sense," he said, his eyes squinting as the smoke filled his immediate space. "This will be the last one I have."

"No way," Christine laughed, tapping the thick, brown stogie and watching the ash glow all the way down to the pavement four stories below before it scattered as it hit the sidewalk. "You quitting the stogies? Not likely."

"No, I mean it." She glanced over at her friend, hearing how serious he really was. "I have to."

"Why?" She was serious now, too, beginning to get more worried. Adam had started smoking his mother's boyfriend's Camels at the age of eight.

"I need to tell you something, Chris," he said, his voice very quiet. He fixed his gaze on the stogie in his hand. "This has been the only bad habit I kept, and that was to help me feel somewhat normal, somewhat like I had a bit of control left, you know?" He glanced over at her, seeing her shake her head.

"No. Explain it to me." She drew her legs in, crossing them and turning to face him. "What's going on, Adam?" she asked, her voice soft and encouraging.

He sighed. "Eight years ago I went to donate at a local blood drive."

"Okay."

Adam met her eyes finally. "Chris, I tested positive for HIV."

Christine felt the breath sucked from her lungs. A wave of dread smashed through her body, and she felt as though she was going to throw up.

"Why didn't you tell me this eight years ago, Adam?" Her voice was shaky and low.

"Because you had your own shit to deal with, and I didn't want to worry you."

"Didn't want to worry me?" she exclaimed, pinning him with an electric gaze. He stared helplessly back. "So why are you telling me this now?" She was unsure whether she was feeling profound sadness or was absolutely pissed off. Probably a volatile mixture of both.

"I'm telling you now because I'm in full blown AIDS." It was his turn to pin her with his gaze. She froze, words of recrimination lost on her lips. There was no point now.

"When?"

"I found out last week."

The silence was only broken by the quiet music on the truck radio, some country tune that Willow would rather not hear anyway. She looked out her window, her forehead resting against the cool glass.

"I figure maybe next weekend we can go shopping for furniture or something," Kevin said quietly, glancing at her.

She looked at him, brows furrowed. "Furniture for what?"

"Well, for baby stuff. Cribs and stuff." He smiled, though it was forced, and they both knew it. Willow realized that he was trying to make up in some way, but it was all so contrived that it left her cold. He was only saying what he thought she wanted to hear.

"Forget it," she muttered, looking back out the window.

"What? Forget what?" He looked at her for a long moment, then remembered the road ahead of him and looked away from Willow's sullen form.

"I know you don't give a crap, Kevin, so don't try and pretend that you do. The last thing on earth you want to do is go shopping for baby anything, and we both know it."

"Honey, you know I don't like to shop..."

"Save it, Kevin," she growled, feeling her stomach beginning to churn. Another bout of nausea was on its way, and there was no way to stop it.

"Save what?" he yelled, his voice loud and booming in the truck's cab. "Jesus, Willow! I'm trying to be what you want me to be, and you're shooting me down!" He looked at her, his face contorted by anger.

"You're not my pet, you're my husband and this baby's father!" She laid her hand on her belly, feeling very protective of what lay inside. "Don't do what you think I want you to do. My God! What the hell kind of logic is that?" Her voice was rising with her frustration level. Why couldn't he just understand?

"'What kind of logic'? What the...Goddamn! I can't win with you!"

"Watch the road, Kevin!" Willow yelled, noting that he was beginning to weave in his lane as his attention was drifting further away from his driving. He straightened the wheel, but there was still fire in him.

"I react in a way that's natural for me, that's not right. I tell you what I think and feel, which you tell me all the goddamn time to do, so I do it, and it's not right, either!" He slammed the heel of his hand against the wheel, making the truck jerk slightly. "What do you want from me?" He glared at her with an intensity that was scary.

"I want you to be happy that you've helped to create a new life, and I want you to be a part of it, but because you want to be and not because you feel forced."

"I've tried..."

"You have *not* tried. I know you, Kevin, and know how you work. The first idea that pops into your head is what you stick with. This is no different."

Kevin was quiet for a moment, though a vein in his neck was sticking out dangerously and a muscle in his jaw was working like mad. Willow was expecting him to explode any minute.

"You want me to be honest? You want me to tell you how I'm feeling and all that psychobabble shit? Alright, fine." His voice was so calm, it sent a chill down Willow's spine. "I'll tell you." His breathing was unsteady, heavy and jagged. He looked at her, eyes ablaze. "I don't want this fucking kid, I never did. I don't want it disrupting our life. I do *not* want to be a father!" This last was yelled, making Willow almost crawl into the corner of the cab.

Her gaze turned to the road, just in time to see a pair of bright red brake lights, not six feet away.

"Kevin!" she screeched.

Stuffing her hands into the pockets of her jeans, Christine walked the streets of the vibrant city. It truly was the city that never sleeps. With her cap pulled low, she blended in well. She didn't want to be bothered tonight. No, not tonight.

Adam and Alice had been asleep when she'd snuck out of the apartment, locking the many locks with the set of keys she'd been given years ago. More than once she'd been able to duck out of the public's eye into the safety of those walls.

Tonight it felt anything *but* safe; it felt like a prison and she like its prisoner, forced to wallow in sorrow at the death sentence given to her best friend.

She found a bench and sat, watching the stream of humanity flow by, some glancing her way, most walking by as though she were part of the scenery.

Feeling an uncomfortable lump at her hip, she placed her hand over the cell phone clipped there. Plucking it from her belt loop, she held it in her lap, looking down at it. Running her thumb over the display window, over and over again, she felt just how heavy her soul was. It felt as though her shoulders were being pushed together by this great burden, slowly driving her down to a slouch on the bench. Her thumb continued to caress the little window.

Absently her fingers flipped the phone open, the display screen and keypad lighting up in a bright blue. She glanced down, seeing that it was after one in the morning New York time. She saw the little symbol at the top right hand corner for her address book, and, of its own accord, her thumb hit the button that would illuminate that. The numbers marched down the screen, curser blinking on the first name.

Scanning down the list, she saw the names, Melissa, Sandra, Robert, Julia, Meg, Elton, Mick, Hef. Nothing that would do her any good. None of those people could help her. None would understand or listen in the way she needed.

Willow. The name was like a beacon, a guiding light to her emotional salvation.

She hit the send button, Willow's number appeared on the blue screen, and the phone began to ring.

Time slowed, the taillights getting closer and closer until she could no longer see them, but only the truck's headlight beams illuminating the car's interior and its two occupants as they plowed into them.

The seatbelt dug into Willow's middle, making her cry out in pain. It felt as though her insides were being squeezed in a steel vice. She heard a terrible crash and realized it was the truck's windshield shattering as it collided with the frame of the car's back window.

Shards of glass showered upon her and Kevin, sticking in their hair and to the skin of their face and arms.

It was all over within seconds, though to Willow it felt like hours. She heard sirens, and somewhere Kevin's voice, though what he said made no sense to her. She had one thing on her mind.

"My baby!"

"Hey. Uh, well, I know it's late and I'm really sorry. Um, I guess I just needed to talk. I'm really sorry if I bothered you or woke you up or anything. Um, I'm fine, so don't worry. I guess just give me a buzz whenever. I, uh, I'll talk to you later."

She snapped the phone shut and got up from her bench. Turning in a slow circle, she saw a café not far down the sidewalk. Eddie's. She'd give Eddie a try. Coffee would be good.

The bell above the door rang loudly as she pushed it open. Looking around, she saw a few customers sitting at scattered tables and a man behind the counter wearing a white apron with the Eddie's logo proudly splayed across it in large red letters. She noted that the bright lights directly above him put strange shadows on his worn face and made him look unnaturally pale. He looked at her with old, droopy eyes, wrinkled before their time.

He reminded her of Archie Bunker before Carroll O'Connor went totally white.

This realization made her giggle a little, a slight burp in emotion. As she stared at Archie/Eddie, her eyes locked with his for just a moment. It was just the barest connection to another human being.

"You alright, miss?"

That's all it took. A few words of kindness, one single moment of a complete stranger's concern. She felt her face fall, and her hands came up to hide her pain, even though it seeped out through her fingers.

She felt gentle hands on her arm and shoulder, and she was led blindly to a chair, where she sat down hard on the plastic seat. She couldn't hold it in any longer. The floodgates were washed out of the way and a wave of tears filled the void, as a concerned hand lay warmly on her back.

Chapter 8

"That son of a bitch," Rachel muttered, pushing through the ER doors into the waiting room. That's where she found her target.

He sat in one of the hard plastic chairs with his head back against the wall, a Band-Aid covering the lone boo-boo on his forehead. Rachel consoled herself at the thought of the headache he must have from hitting the steering wheel with his worthless noggin.

"Well, I don't really think you give a damn, but your wife is going to live, and so is her baby. At least, as of this moment."

Kevin looked up to see Rachel with her hands on her hips, ready to do battle.

For a moment, albeit a very *short* moment, Rachel almost felt bad at the utterly pitiful look on his face. Luckily the moment passed quickly.

"Can I see her?" he asked, getting ready to stand. He "oomphed" as a hand pushed him back into his chair.

"Not on your life, pal. She doesn't want to see you. Besides, she's sleeping. We had to give her a sedative because she was so worried that her baby was dead." She looked at the man with hard, accusing eyes. "And just so you know, that nice officer over there would like to have a word with you."

Rachel turned and headed back into the ER. Perhaps she was getting a little too much satisfaction from this, but she couldn't help it. From what she'd gathered from her friend, they had been fighting over Kevin's immaturity in not taking responsibility for the child he helped to create. *Ungrateful bastard. He has one of the finest women God had ever created, and he's letting her get away. Dumbass.*

She walked down the hall, hearing the chaos of a new arrival in progress. Seeing it was under control, she went to the cubical where Willow slept.

She felt her anger grow as she thought back to just how hysterical Willow had been, terrified that her baby hadn't made it, had been killed by the impact of the seatbelt against her midsection.

"Bastard," she muttered, pushing the curtain aside.

Kevin watched Rachel leave, dread and fear creeping up his spine to fill him with a sense of loss. He was stunned to find out his wife didn't want to see him and suddenly felt panicked, like a little boy who wasn't allowed to join in the game.

"Shit," he muttered. He'd really fucked up this time.

"Kevin Bowman?" the police officer asked, his notebook in his hand.

Kevin turned to the tall, black cop. His sense of dread intensified.

Willow moaned slightly, her head turning to the side, her hand automatically resting on her stomach. Her eyes popped open.

"My baby," she whispered.

"Is fine. Honey, you and your baby are okay."

Willow turned to see Rachel sitting at her bedside and realized the red-head was holding her hand. She squeezed the cool fingers wrapped around her own, then settled back onto the scratchy pillow.

"Are you sure, Rach?" she asked, in a voice just as scratchy.

"Yeah. We're sure, honey. How are you feeling?" Rachel brought her other hand up, checking Willow's temperature; she was still deathly pale.

"Well, as you said, I'll live. Is he still here?"

"No. He left once the cops were through with him. Some big, burly guy came and got him."

"His brother Joe." Willow readjusted her aching body, sighing heavily. "Did he say anything?"

"Not much. He asked to see you. That was about it."

"Can I crash at your place for a little while?" Willow asked, her voice very quiet.

"Of course you can, honey. I was going to insist on it, actually." Rachel flashed a brilliant smile at her friend, who weakly returned it.

"Thanks, Rachel."

"Anytime, sweetie. I have to get back to work. You relax and allow yourself to sleep, okay? Everything will be fine, sweetie. I promise." Rachel stood, then leaned over and placed a gentle kiss on her friend's forehead.

Once left alone, Willow stared at the dimmed light above her. Rachel wanted her to sleep and relax. How on earth was she supposed to do that? Kevin's words echoed through her head: *"I don't want this fucking kid, I never did...I do not want to be a father!"*

The sting of fresh tears made her squeeze her eyes shut once more. She was tired of crying. Her eyes hurt and trails of salt made the skin of her face stiff and tight.

She had some serious decisions to make.

"Is there anything else you need, sweetie?" Rachel asked, sitting on the edge of the bed. Willow looked just like a little girl, all tucked in, covers up to her chin. Rachel thought it was adorable.

"Yeah, for you to let me give you your bed back," Willow grumbled.

"Nonsense." Rachel stood, patting Willow's foot. "I want you to be as comfortable as possible, got me? TV's right there, remote is on the table next to you, glass of ice-cold iced tea next to it. Um, I think that's it. You just rest. You need it, honey."

Willow was left alone to toss and turn, trying to sleep. But sleep would not come. Her mind was everywhere at once, and it seemed as though there were a million voices all talking to her at the same time.

Finally giving up, she sat herself up, wincing at her sore muscles and bruised midsection. Glancing at the illuminated red numbers on the alarm clock across the room, Willow saw that it was just after three in the afternoon. The OB/GYN had insisted that Willow stay overnight in the hospital for observation, just to make sure nothing unexpected came up with the pregnancy. Everything had been fine, so she had been released the following morning.

Reaching for the iced tea on the bedside table, her fingers bumped against the remote for the mounted television, so she grabbed it.

"Who cares who the father of your kid is," she muttered bitterly as she passed the Maury Povich show. "Even when you know, it doesn't matter." Having no desire to see a pride of lionesses stalk and kill an antelope, she also bypassed Animal Planet.

"She was real upset. Don't know what it was all about, but she stayed for like two hours, bought everyone in the place my award-winning cinnamon rolls," said a guy in an apron who kind of reminded Willow of that guy who was in that show her dad used to watch all the time...something night, heat? *Heat of the Night*, that was it.

About to change the channel, she stopped as images of Christine greeting a crowd, then onstage, flashed up on the screen.

"She was in a hospital for fatigue earlier in the year, wasn't she?" one anchor asked the other on the entertainment program.

"Maybe she's pulling a Mariah Carey." They both laughed, then the man turned back to the camera. "In Wacko Jacko news..."

"Christine." With a grunt, Willow pushed the heavy layer of covers off, a chill hitting her bare legs. At the end of the summer, Rachel kept her house at an ice-age temperature.

Finding her clothes neatly hung up in the closet, Rachel's own clothes shoved aside, she tugged on her jeans, leaving on the tank she slept in, and went looking for her purse and phone.

"Willow! What are you doing up? I don't recall giving you permission to sleep for only..." she checked the stovetop clock, "...four hours." Rachel set her cup of coffee down on the kitchen table, where she'd been working on bills.

"Yeah, and I don't recall giving you permission to freeze me out of your house."

"Eh, stop whining. A colder environment is better for you, and you get used to it." Rachel smiled, as Willow muttered a comment about polar bears. She could see that her friend was obviously on a mission, looking under couch pillows, in the pantry and even glancing out the window. "Uh, honey, what are you looking for?"

"My purse," Willow murmured as she opened the slatted door once more.

"Yeah, 'cause I always keep mine in the pantry." Rachel chuckled as she got up and walked into the small office off the living room. Returning, she handed the small, brown bag to her friend. "What's up? Are you okay?"

"Yeah." Willow took the bag, then began to look through the leather compartments frantically. "Got it!" Raising the phone in victory, she flipped it open.

"Whoa, no. You are *not* calling him." Rachel was over there in a second, trying to grab the phone from Willow, who yanked it away.

"Kevin? Are you out of your mind? No, I'm calling Christine." She turned her attention back to the phone, seeing she had a missed message.

"Gray?"

"The one and only." Willow put the phone to her ear and listened to her message. Rachel watched in fascination as her friend's facial expression went from surprise to worry to outright upset. "Oh, Christine," she whispered, searching through the address book until she came up with the singer's number, then quickly hitting send.

"What's going on?" Rachel asked, all humor gone.

"I don't know. I think something's happened. I saw on TV that...hey!" The call was picked up. Realizing that their conversation was over, Rachel left the room.

Christine spread her hands out on the smooth, polished surface of the grand piano. Shoulders hunched, she hung her head.

"Fuck," she whispered. "What was I thinking? Stupid, stupid, stupid."

"Indeed."

Christine whirled round, her eyes full of tears and her face red with upset and rage at the invasion of her privacy.

"Not now, Bob. If you know what's good for you, you'll leave me the fuck alone," she growled, her body tense. Bob stopped in mid-step.

"I don't think it would be wise for you to threaten me right now, Christine," he said, his voice a low purr.

"What are you going to do?" she asked, taking a step toward him, satisfied as he took a step back. She needed to see that flicker of fear in his hard, cold eyes. She needed to feel there was some control for her, that she affected him in some way, other than as a living checkbook.

"What were you thinking, Christine?" he asked, backing up another step in their little tango of power. "It's all over the news and the papers. The public is starting to think you're losing your mind. I'm wondering if they're not right." A smirk touched his lips when the singer faltered, but only for a step.

"What do you know, Bob? You're nothing but a heartless bastard," she hissed.

"What had you so upset?" he asked, struggling to regain the upper hand. "Forget to take your anti-depressants again, did you?"

"Go to hell, you son of a bitch. How about I tell you that your friend — shit you don't have any — okay, your *accountant* was dying of AIDS?" She gave him one last glare, then started past him.

"That little faggot got the gay cancer, huh?"

Christine's blood froze. She turned to him and, without another thought, her fist flew through the air. The sickening smack that followed was punctuated with first a grunt of impact, then a yelp of pain.

"Christine!"

Halting her fist in mid-air, she turned to see Sandra run into the room, her heels clacking noisily against the hardwood.

"No!" She put herself between Robert, who was holding his bloodied nose, and one enraged ex-street fighter. "No," she repeated, putting a hand on Christine's arm. "This isn't the way to go about this. Please, stop." The women glared at each other. "Please," Sandra whispered, praying she could get through. She knew Robert would ruin Christine in any way he could to make up for this humiliation.

Blinking several times, Christine came back into herself. Shaking visibly, she hurried out of the room.

"That fucking bitch," Bob muttered through his fingers. "Fucking bitch."

"You deserved it, Robert," said Sandra. "Jesus." The lower half of his face was covered in blood, and she grimaced at the sight of his ruined nose. "I hope you didn't pay a lot for that nose job or that at the very least you have full coverage on it."

"Get the fuck away from me," Robert growled, pushing past her to the wet bar at the far end of the room. "Do something useful and call Dr. Rae for me. Here," he tossed her his cell phone. "He's on speed dial 1."

"Good to know where I rank in the scheme of things," Sandra muttered, doing as she was asked. Robert grabbed a white bar towel, ran it under cold water, then put it to his nose. The coppery taste of blood in his mouth was making him nauseous, as was the pain.

He looked up at his reflection in the mirror above the small, stainless steel sink. The white Prada shirt he wore was ruined, the pressed, yet "casually" open collar stained pink from diluted blood and water. There was a reddish brown stain on the side of his neck, making his skin feel tight.

"Fucking cunt."

He straightened, keeping the towel to his nose as he heard the soft murmurings of Sandra on the phone with his plastic surgeon, or more accurately, his surgeon's secretary. The phone was snapped shut.

"If you can get there in fifteen minutes he can see you." Sandra walked over to him, tucking his phone into his hip pocket. "Robert, you really should go to the—"

"No! There will be no fucking photographers to see that my fucking client broke my fucking nose."

Rolling her eyes, she grabbed him by the arm, only to have him snatch it away. "Stop being such a baby." She grabbed it again, this time digging her perfectly manicured nails in for good measure, and led him out to the car.

"Hello?" Christine barked into the phone.

"Hey! Are you okay?"

Christine's mood immediately improved at the soft words of her friend.

"Hey," she replied, though her rage was still there and her hand ached badly; she figured she'd probably broken it.

"What's going on? I saw this thing on TV, and then I got your message." Willow took a breath. "Are you okay?" she was truly worried, hearing something in the singer's voice that was unsettling.

"Can you take some time off?" Christine asked, though she had no idea why. Spontaneity was a shortfall for her sometimes.

"Oh, uh," Willow was struck by the question, not expecting it at all, nor the very straightforward, almost hard, tone it was asked in. "Yes, I can. Well, have already, actually."

"Good. Pack for a few days, a little bit of everything, shorts, pants, but keep it casual. A car will be around to pick you up in about," Christine studied the clock in the hall, "four hours."

"Oh, um, alright. Oh, wait, I won't be at home. You'll have to come to Rachel's house."

Christine faltered for a moment, finally taking in that Willow didn't sound so great herself. "Are you okay? I'm sorry, I'm so preoccupied right now, I should have..."

"I'm fine. I'll be okay." Willow smiled into the phone, not feeling a word of what she said. Neither did Christine.

"Well, tell me where Rachel lives."

"Have you lost your mind, Willow?" Rachel asked, following her frantic friend around her house. "You need to rest, not go globetrotting with this singer!" Rachel grabbed Willow's shoulder, turning her so she was forced to look at her. "Honey, what are you doing?" she asked, her voice full of quiet concern.

"I need to get out of here for a little while, Rachel. Honey, you have been so good to me, but I need a change of scenery." Willow sat heavily on the bed behind her. "I've been so stressed since I found out I was pregnant."

"And you trust this woman?" Rachel sat next to her.

Willow sighed, then nodded. "Yeah, I do. I can't explain why, but I trust her implicitly. And," she chuckled lightly, "it seems like she needs to get away as much as I do."

"Where are you going? How long?"

"I don't know, and a few days."

The conversation was cut off by the sound of a car pulling to a stop out front. They rushed to the window.

"Holy shit," Rachel whispered, looking at the tiny, red convertible sports car. "Looks like a Porsche of some kind."

The driver's door opened, and a tall figure pulled herself out. Willow chuckled, wondering why on earth Christine would get such a tiny car.

"Well, I guess this is it. You all packed?" Rachel asked.

"Yes, Mom. Ow." Willow held her arm where she had just been smacked. "Be nice."

Willow found herself pulled into a warm embrace, her eyes closing at the content that filled her. They parted at the sound of the doorbell.

Willow was nervous as she tugged the strap of her bag onto her shoulder and followed Rachel down the stairs.

"Hi, Christine." Rachel opened the door wide, inviting the singer inside. Christine pulled her sunglasses off and smiled at her.

"Hello. Nice to see you again." She stopped into the small foyer, her hands clasped before her, looking for the world like she was there to collect her date. Rachel laughed internally at the thought. Willow stepped around her and was caught up in a quick, tight hug.

"You two crazy gals have fun."

"We will," Willow laughed, rolling her eyes at her friend's antics.

Once outside, Christine took the bag from Willow's shoulder.

"Hey, now, can't have the mommy-to-be doing hard labor." Christine opened tiny bitty trunk at the front of the car, gently setting the duffel inside, then slamming it shut. Chuckling, Willow stepped into the car, sinking into the black leather, almost afraid to breathe.

"This is one heck of a car," she whispered, reverence in her voice. Christine smiled as she tucked herself behind the wheel.

"Well, I decided to pick you up in style. I mean, it's not like I could really bring mine along." She turned the ignition, and the powerful engine roared to life.

"Uh, you have one of these?" Willow quickly strapped herself in as the car sped off down the street.

"I do. This baby is a 2005 Porsche 911 Carrera S Coupe. It will do zero to sixty-two in five point two." She grinned with pride, glancing over at her passenger, who looked just a little frightened.

"So, did you rent this?" Willow asked, looking around the inside of the tiny car, taking in all the instruments and plush settings.

"Nah. Borrowed it from a friend. It's just to get us to the airport. Do you like to fly?" Christine pulled the red blur up to a stop light, glancing over at Willow once she was stopped.

"I do."

"Excellent. I hope you like sun, sand, and surf." The Porsche was put into gear and buzzed through the green light, turning off toward the highway where Christine would show Willow what the little car could really do.

"Where are we going? And that sounds wonderful!"

"Good!" Christine yelled above the howl of the wind. "We're going to my summer house."

"Really? Where is it?" Willow was thankful she had short hair as she watched Christine's long, dark hair dancing around like black flames. She could only imagine the tangled mass she'd have once they were stopped.

"You'll see." Christine grinned, slightly devilishly.

"I can't believe you have a second house! Shoot, I'm just pleased as punch to have *one* house!"

Christine grinned, her eyes planted firmly on the road. "Does it bother you?"

"What, that you've got more money than God? No. As long as it doesn't bother you that I don't." The car pulled up at another red light, and Christine looked at her over the tops of her Ray Bans. "What?" Willow asked at the near glare she was receiving.

"Of course, it doesn't bother me." Christine got the car moving again.

"So, why do you need a summer house? I mean, you live in California, right? It's not like you need to escape the snow."

"No, but I do need to escape my life sometimes. Where we're going, it's quiet and peaceful. Somehow I get the feeling you and I could both use a bit of peace and quiet right now." Christine's voice was quiet, almost sad. Willow had to put the scattered words together to even understand what was said, as the wind was stealing most of Christine's voice.

"I think you're right," she said finally. "I saw something on the news about you. I've been worried about you, Christine." She looked at her friend's profile, the sleek, classic lines and perfect features. How was it possible for someone to be so completely beautiful and amazingly talented? And even Willow's inexperienced eye could tell that Christine Gray's beauty had nothing to do with makeup or money but was entirely natural. Some girls had all the luck.

Christine sighed. "Willow, please don't be offended, but can we perhaps have that conversation another day? Today I just want to enjoy a bit of freedom and your company. Okay?" Their gazes met, reflected in two sets of mirrored sunglasses. Willow nodded with a smile.

"You've got it."

Christine smiled and floored it, and the tiny car sped off like a shot. Willow screeched.

Willow looked around, her eyes widening as she took in everything. The long flight in a plush private jet had brought them to a tiny island that looked from the air like she could skip from one side of it to the other. Once the jet had touched down, a small army of assistants and crew had swarmed around the small hangar.

Now Christine was driving them in a black Jeep Wrangler over rough terrain and dirt paths that led deep into what could only be described as a jungle. Willow held onto the roll bar next to her head for dear life.

Christine glanced over at her, grinning. "You alright there?"

"Oh yeah, just fine." Willow was doing her best not to lean her head out of the open door and puke. Since she'd gotten pregnant, her once iron stomach had turned to fine porcelain.

"I can tell by the fine pea-green color you're sporting." Christine laughed loudly at the glare she got in response. She was in a wonderful mood, which was usually the case when she was on Quenby Island.

"So now can you tell me where we are?" As if reading her mind, Willow was trying to figure out where their very long flight had ended up.

"We are on a private island called Quenby, which means 'womanly'. We're not far from Belize, which is in the Caribbean."

"Oh my God." Willow really began to look around now, though she couldn't see anything but trees. The sun was setting. Christine was trying to get them to the house before that happened so that Willow could see the sunset over the water.

"Just wait until we get clear of all this and onto my property."

"Do you own this island?" Willow asked, holding on tighter as the Jeep plowed over a huge set of ruts in the primitive trail.

"Well, let's just say I own my little part of paradise."

The rough terrain made further talking difficult, but finally they made it through the jungle, and the big tires of the Jeep found purchase on the flagstone drive that led up to an amazing house on the cliffs.

Willow leaned forward in her seat.

The house was two stories, facing out to sea. The long drive curved around the side to a set of unusually tall french doors, painted white to match the trim. There was no planned yard to speak of; everything was natural and very tropical. Palm trees and huge, colorful flowers were everywhere.

"God, that's gorgeous," Willow whispered, antsy for Christine to stop the Jeep so she could explore.

"I'm glad you like it."

"What's not to like?" The moment the brakes were applied, Willow was fumbling with her seatbelt, then off and running. Christine pulled the brake, then got out herself, and leaned against the side of the Jeep. She watched the child-like antics of her friend.

Willow ran to the edge of the cliff, stopping short as she looked down the thirty-foot drop to where the sea roared against the rocks.

"Wow," she whispered, her eyes scanning the horizon and seeing the sun melting into molten waves. The breeze rolling in from the ocean felt wonderful, and she lifted her face to the heavens, letting the balmy air run through her hair and wash over her face.

She'd been there for exactly five minutes and felt like she could stay forever. Finally turning away when she heard footsteps behind her, she smiled up at Christine. "This is amazing. No wonder you like to escape here. How often do you come?"

"Not nearly as often as I'd like." Christine sighed, squinting into the dying sun. "A handful of times a year, I guess. Since I've had the place, anyway. Bought it four years ago." She ran a hand through her hair, which was terribly tangled. "Come on. I'll show you around inside."

Willow followed Christine up the path to the base of a long staircase up to a massive deck which jutted out of the back of the house and wrapped around to the other side.

"Does anyone else live here? On the island?" Willow asked, waiting as Christine unlocked a second set of french doors and invited her to enter.

"A few. But not many," Christine answered, tossing a smile over her shoulder.

Again, Willow's mouth hung open as she saw the high rooms, the glass from floor to ceiling, white everywhere, tile, paint, and marble.

"I hope you never have children in here," she grinned.

"Hey, it gets hot here. You have to do what you can. Come on."

Willow was led through the downstairs, which wasn't huge, but was beautiful. Kitchen, living room, bathroom and a game room made up the main floor. Upstairs was comprised of four bedrooms and three bathrooms.

"And, if all looks okay to you, I figure you can stay in here." Christine walked into the second largest bedroom, the other one that had its own bathroom. The room was easily larger than Willow and Kevin's master bedroom back at the ranch.

"Yeah, I think I can hack it. I mean, it *is* only for a few nights," Willow quipped, running a finger disapprovingly across the spotless, shiny surface of the dresser. Christine rolled her eyes.

"Oh, thank you ever so much." She bowed deeply, jumping back laughing to avoid her friend's attack.

"Feed me, will ya?"

"That was fantastic," Willow sat back in the metal, but surprisingly comfortable, chair that belonged with the very contemporary set on the deck. It almost matched the mammoth stainless steel grill that Christine had barbequed their chicken on. Her belly was full, and she felt utterly satisfied.

"Thank you. Glad you enjoyed it." Christine sipped her iced tea, looking out over the water that sparkled in the moonlight like a million little stars.

Willow sighed again, utterly content and happy and thrilled to no end that she had been able to keep her dinner down thus far.

"Why here?" she asked, looking out into the darkness that lay over the cliff and listening to the sound of the ocean far below. "Other than the fact that it's so beautiful it makes you cry, that is."

"That's true. It certainly did me the first time I saw it. But," Christine raised a single finger to show the importance of her coming point, "for me the biggest reason I bought the place is the privacy. The airport is owned by islanders who understand, personally, the importance of privacy for us here. They turn planes away all the time."

"So they protect you guys?"

"Yep. The owners aren't here all the time, but the crew does *not* want to mess with Keller Davies." Christine grinned.

"Tough?"

"Oh, yeah. She doesn't take any shit." She sighed and pushed away from the table. "I'm sorry, Willow, but I'm exhausted." She began to clear away the dishes.

"Oh, of course." Willow automatically stood, taking the plates from her friend, who looked somewhat baffled at the gesture. "Let me do something to repay your kindness."

Christine snorted. "No need, but if you feel the overwhelming need to do dishes, don't let me stop you." She raised her hands in surrender. "I hate dishes." They laughed. "Look, the house is yours, Willow. You know the whole *mi casa es su casa*, or whatever the hell it is. I've got tons of books in the recreation room, food galore, whatever you want."

"Thanks." Willow gathered the dishes, a gentle smile on her features that made Christine feel warm inside.

"If you need anything, anything at all, please don't hesitate to wake me up, okay? I mean, like, I really want you to come get me. I get the distinct feeling that you're usually a strong chick who likes to do it all herself." Christine grinned at the blush that made Willow even more adorable. "Not here. Got me?"

Willow nodded. "Got you."

"Good. Goodnight, Willow." She turned to go, then stopped, her back still to her guest. "We'll talk tomorrow." Then she was gone. Willow stood, the dishes in her hand, looking around the large deck. It was lit with small tiki lights around the top of the railing. They had flared to life all by themselves, so Willow assumed they must be gas fuelled.

Sighing with renewed contentment, she stacked everything, remembering with not much fondness doing just that very task during her college days. She'd been a waitress at various restaurants the entire time she was in school. Stacking plates and other dishes up her arms, just as she had in the old days, she got everything inside and stowed in the dishwasher.

Inside, can and track lighting gave everything a golden hue, with lamps to give more direct lighting where it was needed. She looked around, trying to decide what to do. She was tired, but her mind was still reeling in a million different directions. She knew trying to sleep would be a joke.

Wandering around the main level of the beautiful house, getting ideas for what she might like to do at the ranch, she trailed her hands over the white, leather sofa, the smooth, yet textured material making her sensitive fingertips tingle. She couldn't believe where she was. She had the urge to call Kevin and tell him all about it.

The sting of unshed tears made her nose itch, and she quickly tried to blink them away, shaking her head free of thoughts of him. She couldn't afford to think about him right now, didn't *want* to think about him.

Still the tears came.

Christine had said if she needed anything...did that mean a shoulder, too?

"I'm fine," she whispered, pressing at her moist eyes with the heels of her hands. "I'm fine."

She found her way into the recreation room, where the legs of an antique pool table caught the gleam from the light in the other room. She found the wall switch, and suddenly the room was bathed in soft light. The pool table had a funky pink top, which made Willow smile. Around two walls were various arcade-type games, Pac Man, Frogger, a few fighting games, and Willow's personal favorite, pinball.

Her fingers itched to hit those paddles and slide that ball back only to shoot it like a cannon. But she walked past the machine, not wanting to wake her hostess. The final two walls were lined top to bottom with inlaid shelving filled with books.

Though not a huge reader, Willow did have her favorites, and as she scanned the spines, lined up like soldiers, she found a few of those.

"Oh," she sighed with pleasure, finding the newest novel, *Carmen*, by Parker Davies-Dubois. Turning the book over, she read the blurb, then opened the back cover to look at the author's picture and bio. There was Parker Davies-Dubois, her signature curly blonde hair around a very attractive face, blue eyes twinkling with the brilliance of her smile.

She idly read the bio, which explained that Parker and her son lived in the Boston area.

Decision made, Willow tucked the book to her chest and, turning out lights as she went, made her way up the stairs to her bedroom.

It was a brilliant day! Christine couldn't keep the grin off her face as she made her way back toward the house, her breathing coming in quick gasps as her run came to an end. What could be better? Paradise all around her, her body alive and ready to fly from the wonders of motion and exertion and just all that the human body could do.

Jogging in place, she looked out over the ocean, thinking of when she'd been on the beach below just moments before. Finally turning, she jogged up the two levels of stairs that took her to the deck. The sun was just now starting to blaze down after its slow rising.

Running her hand through her sticky hair and grimacing at the results, she made her way to the kitchen and opened the fridge, moaning in pleasure as the cold air hit her overheated skin. Grabbing a bottle of grape-flavored Fruit2O, she twisted off the cap, guzzling half the drink in one go, then headed up the stairs, taking them two at a time. She needed a shower and badly.

Freshly showered and dressed, she padded back to the kitchen and started on breakfast, her long, wet hair soaking through the thin material of her tank top and cooling her wonderfully from the morning heat. She was glad that Donna had restocked the house with fresh fruit and groceries. She'd have to give the caretaker a raise.

Cutting up cantaloupe, kiwi, mandarin oranges, and apples, she arranged the fruit on a platter with a cup of plain yogurt in the center. She added freshly squeezed orange juice in a big glass and a napkin neatly folded, and she was ready.

Balancing the tray on one hand, she used the other to knock lightly on Willow's bedroom door. After a moment she heard a sound from the other side, then a soft "Come in." Turning the knob, she pushed the door open with her hip as she took the tray in both hands again.

"Hey, sleepyhead," she smiled. She entered the room, which was still dark, its heavy blinds closed against the tropical sun.

"'Morning," Willow said, her voice heavy and thick with sleep. She blinked sleepily, unknowingly charming the hell out of her friend with her sleep-tussled hair and the t-shirt twisted around her small frame.

"Come on, up, up." Christine set the tray on the side table, noting the choice of reading material as she pushed the book aside to make room. She helped Willow pile fluffy pillows behind her. "Settled?" At her nod, Christine placed the tray on her lap.

"Oh, breakfast in bed!" Willow exclaimed, suddenly very awake and very hungry. "Thank you, Christine."

"My pleasure." Standing at the side of the bed, her hands on hips, she looked around, seeing if there was anything else she could do. "Well, then, you enjoy." She turned to leave but was stopped by a warm hand on her arm.

"You're going?"

She looked down at Willow, who was looking almost petulant. Too cute.

"Well, I was going to let you eat in peace..."

"Unh uh, no. You sit your butt down right here and join me." Willow moved over a bit, patting the bed next to her. "There's plenty here."

Happily accepting the invitation that she had secretly hoped would be extended to her, Christine got herself situated against the headboard and smiled as the tray was scooted over so it rested across both their thighs.

"So I see you like Parker Davies-Dubois," she said, as she popped a bit of kiwi into her mouth.

Willow, who was chewing contentedly on a bit of cantaloupe, the tiniest bit of yogurt leaking out the corner of her mouth, nodded. "Love her work," she finally managed.

"Hmm, I do, too." Christine licked some yogurt off her own lip as she thought for a moment. "How long have you read her?"

"Since her first book, *Control.* Loved that one. So I don't know, five years?"

"Weeelllll," Christine watched as Willow dipped an apple piece in the creamy yogurt, leaving a trail in the goo. "How about we have her over for dinner tonight?"

"Come again?"

"Yeah. She's my neighbor. She stays here all summer while her son is with his dad back in Boston."

"You're kidding me, right?" Willow could feel her excitement level rising, though she was a little unsure.

"Not at all. I'm quite serious."

"Holy cow," Willow whispered, realizing that her leg was not being pulled.

"So, what, around six? Seven?" Christine had to stop herself from laughing out loud. "Close your mouth, Willow. You're going to catch flies."

"You got any more surprises up those sleeves of yours?" Willow asked, taking a long drink of her juice.

"Guess you'll have to wait and see, won't you?" She nudged her with her shoulder.

"So what's the special occasion?" Willow indicated the tray on her lap. "What did I do to deserve breakfast in bed?"

Christine shrugged, feeling a bit sheepish. She wished Willow would just accept it quietly. "Guess I just wanted to. That alright with you?"

"Very. Just wondered." She handed Christine the last piece of fruit, which she took gratefully.

"Come on. Let's go outside. I want to show you the beach." Christine took the tray from Willow and got off the bed. Willow followed, quickly pulling up all the covers and tucking them in. Christine watched, shaking her head as she left to take care of their breakfast dishes.

Willow headed into her attached bathroom. Turning on the water for the shower, she found she was smiling. She couldn't wait to explore this amazing place Christine had brought her to. Plus she was excited to spend time with Christine.

As the water turned warmer, then finally hot, she tugged her t-shirt over her head and stepped out of her panties, kicking them aside before climbing into the shower.

"Oh, yeah," she sighed, stepping under the spray and feeling millions of little fingers massaging her skin. Closing her eyes, she tilted her head back, letting the water smooth her hair back from her face, slicking it down to her scalp. She ran her hands over her neck, down over enlarged, sensitive breasts, and finally to her still-flat tummy. She tried not to wince as her fingers trailed over the bruises on her midsection.

Willow knew her baby was not even quite an inch in length yet, as she was only eight weeks along, but she was still there. Yes, *she.* Willow couldn't shake the thought that she was having a daughter.

She smiled a proud smile. Her baby. Her daughter.

Would Kevin ever come around? Would he ever accept that fact that he had fathered a child?

Memories of the accident flooded back.

Her eyes squeezed shut, her face slowly collapsing into itself as the tears fell. A loud, painful sob was pulled from her throat. Her logical side told her it had been just that, an accident. But her emotions had her wondering if Kevin had done it on purpose, if in his mind it was the quickest, easiest way to not have to deal with a tough situation. Had he tried to kill her baby?

No. That was purely the nonsensical musing of a woman who was scared and who had her world shaken to the core. Willow knew that, but the notion was still hard to shake.

Finally feeling clean and able to face the day, Willow turned the water off, automatically wiping down the inside of the spotless cubicle.

With a towel wrapped around her head, she padded naked across the bedroom, hefting her bag up to the bed, unzipping it, and digging around. Figuring they'd be in California at Christine's place, she'd brought a bathing suit.

She slipped the panties of the two-piece up her legs and over her hips, snapping it into place, then spread the top out on the bed. Slipping the halter over her neck, she reached around to tie the ties at mid-back. They were shorter than she remembered. True, she hadn't put the top on in more than a year, but still...

Finally getting the thing tied into place, she walked over to the mirror, making sure she wouldn't offend anyone's sensibilities by showing so much skin and possibly cellulite. What she noticed first, though, were the bruises that still lightly marked her body. She'd have to think of something to say if Christine asked.

Turning this way and that, she noticed her cleavage threatening to spill out of her top. Cupping her enlarged breasts, Willow squeezed them just a bit, feeling their heft. Turning to the side, she looked at her profile, tucking a finger into her cleavage, giggling at the way it disappeared.

Feeling a bit self-conscious, she grabbed a light button-up shirt, tied it around her waist, and headed out.

Christine stood out on the deck, leaning against the railing, a can of ice cold Coke dangling from her fingers. She heard the whir of the air conditioning for a brief moment as the door behind her opened, then closed.

Turning, she was so glad she had sunglasses on, knowing that they'd hide her expression somewhat. She looked up and down Willow's strong, compact body. Her physique was well sculpted from hours of hard work in the gym and on the ranch with the horses.

"What?" Willow looked down at herself, smoothing her hand down her bare midriff, worried she looked far more horrible than she thought.

"Oh, nothing." Christine smiled, mentally slapping herself. Yes, the dark lenses may have hidden her expression, but she'd still been caught staring. She was concerned about the bruises she saw, but decided not to ask. Willow would tell her if there were anything to talk about. "Ready?"

"Yeah. I'm really excited!" Willow followed her friend down the stairs to where the Jeep was parked.

"Want to walk or drive?" Christine asked, placing her hand on the front left fender.

Glancing toward the cliffs and hearing the sea beyond, Willow thought for a moment, then said, "Let's walk."

They walked along the flagstone path that led to a narrow, railed stairway with three flights of ten stairs each and small, cement landings to separate them.

Holding on to the tube railing, Willow descended carefully, following Christine. She was wearing a black tankini, and her skin was evenly tanned and her legs long and beautiful. Well-defined muscles in her back worked with each move she made, and slender hips led into one of the shapeliest behinds Willow had ever seen. She was normally not one for ass gazing — in either gender — but Christine certainly had one that was worthy of attention, Willow thought.

Perfect body. Perfect face. Perfect talent. All this made Willow feel perfectly inferior.

Flipping the two towels she carried over her shoulder, Christine drank the rest of her drink, crushing the can in her hand, then tossing it into the metal trashcan that sat at the base of the stairs.

The beach was, of course, empty, as that particular stretch was Christine's own private playground. She led her friend onto the white sand, away from the rockier ground.

Willow felt the hot sand give underneath her sandaled feet, so perfectly white it was almost blinding.

"God, too amazing for words," she murmured, lifting her glasses to the top of her head to take in everything in its natural, untinted color.

"Yeah, it really is." Christine smiled, pleased to see that the view touched Willow as deeply as it did her.

Finding a good place, Christine spread out their oversized towels. Meanwhile, Willow dug into the bag she'd brought down with her, pulling out a very squashed hat with a big, floppy brim and a tube of sun block.

She felt Christine's questioning gaze.

"What?" she asked, banging the hat against her thigh so it would fall into its regular shape, then plopping it on her head. "I'm fair skinned." To emphasize her point, she grabbed the tube of lotion and popped the top. "You try being a blonde sometime."

"I have," Christine said dryly, finding a comfy spot on her towel and lying on her back with her arms out at her sides. She smirked at the surprised chuckle that produced. What she *wasn't* telling Willow was that she'd already lathered up with SPF 40 back at the house. But she would never, *ever* be caught dead in such a hat.

She rolled onto her side, propping her head up with her palm. Again feeling eyes on her, Willow met her gaze. Christine couldn't keep the slight smile from her lips at the ridiculous picture that bloody hat made.

"Don't even say it," Willow warned, her voice low. "I hate a burned scalp."

"Whatever you say, Farmer Joe."

Willow tipped her sunglasses down, glaring over their rims. Putting the glasses back in place, she turned her face back up to the sun, the fresh coat of sunscreen giving her face a slight ghostly pallor.

"So what happened? Somehow I get the feeling you weren't just at Rachel's house for a how-do-you-do."

Willow met her friend's gaze again, then sighed, also turning to her side. She looked down at some sand that had managed to make its way onto her towel. Picking at the individual granules, she shook her head. "No. It wasn't just a visit." Flicking some sand off, she watched it land back on the beach. "When you called I was being admitted into the hospital Emergency Room."

"What? Why? What happened?" Christine was sitting now, leaning toward her friend, a vision of panic. Willow paused for a moment, temporarily surprised by the concern she heard in her voice, but deep down pleased beyond words. Though she'd never admit that to anyone — not even herself.

"We were in a car accident, Kevin and I." Flashes of that night raced through her mind's eye, the terror and panic she'd felt flowing over her once more and making her stomach flop and a wave of nausea wash over her. Swallowing it all down, she continued. "We were fighting — about the baby, of course. Kevin was yelling at me, and the next thing I know, we're wearing a sedan for a hood ornament." Her voice broke ever so slightly, but she cleared her throat, trying to cover her emotional tracks. Too late: Christine had picked up on it.

Reaching out, she took Willow's hand in her own, stroking the soft, but calloused fingers with her thumb.

"Are you and the baby okay?" she asked, her voice quiet. She was relieved at the nod she received. "That's where the bruises came from, isn't it?"

Again, Willow nodded. "Yeah." To her horror, a sob managed to escape from Willow's throat. She did her damnedest to swallow it down, but it didn't work.

"Come here," said Christine, pulling Willow to her. She cradled her, resting her chin atop the ridiculous hat.

"He doesn't want his own child, Christine," Willow cried, the tears falling now in a way that she hadn't allowed them to before. "How could you not want your own blood?"

"I don't know, sweetie," Christine whispered, understanding that question all too well. "I just don't know." She rocked Willow until she got herself under control a bit. Willow curled her body sideways between Christine's long legs, finally tugging her hat off and tossing it to her own towel. Christine began to run her fingers gently through the soft, golden locks.

Willow decided to just enjoy the safety of Christine's caring and let herself talk. "You know," she began, her voice soft but thick from the tears, "I used to fantasize about what it would be like to have a child."

"Mm hmm," Christine looked out over the ocean as she listened.

"When I was a little girl, it was hard. My mom was so wrapped up in herself, my dad, or whichever boyfriend she found after they divorced. She had it rough as a kid, and I don't think she fully knew how to love, you know?" Willow sniffled, then continued. "I think she did the best she could, but she just wasn't emotionally available."

"Right. I know what you mean."

"Yeah. I think you do. So I decided young that if I ever had kids, I'd give them everything I never had. All the love inside me. And then with Kevin," here her voice gave out a little, spearing through Christine's heart, "I thought, damn, Willow, you got lucky. He's so great, so sensitive and kind, man, what a great father..."

Christine felt her jaw tighten as anger bubbled inside her. What an absolute fool he was. She held on tighter as Willow began to shed new tears, her voice giving way to her grief and profound disappointment.

"He...he doesn't want...his own baby," Willow cried, clutching almost painfully at Christine's arm, so protectively wrapped around her.

"I'm so sorry, honey. So sorry." All Christine's anger slowly drained away, to be replaced by a protective compassion she'd only ever experienced with Adam. This wasn't about Kevin — fuck him. This was about the wonderful, precious woman who was currently nestled in her arms.

Again, Willow began to calm, Christine's heartbeat against her ear working magic. Closing her eyes, she allowed herself to absorb that magic, adjusting her body so she was even closer, with the entire length of her side cuddled up against her friend's front.

"What are you going to do?" Christine whispered into her hair.

Willow sighed, smiling faintly at the tender pressure atop her head that she recognized as a kiss. "Have my baby. Raise him or her, though I think it'll be a her, to the best of my ability."

"You're going to make a wonderful mother, Willow. This child is a very lucky one."

"Thank you."

Together they watched the waves rolling in then swiftly out again, painting the white sand dark.

"What happened, Christine? Why were you so sad?" Willow finally asked, running her thumb along the smooth, warm skin of Christine's arm.

Christine sighed, rubbing her cheek against the soft hair for a moment before speaking. Pulling away just a bit, she looked into Willow's questioning eyes, those beautiful green eyes that every so often would sparkle with a bluish gray tint, as if they had grabbed the color from the sea.

Willow felt slightly nervous at the intense scrutiny. Finally, it seemed as if Christine had made a decision of some sort. She pulled Willow back into her. Knowing that she could trust the nurse completely, Christine began her tale.

"I told you about my parents when I was nine." She felt a nod. "Well, though I was able to stay with my friend Adam and his mother from time to time, things don't always work out. I still needed money and, being the stupid young thing I was, I decided why not add a bit of adventure into my money making." She smiled humorlessly at the ridiculousness of the idea.

"Come on, Adam. It'll be fun!" she begged, tugging on his arm. He looked skeptical at best, chewing on his lip, looking at her over the tops of his taped glasses. "Think about it — lots of money, free sex."

"I don't know, Chris. Sounds kind of dangerous," he hedged.

"Oh, come on, Adam. Be a man! I live for danger."

"But I'm just a kid."

Shaking herself from the past, Christine continued. "At first we started selling anything we could get our hands on, little things we'd steal around the neighborhood, you know? Clothes off clotheslines, fruit, whatever. We almost got caught, so I decided on another angle of attack."

Willow squeezed her eyes shut, her gut instinctively roiling against what she might hear next. Her heart broke for the young, lost girl Christine Gray must have been.

"We had one thing left to sell, and that was ourselves." She sighed, resting her chin on Willow's head. "I talked Adam into joining me on the streets, Willow. We sold ourselves to the highest bidder at first. Then, when we realized we had way too much competition to be picky, we just plain went with whoever had the cash."

"Oh, Christine." Willow hugged her friend, wrapping her arms around her waist and burying her face in her neck.

"See, there's a certain group of men out there who love the company of a young boy," Christine whispered, feeling a shiver wash through Willow. "Adam is a handsome man and was a very handsome boy. He was quite popular," her voice cracked. "And now, because of me, he's paying with his life for that popularity."

Willow was blown away by Christine's quiet words and their implications. She gently pulled away, looking up into the tortured face of the beautiful woman sitting behind her. There was an almost audible crack as things began to really sink in, and Willow's heart split in two.

"He's sick?" she asked, though it was more a statement than a question. She winced at the nod she received.

"Full-blown AIDS. He was diagnosed with HIV eight years ago. He just didn't bother telling me." Christine's head bowed, hair falling forward to create a protective curtain. Willow scrambled out from between her legs, pushing herself up to her knees and taking the silently crying Christine into her arms.

"I'm so sorry, honey," she whispered, gently rocking her and stroking her hair.

Suddenly, and unexpectedly, long, strong arms encircled her waist, and Willow was nearly crushed by the intensity of Christine's hug. They clung to each other, Willow's own tears now joining those of her friend, feeling her pain as well as her own.

The sun continued to shine, the waves to pound the surf. The world lives on, and so does the heart.

Willow was extremely surprised at Christine's extensive cooking talents. Together they prepared a wonderful meal for their dinner guest, who was due to arrive in just under two hours.

The day had been perfect, and Willow felt a bond with Christine that she had never known before. It was wonderful and sorely needed right now, for both of them, she suspected.

"Stop." Christine slapped Willow's hands away. "The table looks perfect already. Leave it be." Willow blew raspberries at her, but she dropped the napkin she was refolding. "Scoot. Go get ready."

"Alright, alright. Jeesh." Rolling her eyes playfully, Willow scurried upstairs. She was nervous with a capital N. Parker Davies-Dubois, tonight, sitting at dinner with her.

"Oh my gosh," she muttered, hurrying into her bedroom and digging through her clothing. She had nothing even remotely nice, even though Christine tried to tell her again and again that it was just a casual dinner between friends.

Finally settling on a pair of fitted khaki shorts and light green cap-sleeve shirt, she jumped into the shower, taking her time, washing and shaving. She felt like a fool trying to impress some woman who probably didn't give a damn anyway. Laughing at herself and her own childish giddiness, she finished dressing and looked herself over in the mirror. She was pleased that the sun she had gotten had turned her skin a nice, golden brown. It helped mask the bruises from the crash.

Taking a deep breath, she looked at the clock. She was surprised to find that Parker would be there in twenty minutes.

"I wondered if you'd fallen in or something," Christine joked, putting the finishing touches to dinner. She looked comfortable in a pair of cut-offs and a white tank top.

"Hey now, be nice. I'm nervous."

"Willow, just relax. Parker is a very sweet woman, very down to earth, and trust me, fanfare makes her uncomfortable." She set down a basket of fresh baked rolls. "Just be you."

"Okay." Willow blew out. "I can do that." But when the door chime sounded, she still jumped and felt her palms grow sweaty. Wiping them on the thighs of her shorts, she took several deep breaths.

Christine answered the door. A wave of salt-scented air rushed inside with their guest.

"Hey, girl! It's been so long." The author's greeting was muffled as the two women hugged.

"Man, you look great," Christine said. "I tell you, hotter and hotter."

"Oh, stop," Parker laughed, playfully smacking her on the arm.

"Come in, I'd like you to meet a very good friend of mine." Christine and Parker Davies-Dubois entered the dining area, where Willow waited with bated breath. "Parker, this is Willow Bowman. Willow, Parker Davies-Dubois."

Parker held out her hand.

"Hi, Willow. What a beautiful name." Parker smiled, her big, blue eyes twinkling with unending merriment. She had her long, blonde curls bound in a thick ponytail, with random escapees curling around her face.

"Oh, uh, thank you." Willow smiled shyly, taking the proffered hand and finding hers engulfed in a gentle, but firm handshake.

"Okay, let's get it out in the open," Christine interjected, standing between the two women. "Parker, Willow is a huge fan of yours and is nervous as hell to meet you." She turned to the blushing Willow, who was looking at the singer with murder in her green eyes. "Willow," Christine continued, ignoring the look of profound embarrassment, "Parker is a woman like you and I and is a hoot to hang out with. She just happens to have a successful hobby."

"Oh, God," Willow squeaked, burying her face in her hands. The author laughed heartily.

"Don't you just love the gall of this woman?" she said, grabbing Willow's hand and pulling it away from her face. Once she had her attention she said, "I thank you, Willow, and I'm pleased that you enjoy my work. Please don't be nervous." Her smile was utterly disarming. "Tonight I just want to have a good time and get to know Christine's new friend, about whom I've heard so much." Keeping hold of Willow's hand, she tugged her toward the table behind her. "I want you to tell me all about you, where you come from, what you do — don't leave anything out."

Once Willow looked into that innocent, most genuine face, she felt her nerves begin to leak out her ears, and a slow smile began to form. "Okay."

Willow wiped her eyes once more, recovering from the last story that Parker had told them. Who knew she'd be so funny?

"Oh, stop," she begged, using her napkin to dab at her eyes, making the other two laugh even harder.

"Oh, ladies, it's been a wonderful evening, and Christine, as usual, I'm stuffed to the gills. I'll have to bring Keller and Garrison by next time. Keller will definitely appreciate your choice in wine." She grinned, then tossed her napkin to the table.

"You're still coming to the Montreal concert, right?" Christine asked, downing the last of her water. She had declined the wine, not wanting to tempt herself.

"Shit yeah!" Parker looked at her as though she'd lost her mind, then pushed back from the table. Christine did the same, and they met for a deep hug. "Don't stay away so long next time," she said quietly into the singer's ear.

"Okay. I promise."

"Good. And you," Parker turned to Willow, who looked on with wide eyes, "up, up." Willow stood, then yelped slightly as she was pulled into an equally tight hug. "It was delightful to meet you," Parker said, smiling from ear to ear.

"You, too." Willow grinned like a fool.

"You're a cool chick," the author poked her playfully in the chest, then let her go and turned to leave.

"Come on. Let's go out," Christine said, a playful gleam in her eye after seeing off their guest. Willow quickly drained the rest of her wine, knowing one glass wouldn't hurt the baby, then joined the singer at the door.

"What about the dishes?"

"Eh." Christine waved airily. "I'll get them in the morning."

The night was gorgeous, the moon a sliver. Carefully making their way down the long staircase, Christine and Willow walked in step along the beach, the sea beyond turned a glowing blue by the reflective light.

"Amazing," Willow whispered, looking up to see a billion stars. "I can't even see this many stars from the ranch."

"Definitely can't from my place in L.A." They stopped walking, both looking up and seeing a falling star. "Make a wish," Christine whispered. Willow closed her eyes, wishing with all her might that everything would be okay and that her heart would find peace. "May your wish come true."

Opening her eyes, Willow saw her friend smiling down at her. "Yours, too."

Christine looked down at the beautiful woman, her eyes turned a dark gray in the near moonless night, the barest beginnings of tiny lines at their corners. The softest smile curved her full lips. She studied those lips and the soft lines of her chin and jaw, leading down to the smooth neck, snow white in this light.

Her eyes flickered back up to Willow's, then back to those lips. As if in a dream, the distance between them closed, though she had no idea how, and suddenly she felt those lips against hers, as soft as they looked, unyielding.

The dream continued as Christine brought her hand up and brushed the backs of her fingers against the cool cheek, smooth and tender.

The mouth under hers moved with her, the lips brushing her own. Just as suddenly they were gone.

Coming to her senses, her hand left to caress the cool night air, Christine opened her eyes. Willow was backing away from her, fingers on her lips, eyes confused at first, then angry.

"What are you doing?" Willow finally asked, getting her bearings. Her lips still tingled from the kiss, and the sensation frightened her. "What do you think? Do you think I came here for that?" The fear turned into rage, which meant she was going to lash out.

"God, I'm sorry, Willow, I didn't mean..."

"Damn it, Christine! Don't I have enough shit to worry about? I don't need this, too!" With that, she turned and blindly made her way back to the stairs, her quiet sobs floating back on the breeze to Christine's ears.

"Fuck, fuck, fuck!" Christine beat herself on the thigh with her fist. "What have I done?" She sank to her knees, her head hanging and her tears making twin dark spots on the sand.

"Are you sure, Chris? This may be a huge mistake, hon—"

"No, I already made my mistake." Christine ran her hands through her hair, then across her nose and eyes, gathering moisture as they went. "God, I fucked up," she whispered, then sniffled noisily, getting her distress under control, at least for the moment.

"What happened?" Parker asked, concern written all over her face, her hand resting on her friend's leg.

"I don't want to talk about it. Just please, do this for me?" Her pleading eyes met Parker's and, after searching that gaze, the author finally agreed.

"Okay."

"Thank you." Gathering Parker in a painful hug, Christine hurriedly left the bungalow.

Chapter 9

Willow's eyes opened, and she looked around the room. The space was dim, all blinds and curtains pulled as tightly closed as possible, shutting out the world and her own fears.

She turned over in the bed, looking out over the mess she'd made. Her clothing lay scattered where she'd pulled it off. The bedside clock said it was almost eight-thirty, which surprised her. She'd been up most the night, either sitting in the chair in the corner thinking or tossing and turning in bed, her mind unable or unwilling to shut off.

She sat up, her eyes closing at the pounding in her temples. Taking slow, deep breaths, she tried to get it under control, feeling the pulse in her neck keeping time with it and making her entire neck hurt. She knew she would have to get rid of this herself; pain medicine was not really an option right now.

"Okay," she moaned, slowly pushing the covers back and dropping her legs over the side of the tall bed, her bare feet making contact with the fuzzy rug placed over the tile. Making slow progress to the bathroom, she rinsed a washcloth under ice-cold water and placed it around her neck. She grimaced at the new pain caused by the cold sensation, but it quickly died down, giving way to slight relief.

Finding some clothes that resembled an outfit, she gathered her courage and strength and tugged them on like a shield, then headed out to face a new day and her host.

Willow had had a lot of time to think about things the night before. Her stomach was filled with nausea and undecided emotions. Yes, she had been angry at Christine for doing that, for kissing her so unexpectedly. So why the unexpected tingle at the loss of that contact?

Why had Christine done that? What end had she hoped for? Willow had gone over the events prior to the kiss again and again — which had led to the migraine she had when she awoke. The perfect evening, the fun they'd had, the comfort they'd felt. The beach, the romance of the ocean. Had it just been something that happened, or had Christine lured her to the island in hopes of just such a thing? Had it all been orchestrated? Is that why a famous, beautiful, rich woman like Christine Gray, who got anything she wanted and whose preferences had been rumored for years, had taken an interest in a faceless nurse removed from the glitz and glamour of Hollywood?

"Uh, stop," Willow groaned, leaning against a wall in the hallway, holding her head in her hands. The march of thoughts through her head again was making her want to throw up.

Making her way down the stairs, she heard nothing but the tick of the huge, round clock on the wall by the kitchen. Coffee had been made, the little green light on the machine glowing in invitation. Luckily Christine only drank decaf, so it all worked out.

Glancing around, Willow realized that everything from the night before had been cleaned up and put away. Impressed, she moved on.

Pouring herself a mug of coffee, she went out to the deck, figuring that's where she'd find the singer. They needed to talk, and they needed to talk badly. She didn't want to lose their friendship, and only understanding the previous night could stop that from happening.

One side of the french doors was open a crack, admitting some sound of the morning ocean. Willow's heart began to beat double-time as she got closer, which made her head pound even more. She closed her eyes, allowing herself a calming moment, willing her blood to slow down and not try to push through the constricted arteries all at once, making the migraine worse.

"Okay," she breathed, feeling everything settle again. She began to move forward once more.

The morning was gorgeous. For just a moment Willow was able to forget everything and get lost in what her grandmother would call God's perfection.

"Beautiful out here, isn't it?"

Willow turned at the voice, the strange, *not* Christine's voice, voice. Parker Davies-Dubois sat in one of the metal chairs, feet up and crossed on the table, cup of coffee cradled against her stomach. She was smiling up at Willow, her eyes squinting against the morning sun.

"Oh, uh, yeah. It really is." Willow managed to smile through her surprise, setting her mug on the deck railing. "Is Christine out running?" She glanced out over the beach far below, looking for the little jogging speck.

Parker chuckled inwardly. Out running. Nice choice of words. "No, she's not."

Willow turned to her, frowning slightly. Something was wrong. "Where is she?" She remembered seeing the bedroom door at the end of the hall open, which meant the singer wasn't in it.

"Please sit down," Parker said, her sandaled feet hitting the deck. Wary, Willow pulled out a chair diagonally to the author's left. She sat down, setting her cup on the tabletop.

"What's going on, Parker?" she asked, her voice quiet and grave.

"Christine left..."

"What?"

"Hold on." Parker raised a hand. "Let me finish. Okay?" Grudgingly Willow nodded, her head pounding even more. "She came to me early this morning, pretty upset. I don't know what happened, she didn't want to talk about it, but she felt awfully bad."

"So bad she couldn't stick around to talk to me about it?" Willow asked bitterly.

"Honey," Parker sat forward in her chair, concern written on her face. "I've known Christine for about four years now, and I know what a good person she is, but she, like everyone, has flaws and faults. One of her most grievous faults is that she tends to run when she feels cornered or upset about something."

Willow looked down at her hands, feeling bad about her comment. She adjusted the rapidly warming washcloth on her neck, knowing she'd have to cool it again soon.

"She asked me to be here when you got up to take you to the airport or to let you know that you're welcome to stay here as long as you want. Or, and this is from me, if you want to talk, I'm certainly willing to listen."

Willow met her eyes, seeing nothing but genuine compassion and concern there. She gave it a serious moment's thought, then shook her head.

"If you don't mind, Parker, I think I want to be alone for a bit." She smiled apologetically and found her hand wrapped in two warm ones.

"I understand. Listen, before I go I want you to know something."

"Alright."

"Christine cares about you, and I know she'd never intentionally do anything to hurt you. She considers you a real friend, and, sadly for her, *real* friends are far and few between, so I know she'd never deliberately do anything to jeopardize that." Having said that and given Willow a kind smile, Parker stood and took her coffee cup inside, returning a few moments later to take her leave via the stairs. At the bottom, she looked up at Willow, who hadn't moved.

"When and if you do need something Willow, I wrote my number on the dry erase board in the kitchen." And she was gone.

Willow sat where she was, absently sipping her coffee, wondering what she should do and battling with her emotions again. Should she be angrier at Christine for the kiss or for abandoning her in paradise?

"Crap," she muttered, then went back to the kitchen. Sure enough, there was a number written in large, balloon numbers and a happy face that made her smile. She dumped the rest of her coffee in the sink, loading the mug into the dishwasher, which she realized belatedly was filled with clean dishes. When had Christine done all this? Cleaned the kitchen, washed all the pans, put the food away, and run the dishwasher?

Maybe she, too, was up all night. When had she left? Willow felt betrayed at finding Christine gone. Why couldn't she have stuck around so they could talk it out? Yeah, Willow had heard Parker's explanation, and she understood it quite well, a little too well, perhaps. After all, she was on Quenby Island, wasn't she? But still.

She rinsed her washcloth out, almost drooling at the cold water that ran over her hands as she did so. Reapplying it to her neck, she headed upstairs. Maybe a nice, cool shower or warm, relaxing bath would help.

The journey into wakefulness was quick and startling. Willow looked around, unsure of where the hell she was for a moment and what had wakened her. She realized she was on one of the white leather couches in the large living room and that there was a string of drool leading from her lips to the pillow beneath her head.

"Crap." She cleaned it off with her hand. Blinking rapidly, she realized finally that someone was at the door.

Making her way over to it, she saw a man dressed in white from head to toe, a bundle at his feet and a smile on his handsome face.

Curious, she opened the french door. "Um, can I help you?"

"If you're Willow Bowman, you certainly can." His smile was as bright as his clothing, which almost glowed in the intense, noonday sun.

"I am."

"Fabulous!" Grabbing his bundle, he pushed past her into the house, talking all the while as he unpacked his equipment. "I'm Freddie Sanchez, and I hear you've got quite the noggin ache, so I'm here to make your day lovely again." He smiled again, his dark eyes twinkling. The little peak that rose from his Caesar hairdo bobbed as he shook out a white sheet, which he spread over the blue, padded table he'd set up.

"What?" Utterly baffled, Willow took a step back. Was he insane?

"Come on, honey. Let's get you out of those clothes and onto my table," he said, pulling out several glass bottles with cork stoppers from the bag he had hung over his shoulder. He lined them up on a small folding table he had also brought with him.

"You want me to undress? I don't under—"

"Honey, I am *not* going put my hands on your sweet skin through cotton, I'm sorry." He looked at her with accusing eyes, hand on hip. Willow sighed relief as understanding dawned.

"Uh, who called you?"

"Parker, of course. Isn't she a doll? I just love her. And her son is going to be a heartbreaker just like his daddy, someday." Freddie had begun to uncork the bottles, pouring a fragrant, thick green liquid onto his palms, then rubbing them vigorously together. "Come on, snap, snap," he ordered, turning his back to her to afford her some privacy.

Still stunned by the handsome whirlwind, Willow thought, *Oh, what the hell?* Quickly, and shyly, shrugging out of her clothes, she snagged the white sheet that Freddie had hooked on his thumb over his shoulder. Wrapping it around herself, she walked over to him and the table.

He turned around, looking her up and down. Oddly, Willow didn't feel uncomfortable with his attention.

"Mm, mm. Fabulous." He grinned disarmingly. Stepping toward her, he raised his strong, manicured hand and rubbed a few strands of blonde between thumb and forefinger. "Who does your hair, sweetling?" he asked, running his hand through the thick strands.

"Uh, Cost Cutters, usually," Willow muttered, wondering what the hell he was doing now. She wasn't used to such focused attention and wasn't entirely sure what to do with it.

"No!" He blew out, bending down to look her in the eye. "You let those oafs touch this gorgeous golden fleece?" She laughed, nodding. "Oh, honey. Now *that* is pure evil sin right there." Dropping his hand, he shocked her by smacking her on the ass. "Okay, girl friend, jump up on that table for me, please."

Doing as he asked, Willow climbed up and lay on her back.

"Turn over, sweetling," he instructed softly, adjusting the sheet for her, keeping her privacy as long as possible.

As Freddie began to work his hands into her tender flesh, yammering on and on about whom his hands had been on, who he wouldn't touch if his life depended on it, and who he'd do anything to get his mitts on, Willow allowed her mind to wander.

She thought about Kevin, wondering where he was today, what he was doing and thinking. What was she going to do once she got home? When was she going home? Where was Christine? Why had she left? She knew what Parker had told her, and she understood that, but why couldn't they just work it out between themselves? Why had Christine dragged Parker into this, then left the poor woman in the dark about what had happened?

Her eyes drifted shut, and she purred softly as Freddie began to find her most tense areas.

"That's right, sweetie," he murmured. "Let Freddie fix everything."

"Hmm," she responded, eyes growing heavier and heavier, mind wandering further and further out into space. Her shoulders relaxed, her fingers uncurled at her sides, and her breathing evened out. Peace.

The sound of the ocean hitting the surf was wonderful, crashing into her ears, the salty air filling her nose. All she could do was sigh in satisfied contentment.

The sand seeped in between her toes, a feeling she hadn't realized she liked so much until she got to paradise.

The palm trees swayed, and the wild flowers made the air fragrant. Down the beach she saw someone, and she smiled, recognizing the nature of movement.

"Kevin!" she yelled out, hurrying her barefoot steps in his direction, though he was still just a shimmer in the heat. She began to run, curious as to why she wasn't getting closer. She was impatient to tell him her big news. She didn't know what her big news was, but she knew it was big, and she knew he needed to know about it.

He raised his hand in greeting, a big arch of a wave. Even though she was running, she was no nearer to him. She felt frustration bearing down on her.

"Bear down, Willow! Push!" he screamed, but she was having trouble doing so. Her body was too relaxed; she couldn't move, she couldn't push. Looking between her spread legs, she saw blue eyes looking back up at her from the apex.

"Christine," she pleaded, breathless fear clenching her gut as Kevin paced restlessly behind her, his eyes never leaving the main attraction between Willow's legs. "Save my baby."

Like a lion ready to pounce, Kevin paced closer to her, fingers flexing and re-flexing, knuckles popping.

"I need you to relax, sweetling," Christine said, though it wasn't her voice. "Sweetling."

Willow's eyes popped open to see a very concerned face looking down at her.

"Are you okay, honey?" Freddie asked, his hand gently combing back the locks of hair that were stuck to Willow's tear-streaked face.

She sniffled, trying to stop the flow of emotion. "I'm sorry."

She tried to sit up. Freddie helped her, keeping her sheet in place. Running her hands through her hair, Willow tried to smile away her embarrassment. The masseur saw right through it.

"Want to talk about it, doll?"

"I don't know," she sniffled, then laughed nervously again. "I bet I'm the first to cry on your table, huh?"

"Well, actually no. It's not horribly uncommon, but it's usually tears of release, not," he gently swiped a falling drop with his fingertip, "tears of pain or distress. I didn't hurt you, did I?"

"No. In fact, I think it's because you had me so relaxed. It felt so good that I couldn't push."

"Say what?"

"I'm pregnant, my husband doesn't want it, so I dreamt Christine was trying to deliver my baby. She kept telling me to push, but I was too relaxed." Her eyes began to leak again at the memory of seeing Kevin's face, so vicious, ready to take her baby away from her.

"Oh, honey." He sat next to her, his shoulder almost brushing hers. "I'm so sorry." The look of compassion she saw on this stranger's face undid her. The dam burst again, and she dissolved into self-pity. The feel of his strong, yet gentle arms around her was so good.

Getting herself together, she sniffled, wiping her hand across her nose before smiling shyly. "I bet you do not deal with this kind of thing often, huh?"

"Are you kidding?" He waved her off. "Honey, I'm like a bartender; when I work, I'm a captive audience, so who better to tell your woes to?" He smiled with a wink, and she smiled back.

"Thank you."

"No worries, beautiful. Let's say I finish up, huh?" He nudged her with his shoulder, and she nudged him back, nodding.

Willow sat on the deck, curled up on a padded lounger tucked against the rail, a cup of decaf cradled against her chest. The sun had set hours ago, and she was basking in the ocean breeze, which was cooling her over-heated skin. She'd spent most of the day on the beach after Freddie had left. It had been nice, but she felt lonelier than she could ever recall.

The massage and relaxing day had helped clear her mind a bit, readying her for the return trip and for getting back into daily life at the hospital.

She also had to meet with Kevin, so they could come up with a plan of action. She felt strongly that they needed a separation until either he could get himself sorted out or she could gather the courage to make a final decision on the fate of her marriage.

In some ways it seemed so sudden to be thinking along those lines. But a powerful force was rising within her, a force that she knew was her maternal instinct kicking in and hard. She knew she'd do anything for this baby, and that included not staying with a man she wasn't sure could love the child. Either Kevin tried, *really* tried, or it was over. Willow needed to respect whoever she loved, and over the past weeks he'd shown her a side of him that made her all but lose that respect.

Sighing, she grabbed the cordless phone from the arm of the lounger and dialed the number she'd memorized from the dry erase board in the kitchen.

"Thanks, doc."

As the door to the small room closed, Robert Knowles examined his face, turning from one side to the other.

"Your plastic surgeon has a nice ass," Sandra said, re-crossing her legs and adjusting her pants to drape over the top of her boot just so.

Bob glared at her through the mirror, then turned back to his own reflection. "This better fucking heal right or I swear I'll take her for everything she has," he muttered, as if to himself. Standing, he put on the lightweight dress jacket that hugged his broad shoulders perfectly. It helped to fuck a clothing designer. "Let's go," he said, hating that the bandage on his nose was so stark against his tan, making it all the more conspicuous.

Sandra stood, pulling the thin straps of her purse onto her shoulder and digging out her car keys. "How does it feel?" she asked, stepping through the examination room door that Robert held open for her.

"It's fine. It feels just fucking peachy," he grumbled, following her down the hall that led to the private exit of Dr. Rae's office, the one that was used by important clients like himself who didn't want it splashed all over the fucking newspaper the next day that they'd had a bit of medical help.

"Well, perhaps you can learn to keep your tactless comments to yourself," Sandra suggested, hitting the button on the private elevator, glancing over her shoulder at the smoldering man at her side.

He glared at her. "Don't start, Sandra." The warning was low, dangerous.

The designer laughed but shut her mouth all the same.

After being dropped off at his Los Angeles offices, others being spread out in the Bay Area and New York, Knowles caught the elevator, groaning internally as the sleek, polished elevator car halted short of his twenty-first floor stop and opened at seventeen. A man of short stature and big attitude stepped inside.

"Hey, Bob. How are you?" Dennis Weinz asked, his bushy brows narrowing to form a furry caterpillar above the bridge of his nose. "What happened?"

"Tennis accident," Bob said lightly, secretly despising the Fox executive.

"Ah." Weinz drew out his single syllable reply, obviously not believing a damn word, but knowing full well he would use the same lame excuse if he himself had to undergo a putty job. The doors dinged open on nineteen, and he smiled. "Watch that serve, huh?" He disappeared with the sound of his own laughter.

"Prick," Bob muttered, unnecessarily punching the button for twenty-one again. As he stepped into his offices, he was greeted by Katrina, the newest cool, drink of water hired at Knowles Group. "Good afternoon, Mr. Knowles," she said, her light brown eyes twinkling with a knowing glint.

"Kat." He remembered how those long, nineteen-year-old legs had felt wrapped around him. She might not be able to carry a tune in a tin bucket, but was she ever a good fuck.

He collected the latest calls and messages from her flirtatious fingers, fighting the urge to take her right there on the desk she sat at, her tight pencil skirt hiked up around her hips. He shivered at the thought, forcing it away; he had work to do.

Once in his office, he sorted through the messages, tossing most into the trash. Everyone wanted something for nothing. The important ones were given a place of honor in the center of his blotter calendar. There were none from Christine.

"Bitch," he muttered. He had given her a week to contact him and apologize. She hadn't. Alright. She had had her chance. Sitting in the expensive chair behind his even more expensive desk, liking the sound of the leather creaking under his weight, he booted his computer and grabbed his PDA from the briefcase he'd brought in. Using the stylus, he scrolled through his address book until he found what he was looking for.

Grabbing the phone, he quickly dialed.

"This is Brine."

"Mr. Brine." Bob leaned back in his chair, the spring bouncing his weight. "Robert Knowles with Knowles Group Agency here."

"Right, how are you, Mr. Knowles?"

"Fine, fine. Quite well, actually. How quickly can you meet me at my downtown office?"

"Well, if you can give me an hour to get past deadline..."

"Fine. Then I'll see you at," Bob glanced at his Rolex, "two-thirty."

"I'll be there."

"Wonderful. Come ready for a cover story." With a wicked grin, Knowles gently laid the receiver in its cradle.

The streets were quiet finally. Many of the tourists gone home for the weekend, and the locals were at home. Aspen nights were chilly at the end of summer. All the same, Christine strolled with her hands in the pockets of her loose cords, with her shirt untucked and its top three buttons undone.

She gazed at the closed shop, seeing its displays of mugs, artwork, pottery and "local clothing". Most of it was highly overpriced and of poor quality.

Moving on, Christine ran a hand through her hair, the thick, dark strands falling back into place with no frizz. That was the great thing about having her hair professionally treated once a week. She remembered the days when after a good rain she looked like a rose bush.

Smiling at the memory and the image that conjured, she crossed the street, pausing for a Lexus to pass, then went into Sonny's, a wonderful little bakery that stayed open late. They had the best mocha breves in the world, so rich and smooth. Her mouth watered just thinking about them.

Bearing a white bag of croissants in one hand and a twenty-ounce mocha breve with extra whipped cream in the other, she headed back to the street where she'd left the rented yellow Hummer. Sliding into the huge vehicle, she set the bag on the console between the two front seats and sipped her drink, wincing as it stung her tongue.

"Damn it," she hissed, sucking in mouthfuls of cool night air to chill the inside of her mouth. "Well, there go about a hundred taste buds," she muttered, sliding the large cup into one of the many cup holders in the big truck. Turning the ignition, she got the beast rumbling beneath her and pulled away from the curb.

Flying directly into Denver, after randomly picking a state from a map, she'd found the nearest place that rented the big vehicles, and off she went, traveling around the state, killing time and thinking. Ending up in Aspen for a couple days, she'd enjoyed the atmosphere. It had been a while since she had been there, maybe three years since she'd hit the slopes, not having a chance to do during her Red Rocks gig not long ago.

It was after ten and traffic was light. Christine turned the CD player up to near deafening levels and sang along with whoever came up on her MP3 player.

She fumbled with the GPS, and a map of the United States popped up, the camera zooming in to where she was, listing surrounding states as it did. Oklahoma flashed on the screen for a second, then was gone.

A stabbing pain hit her heart, nearly making her choke up. Again. Sighing heavily, she grabbed her cell phone from one of the drink holders, flipped it open, not even glanced at it as she hit the number 7 key. Putting the phone to her ear, she listened to the pause as the long distance was covered, then finally a ring. Then two, followed by a third, a click, and then the sound of her own voice.

"Hi, you've reached out, but you can't quite touch me as I'm not available to take your call. Leave something at the beep. Bye."

Christine waited a heartbeat, then spoke. "Willow? Are you there? If you are, please pick up." She waited another beat, two. Sighing, her shoulders slumped. "Guess I missed you." Clapping the phone shut, she tossed it to the seat next to her, not caring as it smashed into the bag of croissants. She thought about the thing that had haunted her every step of her journey over the past week. How had she managed to fuck things up so horribly? She knew better, and yet she had let her emotions lead her anyway.

What got her the most, though, was knowing that Willow thought she'd done it on purpose. If only she knew how far from the truth that statement was. If only Willow knew that she'd been the first person Christine had ever kissed because she really wanted to. If only Willow knew...

"Stupid," she hissed for the zillionth time. Willow was right — all the shit she was going through and all Christine could do was make it worse. How could she have kissed her? She knew Willow wasn't into that, and even if she were, she was married!

Christine raised a hand, swiping at the tear that tickled the skin of her left cheek. She worried that she'd ruined what she knew intuitively would have been a wonderful, lifelong friendship, the kind she'd never thought she'd find again. When she had met Adam, they had had the innocence of youth and desperation to act as the glue for them. As an adult, friendships like that were next to impossible. Adults learned not to trust readily and not to let anyone in to that emotional level.

Willow was different. The singer knew that she could trust Willow with anything, tell her anything, unburden herself of a past that still dogged her steps. A past she had had to lie about almost every time she was asked about where she came from, about her parents, her siblings.

Willow knew the truth now and still hadn't turned her back. No, instead Christine had betrayed that mutual trust, stepping over a line that should *never* have even been drawn, let alone crossed.

It was better this way, Christine told herself, sniffling back the rest of the threatened tears. Willow could go back to her life in Oklahoma, work things out with Kevin, or move on in her life and not have such a troublesome burden tagging along. With friends like her...

Christine turned the music up to a level that almost hurt her head, using the sound to try to push out her thoughts.

"Kevin, I mean it." Rachel pushed firmly against his chest of the man who had shown up for the past three nights. "She's trying to work and you're going to get her in trouble if you keep hanging out here, hoping to see her."

"She won't return my calls, Rachel," he said. "Damn it, how are we supposed to work on this if she won't talk to me?" He threw his arms out in exasperation. Rachel felt bad for what she was about to say, but it needed to be said.

"Maybe she doesn't want to work it out, Kevin." Her voice was quiet, almost gentle. His face crumpled, but he took a deep breath, keeping himself together.

"I see." He stood straighter, backing away from her. "I can't believe she won't give us another chance. She really wants to throw it all away? Just like that?" He snapped his fingers. When Rachel didn't respond, he nodded. "Well, she needs to get hold of me. She and I need to talk, regardless."

Rachel nodded. "I'll talk to her."

"You do that." With that, he turned and strode out the main entrance. Rachel watched him go. She sighed, hating the position she had been put into. It wasn't fair to her or to Kevin, for that matter. She went off in search of her cowardly friend.

"Stay out of it, Rachel," Willow muttered, looking at a chart for a ten-year-old who had just been brought in with seizures that they couldn't get to stop. Her epilepsy medication was all out of whack. What the hell was her neurologist thinking, putting her on Tegretol, Dilantin and Diezepam all at the same time?

"I can't stay out of it — because you won't talk to your damn husband!"

"Would you lower your voice?" Willow hissed, looking around the bustling hall of pediatrics. Clearing her throat apologetically, Rachel continued.

"Look, Willow, I don't agree with what he's been doing and what he did, but the guy deserves an answer or at the very least a decision. No matter what that is, you both need to be able to move on from this."

Willow sighed, shaking her head. She had no idea what she wanted to do.

"What's going on with you lately? You've been so secretive and indecisive. It's not like you at all, Wills. How can I help you if you won't let me in? Ever since you got back from your trip three weeks ago, you've been like a zombie. You came back upset; you don't want to talk about it. Fine. Kevin comes in nightly; you won't talk to him. Fine. But now you won't even talk to *me. Not* fine." She studied her friend's profile, waiting for Willow to look at her. When she didn't, she sighed in frustration and threw her hands up. "Okay. Whatever, Willow. I'll see you later."

Willow watched her friend huff down the hall. If she hadn't been the cause, she would have found it amusing. As it was, she did indeed feel like a zombie, unsure of which way to turn and doubting her anger at Christine more and more each day. No, the singer shouldn't have done what she did, but in retrospect, Willow believed it was just a heat of the moment thing and that nothing had been expected or planned. She also had to come to grips with the simple fact that Christine had been a handy outlet for a lot of pent-up anger and hurt with Kevin.

"Great," she muttered, turning back to the chart. "Pissing everyone off."

When her long day finally came to an end, she found Rachel, and they headed home together. Sitting in Willow's truck, both were quiet. Rachel stared out of the window, watching the dawn of a new day. Willow glanced over at her a few times, trying to decide what to say. She knew she had to say *something*.

Sighing, she began. "Okay. You're right, you do deserve an explanation." Rachel looked at her with blank eyes. Willow chewed on her lip for a moment, staring out the windshield, trying to decide where to start.

"Alright," Rachel said, her voice very quiet.

"What I'm going to tell you cannot leave this truck, Rachel." Stopping at a red light, she looked at her friend, her expression absolutely serious, demanding acceptance of these terms.

"Okay. I promise." Rachel would stand by that promise, but the gossip in her was now standing at full alert and curiosity was gnawing at her.

"Okay. Here goes. Christine took me to an island off the coast of Belize, a private island that she and a few other very rich folks bought for privacy."

"Oh, wow," Rachel breathed. "Where the hell is Belize?"

"In the Caribbean."

"She took you to a goddamn tropical island?"

Willow laughed, nodding. "Yes, now shut up. Anyway, so it was wonderful, amazingly beautiful, and I *want* her house there. I mean, she is so generous. She offered me anything in the house, use of anything, just amazing."

"Wow."

"Yeah, and she brought me breakfast in bed! Fresh fruit, it was fantastic." Willow smiled at the memory, a wave of sadness washing over her. "God, she is such a sweet woman," she almost whispered. Rachel glanced over at her, surprised by the vehemence of that simple statement. "She introduced me to a friend and neighbor." She smiled. "This may not mean much to you as I know you are not much of a reader. But do you know who Parker Davies-Dubois is?"

Rachel frowned in concentration. "Author, right? I saw her on Oprah one day."

"Yeah and one of my favorites to boot. Anyway, we had dinner with her and had a great time. When she left, Christine suggested we go walk on the beach, so we did."

Here she paused as her mind wandered back to that night, how beautiful and magical it had been, with the moon just right and the ocean teeming with life and mystery. She sighed.

"It was perfect, Rachel." Her friend had to really listen; Willow's voice was almost a whisper. "Romantic in another life." She sighed again. "She kissed me."

"Hmm," Rachel said absently, then she realized what Willow had said. Her head snapped around. "What?"

"Yeah. I said some bad things, Rach. Some things I regret now."

"Like what? Why did she do that? Is she after you?"

Willow shook her head, her bangs falling into her eyes. She brushed them away. "I don't think so. I did at first, like when it happened, you know? I accused her of that very thing, in fact."

"What did she say?" Rachel's voice was also quiet. She knew that this was a huge hurdle in the burgeoning friendship.

"Not much, really. But I could see it in her eyes, Rach." She risked a glance at her friend. "She was just as stunned at her actions as I was."

"Then why did you get upset? Why do you think she did it?"

"I got upset because that was my knee-jerk reaction. I think I let everything that had been simmering in the last weeks spill over onto her. She didn't deserve that. And as for why, well, like I said, it was a beautiful, romantic night; I think she got caught up in it."

"Oh boy." They were quiet for a moment, each in her own head, thinking the situation through. "Have you apologized?" Rachel asked finally. Willow shook her head again, the hair falling back into her eyes. She was amazed at how fast her hair grew now — all those wonderful hormones.

"What would I say? She hasn't gotten hold of me either, so my guess is she's done with me. I was a bitch and accused her of something that was really messed up. How can I take that back?" Willow clicked on the turn signal, waited for two cars to go by, then turned onto Rachel's street.

"Well, you can't. But you can try and make things right."

"No, I can't. It is as it is, and now I get to live with it." Turning into the driveway, Willow pulled the parking brake and cut the engine. She turned to find her friend's gaze on her. "What?"

"Nothing." Shaking her head, Rachel got out of the truck, tugging her massive, everything-but-the-kitchen-sink bag with her.

"No, what's on your mind?" Willow asked, following her, closing the front door behind them. "Come on, Rachel, out with it."

"Alright, fine." Rachel set her bag on the sofa, then turned to her friend. "I think Christine was turning out to be a great friend to you. Intuitively, I think she would have been a big part of your life. I think you're throwing it away and all for stubbornness."

"I am *not* being stubborn."

"Aren't you?"

"No, I don't feel that I am." Willow held her ground, but it was shifting under her feet.

"Willow! What are you always telling me? You won't know unless you try, right? I mean, shit, take your own advice. If she slams the phone down, at least you'll know, and you won't be throwing a friendship away unnecessarily. Right?" Willow muttered something under her breath. "What?" Rachel cupped her ear, making a show of making her friend repeat the comment.

"I *said* I know you're right."

"Good. I'm glad we finally agree." Rachel smiled wide and satisfied, making her friend roll her eyes. "Now, what do you want for breakfast?"

Willow muttered something else under her breath as she followed the pesky woman to the kitchen, though this time she didn't repeat it.

The white man in the cheap gray suit stuck out like a sore thumb.

Residents of the neighborhood sat in the cool shadow of tenement archways and decaying porches, smirking at the shoes the yahoo was wearing. Their slippery soles were not practical for the streets of Queens. Dumb shit.

Notebook in hand, the man walked up to a woman on the corner, her long, thin black hair piled unskillfully on her head, a smattering of love marks mingling with scars on her neck and bare shoulders.

Molly Tamale turned and looked the white boy up and down. His hair, strawberry blond, was combed back to look slick and sophisticated. Instead it made him look like Howdy Doody mated with the mob. She turned away. No way would she sleep with that.

"Excuse me," he said, his voice soft and filled with California sun. She graced him with another dark-eyed appraisal. "Hello." He extended a thin-fingered, very pale and freckly hand. "I'm Kenneth Brine, and I'd like to ask you some questions if I might."

She studied his hand, trying to figure out what his game was. No way was he a cop, or if he was, he wouldn't be lasting long.

"So what?" she said, turning her attention back to the street before her.

"Uh, well, uh, Ms. Tamale, is it? I can compensate you for your time."

A flash of green caught Molly's eye. He had her full attention now.

Sighing in relief, Kenneth continued. "Do you know her?" He pulled out a five-by-seven glossy. Molly looked at the woman in the picture, so familiar to everyone in the neighborhood for one reason or another.

"Who don't?" she asked, flipping wisps of hair over her brown shoulder.

"Uh, true. Um, how well do you know her?"

Molly met his desperate blue eyes and smirked.

"How well you *want* me to know her?"

Kenneth Brine grinned. "If you'll step into my office?" and he led her toward his rented car.

Willow's stomach was in knots. She feared that her lunch was ready to make an encore appearance. Lifting her face to the light streaming through the sky-lights in the kitchen, she sniffled, her tears glistening in the late afternoon sun.

A card reading "Mackenzie Deaton, Century 21" lay on the table. She looked at it through liquid eyes. How could this have happened?

Wiping her face, she pushed back from the table, the chair gliding easily over the wood floor on its coasters. She remembered Mac's message on her voice mail. He'd be by later that afternoon — they needed to talk — or so he said.

Walking over to the window above the sink, she looked out toward the stables, seeing the lone horse, head bent, munching on hay.

"I'm sorry, girl," she whispered, swiping yet again at her wet cheeks.

"Thank you for coming," Kevin said, standing from the recliner by the fireplace. He looked good, though tired.

"It's my house, Kevin," Willow said, her voice probably more harsh than she intended, as was her comment. She could tell it stung. He got quiet, his jaw muscles working.

"Well," he said finally, "thanks for agreeing to talk." Sitting again, he rested his hands on his knees, almost as though he were ready to bolt at any moment. Willow figured he probably was, he was so nervous. They hadn't spoken since the night of the accident nearly a month earlier.

Deciding to rein in her anger, bitterness, and profound disappointment, she sat on the couch. If this were a different situation, she would have laughed at her posture — legs pressed firmly together, back ramrod straight, and arms almost wrapped around herself. She was nervous, too, and needed reassurance from the only person in the room that she knew she could count on — herself.

"How have you been?" Kevin asked, his question derailing her amused thoughts.

"I'm alive," Willow hedged. "And yourself?" He shrugged, glancing out the window, then down at his hands, which were working nervously on his knees.

"I'm okay. It's been tough, trying to keep up with work and this place."

"Yes, it is hard work. The house hasn't burned down, though, so I guess you've managed."

He didn't find her little joke funny. "Are you coming home? I don't see any bags with you," he said instead, eyes pinning Willow to her seat.

She looked back at him, realizing that he hadn't asked a single question about the baby. Is it okay, how's the pregnancy going, can I be a daddy?

"Do you still mean it?" *she countered, looking at him just as intensely. His brow wrinkled in confusion.*

"Do I still mean what?"

"What you said about the baby, that you don't want it, don't want to be a father."

He sighed, running a hand through his newly cut hair, the short strands spiking in its wake. His Adam's apple bobbed as he swallowed hard. "I can try—"

"No try, Kevin. You either do or you don't." *Feeling her confidence and resolution returning in full force, Willow raised her chin a tad, just enough to exert control over the situation. He looked up — eyes filled with...tears?*

"So that's it? Just like that," *he snapped his fingers,* "you can make ultimatums about this? Either I be the perfect Hallmark Card father in two point three seconds or we're finished?"

"Try three months, Kevin," *she said, her voice rising just a bit.* "You've known about this child for three months and yet you couldn't bring yourself to even care, let alone become Father of the Year."

"I do care!" *he exclaimed, pounding his fist on the arm of his chair. Willow shook her head.*

"No, you don't."

"Damn it, I love you, Willow. I was at the fucking hospital every day to see if you were okay or if I could talk to you." *His eyes were a vibrant blue as his anger rose.*

"Kevin, it's not just about me anymore." *She wondered if she sounded as hopeless as she felt.* "What about this child?" *Willow rested her hand on her belly, still mostly flat.* "We're a package deal now."

He said nothing, resting his chin on his knuckles and looking out the window again.

She studied his strong, rugged features. He truly was a handsome man. She had thought they'd be together forever. The seconds ticked by, the crack in her heart growing wider and wider.

"I think we need to separate." *Kevin's head snapped around at her words, but she held up a hand to stop anything he had to say.* "You make far more than I do, so I think it's only fair you find another place to live."

"Don't do this to us," *he said, his voice trembling. For a moment Willow was ashamed at how calm she felt, how right this decision felt. What she said was true, though — it was not just about her anymore.*

"I didn't do this to us." *She said nothing more, letting her words hit their mark. She didn't want to hurt him, to be a cruel, uncaring woman. She just needed for him to understand the breadth of what he had done and the profound betrayal she felt.*

It had started slowly, the money running out. Refinancing the paid-off ranch had seemed like such a good idea four years ago. It had meant they could make all the repairs that were needed and get a new truck for Kevin. And there was that trip to Greece...

She had sold Buster as a stud horse, which had helped. Then she started shaving off small pieces of the land, then bigger pieces, and then another horse. Now Willow was faced with making the most difficult decision of her life — selling the ranch itself.

"Damn it!" she exclaimed, pounding her fist on the table, shattering the quiet in the house. Various folks had tromped through her sanctuary, cheapening it. And now... If what Max wanted to talk to her about was that he had, in fact had a prospective buyer, they would undoubtedly want Star in the deal, and how was a desperate Willow to say no? Besides, it wasn't as if she could really take the mare to an apartment complex or a house in the city.

She heard gravel under car tires. Hurrying over to the kitchen sink, she wet a dishtowel and scrubbed at her face, trying to hide her utter devastation. Clearing her throat, she ran her hand through her shaggy hair a few times, then after a deep breath, headed toward the front door where her unwanted guest would be entering.

Sure enough, within moments muffled voices got louder, Mac's very easy to pick out, loud, boisterous and deep. But who was with him? He hadn't mentioned bringing anyone. Willow's heart sank.

"I agree, it is lovely," he said, knocking several times. The door opened, and Mackenzie Deaton burst into the house, cheeks tinted rosy red from the bright, Oklahoma sun. "Hello, hello, hello!" he bellowed, spying his client and quickly making his way over to her. "How are you? You look beautiful today," he gushed. Willow smiled shyly, always overwhelmed by his personality.

"Thank you, Mac."

He leaned in conspiratorially. "You are going to die when you see the surprise I have for you." He winked, then stood at his full height. "Willow Bowman, may I introduce to you the woman who has saved your lovely behind?"

A tall figure stepped inside the entryway, casual in faded, comfortable jeans and boots and a fitted spring yellow t-shirt. Willow blinked a few times, struck dumb by what her eyes were showing her.

Chapter 10

"Hello, Ms. Bowman," Christine said quietly.

"Ms. Gray — oh, to hell with it!" Willow turned to the realtor, who was befuddled by what was unfolding. "Mac, we need a few moments."

"Oh, uh," Mackenzie looked from one to the other, then back to Willow. "Certainly." He made himself busy in the living room. Willow grabbed Christine's hand and dragged her to the privacy of the kitchen. She whirled to face her, hands on hips.

"What are you doing?" she demanded. Christine leaned against the counter, arms casually crossed over her chest.

"Seems I've paid off your debt."

"But why? How could you!" Willow's pride was pricklier than the cactus outside. Her shock was turning to irrational anger.

"Because I'm not about to let you lose your home!" Christine fired back. Willow's mouth was open to spit something back, but the words got caught in her throat.

"What?" She would have stumbled backwards if she hadn't been already leaning against the island. Recovering, she said, "Christine, you can't buy me."

Christine was stung. "I would never do that, Willow," she said quietly. "I never have."

Looking as regretful as she felt, Willow nodded. "I'm sorry."

"Think of it this way," Christine said, pushing past the hurtful comment and brightening the room with her smile. "Think of it as a gift for the baby, the ultimate crib." She grinned, her eyes twinkling. Willow caught the spark and grinned back.

"Christine, I can't…"

"Too much, huh? Hmm. I was afraid of that." She made a show of rubbing her chin. "How about this, then? I know of a lender I can direct you to. No interest and no penalty for early repayment. Ten dollars will pay it in full; check made out to me, please."

Willow looked up at her, smile fading into genuine curiosity. "Why are you doing this?" Christine's own smile faded into a look of affection.

"Because I can't stand to think of you losing something that I know means so much to you," she said gently.

"How did you know?"

"I came by here a couple weeks ago, planning to visit, when I saw the 'For Sale' sign. I did some investigating and found out what was happening, so," she shrugged, "here we are."

Overwhelmed by emotion and gratitude, Willow threw herself at the singer, finding herself engulfed in strong arms.

"Thank you," she whispered.

"You're welcome," Christine whispered back, eyes closing in the relief at the day's events. "I'm so sorry, Willow."

"No, I'm sorry." Pulling back a bit, she looked up. "I was cruel, I'm so sorry..."

"No." Christine held up a hand. "My actions were completely inappropriate, and I'm forever sorry."

Willow smiled through her tears. "Let's just agree that it was not a good thing all around and move on, okay?"

Christine smiled, too, and nodded. "Agreed." One final hug, and she pulled totally away. "Come on, let's go finish this deal."

Christine handed over a check in the amount that Willow needed to pay the ranch off, and received a check for ten dollars in return. Christine then surprised both the realtor and blonde when she handed the man a check for what his commission would have been had the ranch actually been sold. A most confused, but happy, Mackenzie Deaton left the two women alone.

"I'm sorry I couldn't get here before you sold the other horses," Christine said quietly, leaning against the rail fence next to Willow, who was watching her Star frolicking. "If you know where they are..." Christine's voice trailed off. Willow sighed, slowly shaking her head, her eyes never leaving her lone remaining horse.

"Nah. Some things just have to change."

Bob turned to the left, then to the right, examining himself in the large, round handheld mirror.

"I have to tell you, Joel, you are a master artist." He grinned at the good-looking doctor who stood back, Armani'd arms crossed over a well-developed chest.

"It looks fabulous, Bob," the plastic surgeon said, his slight Brazilian accent smoothing his words. "Better than before."

"Hmm," he said absently, still checking out the new look and new nose.

"When am I going to get my scalpel on the gorgeous Christine Gray?" the doctor asked, wiggling his dark brows.

Bob chuckled, re-slicking a piece of hair that had flopped over his forehead. "You're a married man, Joel."

"Eh, just a simple procedure, Bob."

"Well, I wouldn't count on that, my friend." He tugged on his suit jacket, adjusting the lapels. "You don't have the right equipment to get her on your operating table."

"So the rumors are true, eh?"

"Well, you know what they say, there's a kernel of truth in *all* rumors."

"Really?" Intrigued, Joel Rae leaned forward on his stool. "Perhaps something could be worked out...?" An elegant brow rose in question.

Again, Bob chuckled bitterly. "To my knowledge, *Mizz* Gray hasn't been with a man since...well," he feigned protective silence, "that's not for me to tell."

"Hmm." Dr Rae was disbelieving. "How about a drink between old friends, eh?"

"Sounds wonderful. I know of a great place on the strip."

"Lead the way."

Trista Metzger ran as fast as her short legs would allow, her long dark hair trailing behind her. She nearly twisted an ankle as she turned the sharp corner and her boot slid on the Berber carpeting. She shot out a hand to the wall to steady herself, then sprinted down the final hall, headed for the room at the end.

Bursting through the heavy oak door, she slapped a magazine down on the large desk, holding up a finger as she tried to catch her breath, her lungs burning from the exertion. She really did need to stop smoking.

"Where's the fire, Trista?" Christine asked, a half smile on her face until she recognized the look of horror on her assistant's face. Gazing down at the copy of the *Enquirer* that had almost slid into her lap, her own eyes widened with shock. "No," she breathed.

"Mary brought that in to me just now," Trista managed to say, plopping down in one of the leather chairs in front of the desk. Christine liked to keep an office downtown so business didn't have to be done at her house or in rented conference rooms.

"What have they done?" She read the headline: ROCKER CHICK BY THE HOUR? There was a fuzzy, and obviously doctored, picture of a much younger Christine Gray standing on a street corner in a tiny dress, hand on hip, leaning slightly forward as she talked to someone in a car.

Frantically opening the magazine, she found the article right away, filled with pictures of her in concert, press release photos, and candid shots taken of her over the years. Some she didn't recognize, and she wondered if the *Enquirer* had been keeping them for just such an article.

"They've really gone too far this time, Chris. You should sue their asses for slander," Trista was saying, but her words were only a murmur in Christine's fear- and disgust-filled mind.

Christine read a "first-hand account" from some woman named Molly Tamale who claimed to remember the singer as a young girl working the streets, going with Johns when she was as young as seven.

"Jesus," she moaned. "Who wrote this piece of shit?" She flipped to the first page of the article, seeing Kenneth Brine's byline. "Get me this bastard on the phone," she growled, tossing the magazine back across her desk, turning in her chair to look out the window. She felt sick, the bile rising with each panicked thought.

"You got it, boss."

Once alone again, Christine stood, running her hands through her hair, shaking out the long strands. "Fuck, fuck, fuck." This could ruin her. The story was crap, and most probably wouldn't believe it, but fuck! It was very, *very* close to the truth. Who could have found out about this? Where did it come from?

"Chris?" the tinny voice in her intercom said.

"Yeah, Trista?" She had to force her voice to be calm.

"Myron Reyes on line one. He's the editor-in-chief. They won't let me talk to Brine."

"Fine. Patch the line." Christine sat heavily back in her chair, her face turning to stone.

"Ms. Gray, what an honest to God pleasure," a deep voice intoned. She ignored his pleasantries. She'd had smut published about her before — hell, who hadn't in this business? — but this was an outrage.

"What is this *shit* in your magazine, Mr. Reyes? A term I use advisedly."

"I stand by the article, Ms. Gray." His voice and demeanor had changed in the blink of an eye — now, he was all business and hard and as unyielding as stone. "We have reliable and reputable sources, I assure you."

"What, like Molly Tamale!" Christine stood, the rage seeping out through her pores. "And that I was allegedly on the streets at *seven*? Mr. Reyes, I was living in an apartment with my goddamn parents at seven. And as for this Tamale character, I have never even *met* this woman, let alone her knowing a damn thing about where I was in grammar school!"

Myron Reyes was silent, a sliver of panic shooting through his veins before he recovered.

"We stand by every word that Mr. Brine wrote. He did his research and found the dirt. I'm sorry if it was dirt you'd hoped would not be uncovered. Guess our methods are better than yours, eh?" he chuckled softly, only infuriating Christine even more.

"Who sent you on this wild goose chase?" Christine growled, picking up the receiver so she'd have something to wrap her fingers around and squeeze.

"Goose chase, Ms. Gr—"

"Who?" She was finished with his fucking games. She had a cold feeling in her gut that the *Enquirer* had been spoon-fed this garbage.

"We protect our sources, Ms. Gray."

"I will take everything you've got for this, Reyes. Bet your ass on it." Her voice was like a razor. The office rang with the noise of her slamming down the receiver. She was furious, and she was hurt. Who could have done this to her? No one knew...

Her line of thought screeched to a halt. Besides her, only three people knew enough about her past to have tipped the *Enquirer* on where to look. One was Adam, and he would *never* betray her like that, nor would Willow. The third was...

"You can't go in there!" Kat hurried after the tall whirlwind that had just pushed past her desk. "He's in a meeting!" The young secretary's cries were cut short as the frosted glass office door was slammed open, the crack from the force filling the office like a clap of thunder.

"It's alright, Katrina. I'll take it from here," Bob Knowles said, phone still held in his hands. His dark eyes never left the beast before him as he murmured his goodbyes, then gently replaced the receiver in its cradle.

Katrina was trembling in the stilettos Bob loved so much as she returned to her desk.

Bob got up, his eyes still never leaving Christine Gray as he made his way to the ruined door and closed it for some sort of privacy. He had never seen her like this, and in truth, he was frightened of the hatred oozing from her.

"How could you?" she growled as he made his way back behind his desk again, feeling better with something strong and sturdy between them. His biggest client stood before him, eyes sexy as hell in all their rage, hands splayed out as she leaned over his desk, taking some of that safe space away from him.

He swallowed, as quietly and with as little show as possible. He didn't want her to know how frightened he really was.

"What are you talking about?" he said, quite impressed with how calm his voice was.

"Do *not* attempt to lie to me, Bob. I know you did it. I want to know why."

He stared back at her, dark eyes cool and calm, though Christine knew he was a coward at heart and was quaking in his perfectly shined Guccis. He said nothing, and she knew he'd never admit to it. But his silence said everything.

"You'll not get away with this," she hissed, standing up straight again. "Mark my words, Bob." She was slowly backing out of the office. "The ruin you've just visited upon me is one and the same for yourself. You're fired." With that, she turned and stalked down the hall.

Her world was almost as quiet as the empty road before her, the sound of the trees whipping by the open window the only thing interrupting the almost perfect isolation. The sky was getting darker and darker, as clouds heavy and pregnant, gathered.

She brought a hand up, swiping at a new flow of tears, the betrayal ripping at her insides. She felt lost. Her music, her face and body, her voice, her name had not been enough. Now they wanted her soul. There seemed only one safe place in this dark night, and the turn that led to it was coming up.

The rain was coming down in earnest now. Willow was just thrilled that she'd taken care of Star earlier and the mare was tucked safely in her dry stable.

She headed back toward the stairs, retying the doo-rag she'd put on her head to keep paint from getting in her hair. Hand on the banister, she heard something and glanced out the beveled glass that lined the sides of the tightly locked front door. Headlights shone across her face for a moment as a car pulled into the circular drive.

Turning away from the stairs, she peered out of the window, catching images in prism of someone opening a car door, slamming it shut, and walking toward the porch stairs.

Willow unlocked and opened the door, light spilling out into the storm-dark night. Pushing open the wooden screen door, she went out. There stood Christine, her hair plastered to her head and her clothing like a second skin, soaked from her short walk to the porch from her rental car. The look on her face was what really got Willow moving — absolute anguish.

A sob ripped through the night. Christine found herself engulfed in those safe arms, resting her head on a sturdy shoulder. "Come inside," Willow said into her ear. "Come inside, Christine."

Christine had driven straight through — making the 1,300-mile trip in a day. Now she was sleeping soundlessly in the guestroom. Willow checked on her often, wishing so badly that there was something, *anything* she could do. She thought about earlier that day.

"Wolf man eats his wife," Rachel smirked as she shoved the smut mag back into its rack at the register of the Safeway she and Willow were waiting in line at.

"Shouldn't it be wolf woman eats her husband?" Willow said, and they both chuckled. She was fingering a tin bubble gum container, the little pieces of gum inside shaped like dolphins. She was intrigued, just like a child.

"Oh, no," Rachel said, her voice filled with foreboding.

"What?" Willow asked, checking the calorie count on the little fishy gum.

"Look, Wills," Rachel shoved the magazine in front of her face, and her eyes immediately settled on what looked to be a very young Christine Gray: ROCKER CHICK BY THE HOUR?

Willow felt her blood go cold.

"Oh God," she gasped, taking the tabloid from her friend's hand. "God, I hope she hasn't seen this."

"Who could do such a thing?" Willow whispered, gently brushing locks of dark hair from a pale forehead with feather-light touches, not wanting to wake the troubled woman. With a sad sigh, she stood, heading downstairs where Rachel was making coffee for them.

"God, how can you drink this stuff?" she asked, handing Willow a steaming mug.

"It doesn't taste any different, you pain in the ass."

"Yeah, but where do you get your little extra oomph from?" The women sat at the breakfast nook, Rachel's painted nails clicking lightly against the ceramic mug.

"Oomph? You're kidding, right? Shoot, my energy is being sucked down into my gut." Willow grinned.

"How is she?" Rachel asked, sobering. Willow sighed and shrugged.

"She's still asleep. God, Rachel, you should have seen her." Willow shook her head, looking out at the muddy morning. "Drenched to the bone, but I swear it was like the sky was crying for her. She was devastated."

"The sky was crying for her, huh?" Rachel grinned. "Methinks you've been hanging out with the songstress a little too much."

"Oh, hush." Willow playfully smacked her giggling friend. "I know that was corny, but it's true. I just want to protect her from the world, you know?"

"That's probably why she came here, Wills. I'm sure she feels safe here, with you."

"I hope so. If I can keep her out of the public eye for even just a few days, you know?" Willow stirred in a packet of Splenda.

"Yeah. What is she going to do?"

"I have no idea. She crashed within twenty minutes of showing up. All I know is that she drove here from L.A." Willow walked to the fridge, pulling out a couple of containers of yogurt.

"Thanks." Rachel opened the container put before her, then grabbed the spoon set next to it. "You still craving this stuff?" she chuckled, stirring the fruit up to the top.

Willow rolled her eyes. "God, it's been weird. At least I know I won't be having any yeast infections."

"Monistat 7, ladies. Works wonders."

Both nurses turned to see Christine grinning from the doorway. Willow thought she looked adorable, her hair disheveled in every which way, t-shirt slightly askew, and one leg of her shorts longer than the other from shifting around in her sleep.

"Hey, you." Willow smiled, standing. "Are you hungry? Thirsty? Can I get you anything?" She was stopped with a hand to her arm and a gentle smile.

"I can get it. Take a load off." Christine squeezed her arm affectionately until she got a nod.

"Help yourself to anything, okay?" Willow said quietly.

Rachel was surprised to find a sting of jealousy rushing quickly through her veins, then dissipating just as quickly. Watching the interaction between her friend and Christine was most interesting. There was an easy trust between them, a comfort level that was quite surprising considering firstly, how they met, and secondly, that Christine Gray was one of the top female recording artists in the world.

Willow took her seat across from Rachel again, hearing the rustle and clinking in the kitchen of pans being pulled, fridge being opened, items removed and arranged on the counter.

"You ladies like omelets?" Christine asked, glancing at the pair.

"You any good at making them?" Rachel teased. "I'm pretty damn picky when it comes to my eggs."

"Well, lucky you; so am I." Christine winked, then began to crack shells.

One hour and eight eggs later, the three sat in the living room, each nursing a cup of hot decaf.

"I need you both to understand that now this story has broken, they'll stop at nothing to find more, which will ultimately lead here," she pointed down, "to your hospital and to the events that happened last February."

"We won't say anything," Rachel said, indicating herself and Willow.

"Say what you will, Rachel. That's what these bastards do for a living — find the dirt. Mark my words," she sipped her brew, "the hospital is going to be bombarded by questions." She sighed, that sadness clouding her features again. "I'm really sorry to put you guys through this."

Willow and Rachel shared a quick look, then Willow went to her, sitting down next to the singer. "Please don't apologize, Christine," she said quietly, taking the large, calloused hand in her own. "You don't deserve this. I really hope you don't think that you do."

Christine raised her sad eyes to meet those of the beautiful nurse. "I did all this, Willow. What they're accusing me of, I did."

"I know that. But look what you've done with your life since! Look how many people you've touched out there all over the world. With your music and your talent, you've reached inside millions and made them smile, made them forget their problems for just a short while." She smiled. "I speak from personal experience here, okay?"

Christine studied those eyes, seeing nothing but truth. Rachel nodded in agreement, though Christine never saw it. Finally she conceded.

Rachel waited a heartbeat, not wanting to interrupt the silent conversation, but then she downed the rest of her coffee, gently setting the mug on the end table next to the loveseat where she sat.

"I have to get going, girls. Connor's waiting."

Shaking herself out of her almost trance-like state, Willow stood and walked over to her friend. "Thanks for coming," she said quietly, taking her in a tight hug.

"Anytime, sweetie." Rachel turned to look at Christine, surprised to see the singer had made her way over to them. She squeaked quietly as she found herself engulfed in warm arms; she grinned up her. "You've got a hell of a hug machine there, Gray."

Christine grinned. "Why thank you. Never had any complaints before."

"Hmm, bet not," Rachel muttered, then she headed out.

Holding the brush between her teeth, Christine readjusted the rag covering her dark hair, then took the handle between nimble fingers and began to work the delicate blue paint into the wall.

"This is all going to be *so* cute," she gushed, unable to keep the grin from her face.

"Thank you. I'm glad you like it."

"I'm surprised you're starting this so soon," Christine glanced down at Willow, working around the floorboards while she handled the area closer to the ceiling, not wanting the mother-to-be to climb the ladder.

"Well," Willow shrugged, "I figure I might as well just get this stuff started now, the stuff I won't really be able to do later, you know?" Glancing up, she saw Christine's nod. "And now that Kevin won't be helping me," she shrugged again, "it's all me." This last part was more muttered to herself than meant to add to the conversation.

"Not if I have anything to do with it."

Willow looked questioning. "Oh?"

"That's right," Christine said with determination, dipping the small brush into the plastic pan balanced at the top of the ladder. "I'm going to make sure you get all the help you need, my friend. Don't worry about a thing."

"Oh, well thank you very much." Willow wiggled her brows at the singer, making her chuckle.

They worked in silence, each lost in her own thoughts. Willow wanted to get to the heart of the matter, but she wasn't sure if she should broach the painful subject.

As if reading her thoughts, Christine asked quietly, "What are you thinking about down there?"

Willow sighed, brushing a stray lock behind her ear with her pinky, one of the only fingers still paintless. "Who did this to you?" For a moment she wasn't sure Christine had understood the question, but finally she replied.

"Bob Knowles."

"That son of a..."

"I know." Christine smiled at Willow's vehemence.

"Why'd he do that to you?" Willow stood, stretching out her aching back and tossing her brush into the pan not far from where she'd just finished up.

"Because he's a bastard who was angry that I laid him out," Christine said, leaning in close as she painted a tight spot, making sure she didn't paint the ceiling, which, like the woodwork, would stay white. "He was unfortunate enough to be born with little-to-no tact and made a very stupid and thoughtless comment."

"I'm sorry."

"So was he." Christine gave Willow a shit-eating grin then turned back to her task at hand.

"So what are you going to do?"

"That is the question, isn't it?" She painted a little more. "I don't really know. Disappear off the face of the earth, maybe? Pretend it never happened? Lie? I don't know."

"Why not call him on his own methods?"

"What do you mean?" Christine stopped painting and leaned on the ladder.

"Well," Willow drawled, crossing her arms over her growing chest. "Play his game, Christine. You have *tons* of high-powered friends out there. Make them work for you. Tell *your* story. The *true* story." She stared up at her, letting the words sink in. "The truth shall set you free." She grinned.

"He is as smug as a bug in a rug, Chris," Trista said, flopping down in one of the chairs in front of the desk.

"Hmm," Christine said, staring down at the bustling city below. "I'm not surprised. Is everything arranged?"

"Yeah. Oh my God, yeah! Her people were nearly peeing in their pants with excitement to get such an exclusive." She rolled her eyes. "You should hear what Katrina says about him. The guy's going way over the top with this. That son of a bitch is talking to *anyone* who's willing to listen to his garbage." She crossed a bare knee over the other, lazily swinging her high-heeled foot.

"No, I'm not surprised in the least. He wants the spotlight — always has." With a sigh, Christine turned to her assistant, hands tucked into the pockets of her jeans. "When are we on?"

"Wednesday night, your place."

"Good."

"I'm nervous," Willow gushed, laughing with nervous energy.

"I know. Me, too." Rachel patted her on the knee, then began to tuck into the freshly popped bag of Orville Redenbacher with extra butter.

The sitcom they'd been watching ended, and an advertisement came on for the Barbara Walters Special, an exclusive with Christine Gray.

Christine was surprised at how warm the legendary journalist was. She'd heard a lot of folks call her a diva but had found no such thing herself.

She had happily showed Barbara around her house and its perfectly kept grounds in the hills overlooking L.A. She knew from previous specials she had seen that much of it would be edited out, with only a few scenes being used for visual effect during Barbara's narrative.

Sitting compliantly in one of the extremely comfortable wingbacks brought to the music room from the formal living room, Christine waited for the makeup girl to finish, listening to the murmured orders and requests from the crew. They were slowly turning her room into a theatrical production space meant to look like a sanctuary suitable for intimate conversation.

"And in five," the producer, headset in place, counted backward to three, then fell silent, fingers counting down the rest of the way.

"There has been much said of late about your past, Christine," Barbara said, a soft smile on her lightly painted lips. Her tone was almost maternal, but with a reproving edge to it.

"Tell me about it!" Christine said, rolling her eyes and offering a playful smile, which earned her a small chuckle from the journalist.

"Turn that up, please, Raymond. Thank you." Robert adjusted his head against the padded rest, his face gooey and stiff from the mud mask, and his eyes closed by the slices of cucumber resting upon his lids.

His masseur did as bade, and the television's sound and light filled the small, darkened room.

He had heard from some of his friends, and even a couple of clients, that Christine would be doing a Walters' special. "Special, my ass," he murmured, hearing Raymond leaving him to "soak". "You want special you should've come to me, Walters."

"How did the story in the tabloid make you feel?" Barbara asked, her hands resting peacefully on the yellow legal pad of notes on her skirted lap.

Christine sighed, thinking of the best way to answer that. "Truth of the matter is, Barbara, the story is true." She noted the slight widening of the journalist's eyes but nothing more. "It was a very painful time for me, and certainly one I wanted to forget." She shrugged, a sad little smile tugging at her lips. "It wasn't to be so."

"Do you want to tell your story? Here and now? *Your* side of things?"

"Yes. What that tabloid printed was based on truth, yes, but it made a mockery of human pain. That pain was mine, so now I'm here to set things straight."

"She's so brave," he said, mesmerized by the strongest woman he knew, the woman who dominated his twenty-seven inch screen.

Alice held his hand tightly in her own as he lay with his head in her lap. "Yes, she is," Alice said quietly, leaning down to gently kiss his temple, which was slightly damp from sweat. "How are you feeling, my love?"

"I'm fine," Adam said absently, still waiting almost breathlessly for Christine to speak.

The front door opened, and Rachel's finger automatically went to her lips. Connor looked at her like she'd lost her mind.

"Have a seat," she whispered, patting the couch next to her.

The man entered the room where Rachel and Willow sat, glancing at the light from the tube, his face falling in disappointment. "But Rach, the first game of the season is on," he whined.

"Then go watch it upstairs," she hissed, noting Willow's eyes were pinned to the screen.

"But this has the surround sound..."

"Then go to your own damn place to watch it!" she snapped, irritated that he wouldn't watch this with her, something that was far more important than stupid football.

Knowing a losing battle when he saw one, he clicked his tongue like a child and stomped upstairs.

"God, such little boys," Rachel muttered, shoveling anther handful of popcorn into her mouth.

Willow didn't answer.

"So tell us, in your own words, the true story of Christine Gray."

"Oh, where to begin," Christine breathed, raising a hand to run through her hair before she remembered it was plastered with product and they'd have to shut down, allow time for her hair to be fixed, then start up again. She'd have to find a new nervous habit for this journey.

She began her tale, beginning with her parents and their abandonment and her fortuitous meeting with Adam.

"I can't, Adam," Christine hissed, being pulled along by her wrist, the third flight of stairs before them.

"Come on, Christine. Don't worry."

"Will she get mad?" she asked, looking around, waiting for her friend's mom to pop out of the walls somewhere.

"Why would she? She probably ain't even here. God, you worry all the time."

They continued in silence. What she'd heard about Toni "Machete" Mischetti was not pleasant, and it scared Christine. Word on the street was she was with Derrick Zolna, a real tough guy, who had suddenly disappeared after they had been seen fighting.

Their feet slammed onto the landing for the third floor of the old brick tenement, and they headed down the hallway, the carpet almost totally worn through in places.

Adam stopped at his door, struggling with the knob that liked to stick, then finally kicked the door open, adding another mark to the multiple shoe prints at the bottom of the stained wooden door. The apartment was tiny and stuffy with the smell of stale cigarette smoke and vomit.

Fighting the urge to hold her nose, Christine followed him inside and looked around. The furniture was old; holes eaten through to the stuffing, either by mice, a huge problem in New York, or from some evil pet. She'd bet on the mice.

"Rosco, honey, that you?" a woman called out from the bedroom.

Christine's spine stiffened and she turned to face Adam. "Rosco?"

"Shut it," he hissed.

She stifled a giggle.

Toni came into the living area, which doubled as a kitchen. Flopping down on the couch, she ran her heavily ringed fingers through a mane of wild black hair and brushed it back from her face. She was not what Christine would call pretty, but she wasn't exactly unattractive, either. Toni looked older than her twenty-four years, her face lined from years of hard drinking and smoking. Her eyes were a dark gray and probably would have been pretty if they hadn't been so red-rimmed and bloodshot.

"Where you been, son? Who's this?" she asked, snagging a pack of Camels off the badly scarred blond wood coffee table. Shaking one loose, she grabbed it with dry, cracked lips, and then quickly lit it with a red plastic lighter. A cloud of smoke billowed out around her head. She eyed them both through the haze.

"Ma, this is Christine. That girl I told you about," Adam said, standing next to her.

Toni eyed her, inhaling another drag and squinting her eyes. "Nice to meet you, Christine." She exhaled. "I got company tonight, Rosco. Be a good boy and you and your little friend go play, huh?"

"Yeah, okay. Can she stay with us for a little while?" he asked, his young voice rising in hope.

"Adam," Christine hissed.

He shoved her with his shoulder, his eyes never leaving his mother.

Inhale, exhale. "Sure, why not. You two be quiet and use the back door. James will be here soon."

"Ah, mom, I can't stand James," Adam whined.

"You watch your mouth, son," Toni said, pointing at him with her cigarette fingers. "He been nothing but nice to you."

"Yeah, till he gets mad," he muttered and tugged Christine by the sleeve back out the door.

And so it went. Toni still scared Christine. She was a nice enough lady, but don't get her mad! Bad idea. Christine entered the apartment more than once to a screaming match between Adam and his mom.

He never did tell her what was up with the Rosco bit. Christine thought it had something to do with some dead relative. Things seemed okay until after her eleventh birthday. That was when things began to change.

She and Adam were sitting on the living room floor, fighting over the one Nintendo controller.

"You are so full of shit!" Adam yelled, shoving her.

Christine, tall for her age, quickly shoved him back.

"Hey," Bernie, Toni's latest squeeze, smacked Adam upside the head. "Shut that hole of yours."

They both looked up at him, surprised.

Bernie winked at Christine causing her to shiver in disgust. He had been watching her all week, and it was giving her the creeps. She would have said something to Toni, but Toni had been watching her, too. A totally different kind of watching. Bernie's was filled with that lust she had seen in those movies Toni used to watch all the time. Toni, however, looked at her like she was some rival or something.

Weeks later, with Adam and Toni out of the apartment, Christine was sitting on the couch watching television when Bernie jumped her and started kissing her. His big hand, greasy from a day working at the shop, fondled and squeezed her hard.

Toni walked in and all hell broke loose. "What the fuck!" Toni's voice boomed and, before she knew what was happening, Christine was grabbed by her ear and pulled off the couch. Toni called her horrible names as Christine tried to explain that it was Bernie who started it all, not her.

Toni finally screamed, "Get out! Get out of my fucking house right now!" She stormed after Christine, who backed away, trying not to give Toni the chance to grab her again. Christine's back hit the apartment door. "I took you in, you little slut, and look how you repay me," Toni hissed, her breath reeking of the rum and grape juice she liked so much.

Christine turned and fumbled with the locks, trying desperately to get away. Finally the door opened, and she literally fell out into the hall, hitting the hard and unforgiving floor. She scrambled up and stumbled down the hall, running headlong into Adam, coming back with a bag of groceries.

"Whoa, fuck, Chris!" he yelled, picking himself up off the floor.

"Sorry," she grumbled, jumping back to her feet. She ran down the hall and hit the stairs.

"Hey! Wait!" he yelled after her.

She kept going, not wanting him to see the tears that were freely falling.

The door at the top of the stairs banged open, and footfalls echoed a flight and a half up. "Damn it, wait up, Chris!"

Christine pushed through the door that led to the main hall, using her long legs to her advantage.

Running Adam finally caught up to her four doors down. "What happened?" he gasped, as she stopped and nervously paced the sidewalk. He bent over and placed his hands on his knees to catch his breath.

"She kicked me out," she yelled, bitterly swiping at the tears that ran down her cheeks.

"What?" He stood straight again, looking at her with narrowed eyes. "Why?"

"That asshole boyfriend of hers fucking attacked me, and she blamed me!"

"No way!"

"Way." Christine started walking again, wiping away the last of the tears. She could make it on her own just fine. She didn't need Toni. Yeah. She did not need anyone.

Television viewers across America watched in rapt silence as one of the greatest musicians of her time told a story of innocence corrupted. Nielson would later report that as many people watched the special as had watched the previous Super Bowl.

A blonde in Oklahoma sat with her legs drawn up, and her arms wrapped around her shins, eyes wide, unnoticed tears gently streaking the smooth skin of her cheeks.

A man sat on a padded table, his face like wood where a mud mask had completely dried, forgotten, with two pink circles around his eyes where two slices of cucumber had once been. He watched as faded snapshots accompanied Christine's story of a childhood gone terribly wrong. He was transfixed.

A couple cuddled on an olive green couch, a light breeze rolling in through their open fire escape window. One gently combed her fingers through soft, thick hair, while the other felt his stomach roil at what he knew was to come.

Christine sat in her chair, silent for a moment, all the memories attacking her at once.

"Do you need a break?" Barbara asked, reaching across the distance between them to gently cover a pale, trembling hand.

"No," she smiled weakly, then sipped the goblet of water on the small, oval table next to the chair. Taking several deep breaths, she continued. "Well, I got myself into this mess; I had to go through with it. If for no other reason than I didn't want Adam to think I was a loser."

"Come on, honey. I don't have all night," he called from the main room of the cheesy motel.

Closing her eyes, fingers trembling, she tried to undo the top button of her shirt. "Come on," Christine tried to encourage herself. He seemed nice enough…but, God, he was old.

Finally the button went through the sliver of a hole, followed by the next and the white of her very first bra came into view. Having outgrown it, Toni had given it to Christine. She hastily threw the stuffing out before the old guy saw it.

Her mind flashed to the guy in the other room. Did he have light hair or dark? The only thing she remembered seeing clearly was the massive gold belt buckle with a gaudy J written in rhinestones.

Christine jumped at the knock on the other side of the door.

"Look, honey, are we gonna do this or not?"

"Yes," she whispered. She looked in the mirror at her eyes, her face, willing herself to look more grown up. She took several deep breaths, clenching and unclenching her hands, and then unbuttoned the rest of her shirt. She let the material slide down her shoulders a bit, hoping it looked sexy. "Here we go," she whispered to herself.

After another pause to allow Christine to compose herself, Barbara Walters explored with the singer how her talent and drive had finally provided a way out of the hellhole that had been her young life. How she'd bought a used guitar and taught herself to play it. How she had gotten a break at age 14 and — until someone had fed this disgusting and hurtful story to the tabloids — how she had never looked back, except to support a number of programs for homeless and disadvantaged kids in Queens. On that note, and with a comforting pat of the hand from Barbara to her interviewee, the special ended, and the credits rolled.

"Fuck!" Robert Knowles shouted.

Chapter 11

Jack Renovich looked at his client, and, truthfully, boss, with his mouth open, his jaw slack and eyes glazed.

"What?" He wasn't sure if he'd heard correctly.

Dark eyes turned to glare at the slight man. "What part of 'Call Foster' don't you understand?" Robert Knowles turned to face the attorney in the expensive suit, a suit that had he basically paid for in the exorbitant fees Renovich charged. "If he could help bring that whore, Fleiss, down, then he can do the same to Christine Gray."

"Bob, this is crazy." Jack tried to reason with the man, but he was having a hard time keeping his eyes off Bob's new nose. It changed his entire face. He'd heard a watered-down version of the story behind it, but wasn't up on the actual circumstances. Clearing his throat, he emptied his mind, a little technique he'd picked up at Harvard Law. "You're risking career suicide..."

"Goddamn it, Jack, just fucking do it!" Knowles thundered, slamming a well-manicured hand down on the expansive mahogany desk, the thud echoing round the spacious office. The two men locked gazes, engaging in a cock fight of wills.

Finally with a heavy sigh, Renovich nodded. "Alright, Bob. However," he raised his eyes and a finger of warning, "any backlash is yours and yours alone."

"Nonsense." Knowles gave his trademark dimpled smile, filled with charm and confidence. "That's what I pay you for, Jack. You can handle the heat." He grabbed his Ray Bans off the desk, sliding them into his jacket pocket. "We still have an eight o'clock tee time?"

"Uh, yeah, we sure do." Jack tried not to look at the man standing in front of his desk as if he were the bastard he really was. It was getting harder and harder to continue working for Bob Knowles. The money he'd made off the man almost wasn't enough anymore. Almost.

Long, knowing fingers worked their way across the smooth, white keys, bringing an emotional jolt to the music as its creator swayed with it, her eyes closed to block out her world, which felt as though it were crumbling around her feet.

The swell of the piece made her chest swell in sympathy, her throat tighten, and her breathing hitch, then everything combined in a peaceful, satisfying climax.

Music such as this had always seemed to Christine to be what making love must be like. The caress of fingers brought the body of the music alive, starting slow and sweet, working toward a more chaotic level of excitement that only the release of the intensity could bring about, sending a lava flow of emotion and sensation through everyone lucky enough to be an auditory participant.

The last few notes died away, and her blue eyes slowly opened, staring off into the spacious room, absently noting the high ceiling and the special soundproofing built into the walls by a previous owner.

Christine sighed, her hands falling limply to her lap. Her body felt like Jell-O — not just because of the emotional release she'd received from the music, but also because of the interview. Three days had passed, and while the initial response of the media and her fans had been fairly good thus far, only time would tell what the eventual fallout would be. She wasn't sure she cared anymore.

She stood and made her way over to the bar that ran along the back wall of the music room, to where glass shelves of various bottles of liquor once had stood. This was her third visit in as many hours. Her tongue snaked out, the craving for a tequila sunrise making her mouth water. It would take nothing to send Bradley, her gardener, out on a little shopping trip.

For the third time, she shook off the want, grabbing a bottle of raspberry Fruit2O instead.

Walking over to the french doors that opened on to the grounds of her estate, she twisted off the bottle's white cap, taking a long swig of the flavored water, smiling at the taste and at the pride she felt for once again denying the demons she knew would snap at her heels for life. There was a time, not too long ago, when she would have been proud for having a tequila sunrise instead of straight tequila or vodka.

Baby steps.

She did, however, allow herself one small indulgence. Pulling a pack of Camels from the breast pocket of her button-up shirt, she shook out a long, white cigarette, tucking the gold tip between her lips. She could feel the slight weight of the silver Zippo in her hip pocket, but she left the lighter where it was tucked. Tonguing the cigarette, making it dance, she looked out over the beautifully kept grounds. Bradley did a wonderful job, but someday she'd like to do that work herself, making her very own green thumb master-piece.

She thought back to the tearful phone conversation she'd had with Adam earlier that day. He and Alice had watched the Barbara Walters' special, of course, and it had been hard for him. Though Christine had left out any partic-ulars involving him, trying to shield him from media scrutiny, *he* knew, and *he* remembered, and it broke his heart all over again. To her great relief, he hadn't been angry with her but had instead stood behind her one hundred per-cent, as she had hoped he would.

She was working on a way to repay him for everything he'd done for her, all the sacrifices he'd made. There was nothing she could do to make him well, but she could make sure that his work continued and that he knew Alice would never have to worry about anything.

"Oh, Adam," she whispered, removing the Camel from her mouth. She held it between her fingers, turning it this way and that, thinking about the fact that Adam, once a heavy smoker, had given up the habit in order to maxi-mize what precious little life he had left.

She snapped the cigarette in two and dropped the pieces onto a nearby table. Sighing, she sat and swung her booted feet up to the table's top, snaking her hands behind her head and looking out into the dying sunlight of the day. She'd stick around California for a few more days, make sure she wasn't needed anywhere or didn't have to fix any more messes, then maybe she'd take a trip toward the south and east.

She was scheduled to be back in the studio in three weeks to record the last album she was contracted for. For the first time in her career, she was dreading it. She felt stifled, having been restricted to a certain formulaic sound for nearly two decades. She had the distinct feeling that her fans weren't being given enough credit, that they would probably happily follow her along in a creative journey. And if not — well, Christine was at a point in her life where that didn't matter much any more.

As she sipped her water, she realized that she'd stuffed herself into a bottle and now the genie wanted out. She had stopped performing or creating for herself, but instead was writing and playing for the fans, what *they* would want or buy — or at least what Bob had said they would. Bob Knowles was no longer in her professional picture, however. So what was stopping her from following her own instincts?

She sighed in confusion. Something had to be done before her muse left her for good. The adoration and money were fantastic, for sure, but now all that was for Christine Gray the image, not Christine the person.

"A change is definitely in order," she muttered, bottle to her lips.

The night seemed to drag on. They had an emergency involving an eight-year-old boy, pulled out of his father's truck by firemen with the help of the Jaws of Life, but only after he had sat in that tin can of a truck, staring at his father's lifeless eyes for more than an hour. To say the boy was going to need some counseling after he healed up was a serious understatement.

Willow sighed, tugging off her mint green scrub top, wadding it up, and tossing it into the small wicker basket she'd brought with her to gather up her dirty work clothes. She'd be doing laundry for days with the amount she had, but that was alright. It wasn't like she had anything else of importance to do on the eve of her three days off.

Rachel and Connor had hit the slopes to mountain bike down in Colorado for a few days, so it was up to her to occupy her own time. Willow smiled when she thought of last Wednesday. She'd dropped by Rachel's place, intending to only stay for a short time, but then just stayed on. Finally on Thursday afternoon, Rachel had turned to her.

"Okay, hon, you know I love you, but are you going to leave at some point or should Connor and I go have sex at your place?"

How pathetic. As an only child, she'd had to figure out how to keep herself entertained, and she'd done a fine job of it, loving the solitude. Heck, even when she'd been in college and she and Kevin had first gotten together, they used to fight because she still wanted that alone time and he wanted to spend all his time with her.

Willow sighed. When had all that changed? Maybe it was because when she was with Kevin, she knew she had the option of having company if she'd wanted it and had taken that option for granted. Now it was just her and her alone. You could only talk to an unborn baby for so long before the one-sided conversation got boring. Gathering up her belongings and the wicker basket, she headed out to her truck.

The ranch was quiet, apart from Star whinnying and snorting quietly as the sun just began to peek over the horizon. Willow pulled the truck up to the garage, parking in front of the closed door.

She had been contemplating trying for a different shift at work, the day shift maybe, or at least the mid. She didn't think it would be too wonderful coming home at six in the morning in the cold of winter when she was six or seven months pregnant.

The house seemed even more quiet and dark than usual. Willow flicked on lights as she went, even ones that weren't necessary for her to move around. She switched on the television in the kitchen, then the one upstairs in her bedroom as she gathered the laundry from her home laundry basket. She had no idea what was on TV, just that she needed to feel as though there were someone else in the house with her, that someone else knew she was there, knew she was alive, and cared enough to spend time with her.

She tried to clear her head and her emotions. One of the things she was looking forward to losing after having the baby was the feeling that she was PMSing all the time, her emotions and feelings flying every which way. She angrily shoved everything into the wicker basket, then whimpered in frustration when she realized that she had just buried the badge, keys, and sunglasses she had set atop her scrubs when she was coming into the house. Digging them out, she headed downstairs to the washer and dryer. She automatically grabbed the cordless phone, clipping it to her pocket on the way down to the unfinished basement, the main function of which was to house the washer and dryer and innumerable bugs.

The bare bulb came to life with a tug on its chain, illuminating the cool gray of the basement. Willow hated going down there. The starkness of the area reminded her of a terrifying moment in her childhood.

Her parents, while they were still together, had moved into a ranch-style house in Denver, one that had an unfinished basement. The walls had already been framed, turning the dungeon into a maze of two-by-fours. A four-year-old Willow had been instructed to go downstairs and grab a piece of luggage that was kept in the angular alcove beneath the bare, wooden stairs.

The smell of raw wood and moldy cement met her nose, making her wrinkle it, screwing her whole face up. Her saddle shoes made little hollow sounds on each step, her weight being too slight to really make them creak. She followed the wall, which was mostly smooth until the rough seams scraped her palm. The first one made her jump in surprise. Gathering her courage with a deep breath, she continued down into the abyss.

She had asked her mom for a light or something so she could see going down, since the light switch at the top of the stairs didn't work. Her mom said she was fine, to get on down there and not be such a baby. Willow swallowed her tears, her eyes stinging with fear, but she did as her mother asked, wanting to be a big girl.

She finally reached the bottom of the stairs and started to feel around for the wall switch her mom had told her was there. She couldn't find it, and her panic began to grow as the purest darkness she had ever known engulfed her, swallowing her whole.

Her breathing echoed in her own ears, rising with each blind second, the skin of her palms and fingers being rasped by more rough seams and then a splinter from part of the framing. She cried out, then whimpered; she was sure she heard a monster in the pitch black, come to gobble her up.

"Mommy!" she cried, frantic to find that switch. She could hear her mother's music upstairs. She knew she couldn't hear her cries, that she would never know that the monster had killed her. "Mommy!" she cried again, louder, crying out as she backed into something. Whirling, hands in front of her, she latched onto not a slimy, scaly hand, but framing. Relieved for a heartbeat, she heard something deeper in the room, making her whirl again, desperately trying to see through the sea of ink.

Her heart was about to beat out of her chest. Shivers passed through her in waves, her eyes as wide and dilated as possible, almost painfully so.

She began to plow ahead, fear driving her forward, trying to find the light, the precious little light that trickled down from the open basement door. She heard constant whimpers and cries, and it was not until later that she realized they were her own. At that point, they were propelling her to get out, convincing her that the monster was catching up to her, getting closer.

She tripped over something, hitting her chin, and clicked her teeth painfully together. She felt something wet and gooey on her face, but she didn't care. Realizing that she'd found the stairs again, she scrambled up them into the world of light.

"Mommy!" she cried, spotting her in the dining room, wiping smudges from the glass front of the china cabinet.

"What?" her mother said, turning. Willow flung herself into her arms, her heart only now beginning to calm. It was also then that she finally felt the pain in her jaw. "What happened? What did you do? Where is the bag I asked you to get?"

Willow brought a finger up, tracing the tiny, almost invisible scar at the very roundest part of her chin.

The whole thing was laughable now, twenty-four years later, but it had been terrifying at the time and had scarred more than her chin.

Shaking the memory away, not wanting the oppressive grayness to close in on her now, she set the basket on the folding table next to the dryer and began to sort the clothing in the basket, creating little piles on the cement floor.

Kevin had promised two years ago to finish the basement for her, but had never gotten around to it. Willow's grandmother had used it as a root cellar. She smiled at the shelves that lined every wall in the large basement, some still holding large, sealed Mason jars of God only knew what.

Her smile grew even wider, remembering the summers spent here at the ranch, helping her grandmother can all the peaches and plums, then tomatoes and pickles. For the first couple of years after Willow and Kevin had taken over the ranch, she had canned, too, but after awhile, she hadn't had the time anymore. Maybe it was time to pull out the massive stainless steel pressure cooker again.

Willow poured in a measured cup of Tide, slammed the lid shut, turned the dial to the correct setting, and pulled it out, the machine roaring to life as it filled with warm water.

Glad to be finished, Willow hurried up the stairs, the hair standing on the back of her neck as it always did and a shiver of relief passing through her as she stepped into the kitchen. She always felt foolish for getting so spooked, but it happened every time she went to the basement nonetheless.

Outside the sun was beginning to break the horizon. What now? Deciding breakfast might be a good place to start, she headed to the fridge, checking to see what she had, and out of that list, what actually sounded good. Eggs, waffles, leftover spaghetti. With a sigh, the nurse grabbed a peach and slammed the door home with her hip. Rinsing the fruit off in the sink, she watched as, outside the kitchen window, a new day spread its light over the miles and miles of space surrounding her.

It was such a lonely time to own a ranch.

Christine paced, her hands tucked into the pockets of her cords, waiting, rehearsing what she was going to say. She looked at the same blocks of sound-proofing, at the same kit of drums, red, banded in chrome.

The minutes congealed into a half an hour. Finally the inner doors of the studio opened, preceded by the laughing and hooting of her bandmates. "Hey, girl," Joey gushed, grabbing the singer up in a bear hug that left her ribs aching. After similar greetings by all the boys, Christine decided it was time to get down to business.

"Okay, guys, settle down. I need to talk to you." She leaned against the wall, watching as her beloved friends got settled.

"What's up?" Eli asked, lightly tapping his sticks on a denim-clad thigh.

"Well," Christine sighed. "I've got good news, and I've got bad news. This time around I'll give you the good news first." She hiked a thumb toward the huge window behind and to the right of her. "You'll notice behind me, gentlemen, that there is someone missing from the engineers' booth."

On the other side of the glass sat two men. They were talking, judging from the movement of their mouths. There was no sound, though. All microphones had been turned off — at Christine's request. She needed some privacy for this. "Only Ronny and Evan," she said, smirking as realization dawned on her boys.

"Fucking A, so it is true? You really got rid of that mother fucker. It's been all over the news, but we weren't sure 'cause you hadn't said anything to us," Davies asked.

"Sorry to keep you guys in the dark, but Robert Knowles has been fired, yes."

"Woohoo!" Joey yelled, pumping his fist in the air. "About time."

"Yes, yes, I know. Bottom line, it means that we can chart our own path for this album. I've spent the last three weeks composing songs to substitute for some of the pap he insisted we play." There were more hoots of joy.

"Okay, now for the bad news." Christine made eye contact with each of the men, making sure she had their full and undivided attention. "As you guys know, this album is the last one Twilight needs to complete to fulfill our contract." She paused again, once again scanning her bandmates. "After we finish recording this and do all the touring shit, I'm retiring."

Christine wasn't surprised at the uproar that ensued after her revelation. She stayed quiet, letting the worst of the storm pass. She eyed Joey as he rose from his perch on a stool and walked over to her. He said nothing at first, leaning his shoulder against the wall, looking down at the floor, chewing his bottom lip in thought. Finally he cleared his throat and looked at her profile.

"Why are you doing this, Chris?" His voice was soft, though the hurt was evident. She met his gaze of concern and confusion.

"You know, Joey, there comes a point when your heart just isn't in it anymore. Yeah, we've had a great go, broken attendance records, been on Leno, Letterman, all of that. Won the awards and accolades, but when it all boils down to it, I ended up making music for them, not for me." She waved her hand to indicate unseen fans. "My heart isn't in this anymore, Joe."

He stared at her, reading her, trying to understand. Finally he nodded with a sigh. "I think I've seen this coming." He began to pick at a thumbnail. "Shit, the events of Oklahoma City almost a year ago should have been the first clue, huh?" he said, smiling weakly.

"Yeah. I think so." She returned his smile, but it faded quickly. "I'm sorry, Jo-Jo. I'd never do anything to hurt you all, but ultimately my apathy would have hurt the band, anyway. I don't want us to turn into a joke or a bunch of has-beens."

"Yeah. I know. It's just hard to hear. An era coming to an end." He shook his head. "Just real hard to swallow."

"I know, Joey. I know." She took the guitarist in a quick, but tight hug.

Christine felt a combination of profound sadness and elation when the recording sessions were over. Everything she had worked so hard for, dedicated eighteen of her thirty-two years to, was gone, finished, with a snap of her decisive fingers. She had no doubt it was the right decision, had no regrets, but she was astonished that the time had gone by so quickly. It seemed just yesterday she'd been a kid on the streets in Queens, praying to find a fiver on the street so she could get some breakfast. Now her only limits were her own boredom and discontent.

Christine knew if the press got wind of her retirement, they'd tie it to the recent scandal started by Knowles. She'd look like she was running. She really didn't care. She was tired of living her life in the public eye, doing what worked best for *them,* and not what she herself needed to do.

Still, there was no point in giving the tabloids more ammunition, even if a "farewell tour" would probably boost box office sales. She'd managed to convince her bandmates of that after some heated discussion — and a promise to forego her share of the album proceeds if they kept their mouths shut. It had pained her that she'd had to resort to that, but she could see their point: her retirement pretty much meant their retirement, at least as a group. They deserved some compensation, she guessed, and hell, she didn't give a crap about the money anymore. She just wanted to be done with it.

"Fuck 'em," she muttered.

Willow bared her teeth as she tugged on the ends of the shirt, trying to bring them together so that she could button the darn thing.

"You fit two weeks ago," she hissed, finally giving up when she heard the seams straining. "Dang it!" She looked down at herself, the burgundy shirt hanging open, exposing very exaggerated breasts contained in a white satin bra. The beginnings of her bump made her pants slightly uncomfortable. "Have to go to the dang fat store." She pouted, not liking this at all. Stalking over to the closet, she shed the shirt and grabbed a loose-fitting long-sleeve cotton t-shirt.

Walking back to the mirror, she turned this way and that, studying her profile as well as her front and rear views. She was shocked.

"My God," she murmured. Her misery was cut short by the ringing of the phone.

"Hey, you coming or not?" Rachel said on the other end, irritation marking her voice.

"Yes, I'm sorry. I can't find a darn thing to wear!"

"What? In the two closets you have, filled to the brim? You're only coming over here, Wills. It's not like you need to dress for a friggin' cocktail party."

"No, it's not that." Willow plopped down on the end of the bed. "I look like a damn Barbie doll. Everything is extremely out of proportion."

"Oh, you mean 'cause your breasts are huge now?" Rachel chuckled at the moan that got. "Come on, Willow. It's all part of it. You look beautiful."

"I look like a hooker!" Willow threw herself backward onto the bed, one hand covering her face, the other one holding the cordless to her ear. She grimaced at the laugh on the other end of the line.

"Hey, most women would kill for breasts like yours, even before you were preggers. Enjoy it while it lasts. From what I hear, it's all downhill from here." She winced at the loud cry that filled her head. Oops. Getting serious, Rachel softened her voice. "Willow, I'm sorry, honey. I was only teasing. You are a beautiful woman, and having that baby inside you has made you even more so."

"Really?" Willow said hopefully, uncovering her eyes.

"Yes, really. I wouldn't lie to you about this. You have nothing to worry about. You're one of those damn women I hate, the ones who look good no matter what they're wearing or what they're going through. You have to believe that."

"I don't, Rachel. I feel like the ugliest, dumpiest woman to walk the earth." Willow sat up, running a hand across her ever-seeping eyes.

"I know, and I could kill Kevin for doing this to you. But you know I think you're gorgeous and always have. Heck, even Connor has mentioned it."

"You're so full of crap."

"No, really. Honestly. I had to smack him for staring at your breasts."

"Well, that's not surprising since they're the size of basketballs." Willow stood, tucking the phone into her neck as she fastened her watch and slid on the couple of rings she wore.

"Oh, stop. They are not. Come on. Connor is going to be putting steaks on in a few minutes."

"Okay. Why are you guys barbequing in the middle of October?"

"Because my honey is a dork."

"Ah, okay. See you soon." Willow ended the call. She lightly misted on her perfume before grabbing her keys and heavy jacket. It had been cold and windy all day, and she knew by the time she got home that night it would be even worse.

The drive was slow; the wind blew Willow's two-ton all over the road. She grasped the wheel with both hands, fingers tightly wrapped around the leather-covered steering wheel. Easing up to the main road that would get her to Rachel's, she braked, looking over her shoulder, creeping forward as a big rig rushed by, whipping her truck into a rocking frenzy. In its wake, she merged.

As another car roared by, a chirping filled the cab of her truck. Glancing at her cell phone, which was resting in a drink holder in the console, she tried to see who the caller was. Probably Rachel, yet again, wondering where the heck she was. She almost veered into a car in the other lane when she spotted the California area code and grabbed for the phone.

"Sorry!" she hollered out as the car blared its horn. Straightening her wheel, she used her chin to open the flip phone. "Hi!" Willow grinned from ear to ear at the chuckle that received.

"Hi, yourself. How are you?"

"I'm doing fine. But you know, there's this friend I have, she's kind of been AWOL. Think you can help me find her?"

"I know, I know. I'm sorry. I've only had time to write those few emails. Forgive me?"

"Hmm, well..." Willow pretended to think, drawing out the angst, "...okay." She grinned at her own silliness. "How has the touring circuit been? Had any more bras thrown at you?"

"Oh God!" Willow just knew those amazing eyes were rolling. "Crazy people, I tell you."

"Oh yes, I'm sure it's horrible to be so loved and adored. Please, please, what can I do to help?"

Christine laughed at the sarcasm in her friend's voice. "Yes, I know. It's a hard life, but alas, I've decided to end it."

"What?" Willow pulled to the side of the road to avoid crashing.

"The tour life, Willow. Just the tour life." Christine's voice was soft, understanding. Willow put a trembling hand to her head, sighing deeply. "I didn't mean to scare you." She knew how easy it was to upset the pregnant woman, and she often felt she was walking on eggshells. She tried to be as understanding as possible.

"God, I don't know, guess I just had a flashback or something." Taking several shaky breaths, Willow laughed at herself. "That was pretty silly. I'm sorry."

"Don't be. That was a scary night. I should have worded it differently."

"Wait a second." Willow's mind finally began to catch up to the news. "You're not going to tour anymore?"

"Yeah. We've made our final album as Twilight, Willow." Christine looked out the window of her hotel room, seeing the city lights of Miami below her. "I've had it. After this tour, I'm retiring."

"Oh, Christine." Willow reached up, brushing her fingers across the smooth surface of the tiny phone, wishing she were caressing her friend's hand instead. "I don't doubt your wisdom in this; only you know what's best. But I do hope it works out how you want it to."

"Thank you, Willow." Christine walked over to the bed, lay down, and curled up on her side around Willow's voice. "Can you get a few days off the weekend of November tenth through the twelfth?"

"I imagine so. Why?"

"Well," Christine groaned as she turned onto her back, stretching out her long legs, her free hand playing with the material of her thin, ribbed sweater, "we're going to be in your neck of the woods — Houston, Austin, and finally San Antonio. I'd like you to come."

"See you in concert?" Willow maneuvered the truck back onto the road, seeing a mental picture of Rachel glaring at her and tapping her toe.

"Well, kind of. I was thinking actually that you could tour around Texas with us. We'll be in the Lone Star State for a bit..." her voice trailed off, hoping Willow would say yes.

"Yes."

"Fantastic!"

Grinning from ear to ear, Christine gave Willow a sketchy itinerary, promising more solid details as they became available.

"I'm so excited!" Willow gushed, also grinning from ear to ear. Sometimes she worried her grin would one day become irreversible.

"So how are you doing? How's little you?" Christine asked, trying to imagine if her friend would be showing yet or not.

"Oh God." Willow blew out in exasperation. "My boobs are the size of a damn house."

"Wow. That must make life interesting," Christine teased.

"You have *no* idea. It sucks."

"Well, I can't wait to see you." Christine paused, trying to decide if she should say the next part. "I miss you, Willow."

Willow noted the way the singer's voice had softened, and it put a warm place in her heart and a broad smile on her face. "I miss you, too, Christine. And I can't wait to see you, either."

Christine blew out a relieved breath. "Well, I should go. Gotta get up early tomorrow for sound checks and a tour of Miami. We've not hit this venue before. We usually skitter around Orlando, Daytona, that kind of thing."

"Well, happy dreams to you, and I hope you enjoy your tour. Pick me up something cool, will you? I've never been to Florida at all."

"You got it. Goodnight, Willow. Keep you and little you safe, okay?"

"Will do. Goodnight." With a mixture of contentment, happiness, and sadness at saying goodbye, Willow replaced the phone in the drink holder and hummed the rest of the way to Rachel's house.

Christine paced, her hands clasped behind her back. She felt ridiculous, but she was anxious. She only wished she'd had time to fly out and pick Willow up herself. Rush, rush, rush. That was life on a tour. Very little time to herself, save for the middle of the night, when thoughts rattled around her brain: Had she sounded good? Had she looked good? Was she entertaining enough?

It never ended until the day she stepped through her own door in Beverly Hills.

They had played at Reliant Stadium the night before, and it had been amazing. Christine had watched countless football games played there. Never did she think she'd be playing there, too.

She was keyed up from the show and from lack of sleep and food. But mostly she was keyed up with anticipation.

"Yo, I've been calling you for five goddamn minutes!" Stone yelled out.

"What? I'm sorry. What, Taylor?" Snapped out of her reverie, Christine turned toward her red-faced road manager.

"I asked if you wanted to put that last song in tonight or not."

"Oh, sorry. Uh, yeah. I do." She was momentarily angry with herself for her indecisiveness. It had been less than a year since she'd taken the plunge and started playing what she wanted to. It was hard to break the habit of expecting Bob to come screaming from the wings at her when she decided things for herself. She craved and enjoyed the creative freedom, but had as yet to get used to it.

"Good. It was a huge hit in Houston." The short, balding man turned, cupping the side of his mouth with his hand. "Cue up the lights for that number, Roger!" he yelled up at the lighting engineer, who was in the very back of the large auditorium. A light flickered briefly to let Stone know his order had been heard and followed.

Christine soon grew bored with the light show that she'd been part of every night for the past month. She resumed her pacing.

"I'm wondering how many more steps it'll take before you fall right off and onto your head."

Christine stopped pacing abruptly, her booted toe skidding over the time-slicked wood of the apron of the stage. She brought a hand up to try and see into the darkened house, but the stage lights were blinding.

Out of the darkness came a small, smiling blonde woman, an overnight bag held in one hand and a Mason jar in the other.

Wide-eyed like a little kid, Christine hopped down, running past the first rows of folding, padded chairs until she reached her friend, grabbing her in a crushing embrace. Willow almost dropped her grandmother's prized peach jam in the exuberant show of affection, but she didn't mind.

"You look wonderful!" Christine gushed, finally holding Willow at arms' length. "How was your flight? Did little you do okay?" Her gaze flickered to the slightest paunch in Willow's shirt, then she noticed Willow looking amused. "What?"

"Nothing." Willow felt warmed, not only by the stage lights, but also by the genuine concern from the remarkable woman, who was still looking at her with suspicious eyes. "The flight was fine. I mean, how bad can it be on a private jet?" she said accusingly. Christine looked down sheepishly.

"Yeah, well, if you think I'm going to let you fly here coach, you're out of your tree."

"I'm already out of my tree. But, nonetheless, little me, as you insist on calling her, is doing just fine. And here," she raised the hand that held the Mason jar, "my grandmother says hello."

Christine took the jam, chuckling at the thoughtfulness of a woman she'd never met. "This better be as good as you say," she warned, with a waggling finger.

"Oh, you have no idea what you're in for. I'm going to make you French toast, Grandma's recipe, and then you," said with a poke to Christine's chest, "are going to absolutely smother it with this, and then you'll know what Heaven on earth is."

"What?" Christine looked at her like she'd lost her mind. "What the hell do peach jam and French toast have in common? A match made in Heaven, this is not."

"Don't knock it until you've tried it, woman."

Christine knew better than to argue with Willow, so she nodded like a good little girl. She hugged her friend with one arm and led her toward the stage.

"So this is where you'll perform tonight?" Willow asked, taking in the giant screen being installed behind where the drum kit platform had been constructed. Two men shouted instructions back and forth across its impressive breadth, tweaking here and there, making sure the screen was secure and operable.

"Sure is." Christine also took in her surroundings, seeing it anew through Willow's eyes. It really was quite impressive. She turned to see her friend grinning up at her. "What?"

"I'm so excited to see the show," Willow said, her chest about to burst with pride.

"Glad to hear it. So, ready to get settled? I'm going to be stuck here for awhile, so how about you head to the hotel, get comfortable, and I'll see you later?"

"Sounds great."

Chuck Maggio glanced into his rearview mirror for the third time in as many traffic lights. His passenger, an entire car-length back, was a hottie to be sure. She had the best set of tits he'd seen in a while and curves to match. He could imagine gathering a handful of that blonde hair as he took her from behind.

He focused on the road, not wanting to wreck the limo again. Frank would kick his ass. Besides, he was working for Christine Gray this weekend and wanted a good tip. Who was this little piece of hair pie to the singer, anyway? Chuck had heard all the rumors, hell, who hadn't? Maybe this chick was her lover or something.

He glanced at his passenger again. Shaking his head, he focused on the street again. What a waste.

"Miss." Chuck extended his hand to help Willow out of the back of the limo. He couldn't help letting his eyes wander behind the dark lenses of his sunglasses.

"Thank you," Willow said, getting out of the long car.

"May I take that for you, ma'am?" He indicated the bag she held.

"No, I'm fine, thanks." Willow was amazed at how kind and polite the driver was.

"Enjoy your night, ma'am." Tipping his hat, Chuck turned to head back to the driver's side of the car, watching Willow's ass in the side mirror as she headed toward the plush Hilton hotel.

Willow hoisted her bag onto her shoulder, smiling at the doorman who opened the heavy glass door for her.

"Excuse me."

Chuck hesitated, hand on the car door handle. He looked over his shoulder to see a man hurrying over to him.

"What do you want, buddy? I got a schedule to keep." Chuck leaned against the car. The man, breathless from the exertion, finally reached the chauffeur.

"Y'all the driver for Mizz Christine Gray?" the man asked, his southern Texas accent grating on Maggio's nerves.

"Yeah. What of it?"

"Well, my name is David Sumter. Ya see, sir, my employah wants a story on Mizz Gray in this fine city of ours."

"And who would your employer be, Mr. Sumter?" Chuck asked, already having an inkling of what he was dealing with.

"Well, let us say my employah is willing to pay for good information for our readers."

"Oh yeah?" Chuck was listening now.

"Oh, yeah."

Chuck pushed off the side of the car and opened the back door of the car.

"Get in. We'll talk."
"Yes, sir!"

Willow was stunned as she stood in the large room, which the bellboy informed her was the living area of the hotel suite she would be sharing with Christine.

The space was almost as large as the entire first floor of Willow's house back in Oklahoma. The decorating was beautiful, though, not gaudy or ostentatious in spite of the sheer size of the place.

There were three bathrooms on the main floor, as well as a kitchen, complete with stocked pantry, and a large, beautifully appointed dining room. Upstairs were two bedrooms, both the size of large apartments. It was easy to figure out which one was to be Willow's.

She sat on the bed, a huge bouquet of flowers in her lap. Plucking the card from the clear plastic pitchfork, she tugged it out of its tiny envelope.

Willow—
Welcome, and I hope you like the rooms. Please feel free to use
the entire suite, and don't hesitate to ask for anything.
I'm glad you came.
Me

Touched by the gesture, Willow stood, setting the fragrant gift onto a nearby table, where she'd be able to see and smell it everyday.

Quickly getting settled, she explored the beautiful hotel.

The night was filled with the intense beat and rhythm of Christine Gray and Twilight, in what was their third to last performance of their final concert tour, although the audience didn't know it.

Willow sat in the wings; Christine had given her the option of sitting in the front row with the raving fans or having her very own personal seat, basically on stage.

Her blonde hair flew into her eyes over and over again as she jammed with the thousands of other people filling the auditorium. She had heard the music hundreds of times before, and still the words and tunes filled her with a joy that no other artist had ever been able to inspire in her.

She opened her eyes and peeked out into the darkened house. Hundreds of lighters began to flick on as the stage lights went down, and Christine was reduced to a silhouette backed by purple light.

Twilight.

The music started, slow and sure, getting the listeners ready, making them crave the unbelievable voice of their hero or object of lust. Christine fed that lust, her voice, smooth and sure as silk, filling the auditorium.

Willow watched, leaning forward in the one of the most comfortable armchairs she'd ever sat in, taken directly from Christine's dressing room.

Finally giving in, she sat back and closed her eyes, her head leaning against the cushioned back, allowing that voice to fill her, to reach in and touch her deepest, most vulnerable places. It wasn't long before she felt a tickling wetness at the corner of her eyes. All she needed to do was blink or open her green eyes and her tears would escape.

Amazing. How could one person, one human being, mortal as anyone else, reach inside someone else and take control of something so personal as emotion and feeling? Even without seeing it with her own eyes, Willow knew that everyone in that auditorium was experiencing the same thing, that the music was traveling into the same place, causing the same effect. Yes, everyone handled things differently and more than likely not everyone was sitting there crying as Willow was, but they felt it.

She opened her eyes, her lashes flicking those errant tears down her cheeks, but she didn't care. She looked at the cause of that precious emotion, Christine at center stage, sitting on a stool, one booted foot on the floor, the heel of the other hooked onto the bottom rung of the stool. She held the microphone, free of its stand, in her left hand; her right rested casually on her leather-clad thigh.

At that moment, those beautiful blue eyes were closed, and the fingers of her right hand were tapping softly to the beat.

Willow studied her profile, the perfect lines, the way the purple light caught the flyaway hairs caused by the static from the microphone and electronic equipment, giving Christine a halo.

She thought about the response from the audience and from herself. The knowledge that Christine had touched every person in that place. That they'd go home talking about the amazing concert they'd just attended or that they'd make their friends go out and buy a Christine Gray CD just because of the way they had gushed. The way that everyone had been changed in this moment, thousands of fans united for a single moment, everyone in the same place, thinking and feeling the same things.

Willow had never felt prouder to know anyone in her entire life. Chills spread through her body, bringing a smile to her lips and peace to her heart. She was grateful to have such an amazing person in her life, and she would do everything in her power to make sure things stayed that way.

"Hey, you. Wakey, wakey."

Willow blinked, trying to figure out where she was and who was rubbing her arm. Looking up, she was almost blinded by the stage lights, all turned up now and very bright.

Blinking rapidly again, she looked away. "Welcome back, Sleeping Beauty." Christine smiled, kneeling down on her haunches next to the chair Willow was sprawled out in. The singer knew she would die if she knew just how unladylike she had looked in that moment.

"God, I had no idea I'd fallen asleep," Willow mumbled, pulling herself up into a sitting position. "That was an amazing concert, Christine."

"Hmm, I must say I'm not entirely convinced you saw it," Christine teased, as her friend tried to stand, only to fall back into the cloud-like cushion of her chair. "Come on. We're done taking everything down, and the boys are loading up. I think there's a bed with your name on it back at the hotel."

"Mm, that sounds wonderful."

The two women headed down the main aisle of the theater, through the double doors, and out into the late Texas night. There were cars everywhere and hundreds of people still trying to get out, though the majority of the crowd was gone and it was now safe for Christine and her band to leave.

The limo was waiting. Willow recognized the man from earlier waiting for them with the door open. The darkness of the car was inviting. The driver smiled and nodded at them, and they both smiled in return.

"So, you really liked it?" Christine asked, once they were settled.

Willow glanced at her, surprised, to see a twinge of uncertainty in her face. "Yes. It was the best concert I've ever been to. Really. Truly amazing. And I loved that new stuff you threw in at the end."

"Thank you." Christine smiled with pride as she looked out her window, the city lights passing rapidly.

She looked at the cars around them, next to them, passing them. As a kid she used to see limos pass through the city all the time and always wondered who sat behind those dark windows, which celebrity or person of power. Now, from the looks she got, she knew others were thinking the same thing, and it made her smile.

"I've been working on that new stuff for a while, wanting to bring it into the act, but Bob would never let me," she explained.

"Well, I think he was a fool. It's wonderful."

"Thank you, Willow," Christine said, her voice soft as she looked at her friend. Willow looked so tired. She reached over, gently brushing a strand of blonde hair away from Willow's cheek, tucking it behind her ear. "Your hair has really grown," she said absently, quite unaware of the pair of eyes watching the gesture in the rearview mirror.

"Yeah," Willow said, nodding, then laying her head back against the leather headrest. "I can't keep it under control," she smiled drowsily. "My doctor warned me of that, which sucks, you see, as my hair grows ridiculously fast anyway. All those out of control hormones, plus the vitamins I've been scarfing down."

"No doubt. Thanks for coming."

"You're most welcome. Thanks for inviting me."

"*You're* most welcome."

Willow started again, turning over in bed with a heavy sigh, then turning back to her other side. She attempted to roll on her back, when her eyes flew open. What the hell was that?

Sitting up, she listened. Not hearing anything, she was about lie back down when a wisp of noise came to her, like smoke through a crack. She got out of bed and shrugged into a sweatshirt and mesh shorts, then padded out to the sitting room of her suite within a suite, pressing her ear to the door. Sure enough — music.

Lights blazed downstairs, and there were sounds of conversation and laughter and the smell of smoke — which wasn't all tobacco.

Willow saw Christine's band members in various states of undress; there were girls everywhere, and on almost every horizontal surface beer cans and bottles were scattered, some of them empty, some full, most in the process of being drunk.

At the center of activity stood a glass table on which sat a mirror, maybe two feet by one foot, remnants of lines of white powder on its reflective surface.

Willow felt sick, her stomach revolting at the scene before her, especially when she saw Joey in the corner. He was pinching his nose and sniffing repeatedly, a gorgeous, half-naked blonde on her knees before him, happily licking away at the head of his penis.

"Where's Christine?" Willow asked of no one in particular. Someone answered that the singer had been last seen on the balcony. She headed in that direction, feeling numb and as if she were walking through gauze in a dream world.

The doors were partially open, and she stumbled her way over to them, feeling the cool, early morning breeze coming in.

Christine stood at the railing, a brown glass bottle held by the neck between her thumb and forefinger. She was leaning on her elbows, overlooking downtown.

Willow felt her nausea return as she saw that bottle, together with a small line of empty bottles just like it on the railing next to Christine, like soldiers marching off to war.

"I can't believe you're doing this," she whispered, shock steeling her voice.

Christine slowly turned her head, looking at her guest over her shoulder. "Doing what? Why are you up?" Turning around, Christine leaned her back where her elbows had just been, bottle dangling next to her thigh.

"Because of that!" Willow hissed, pointing back toward the party. "I can't believe you." She shook her head, accusation written all over her features.

"What have I done?" Christine asked, taking a tentative step toward her friend. "I'm sorry the boys woke..."

"Yeah, I bet you're sorry they woke me." Willow's anger was building with every word. She snatched the bottle out of Christine's hand. "How can you go back to this stuff?" She walked over to the large potted tree standing next to the balcony doors and poured the contents, fizzing, into the rich, dark soil. Then she tossed the bottle off the balcony.

Christine watched with a mixture of annoyance and amusement. "You just poured out my A&W." She hurried over to the railing, watching as the glass bottle exploded in the courtyard dozens of stories below.

"What?" Puzzled, Willow walked over to the railing and grabbed one of the empty bottles.

"My goddamn root beer," Christine said, her annoyance starting to gain an edge over her amusement. Turning the bottle in her fingers, Willow saw that it was, in fact, A&W root beer. She looked up into Christine's narrowed eyes.

"I..." Willow cut herself off, feeling ridiculous, but then she remembered what she'd seen in the suite. She couldn't shake the image of the cocaine spread out on that mirror on the table. Bringing the bottle to her nose, she took a deep whiff.

"I see," Christine said, her voice dry as she turned toward the balcony doors.

"What am I supposed to think?" Willow asked, relieved to smell only the sweetness of the soda. "What the hell do you think you're doing, Christine?" she hissed, "letting those guys do that...well, that *shit* in your hotel room!"

Christine whirled on her friend, her eyes blazing. "No, I don't do that shit anymore, Willow. No, I don't like it, and no, they're not children. I can't control what they do, but at least they're not out there being stupid in a dangerous environment where they could get hurt, arrested, or recognized." Her voice was a low, dangerous purr. "I didn't bring you along as a chaperone, Willow. You'd be wise to remember that." And with that, Christine was gone.

Willow stood alone on the balcony, frozen to the spot. The obvious anger and hurt in Christine's voice burned into her soul.

Sighing heavily, she made her way back into the suite. Christine was nowhere to be seen, and Willow decided it was best not to look for her. She'd done enough for one night. She went back up to her room.

Christine nodded at the doorman, shivering as she came out of the November chill. It may have been Texas, but winter hit there, too.

Pushing the button that would take her back to her floor, she waited for the elevator doors to slide open, staring at her reflection in the highly polished stainless steel of the outer doors. She had escaped her suite in just what she'd had on — jeans and a long-sleeve t-shirt. Her hair was less than perfect, the tennis shoe on her right foot untied.

As she knelt down to tie it, she thought of what had driven her from her own rooms to begin with.

When the knock had come on her suite door, Christine had known who it was and what they wanted. The boys didn't have a suite, each only having a room, which although luxurious, was not big enough to party in. They'd brought their booze, drugs, and women to her door, wanting her to join in the fun, but she'd refused. Joey, figuring this would be the case, raised a six-pack of her favorite and asked to come in.

Christine had hidden out on the balcony, knowing full well she wouldn't be able to sleep upstairs with what was going on downstairs. Popping the top of her first A&W, she'd taken a satisfying swig and then had taken a seat on the wrought iron balcony furniture, putting her feet up on the railing and taking in the sights of the city around her.

She'd let her mind wander, not really thinking about anything in particular — replaying the performance, things she would have done differently, things that had gone better than she'd hoped or thought. She'd also thought of her friend and how cute she'd looked, asleep in that big chair with her mouth hanging slightly open.

Never had she thought Willow would awaken to the debauchery that was their hotel suite. Never did she think Willow would know. She didn't want her to see it or know that the boys even did that sort of thing. But alas, it hadn't worked out that way.

Christine knew that Willow was right in her accusations and anger. If their suite were to be raided, they'd all go to jail, and it would be a disaster. Willow's opinion meant the world to Christine, especially after the way they'd met and the condition she had seen Christine in on the worse night of her life. To hear what Willow thought, to see the disappointment in her eyes and hear it in her voice, had been more than Christine could bear. The kicker, though, had been when Willow hadn't believed the innocence of Christine's beverage of choice and had sniffed it for traces of alcohol.

The elevator dinged, then the doors slid open, revealing the elevator operator. He smiled at her as she entered, then pushed the right buttons for her floor.

Christine had worked so hard to beat her addictions and stay clean in a world where temptation was everywhere, offered by everyone. In the entertainment business, you were more likely to be offered a nose full of blow than a glass of water. She had declined, she had managed to stay strong and not give in to a habit she'd had most of her life.

She sighed heavily, glad when they reached her floor and she could escape the presence of the unobtrusive elevator operator. Sometimes she hated that in the nicer hotels. Her short few moments in an elevator were often her only time alone.

Making her way down the hall, she pulled out her keycard, glad to hear silence on the other side of the door to her suite.

All the lights were still on, but the music was off, and all traces of the drugs were gone. By the looks of everything else, though, there would be another interesting story about Christine Gray's partying habits.

Making her way up the stairs, Christine rubbed her eyes, the rising sun outside making her realize just how long she'd been up and just how exhausted she really was.

Heading down the hall that would take her to her own rooms, she stopped, seeing the closed door of Willow's room. She reached for the doorknob.

The room was dark and quiet, light just barely making its way in through the sheer curtains.

Willow was lying on her side with her back to the room, curled up around the second pillow on the king-sized bed. Her eyes were closed, and her breathing was even and calm. Christine stared down at her, a soft smile forming on her lips without her even realizing it.

After debating for a couple of minutes, Christine finally sat on the edge of the bed, trying to take up as little space as possible. She watched her friend for a few more minutes, then reached out, brushing the ever-errant strands of hair from Willow's beautiful face.

"Willow?" she whispered, petting the thick hair. "Wake up."

Willow's eyes fluttered open, then closed again with a soft sigh as she reveled in the touch. She turned onto her back, looking at her friend perched on the edge of her bed.

"You okay?" she murmured.

Christine nodded. "Yeah. Well, no."

"What's wrong?" Willow, about to sit up, felt a gentle hand on her shoulder, keeping her down.

"Shh, everything's okay. I just wanted to tell you I'm sorry."

"Sorry? For what?"

"For going off on you like that. For making you witness all that. I really didn't want you to see it," Christine said, feeling like an ass even as she spoke.

"No." Willow shook her head, turning onto her other side to face the singer. She caught the hand that had been in her hair, hugging it to her, tucking it under her chin. "I'm not your mother, you're right. I had no right to say any of those things or treat you that way. You and the guys..."

"It wasn't me. Hell, I just wanted to go to bed." Christine smiled ruefully, looking down at her other hand that rested on her leg. "I shouldn't have allowed that to go on here. I put us both at risk. I'm sorry."

"It's okay," Willow whispered, tugging on the arm that was attached to the hand she cradled. Christine looked at her, brows drawn. "Lay down with me. You look so tired."

Not needing another invitation, Christine laid herself down with her back to Willow. She smiled as she felt a warm body curl up against hers and the covers being brought up over both their bodies. She closed her eyes.

"Christine?"

"Hmm?"

"I'm proud of you."

"For what?"

"For drinking root beer."

With a smile on her lips, Christine fell asleep.

Chapter 12

Bob Knowles absently raised the tumbler to his lips, only glancing into the glass when the ice clinked against the crystal, but nothing else happened. Remembering he'd drunk the last of the scotch ten minutes before, he set the heavy glass on the top of the desk in his office in San Francisco.

He looked out over the bay at the fog moving in, muffling the traffic and the horn of a lonely fishing vessel.

Tearing his attention away from the window, he looked down at the newspaper sitting next to the abandoned glass on his desk, the headline bold and mocking: MUSIC HEAVY HITTER STRIKES OUT

The phone call he'd had with Jack earlier in the day weighed heavily on his shoulders, too, causing them to slump, wrapped in the crisp, starched button-up from Prada, designed with his form and tastes in mind. A shirt even named after him.

So they were all bugging out. Didn't trust him. They'd heard what he'd done to Christine Gray and were worried he'd do the same to them. Worried he'd open their closets and let their skeletons dance around like a live chicken in a frying pan.

Knowles walked around his desk, taking the tumbler with him. He filled it to the rim, nearly emptying the bottle, which he set back on the marble bartop. Downing half the glass in one swig, he nearly choked as another thing Jack had told him came back to him. According to Foster, those pricks at Mercy Hospital wouldn't say a fucking word about the condition Christine had been in when she was hospitalized last February or about the drugs that had been in her system at the time. They were protecting that little bleached blonde nurse, who, no doubt, was fucking the star singer.

"Bitches," he breathed into the glass, taking the rest of the liquid fire down, the ice sliding against his perfect, capped teeth. "Fuck you all." He slammed the tumbler down on the bar with finality.

A green eye cracked open, as nearby whispering tugged her from the warm web of peaceful sleep. Willow couldn't make out what was being whispered or who was whispering, but the words "cute" and "hot" did lodge in her brain.

As the haze of sleep wore off a bit more, she realized that she was still cuddled up with Christine, her head resting against a steadily rising and falling chest, her arm tucked up close to her face, fingers spread out over a somewhat pronounced ribcage.

"What the hell are you guys doing?" Christine muttered, her voice rumbling through Willow's entire body, making both green eyes flutter open. There, at the foot of the bed, stood Eli, Davies, and Joey. Eli held a harmonica in his hand.

"Eli," Joey said, causing the drummer to blow a note on the instrument, thus launching the boys into an *a cappella* version of Brenda Lee's "I'm Sorry."

"Get out of here!" Christine laughed, throwing one of the shoes she'd taken off sometime during the night at the retreating musicians. "I swear," she muttered, resettling herself and wrapping her arm around Willow.

"Goofy bunch," Willow murmured, basking in the warmth and comfort of her human pillow.

"I'll say."

"That was really sweet of them, though." Willow raised her head to see a small smile play across Christine's lips, her eyes closed.

Christine nodded. "Yeah."

Willow lowered her head again, snuggling in. Heaven. Pure heaven. She forgot all the months she'd been missing human contact. She felt so safe, so cared for. Did she dare say, happy?

"So what's the plan today?" she asked, her eyes opening to get a very up close view of Christine's t-shirt. She looked at the cotton fibers at an almost microscopic level, seeing the tiny fibers crisscrossing and the occasional piece of lint, which she picked off.

"Mm," Christine groaned. "The fun starts. We pack up and head out." She took a deep breath, letting it out slowly and steadily, raising Willow's head along with it. "How are you doing this morning?" she asked, bringing her hand up to play with a few flyaway strands of hair.

"I'm good." Willow raised her head, holding it up on her hand and smiling down at her friend. "You make a great pillow, you know."

Christine snorted. "I've been called a lot of things in my time, but pillow isn't one of them."

"Well, now you have, so deal. And I'm fine. You?"

The smiles were gone as the seriousness of the night before came flooding back. Christine looked deeply into Willow's eyes, trying to read her, to see if she truly was fine. Seeing nothing but truth, her smile returned. "I'm okay."

"Come on. Feed me." Willow climbed off Christine, then the bed, running her hand through a very interesting do. "One thing I've always hated about short hair," she grumbled.

"I think it's adorable." Christine walked over to her and grabbed some of the strands that were obviously out of place.

"Stop it!" Willow smacked at Christine's hands and backed away with a glare. "Pain in the butt. Go to your room." She pointed out the door.

"Oh, the little mother in you emerges."

"Out!" Willow's lips twitched. She tried to keep the glare in place, but she was losing the battle. Finally a smile burst into full bloom. "Unless you want to see a fat woman shower, go away."

"In that case," Christine headed back toward her friend before giggling as she started to run, a growling Willow chasing her.

"Some people's kids," Willow muttered as she turned back toward her bedroom.

"You're not fat."

Willow swung around to see Christine leaning against the doorframe. With a yelp, the singer disappeared.

Samantha Cox pushed her dark-framed glasses a bit further onto her nose, sighing as she re-read her copy for the next day's paper. The story was shit, and she knew it. The editor was a chauvinistic ass, and every woman in the building knew that. She should have taken that job as a stringer for the Times.

Finally giving up, deciding the story on the runaway pet potbelly pig was as good as it got, she clicked the mouse, sending the story to the editor's queue and pushing away from her desk.

"Stacy, you want anything from Starbucks?" she asked as she slid into her light suit jacket.

"Yeah. Get me a mocha breve with extra chocolate and whipped cream. Grande!" the photographer called out to the retreating back of the young reporter.

"How the hell does she get any coffee with all that chocolate?" Samantha muttered as she made her way through the maze of desks that was the small Bay Area paper she worked for. Climbing into her Honda Accord, Samantha gave it some gas and sputtered out of the parking lot.

One of the only good things about the job was the view. The Golden Gate Bridge was just off to the left, and it was amazing. Samantha had only moved to the area a few months ago, having grown up further south in San Diego. She certainly loved the area, even if it did cost her an arm and a leg to live there. She lived in a tiny, crackerjack apartment and paid triple what she paid back home.

Singing to herself, as the radio was being stubborn again, she headed down the street, the big Starbucks sign in view. Glancing again toward the bridge, she noticed a bunch of emergency vehicles, lights flashing.

Slowing to turn into the coffee house parking lot, she quickly changed her mind, cutting off a Ford Taurus as she gunned the engine and headed toward the bridge. Her reporter instincts were telling her to investigate. She saw a bundle being pulled out of the water, two hundred and twenty feet below the landmark, and gave her little car even more gas.

"Shit, a jumper," she murmured, driving like a lunatic to get there as quickly as possible. "Yes!"

"You are so full of shit!" Christine accused, throwing the guitar pick she had been using at Eli. The group laughed, including Eli who chased the pick down. "Give me my damn pick back."

"No way. You threw it at me, so *obviously* you don't want it anymore." He grinned, waggling the little piece of plastic tauntingly at her.

"Jerk."

Joey jumped up as his cell phone rang; he'd left it at the back of the bus. As he hurried down the main aisle to answer it, he snagged the pick out of Eli's hand.

"Hey!" the drummer yelped in surprise. Joey grinned, tossing the pick to Christine before disappearing into one of the back rooms.

"Brown nose!" Eli yelled after Joey's retreating back.

Willow sat curled up on one of the numerous comfy sofas that lined the outer walls of the bus. The play between Christine and her bandmates kept a constant smile on her lips. She was amused and touched by how close they were. A part of her felt sad for the boys, losing their lead singer, and she wondered what they would all end up doing. Including Christine. Willow wondered if someday the singer would regret her decision.

"Uh, Chris," Joey said, his face pale as he took his cell phone away from his ear. "You need to hear this." He handed her the small, silver flip phone. Her eyes remained on his face, worry furrowing her forehead.

"Hello?"

"Christine, this is Trista," the woman on the other end of the line said, her voice low and slightly thick.

"Hey, Trista. What's up?"

All conversation had stopped. The boys and Willow watched and listened intently, trying to figure out what was going on; Joey wasn't saying a word. Instead, he took Christine's guitar from her and quietly began to strum a mindless tune on it.

"I tried to call your cell, but it wasn't on."

"Oh, shit, sorry. I was charging it and forgot to turn it back on."

"It's okay. Listen, boss, this morning Bob Knowles' body was dragged out of San Francisco Bay."

"What?" Christine stood, shock sending a wave of energy through her body.

"He jumped," Trista clarified.

"Ah, Jesus." Christine sank to the couch next to Willow, her free hand going to her forehead. "Is he..." she couldn't bring herself to say it.

"Very much so." Trista sighed. "I can't believe he did that."

"Yeah." Christine felt an uncomfortable numbness begin to envelop her. "Thanks for letting me know." With that, she slapped the phone shut, tossing it back to Joey, and headed toward her sleeping quarters at the back of the bus.

Willow looked around, confused.

"What happened?" Davies asked the question on everyone's mind.

"Knowles committed suicide off the Golden Gate Bridge this morning," Joey said quietly, watching his fingers needlessly adjust the pegs of the perfectly tuned guitar.

"Serves the fucker right," Eli said, grinning at everyone, only to be met with disapproving glares from his bandmates.

"Dude, that's not cool," Joey said, voice low.

"What? The guy was an asshole from the word go. Good riddance." Refusing to feel bad or take back his comment, Eli stood, walking over to the bar. "Hey, where's the rum?" He looked over his shoulder for answers, but none were forthcoming. "You guys take off with the booze?" he tried again.

"Chris threw it all out," Davies finally answered.

"Fuck. Goddamn puritanical..."

"I'm going to make sure she's okay," Willow said softly, cutting off Eli's muttered remarks. She couldn't stand hearing him talk badly about the singer, who was only trying to live better. She didn't feel it was her place to lecture Christine's friend, however, so she said nothing.

Fighting her nausea as the bus jerked her from side to side, Willow made her way down the aisle to Christine's closed bedroom door. She walked up to the dark paneling, fingers running lightly over the smooth wood. For a moment she thought about walking away, leaving the singer alone, but she needed to be there for her. If Christine sent her away, she sent her away. But she had to try.

Knocking lightly, she called out Christine's name. Not hearing anything, she decided to take a chance. Turning the knob, she was glad to find it unlocked and pushed the door open.

"Christine," she whispered, pushing her way into the small space. Christine sat on the edge of her bed with her legs curled under her and her hands resting in her lap. She didn't answer. Walking over to her, Willow stood before her friend, seeing the faraway look in her blue eyes. "Christine," she whispered again, tentatively touching her shoulder and then yelping in surprise when she was suddenly gathered in needing arms and pulled to the edge of the bed.

Regaining her balance, Willow wrapped her arms around Christine, cradling her head against her chest, running her fingers through her long, dark hair. She felt Christine's hands clasp at her lower back.

No words were spoken. None were needed. Willow could feel the sorrow radiating off Christine in waves. She hoped the singer would want to talk about what had happened, knowing she needed to, but she wasn't about to push the issue.

As they stood there, Willow couldn't keep the image out of her mind of a cold, February night and the Dittman Bridge. She remembered how blue Christine's face had been, how lifeless her body. She held her friend a little closer, her protective instincts kicking in like mad. But today this wasn't about Willow, and it wasn't about what Christine had attempted to do. It was about Christine's pain over what her long-time manager had done. He may have been an ass, but they still had a history, for better or for worse.

Willow rested her cheek atop the wonderful smelling dark hair, tiny wisps tickling her skin.

They stayed like for so long that Willow's legs were beginning to ache. Finally Christine spoke.

"Willow?" she said quietly, her head pressed against her friend's chest, listening to the steady heartbeat.

"Yeah?" Willow said softly, finger-combing Christine's hair.

"Do you think that my firing Bob had anything to do with his...with what he did?" She pulled away from Willow, looking up at her with the saddest expression on her face. Willow's heart broke at the sight. She smiled sweetly, shaking her head.

"No, honey, I don't. I think he did it to himself," Willow said, her voice soft, with no malice in her words. She contemplated whether she should tell her friend what she'd heard at the hospital and decided it might be best. Christine deserved to know the whole truth. "Honey, he was trying to ruin you."

"Perhaps, but I got him back..."

"No," Willow said. "He was trying to find someone at Mercy to speak against you, Christine." She gently caressed her shoulder, trying to take the sting out of the words.

"What? What do you mean? When?"

"A couple of weeks ago. He wanted to expose what happened last winter."

"God." Christine looked down at her lap, stunned. "Why haven't I heard anything about this?"

"Because no one would talk." Christine looked up again, meeting Willow's gaze. Willow smiled. "We weren't going to turn on our hometown hero."

Christine chuckled, then hugged Willow to her again, quick and tight.

"I need to make some calls," she said, pulling away and standing up.

"Okay. If you need anything, don't hesitate, alright?" Willow said, halfway to the door. Christine nodded, then smiled. Willow heard the cell phone come to life as she clicked the door gently closed.

They stood at the foot of the stairs that led onto the small jet. Christine pushed her hair back, the wind immediately blowing it back into her face.

"Thank you so much for coming," she said, lightly rubbing Willow's jacket-covered arm.

"Thank you so much for inviting me. It was," Willow chewed on her lower lip for a moment, looking out over the tarmac as she tried to think of the words, "the trip of a lifetime," she finally said.

"Well, I don't know about that."

"No, really." She hugged Christine close. "It was truly amazing. Thank you." Pulling away, she smiled.

"I'm going to miss you," Christine said, holding her hand.

"I'll miss you, too. When will I see you again?"

"I'll come visit for a bit. How would you like that?" Christine glanced at the plane as the engine began to spin to life. "You better get going."

"Yeah." Willow stepped up onto the first stair, bringing her to Christine's eye level. "And I'd love that. You better keep your promise," she poked her.

"I promise. I need to take care of some stuff back home, then I'll be out."

"Okay." About to head up to the next stair, Willow quickly threw herself into Christine's arms, hugging her tight. Christine squeezed her eyes shut as she allowed herself to be enveloped in Willow's warmth.

"If you need anything," Willow whispered into her ear, "I've got two good shoulders and a great set of ears, okay?" Looking deeply into her friend's eyes to make sure Christine was listening, she smiled, and with a quick peck on Christine's cheek, she was up the stairs and in the plane.

Christine stepped back from the jet, which was getting ready to taxi out to the runway. She saw her friend getting settled through the small, oval windows. She waved with a smile when Willow spotted her. She didn't feel the smile, however. It was purely for Willow's benefit. She missed her friend on a level she couldn't believe. Just being around her made Christine feel better, feel grounded.

Even Adam didn't have that effect on her.

Shaking those lonely thoughts away, she waved one last time, then turned and walked back to the limo to go and catch her own flight.

Willow watched as her friend walked away, ducking into the back of the limo. The plane began to pull away, and she twisted her head to watch as far as she could until the car was out of sight.

Turning back around in her seat, she sighed and settled in for the short flight back home.

Rachel pushed the grocery cart down the cereal aisle, glancing up from her magazine from time to time to make sure she wasn't running into anything or anyone. Looking back down at the article she was reading, she turned the page and the cart came to a screeching halt against a display of chocolate Lucky Charms. Not even realizing what she'd done, she stared at the magazine in her hands, her mouth catching flies.

Eventually coming back to life, she grappled with her purse until she found her cell phone.

"Of course you can come over. You know better than that." Willow rolled her eyes and wiped her hands off on her jeans as she finished brushing Star down. Shutting the phone, she stuffed it back into her pocket, sweet talked her horse for a few more minutes, then headed back inside. It wasn't long before she heard Rachel's SUV pull into the yard.

The front door opened, and Rachel whooshed in with the wind and snow.

"Close the door! It's freezing out there," she said as she brought a cup of coffee to a shivering Rachel.

"Thank you," Rachel mumbled, her lips half frozen. She took a long, hot drink and began to thaw. Remembering why she was there, she quickly put the cup down on the kitchen counter and tugged her huge purse from her shoulder.

"You are not going to believe this," she said, digging until she found what she was looking for. Tugging the magazine free, she frantically flipped through it until she found the page, then shoved it in front of Willow's face.

"What is this?" Willow took the magazine, frowning as she stared down at her own face. "Oh my God," she breathed when she read the headlines. "They think," she looked up at her friend, who looked just as concerned, "they think Christine and I are...lovers?"

"Why would they say such a thing?" Rachel whispered, picking up her coffee again between her still chilled hands.

"I don't know," Willow said absently, reading the story. The pictures were taken in Houston, and possibly, Willow thought, in Dallas. "I can't believe this." She was horrified to see a picture of Christine and her on the streets of Houston together, Christine's arms around her, their foreheads together. It was the main picture, certainly the largest. The caption underneath read: *Christine Gray and this unidentified woman strolled the streets of Houston together, laughing and cuddling.*

Willow looked up at Rachel, eyes wide and distraught. "How could they do this? It's not true." She smacked the smooth pages of the magazine. "It's not true."

Christine closed the door after sending Millie home for a bit. There was no reason for the housekeeper to stay in an empty house. She'd only be coming twice a week to make sure things were okay and to watch the dates on food.

Jogging up the stairs, she broke into a dead run when she heard the phone ringing. Grabbing the first phone she came to, she answered, out of breath.

"Are you a lesbian?" asked a solemn voice on the other end.

"What?" About to slam the phone down, she stopped.

"Are you? I need to know, Christine."

"Willow?" She lowered herself to a chair, a chill gripping her heart. "Why, where did this come from?"

"Please answer the question. I mean, I'm not stupid, I've heard all the rumors, but I..."

Christine twirled her fingers in the phone cord, hearing the pain in Willow's thick voice. What was going on? "Willow, I don't...well, I don't really stick myself in any categories." She blew out a breath of exasperation, feeling sweat begin to pool between her breasts. "Willow, where is this coming from?" she asked again, her voice soft.

"*Screen Magazine*," Willow said, her voice low and with a quality Christine couldn't quite make out.

"Yeah?" Christine said, not following, filled with dread just the same.

"According to *Screen Magazine*, I — the unidentified woman in the picture — and you are lovers. The latest in a long line..."

"That isn't true, Willow," Christine said, anger beginning to replace the dread.

"So what is true? Why would they say something like this?" Willow leaned against the counter.

"I'm so sorry, Willow. God, I'm sorry. I never wanted you to be dragged into my mess. They do this because I don't give them anything to play with. You understand?" Christine gripped the phone tighter, praying that she could say the right things to fix this.

"No. What do you mean?"

"I mean that I don't give them details of my life. They don't see me at award shows with God only knows who, and I don't flaunt it." She stood, pacing nervously. "I can't apologize enough, Willow. I never meant for anything like this to happen."

"I know," Willow whispered. "I know."

"Do you still want me to come up next week?" Christine held her breath, praying this hadn't ruined one of the most important friendships of her life. Willow stared down at the magazine, looking at her smiling friend's face.

"Yes," she said finally, tossing the magazine into the trash under the sink. Christine smiled and let out a silent breath. "Good."

Willow smiled. "I'll see you soon."

"See you soon."

Walking through the halls of Mercy was an interesting experience to say the least. No one actually said anything, but the looks Willow got said enough. She didn't try and defend herself, figuring that if she were to bring it up, it would make things worse. If someone actually had the guts to ask her, then she would set them straight. No pun intended. Right now she was just trying to concentrate on getting things ready for Christine's visit.

She was thrilled that the singer planned to stay for a couple of weeks. She thought about looking into hiring security for her ranch, but then decided that was ridiculous. If that sort of thing were needed, Christine would say so and probably knew what to do about it, too.

Part of Willow hated Bob Knowles for what he'd done to Christine, in so many ways. He'd brought the hounds of the media down on her, prompting them to sift through every aspect of the reclusive singer's life, even going so far as to make something out of nothing. She shivered, thinking again about that article. She also hated him for being such a coward and dumping that sort of self-blame and guilt on someone as sensitive as Christine.

"Selfish prick," she muttered, heading toward the locker room to get changed and go home.

Everything in the house was perfect, everywhere clean, linens changed, perfect. Willow went to every room, touching up where there was no need to touch up.

Why was she so nervous? After being on tour with Christine for those few days, seeing how people literally threw themselves at her feet, seeing all the things Christine could afford and bought, and all that the singer was used to, Willow felt that her modest house was a shack comparatively. Shoot, the suite they'd stayed in in Texas was bigger than the entire house, just about!

Deep down, Willow didn't think Christine would think that way, but the worry still lingered. The sound of the front door opening broke her from her reverie.

Panicking slightly, she edged into the upstairs hall, making her way toward the staircase, and peeking around the wall. Partly relieved and partly annoyed, she marched down the stairs.

"What the hell are you doing here? And what do you think you're doing just letting yourself in? Give me your key, Kevin."

"Sure," he said, his eyes blazing, "as soon as you explain this shit." He tossed the magazine at her. It fell to the floor before her feet. "What is this shit, Willow? Is that why you left me? For that fucking *dyke*?" There was venom in his voice.

Willow glanced down at the magazine, knowing full well which one it was though it had landed with an advertisement for Grey Goose showing.

"How dare you accuse me of that, Kevin? You know damn well why this marriage failed." Willow was stunned at just how calm she felt. She was proud of herself for not blowing up, which was what usually happened. She had been trying to work on her temper, knowing it wasn't good for her or the baby.

Kevin stared at her for a moment, at a loss what to say. He knew she was right, but there was no way he was going to give it to her. "Is it true?" He nodded toward the rag on the floor, his arms crossed defensively.

"What business is it...?"

"Is it true?" His face was red now, all pretense of a civil discussion gone. A vein throbbed in the center of his forehead, pounding in time with his heart.

"No," Willow said simply.

"Then explain those pictures, Willow. The two of you cuddling, heads together." Kevin was trembling now.

"I'll answer your questions, Kevin, though the Lord knows why, but I'm going to warn you." She pointed a finger at him. "If you blow up, if you lose your temper, you're out of here. Got it? It's not good for me or *my* baby to get upset."

"It took two to create that kid," he growled.

"Really? Well, I seem to be the only one taking responsibility for her, so she's mine. Deal. Now get the information you came here to get, Kevin, because that's all you're going to get."

He took a calming breath, then started to walk past her, toward the kitchen.

"Where do you think you're going?" she asked, stunned.

"To get coffee. It's six-thirty in the damn morning, and I'm tired," he explained, stopping to look at where her hand rested, none-to-gently, on his arm.

"No. This isn't a social call, Kevin, and I don't recall inviting you into my house. Right back to where you were, mister." She snapped her fingers, pointing back to the spot in front of the door.

He looked at her for a moment, incredulous. "You're kidding, right?"

"Do I look like I'm kidding?" she asked.

Blowing out a breath, he followed her orders. "Feel like a goddamn child," he muttered.

"That's what happens when you act like one. See? Practicing being a mother already." Willow smiled sweetly at him. He glared at her.

"Are you fucking that bitch or what?" he asked, getting back to the main purpose for his visit. The other part — winning her back — might or might not come later, considering how his wife was acting. Hell, she wasn't even his *ex* yet. The divorce wasn't going to be final until December. He held his cards close to his chest, though he knew he'd better start behaving if he even planned to *get* to the next part and not thrown out on his ear. Again.

"No, we're just friends. She invited me to go on tour with her in Texas, where those shots were taken." She indicated the magazine between them. "Christine's former manager has been trying to make trouble for her, and this got the news machine purring back to life. They must have tailed us, taking any sort of shot that looked like it could be anything. That's it, end of story, now get out."

"Hold on a minute." He held up a hand in supplication her, his eyes softening. For just a moment, only a small moment, Willow saw the man she'd fallen in love with so many years ago. She swallowed that moment down, bringing her current reality back into sharp focus. "Honey."

"My name is Willow."

"Willow," he sighed sadly, "don't do this to us." He took a step toward her. She didn't step back, and he took that as a good sign. "We really loved each other once, you and me." He smiled, the man she'd married shining through again. "I still love you. The divorce isn't final yet, hon...Willow," he swallowed. "We can turn back the clock, get back what we lost." He stood right in front of her now. She looked up at him, her own eyes softening. "What do you say?"

"Turn back the clock," she murmured, her eyes looking up into his, searching them.

"Yes. Turn back the clock." He leaned in close, inhaling the smell he knew so well — the smell of her hair, which he was glad to see she was letting grow out. She'd had long hair when they'd gotten together, and he loved running his fingers through it. "Find what we used to have," he continued.

"Tell me something, Kevin," Willow asked, her voice soft, gentle. Her heart was racing.

"Anything."

"Do you remember that night when we made love in front of the fire, down here in the living room?" Her voice got even softer.

"Yeah, I do." He could almost get hard thinking about that night. He had been the one to suggest the whole fire thing, knowing how much she got into that Harlequin, romantic nonsense.

"Do you remember how hard you came?" Her voice was softer yet; Kevin almost had to bend closer to hear her.

"Of course. You're so beautiful, Willow, so sexy, how could I not?" He brought a hand up, running the backs of his fingers down the sides of her breasts, just a ghost of a touch. "You still are. God, you're sexy."

"Well, if you want to turn back the clock," her voice gained strength and she caught his hand where it brushed against her, her fingers like cold steel, "then I suggest you go back in time and shoot your load into a condom, because that's the night you got me pregnant."

He froze, his blood like ice as he looked into her eyes, surprised to see the arctic coldness there.

She shoved his hand away from her, turning her back on him and heading up the stairs. "Take that filth with you," she said over her shoulder, glancing down at the magazine, still on the floor. "And leave your key!" she shouted, out of sight.

Kevin stood there, stunned, for a good five minutes, then finally pulled himself together. Grabbing the magazine, he looked down at it, then, quietly and sadly, he placed the key on the balustrade and left.

Christine knocked softly, waiting for the big door to be opened. Finally, after a wait of a few agonizing moments, which she knew were on purpose, the door opened, and Sandra was revealed. The women stared at each other for a moment, then Sandra turned and walked back into her studio, leaving the door open for Christine to follow.

Sandra looked as she always did; calm, cool, impeccably dressed with her hair piled on her head just so. But having known the woman for eighteen years, Christine was aware it was a facade.

Sandra walked over to her worktable, where she had a smattering of drawings, some finished, most not, and picked up her pencil. Not looking at her uninvited guest, she spoke, "What can I do for you, Christine?"

Christine looked around, enjoying the look and feel of the huge space. There were floor to ceiling windows, and the entire room was painted white, including the molding on the ceiling and floor. The floors were hardwood. The place looked more like a dance studio in New York than the workshop of a clothing designer in Beverly Hills.

"How are you doing?" Christine finally asked, settling herself on one of the few pieces of furniture. The majority of the space was taken up with material, tables for cutting, and racks upon racks of clothing in various stages of pinning or sewing. A few life-sized mannequins decorated the corners.

"I'm fine. How are you?" the designer asked, still not bothering to look up from her sketch.

Christine sighed. Sandra was being difficult. "How was it?"

This got Sandra's attention. Her sharp eyes snapped up, grabbing Christine in a brutal gaze. "You'd know if you'd bothered to go, now wouldn't you? You wouldn't have to rely on second-hand descriptions." Her voice was as cold as her eyes.

"I didn't feel it was appropriate for me to go."

"No?" Sandra threw her pencil down, coming around her table, long, flowing material fluttering around her thin body. "And why not?" She stopped in front of the singer, glaring down at her. "He was your manager for eighteen years, Christine. He made you..."

"Stop!" Christine held up a hand, her own anger beginning to build. "Stop right there, Sandra. You and I had this very conversation not six months ago." She met the woman's steely gaze, dagger for dagger. Finally Sandra's eyes dropped, and she turned to one of the many windows.

"When did he turn into such a cowardly ass?" she said absently, watching the traffic down on Ventura Boulevard.

"He always was, Sandra. He just hit an all-time low," Christine said, just as quietly, standing up.

"No pun intended, I'm sure," Sandra muttered. Christine's smile vanished quickly as she moved over to the other woman leaning against the cold, painted brick wall.

"You don't need to lay any sort of guilt trip on me, Sandra. Trust me, I'm doing enough on my own."

Sandra's eyes met hers again, studying her, almost to the point of making Christine uncomfortable.

"He loved you, you know." Christine just looked at her, revealing nothing. Sandra turned back to the window. "Don't feel guilty, Christine. You have absolutely no reason to. Robert did this to himself. He tried to ruin you out of spite, and in so doing, he ruined himself."

"What happened?" Christine asked, almost afraid to hear the answer.

"He lost every client he had. Every last one. Even the has-beens." She laughed bitterly. "They were all afraid he'd send them off to the same fate he'd created for you." She sighed heavily. "I guess he figured since he'd already committed career suicide, he might as well finish it off. Just like him." Her voice cracked slightly. "If you're going to do it, do it right and irreversibly, he used to say."

"I'm so sorry, Sandra," Christine whispered, laying a gentle hand on the normally untouchable woman's shoulder. To her surprise, the designer turned and threw herself into the singer's arms. Christine held her, rubbing her back, staring out at the street below. "I didn't go," she quietly explained, "because I knew I'd be expected to say something that I didn't mean."

Christine was shaken from her rambling thoughts by the feel of soft lips on her neck. Her heart stopped for a moment, then started back up again, double time, as those lips continued, softly, slowly, up toward her ear.

"Sandra," she half said, half moaned.

"He used to talk about you," Sandra said, bringing her tongue into play as she licked a fiery trail down Christine's neck, "when we were in bed. He used to talk about bringing you in to join us."

Christine was torn between two worlds. Torn between what she knew was so very wrong and what her body was pleading for. She didn't mean for her eyes to close or for the long sigh to escape as she felt ringed fingers brush across her breast, her long-neglected nipple instantly flaring to attention.

"You are so beautiful, Christine," Sandra whispered against her skin, kissing along the chiseled jaw line, then finding Christine's mouth. She kissed her, lightly, almost chastely, whetting their appetites. "Let me do this, Christine," Sandra begged, her hand squeezing the breast, getting a feel for the size and shape. "Let me fulfill his wish..."

Christine's eyes flew open, and she shoved away from the woman, her body screaming in protest, but her mind screaming for an entirely different reason.

"Don't," she said, stopping Sandra in her tracks. "Don't use him like that, and don't use me as a replacement for him."

Sandra swallowed, trying to push down her embarrassment and shame. "It's that little blonde from Texas, isn't it?" she finally managed. Her emotions and her body were caught in a whirlwind, and she didn't like it at all.

"Don't do that," Christine whispered, pained. "Don't bring that innocent woman into this. You know me better than that."

"You're right. I do." Sandra brought her hands up, touching her hair to make sure it still looked fabulous, then she straightened her dress unnecessarily. She looked as beautiful and statuesque as ever. "I'm sorry, Christine." She looked away. For the first time in a very long time, she did feel sorry. Christine Gray was one of the few people on the planet who had managed to win her respect and true admiration. "Perhaps you should go."

"Yes, I think I should." Christine walked over to the couch and picked up her coat. She stopped at the door as Sandra's voice called out to her.

"She really is lovely, Christine."

With that, Christine made her exit.

Chapter 13

Willow was almost giddy as she saw the Jeep Wrangler make its way across the winter wonderland that was her ranch. She ran out onto the porch, her breath instantly freezing in the cold evening, but she didn't care.

Christine waved as she pulled to a stop. She barely had the door open when an excited Willow was in her arms.

"I missed you!" Willow exclaimed, nearly squeezing the breath out of Christine, who laughed and squeezed her back.

"I missed you, too." They pulled apart, and immediately Christine's gaze scanned down to a sweater-clad tummy. She placed her hand over it, chewing on her lip as she concentrated on what she was feeling.

Willow grinned. "What are you doing, you goof?"

"Well, I figure since you're starting to show, I want to see if the little imp is doing somersaults yet."

"Ha ha, very funny. This little imp is going to freeze to death if I don't get her into the house. You're welcome to stay out here if you like..." Willow's voice trailed off as she turned toward the house.

"Hey! You going to help me carry in my stuff or what?"

Willow gave her a sly look over her shoulder. "Sorry. I'm already carrying a bundle," she said, cupping her stomach to emphasize her point, as she sashayed up the stairs and into the house.

Christine watched her, mouth hanging open incredulously. "Is she kidding?" she muttered.

"Of course I'm kidding, you nut!" Willow ran back down the steps, playfully slapping her friend's arm. Together they lugged in Christine's four bags and settled her in her room. She was left to unpack as Willow hurried to make some hot chocolate for the poor, frozen woman.

Christine looked around the small room, tastefully decorated in simple, yet very warm colors and themes. There was a four-poster bed in naked oak, with what looked to be a handmade quilt covering the queen-sized surface. Scattered around were pictures which looked to Christine to be mainly family. She examined a few of them closely, recognizing a young Willow at various ages — blowing out candles, sitting atop her horse, Star, arm in arm with a man that looked to be her husband.

Funny that she'd never really paid much attention to the pictures before. Were they there last time she'd stayed in the room?

"I see you've discovered my newest hobby," Willow said softly from the door, two steaming mugs in her hands. "It's not good for me to spend too much time alone — I start getting creative." She smiled, walking into the room and handing Christine one of the mugs. "Marshmallows, just the way you like it."

"Thanks." Christine closed her eyes in pleasure at the taste of the rich chocolate. "I miss this." She raised the mug. "No need for it in California." She walked over to one of the pictures. "This is you?"

Willow nodded. "Yep. Me and my best friend from elementary school and junior high, Scarlet."

"Do you and Scarlet still talk?" Christine asked, taking in all the details of the two young girls, who looked to be around eight or nine, dressed in white dresses with funny looking white, paper hats on their blonde heads. They both had their mouths open, and Scarlet was looking at the photographer.

"No. She moved away during our eighth grade year. We were in a play in that picture." Willow chuckled softly at the memory. "It was one of those ridiculous things where no one really has a role, per se. We were all supposed to be bakers. That's what those things are supposed to be." She tapped the glass over the funny white hats. "Bakers' hats."

"Ah. I was just going to guess that." Christine grinned.

"Do you have any pictures of you? When you were younger?" Willow sat on the edge of the bed, with her hands wrapped around her mug, warming them. Christine snorted, looking at a picture of Willow with her grandparents, during her high school graduation.

"The first picture taken of me was a mug shot when I was eleven years old," she said absently.

"Oh." Willow looked down into her chocolate, watching a marshmallow begin to melt. "I'm sorry."

"Don't be." Christine smiled, sitting next to her friend. "I've had enough pictures taken of me to last a lifetime."

"Yeah, guess you have, huh? Well," Willow said, grinning from ear to ear, "when this baby is born, she's going to have a camera in her face all the time. I'll fill tons of albums with pictures of her." She stared off into space, imagining it.

"You're pretty sure it's a girl, aren't you?" Christine glanced down at the little protrusion in Willow's tummy, tempted to reach out and touch it again, but deciding against it. Once a day was enough.

Willow nodded. "Yeah. It's funny. It's like I just know I'll have a daughter."

"And if it happens to be a boy?"

"Then I'll love him just as much. I'll just have to find a new name for him." They both laughed. "And don't ask," Willow wagged a warning finger at her friend, "I don't want to jinx it by saying her name out loud."

"Fair enough. I won't ask."

"Come on," Willow gently slapped Christine's knee, "let me show you the other stuff I've done to the house."

"Mm, that's good." Christine sighed, bringing the mug back down to rest in her lap.

"Rub it in."

"Hey, I told you to make the decaf," she said, glancing across the sofa to Willow, who was dutifully sipping her mug of decaf hot tea.

"Kevin was here." She looked at Christine. "About a week ago."

"What did he want?"

Willow chuckled. "To see if I was a lesbian."

"Ah, the 'L' word. Not just a show," Christine muttered. "I guess he saw that wonderful work of fiction?"

Willow nodded.

"He also tried to get me to not divorce him." Her voice was bitter, making Christine sad.

"What did you say?" she asked quietly.

"In not so many words, I told him Hell would freeze over first. He made his bed; let him lie in it." Unconsciously she brought her hand down to rest on her stomach, her protective instincts on high alert.

"Are you okay with his visit?" Christine set her mug down, turning a bit so she could face her friend.

Willow didn't say anything for a moment, as she studied the dancing flames in the hearth. Finally she looked at Christine. "Yes and no. It hurt, but I guess in some weird way it was good to see he's okay. You know? God, does that make any sense?" She ran a hand through her hair, turning back to the fire.

"Willow, you loved him, and you guys were together for a long time. It would be crazy for anyone to expect you to just forget about all that. Loving someone becomes almost like a habit."

"It can be hard to break," Willow agreed with a nod.

"No doubt."

"Have you ever been in love?" she asked after a slight pause. Christine shook her head; no thought required. "Never?"

"Never." Christine sighed, thinking that perhaps this might be the perfect segue into the conversation she knew they needed to have. She'd been there for three days, and it hadn't come up. It was time that it did. "Willow, I really want to clear the air about something." Willow said nothing, waiting for her to continue. "That article in the magazine."

Willow nodded, sipping a bit nervously from her cup. "There's really nothing to clear, Christine. It's not like you did anything wrong."

"No, I didn't. But that still affected you, your life, friends, family."

Willow chuckled quietly, staring down into her cup. "I got a few questioning stares, to say the least."

"I bet." Christine sighed, locking her courage into place. "You asked me a question, and I didn't really answer you. It's been bothering me." Their gazes met for a brief moment, a thread of understanding briefly shared.

Setting her mug onto the coffee table, Willow turned into the arm of the sofa, curling her legs under her. She looked at her friend expectantly.

Christine sighed before beginning. "You know, this world loves labels. Humans feel the need to label anything and everything, I guess to be able to relate to it. I'm not sure. Our culture and language is interesting that way, I suppose," she rambled absently. "Anyway," shaking her head, she focused on the topic at hand, "since I came onto the music scene when I was fifteen, the world has wanted to put me somewhere, and I didn't really fit, you know? I wasn't exactly a pop princess, or a diva, whatever you want to say. So, when they couldn't put me in a category of music, they wanted to categorize me personally."

"What do you mean?"

"Well, I had the gay community trying to tuck me under their wing as the next Melissa Etheridge, even though we emerged around the same time." She chuckled lightly. "But you also had the straight community lumping me in with Sheryl Crow or Alannah Myles, or whoever else you can think of. Trust me, I've heard them all."

"Why do they do that?" Willow was fascinated, never having given it a second thought.

"Because everyone needs to stake their claim. Like Bob, for instance. *He* made me, *he* discovered me, never mind it was *my* talent that got us there."

"So, everyone wants a piece of you," Willow said. Christine nodded.

"Yes. I have never been photographed with a man who couldn't be identified as belonging with someone else, or gay, or whatever. Okay, so they move on to women. Same problem, but since I have such a large lesbian following, that *must* be it."

"Why didn't you set the record straight, then? If you're not gay?"

Christine's lips curled into a delicious smile. "What, and ruin the mystery? This may sound cold, Willow, but mystery sells."

"I thought sex sells?"

"Oh, it does. And what better story then a singer whose career has been built on mystery, pure sexuality, but yet who remains sexless. Stumps 'em every time, so then they can't get enough. Sadly," she sighed, picking up her mug again and sipping, "it backfired. Every strange woman I'm seen with automatically becomes my newest conquest." The bitterness was unmistakable. "Including you."

"Christine?" Willow said softly, her hand resting on her friend's ankle. "You still haven't answered the question."

Christine thought about what to say as she took another sip, then held the mug between her hands, back in her lap. She stared down at the dark liquid.

"Both lesbians and straights alike gauge your sexuality by who you're having sex with, agreed?" She glanced at her friend, who nodded.

"Yeah, for the most part, I guess."

"Sure, you have your sticklers out there who claim it's far more than that, but when it comes down to the nuts and bolts of it, it's all about whether you're enjoying a penis or a vagina."

"Okay." Willow frowned, trying to work out where this was going. Christine looked her dead in the eye.

"How can I be labeled if I'm not having sex with either?" They stared at each other for a moment, Christine's blue eyes unflinching. She saw shock and uncertainty cross Willow's face.

"Wait, what?" Willow sat forward, crossing her legs Indian style, elbows resting on her knees. "I don't understand..."

"Willow, to me sex is a dirty word. It's something I peddled on the street, something that's killing my best friend," she explained, her voice soft.

"Honey, it doesn't have to be that way," Willow said, saddened that her friend, who deserved all that was good in life and love, was denying herself something because of a past riddled with imperfections.

"It does for me. I know that what I did isn't all that sex is. Trust me, I've heard this argument before, but I've never, ever made love. It's always been something naughty, up against a wall in some dark, dirty alley, or in some smelly, pay-by-the-hour motel room."

"Okay, so let me get this." Willow readjusted her position, getting more comfortable for what she figured would be a long, in-depth conversation. "You have not had sex with anyone since your days on the streets? You've never made love to someone? Never been made love to?"

Christine shook her head, eyes lowered, feeling shame flush her features. "Since I started all this, I've had people throw themselves at me, you know? All wanting a piece of the pie, so to speak." She sighed heavily, then looked up at her friend with tortured eyes. "Not one of them wanted me for *me*." She tapped herself in the chest. "It was all about the image and what I could do for them."

"Oh, Christine," Willow whispered, taking her hand. "I'm sorry." Christine shrugged.

"You can't miss what you never had. It's just not anything I really waste my time on. Besides I've sold myself to the masses; there's nothing left to give an individual."

"Do you really feel that way?" Willow asked, her voice hoarse, almost feeling guilty for being part of those masses.

Christine nodded sadly. "I didn't used to. It's only been within the past five or so years. I'm just so tired, you know?"

"I can't stand in your shoes, but I can see the wear on you, in your eyes." She squeezed Christine's hand. "I hope this little trip here will give you a bit of peace. I mean, you'll certainly find quiet here." They both laughed. It hadn't escaped Willow's attention that Christine hadn't really answered her question, but she decided to leave it alone. For tonight.

"Well," Christine said, scooting her legs around so her socked feet hit the floor. She drained her coffee, then wiped the back of her mouth. "I'm exhausted." She leaned over and gave Willow a goodnight hug.

"Sleep well," Willow murmured into it, then smiled up at her friend as they parted, and Christine stood.

"You, too. I'll see you in the morning."

Willow watched as she grabbed her mug and Willow's near-empty cup, padded into the kitchen, then headed up the stairs, taking the steps slowly, hand on the banister, almost as if she were tugging herself up.

That night, Willow went to sleep with a smile on her face.

"Connor. Stop it." Rachel gave Christine a clenched teeth smile, then whacked her boyfriend in the leg again.

"Sorry." He lowered his eyes, looking back at his cards, though it was only moments before his eyes flicked back up to the woman sitting across the table from him.

Christine basically ignored his stares, but it wasn't easy. Especially when it was his turn to draw a card, and either Rachel or Willow had to smack him to get him back in the game.

"Uno," Christine said, wiggling the card left in her hand. The other two women growled, while Connor just grinned like a fool.

"You're an embarrassment," Rachel whispered to him. "Can't take you anywhere."

"Okay, you suck," Willow said, ignoring the other nurse. Christine stuck her tongue out at her, holding her one card close to her chest, keeping it away from curious eyes. "We've got to keep her in the game, guys," she said, looking at her hand. Grinning evilly, with her tongue between her teeth, she laid down their one chance of keeping Christine in the game.

"Hey!" Connor yelled, seeing the Draw Four card that had just been laid down for him.

"Sorry, buddy boy," Willow laughed. "That's what you get for sitting there with your tongue hanging out all night." He glared at her as he stubbornly drew his cards.

"What color, Wills? Choose wisely," Rachel warned.

"I know." She chewed on her lip, glancing over at the black, white and red card that Christine had practically made part of her shirt, as though she were trying to see through it. Christine gazed back at her, brow raised in challenge. "Green. No, red. Wait, I think blue..."

"Come on, Willow. Pick one."

"Green. Yeah. I'll go with green."

"Should have gone with yellow," Rachel hissed. "I had a Draw Two card in yellow." She tossed down a green two. All eyes turned to Christine, who looked forlorn as she took in two pairs of expectant eyes and one pair of puppy dog eyes. Finally she sighed.

"Yep, you should have gone with yellow." Christine gave each of them another look, then turned to Willow, her mouth curving up into a lopsided smirk. Without breaking her gaze, she tossed down her card.

"Willow!" Rachel exclaimed, gawking at the red two that topped the pile of cards.

"I'm out," Christine said softly. Willow glared at her. Christine threw her hands up in the air, pumping a victorious fist.

"Beginner's luck," Willow mumbled.

"I still can't believe you've never played Uno before." Rachel shook her head as she tossed her own hand to the table. "Connor, stop it."

"That was fun," Christine said, gathering up their glasses and heading toward the kitchen.

"Yeah, it really was," Willow called back from within. She was busy unloading the last few clean dishes so the dirty ones from the evening could be stowed. "I am really sorry about Connor. He's usually not that obnoxious."

Christine chuckled. "It's okay. I've met his type before."

"Well, somehow I don't think he's met *your* type before, though." Willow took the glasses from Christine, putting them on the upper rack of the washer.

"It happens." She took the dishrag from where it had been left to dry and went back out to the dining room to wipe down the table.

"Quite the card shark, aren't you?" Willow asked, leaning against the archway between the dining room and the hall. Christine grinned.

"Like you said," she quipped, "beginner's luck."

"Uh huh."

"Look, I think I'm going to head back to L.A. this weekend." Christine twisted the rag around her hand, feeling suddenly nervous. Willow fought to keep the deep disappointment from her face, though she wasn't sure how successful she was.

"Oh. Uh, okay." She turned to the china cabinet, opening one of the glass-paneled doors, rearranging a few silver pieces, just to keep herself occupied.

"Well, I've been here almost two weeks now," Christine explained softly. "I've run out of clothes. I only packed enough for the two weeks." She looked at her friend, who was staring down at the silver butter dish in her hands. Willow was softly clicking the top into the bottom, then removing it, only to do it all over again.

"Okay. I understand." Willow glanced at her friend, smiling weakly. She was stunned at how her heart dropped at the sudden news. She felt lost already, and it was only Thursday.

"I figure I could go back, get some more clothes..." Christine's voice trailed off, seeing the light return to Willow's eyes. Without a word, she marched up the stairs, bursting into the room Christine was using. She looked around and saw a black trash bag sitting in a corner, stuffed full of dirty clothes. Grabbing it, she heaved it over her shoulder and went back down the stairs, past a stunned Christine, and down the stairs that would take her into the basement.

Finally getting her bearings, Christine hurried down the stairs after her. Catching up her, she asked, "What are you doing?"

"I'm saving you a plane ticket," Willow said, tossing her friend's clothes onto the cement floor of the washroom, separating them into piles of darks, whites, reds, and delicates.

"Willow, honey, you don't have to wash my clothes." Christine tried to grab her friend's hand, but she was slapped away.

"Mine."

Christine knew better than to try and change the stubborn woman's mind, so she leaned back against the ironing board, watching her work. The washing machine whooshed to life as Willow set the dial, poured in Tide with bleach, and then added a Downy ball.

Wiping her hands together, she turned proudly to the stunned Christine, who held up her hands and said, "Okay. I'll stay."

Willow grinned, walking past her friend and taking her hand in passing. "Come on, mega star. You owe me a rematch of Uno."

The leaves were gone, and the transformation to winter was complete. The days were shorter, quieter, life and sound muffled by the blankets of snow, while light was amplified to a blinding brilliance. The notorious Oklahoma winds blew the snow in sheets, flowing across the land in layers, almost like a sand storm across the desert.

Christine turned from the window, rushing to help when she saw Willow carrying a box with a telltale garland hanging out the side.

"Willow!" she hollered, scaring her friend to death and almost making her drop the heavy box. It was saved when Christine snatched it from her arms.

"What are you doing? Are you crazy?" Willow tried to grab the box back, but Christine was already halfway down the stairs.

"Damn it, Willow. You know what your doctor said." The box was set down at the foot of the stairs. She walked back up the few stairs to the pouting Willow. "Honey, don't do anything that could hurt you or the baby," she said softly, placing a protective hand on Willow's substantial basketball.

Willow sighed, sitting on the stair she stood on. "I hate this," she mumbled, hand automatically going to support her internal bundle.

"I know. But it's temporary." Christine sat next to her. "Use me for this kind of stuff." She pointed to the box. "That's what I'm here for. Okay?" Willow sighed.

"Okay. I know you're right."

"Only two months to go. You're almost there."

"Mind if I hand the baton off to you, and you can finish the race for me?" Willow asked hopefully. Christine grinned.

"I would if I could. Now," she stood, pulling her to her feet, "tell me where you want that stuff, and then you can rifle through it while I get the rest of it."

"I guess." It was a thoughtful compromise, Willow knew, but she still hated feeling useless. Truth be told, she was hugely grateful that Christine had been there over the past month. She'd gotten bigger overnight, her belly seeming to have exploded, and she was beginning to find the simplest of things difficult and trying at best.

Within twenty minutes, all of the holiday stuff had been pulled from the attic, and both women were sorting through it, determining what was broken and what would be put where.

"A little to the left. No, more right. Up. No, down..."

"Woman, make up your mind!" Christine glared down at Willow, porcelain and lace angel in hand, as she teetered over the fake tree.

"I'm trying to get it perfect," Willow explained, tilting her head to the side to get a better mental image of what she was looking for.

"Well, while you're trying to do that, I'm going to fall on the tree and knock the entire thing down. Then it won't matter where it goes."

"Alright, fine. Put it where you had it a few moments ago."

Christine rolled her eyes, having absolutely no clue which of the dozens of positions it had been in a few moments earlier. "Could you be just a smidge more specific?"

"Right," Willow reached up, on her tippy toes, nudging Christine's hand just a centimeter to the left, "there." Smiling proudly at their creation, she took a step back, looking at it. "Come down here! You've got to see this!"

Muttering to herself as she climbed down from the stepladder, Christine stood with her friend, looking at the product of an afternoon's work. Irritation immediately forgotten, she smiled.

"Wow."

"Beautiful, isn't it?" Willow said softly.

"Oh, wait." Christine hurried over to the tree, dropping to her knees, then to her side, and doing a warped, side Army crawl around the back of the tree. With a grunt, she plugged in the lights. She smiled at the gasp she heard from her friend, then the room went dark, the tiny bulbs encircling the tree the only light.

Scooting herself out from behind the tree as quickly, but as carefully as she could, she rejoined her friend.

"You want to know something?" Christine said, her voice soft, as she pulled Willow back against her.

"Hmm?" Willow asked, folding her arms over those that encircled just above her stomach and below her breasts.

"I've never really enjoyed Christmas all that much," she said softly. "Usually the guys were off with their families and stuff, and, I don't know," she shrugged. "I always felt bad interrupting Adam and Alice."

"So what did you do?" Willow said, her voice dreamy as she studied the twinkling lights, letting them lull her almost to sleep.

"Typically just stayed home and wrote. Millie is a Jehovah's Witness, so she and her family don't celebrate it. She and I would chat, maybe bake something." She shrugged again. "That was about it."

"But *you* celebrate Christmas, right?" Willow asked, head lightly leaning back against her friend's shoulder.

"I suppose I do," Christine said quietly. "We used to when I was a kid, anyway," she smiled at the memory, "a really young kid. Before they got into anything really bad. Well, that's not true. They were bad even before I was born. I guess I should say, before they allowed it to really fuck with...wait, sorry. I'm trying to watch my language." She cleared her throat as Willow giggled. "Before they allowed it to really mess with the family. You can take the girl out of the gutter, but you can't take the gutter out of the girl."

"Sounds like the title of a country song," Willow laughed, pulling away and planting herself firmly on the couch. "Come here and keep me warm."

Not having to be asked twice, Christine sat next to her friend, wrapping her up in warm arms and tucking the throw from the back of the couch around Willow's feet, knowing how swollen and cold they got.

"Can I ask you something?" Willow asked after a while.

"Of course."

"Are you bored here?"

It took a moment for the words to sink in, then Christine frowned. "Wait, what?"

"Well, it's not Los Angeles or New York. We don't have the bright lights and big city to keep you occupied. You know?" She glanced up, noting how the brilliance of the Christmas tree lights reflected beautifully in Christine's already beautiful eyes.

She smiled down at Willow, shaking her head. "How can you possibly get bored on such a huge piece of land that requires so much work? And your horse!" She rolled her eyes. "My God, and I thought children were demanding." She winked at Willow's laugh.

"I'm being serious, you goof."

All levity gone, Christine hugged her close. "So am I," she said softly into the blonde hair. "No, I'm not bored. I love it here. It gives me such peace, it's amazing. Really an amazing place. I can understand why you came here as a kid. It must have provided some pretty cool places for an active, precocious child, which you no doubt were, to hide and play."

"Hmm." Willow smiled, feeling safe and content. "My divorce is final tomorrow," she said so softly that Christine almost didn't hear it.

"Are you okay with that?" she asked, suddenly feeling a cold hand finger-walk its way up her spine.

"Yes. Very." Willow sighed deeply. "It'll finally be over, all over, and I can move on."

"Do you think he'll try and fight you for custody?" Christine had to smile to herself, finding that her hand had absently wandered to cover Willow's extended belly. She felt so protective of what lay beneath. The warmth that met her hand filled her heart.

"I don't know."

"Guess we'll just have to cross that bridge when we get to it, huh?" Christine said softly, feeling Willow's nod. She stopped cold, realizing what she'd said. Feeling a fool, she squeezed her eyes shut but said nothing. Fixing it would only bring light to her mistake, as Willow hadn't seemed to notice. How dare she add herself to an equation that was a simple one plus one equals two — Willow and Kevin.

"Christine?"

"Yeah?"

"I have to start Lamaze soon." Willow pulled away, though it took a bit of effort, her belly not allowing her to move as smoothly as she once did. After the grunting, she turned and looked up at her friend. "Would you be my coach?"

"I'd love to." Christine's suddenly dark world was filled with light again. God, Kevin was a fool.

"What? Would you stop? You're making me self-conscious." Christine growled, flipping the turn signal to turn on to Brandy Road, which would lead to the clinic.

"I'm sorry; I just can't get over how different you look. It's mind blowing."

"Yeah, but will it be convincing?" Christine looked over at her.

"Okay, mommies and coaches, find yourselves a comfortable spot, and let's get to work," Heather Yaklich called out, clapping her hands. As her class murmured amongst themselves, she turned to the few late arrivals, getting them signed in and giving then the appropriate brochures and paperwork to take home.

Two lovely blonde women entered, the shorter one obviously the reason for them to be here, and the taller one, with large, lovely brown eyes, the woman's partner.

"Hi. Willow Bowman and Casey." Willow smiled at the instructor.

"Nice to meet you both." Heather shook both their hands and had Casey sign them in. "Okay, ladies, if you'd like to find yourselves a spot, we'll get started."

"You'll do fine," Willow whispered, sensing Christine's nervousness.

"I hope so," she whispered back.

"Now, mommies, soon you will be responsible for taking care of your little one, guiding him or her and nurturing that child to grow into the good, helpful, productive adult you are." Heather smiled at her class, looking at each couple individually. She didn't miss the green coloring to Willow Bowman's face. Must be her first.

Blinking several times, Christine examined her red-rimmed eyes in the mirror, rubbing them with her fingers. Blinking again, she grabbed the bottle of Visine, dropping about a dozen droplets in her hair before she finally got any in her eyes.

What she couldn't figure out was how people wore those evil things day in and day out. On purpose!

Snapping the contact case shut, she turned off the bathroom light, running her fingers over the blonde wig mounted on its Styrofoam head as she passed. Thank God for her connections in the show biz world. She'd been able to get her disguise FedEx'd overnight. No shrieks of surprise or delight had met them, no murmurs of recognition. She figured the disguise was a success.

Besides, who'd be expecting to see Christine Gray in Oklahoma and in a Lamaze class?

About to turn down the hall toward the stairs, she stopped and listened, her hand still on the doorframe of her room.

Identifying the sound, she rushed to Willow's bedroom.

Willow was lying on her side, curled up as small as was possible in view of the beach ball under her shirt. Her face was buried in the pillow, her hands tucked under her chin, and she was crying.

In the five weeks Christine had been there, she'd seen the crying fits often, but it was usually like a child's cry — you could always tell what it was, simple or complex, hormones or something real. This was one of those real times.

"Hey, you," Christine said, her voice as soft as her touch, as she slipped onto the bed, curling her body around Willow. She didn't respond, but cried harder.

Deciding to let her cry the brunt of it out, Christine just held her, pulled back against her body, her arm resting between Willow's breasts and the baby bump.

Willow allowed the body heat behind her to fill her with peace. The tears began to subside, small sniffles taking their place.

"Why are you crying, Willow?" Christine whispered in her ear, once she knew her friend was somewhat under control again.

"It's stupid." Willow sniffled.

"I doubt that. Try me."

"It's what that woman, Heather, said tonight. About us all having to raise these babies, taking all that responsibility on our own heads. God, Christine, how am I going to do this?" Her eyes began to leak again, and she angrily swiped at them. "I don't think I can do it on my own."

"You're not on your own, honey." Christine tried to reason with her. "You've got so many people here who love you and who want to help you. Just last week Rachel told you she was more than willing to kidnap the baby for a few days at a time to give you a break." She squeezed Willow playfully. "Her only ransom request was that you make your double chocolate fudge brownies."

Willow smiled through her tears, but it was short lived. "I guess once I decided I wanted to have kids, I had this picture in my head, a home, parents, dog, all of it. I wanted to be able to give my child everything my parents didn't, wouldn't, or couldn't give to me. I blew it." She began to cry again.

"Oh, honey. No, you didn't."

"I'm alone! A pregnant divorced woman!"

"Oh, sweetie." They rode out a fresh wave of grief and fear, Christine holding her, whispering words of encouragement and comfort into her ear, wishing so bad that she could just climb inside Willow and take her pain.

After awhile, the sobs quieted again, and Christine decided to try a new tactic.

"You know, honey, there are all sorts of families out there. Sometimes when your blood turns their back on you, you have to make a new one. You've got that. No one is going to let you do this alone, and Willow, everything is temporary in life. You remember that. It won't be like this forever, I promise you that. You're a young, gorgeous woman with so much to offer. I know for a fact that someone is going to come down and sweep you up."

Willow sniffled. "Do you really believe that?"

"With everything in me. And Willow, you're going to give this baby what your mother couldn't give you, and that is unconditional love and support. Your mother is a selfish woman who concentrated on herself and her own needs. You won't do that."

"How do you know? Maybe I'll turn out the exact same way." Willow glanced at Christine over her shoulder, eyes wide with hope. Her friend smiled at her, gently running a fingertip down Willow's cheek.

"Because it's not in you. You don't know what it means to be selfish like that. You give everything you've got to whatever you do."

They shared a moment, each searching the other for answers. Finally Willow smiled, laying her head back on the pillow and scooting her body further back into Christine's.

"You're not alone," Christine whispered again. "You have me, too."

"Thank you," Willow whispered back. "You're the best friend I've ever had."

"Come on. Let's go make some of those double chocolate fudge brownies, huh?"

Sniffle. "Okay."

Christine kissed the side of her head, then pulled herself up off the bed. She was surprised when she heard another sob coming from Willow. Turning back to the bed, she leaned over her.

"Honey, what is it?" Panicked, she was about to slide in behind her again.

"I can't get up," Willow whined.

Chapter 14

"Just how much of a beached whale do they think I am?" Willow cursed, plastic Hefty bag in hand. "Oh, I need to sit down." She lowered herself to the couch, feeling like an eighty-year-old man. "I mean, she used half the darn roll of toilet paper!" she continued her tirade, the three remaining women hiding their smiles.

"Whale or wailer?" Rachel muttered.

"I heard that!" Willow yelled to her friend, who was throwing away the paper plates and cups from the party.

"Alright, alright, no picking on the pregnant woman," Christine said, all the while grinning at Rachel and nodding.

"What am I going to do with all this stuff?" Willow sighed, looking around at the piles of boxes and bundles, all wrapped in pink and blue.

"Thank your lucky stars, my love," Myra said, sitting next to her granddaughter and patting her thigh. "When I had your father, they didn't have all this fancy schmancy stuff." She waved her hand at the room. "You're going to do just fine, my love."

"Thanks, Grandma. And thanks for coming." She leaned her head against her grandmother's shoulder, so happy to see her.

"Oh, honey, this is my very first great-grandchild," Myra said softly, running arthritic fingers through the thick, blonde hair that she used to love to comb for a young Willow so many years ago. Long ago, when the girl had her hair down to her waist, she used to call it spun gold, which it was. It nearly broke her heart when all that gold was cut off in favor of the new, shorter styles of today. What were these young women thinking, making themselves look like boys?

"So, what do you think?" Rachel whispered, pouring soap into the little dish in the dishwasher. Slamming the door shut, she turned the dial and sent the machine whirring into life.

"I think now is a good time," Christine whispered back, tying the black Hefty bag shut and setting it by the kitchen door to be taken out later. Rachel grinned, matching Christine's own mischievous look.

"I'm so excited!" she hissed, rubbing her hands together. Giggling like schoolgirls, they headed into the other room.

Clearing her throat, Christine spoke. "Willow, the three of us would like to give you our gifts, now." She indicated Rachel, Myra, and herself. Willow lifted her head from her grandmother's shoulder, looking confused.

"But you guys already gave me a gift."

"Purely a smoke screen, my love," Myra said, continuing the secret smiles and winks of the other two.

"Oh, okay." Willow was wary, but stood, with Rachel's help.

The four of them made a slow trek up the stairs, Rachel helping Willow and Christine holding Myra by the elbow.

"I'm so grateful my granddaughter has you to help her," Myra said softly, tucking her arm into Christine's.

"Thank you, Mrs. Wahl," she said, smiling gently.

"Oh, nonsense! You're family. You call me Grandma, or you don't expect me to answer, you understand?" Blue eyes bore into Christine's, and in that moment Christine knew just exactly where Willow had gotten her spunk.

She nodded. "You got it, Grandma."

"Good girl."

On the outside Christine was the picture of calm, but inside she was bouncing with delight, like a child on Christmas morning. She had never uttered the title "grandma", let alone bestowed it upon someone. The warmth that spread through her made her limbs tingle. That tingle spread to her heart when she saw Willow smile back at her from two steps above. She had obviously heard and approved. Christine smiled back.

"You know," Rachel said, once they had stopped before the closed third bedroom door upstairs, "thank God you've been too exhausted to get nosey." She smiled at her friend, squeezing her hand as she turned the knob, slowly pushing the door open.

Willow's retort was cut off as the smell of fresh paint and stained wood met her nose. Turning to the three grinning women around her, she pushed through the door, then gasped, hands flying to her mouth.

"I hope you still wanted Care Bears," Christine said softly, placing a gentle hand on her shoulder. The fingers were quickly grasped tightly, and her arm was pulled further down and finally wrapped around Willow in its own little nook, between her breasts and the baby bump.

"Oh, Christine," Willow whispered, "it's beautiful." She took in the painted walls, little Care Bears bouncing all over the place, on clouds, sliding down rainbows, and dancing on green grass. Mistily she saw the white crib set up in the corner, next to a matching changing table. Nestled in the other corner was a large, padded rocking chair, a spit-up towel already hung over the tall back. A dresser stood next to the closet, each knob painted a different color of the rainbow, matching the long dresser across the room.

"I figure as the baby gets older, those can be stained or painted to whatever color she wants," Christine explained.

A small sob escaped Willow's throat, and she turned into Christine, burying her face in her neck. Wrapping her up in her arms, Christine rested her cheek against the top of the blonde head.

Rachel stood near the door, her shoulder resting against the Care Bear light switch, and watched the pair. Her face showed a mixture of reactions. A small part of her was jealous; *she* had been the one Willow was close to and would hug. But somehow that jealousy was canceled out by the gut feeling that the bond between Willow and Christine went far beyond any Willow had shared with her. She couldn't quite put her finger on it, but it was heartwarming to see that Willow had such a strong pillar to lean against.

"How did you do all this?" Willow asked, wiping her tears, and looking around again.

"It wasn't just me. We all have been working on it for a while," Christine explained. "It's a good thing you don't like to go down into the basement." She grinned. Willow laughed and squeezed her arm.

Pulling slightly away from Christine, Willow turned to Rachel and her grandmother. "Thank you guys so much. It's so beautiful." Then, overcome by fresh tears, she found herself the center of a group hug.

"Concentrate on Mickey, honey, breathe with me," Christine said softly. Willow's eyes squeezed tightly shut, then opened, focusing on the figurine that stood on the tray over her bed.

"Sing," she panted, "sing to me."

Christine was surprised at the request, but happily complied, her mind spinning for a moment as she tried to think. Nothing came to mind, so she began to hum, her voice soft and soothing, visibly calming the mother-to-be.

Willow cried out as her insides were twisted once again, another contraction seizing her and leaving her breathless. Christine checked her watch — four minutes apart. She stopped humming, softly encouraging her friend to breathe through the pain, to stay focused.

Rachel ran up the stairs, not even bothering with the elevator, her chest heaving in exertion and excitement. Bursting through the stairwell door to the fifth floor, she looked around, seeing Cameron Dawes, a day nurse she used to work with in the ER.

"Cameron," she exclaimed, startling the poor woman. She hurried over to her, out of breath. "What's Willow's status?"

Cameron's eyes immediately lit up, excitement flushing her cheeks. "She's just been wheeled in. She's dilated to eight and a half, so she's just about ready." Her grin was contagious. Rachel took the woman's hands, and they both giggled like little girls for their co-worker and good friend.

"God, I can't wait to see the baby," Rachel exclaimed. "How's security?"

"It's pretty tight. Nobody's getting into this ward without us knowing about it," Cameron said proudly, personally having taken it upon herself to make sure everything was in place. Rachel looked around the ward, seeing uniformed officers everywhere, doing their best to keep the press out. "How the hell did that little fireball get a famous singer as her Lamaze coach?"

Rachel chuckled, patting the woman's arm. "It's a long story."

"Hmm. Do you see her often? I mean, is she all snobby and high and mighty?"

"No, not at all." Rachel and Cameron moved around to the nurses' lounge, grabbing a cup of coffee. "They come over all the time. She's a really great person and a wonderful friend to Willow."

Cameron shook her head, stirring in some creamer. "Crazy, and right here in Oklahoma City."

"I know. It's a crazy world," Rachel grinned, squeezing the woman's arm again, then heading toward the unit's waiting room, to sit with Myra and Willow's mother.

Willow's head slammed back against the gurney, eyes closing, face pale and clammy. She felt light headed after that last push.

"You're almost there, baby," Christine whispered, smoothing back the sweat-soaked hair sticking to Willow's face.

"I can't." Willow panted. "I can't."

"Yes, you can." Christine leaned over, laying a soft kiss on her forehead. "One more, Willow. One more."

"Come on, Willow, give us one more good push," the doctor said from between her legs. "The head has crowned, so just one more good one, and I can do the rest," she encouraged.

"You can do this, Willow. I have faith in you. Come on, baby."

Willow opened her eyes, looking into Christine's, so close to her own, the blue almost matching the scrubs that she wore. Looking into those eyes, focusing on their color and brilliance, focusing on how calm they made her feel, she was able to block out the pain. She could do it. She'd do it for Christine.

Scrunching up her entire face and squeezing her eyes shut again, she used every last little bit of energy she had, yelling out as she pushed, teeth bared, mouth slowly opening into a scream as she felt a sudden release, a numbing pain, followed by the screech of a very unhappy baby.

Her scream turned into a laugh of relief, and she felt Christine's tears on her face as her head was cradled close.

"You did it! Oh, baby, oh, Willow, you did it!"

"You have a healthy baby girl!" the doctor proclaimed, holding out a very long, pair of scissors. "Christine, would you like to do the honors?" she asked, her eyes smiling behind her mask.

A wave of pride swept through Christine as she took the scissors in trembling hands and was guided to the cord by the doctor.

"It's okay," the doctor murmured, "you won't hurt her."

A simple snip and the cord was cut. Christine quickly handed the scissors back, then turned her attention to Willow, who was semi-conscious, pure exhaustion winning over her need to see her daughter.

"Christine," the nurse said softly, walking over to her with the newly cleaned and swathed baby in her arms.

"Oh," she breathed, looking down into the tiny, wrinkled face that looked back up at her as the newborn was placed in her arms. "My God," she breathed, unable to keep the smile from her face, "she's so tiny." The baby's face, her squinty blue eyes blinking rapidly, began to contort as short bursts of upset erupted from the tiniest mouth Christine had ever seen.

The nurse smiled, never tiring of seeing a parent fall in love with their child for the first time. This was no different.

"Oh, listen to you," Christine cooed, suddenly forgetting anyone else in the entire world existed, save for the itty bitty life she held in her arms. "You are beautiful, just like your mommy, yes." Tiny arms waved uselessly, trapped in the blanket. The little bursts stopped for a moment, as if the baby were uncertain what she was supposed to do. Her eyes opened again, big for just a moment, then squinting again as a full-out cry escaped.

Christine moved over to Willow, her heart feeling as though it would burst, love oozing from every pore she possessed.

"Thank you, Willow," she whispered to the sleeping woman. "Thank you for sharing this with me."

"It's a girl!" Christine exclaimed, exploding into the waiting room, still in her scrubs. A dozen faces turned to her, but only three stood and hurried over to her. She found herself wrapped up in a sea of questions and emotional hugs. She answered the questions as best she could — seven pounds, fourteen ounces; twenty inches; blue; dark; fine, but asleep; no, she didn't faint.

Christine felt exhausted; she'd been up with Willow during her labor, all thirty-seven hours of it, and she was drained. She dropped into a chair next to Willow's bed, the noise of excitement all around her fading as blissful dark- ness eased in around the edges of her consciousness. Her head lolled back against the wall, her arms dangled over the chair, her eyelids got heavier and heavier, closing.

Everyone finally cleared out, and Willow, braced against pillows, held her daughter to her breast, listening to her quiet suckling sounds. She spied Chris- tine, who'd been asleep for well over an hour, and a soft smile brushed her lips.

Giving birth had certainly been a trying experience, and there was some of it she couldn't recall, but she remembered Christine there with her, never leaving her side, even leaving the bathroom door open in Willow's room, to make sure she could hear if anything was needed.

Her heart was already so filled with love for the bundle she held, but somehow it expanded to breaking point as she felt a strong love for Christine join that for her daughter. She couldn't help but think of how incomplete the day would have been without her.

She remembered the look in Christine's eyes as she encouraged her in the delivery room, the way she'd kissed her forehead and had done her best to keep Willow's hair and sweat out of her eyes during the difficult delivery.

How was she going to be able to handle it when one day Christine decided to leave, to return to her life? Willow knew it was only a matter of time. She had seen Christine standing before the piano more than once, her fingers absently hitting a key or two and a look so wistful crossing her beauti- ful face that it broke Willow's heart.

There was no way she could compete with that longing.

As she watched, Christine groaned and awoke, unfolding her long body from the uncomfortable chair. She looked around, getting her bearings. When she saw the two in the hospital bed, an instant smile spread across her lips.

"Hey," she said, her voice rough from sleep.

"Hi," Willow said, smiling. She felt bad as she saw how red Christine's eyes were, knowing that she had to be utterly exhausted.

"Where is everyone?" Christine stood, stretching with a groan, arms raised over her head before she walked over to the bed.

"They all went home. It's late."

Looking down at the two, Christine reached her hand out, gently brushing a few brown strands that were scattered across the baby's tiny head. "I can't believe how little she is," she whispered in awe.

"I know." Willow looked down at her daughter, absently reaching for Christine's hand. She winced slightly as she scooted her body over, making room for her to climb up onto the narrow bed beside her. "Come join us," she whispered, never taking her eyes off the baby, who had fallen asleep against her breast.

Carefully climbing onto the bed, Christine stretched her legs out, wrapping an arm around Willow and the baby, watching her sleep.

"I'd like you to meet Emma Christine Bowman," Willow said softly, meeting her friend's eyes. Christine felt the sting of emotion and blinked it away. "Don't look so surprised," Willow smiled. "Without you, very little of this would have been possible today."

"Well," Christine said through her amazement, "I think Kevin deserves some credit."

Willow chuckled softly, leaning forward and resting her lips softly on Christine's cheek. Heads together, the women eventually fell asleep.

A month quickly bled into two, life filled with the blind leading the blind, trying to raise a newborn baby. Christine had no idea something so little could be so smelly. Holding her breath as she dumped yet another tiny diaper into the Diaper Genie, she headed back upstairs, Willow still calling for her to bring the new tube of Desitin from the diaper bag.

"Coming," she called up, taking the stairs two at a time, finally slapping the tube into the waiting mother's hand.

"How's my messy girl?" Christine cooed, making a gaggle of crazy faces at Emma. The little one's eyes, which had steadily turned green, shone, and the little dimples appeared that made Christine's heart melt. "Willow, it's official," Christine said, looking at her seriously.

"What's that?" Willow asked, handing her a fresh diaper to put on Emma.

"I've lost my heart to a female."

"Oh you have, have you?"

"Yes." She looked down at the baby, waggling her tongue at her as she crossed her eyes.

"Hmm. Well, it's about time you made a choice between the sexes."

"I agree. Guess you can call me a baby dyke." Christine burst into laughter. Willow looked at her like she was nuts. "I thought it was funny," she muttered to Emma, who blew raspberries in response.

Willow put all of Emma's diaper stuff back on the shelf above the changing table, chuckling to herself. She loved watching Christine with the baby. She tried to imagine how it would be as Emma got older; she'd have two kids on her hands.

The phone rang. She walked across the hall to her bedroom, grabbing the cordless off its base.

"Christine?"

"Yeah?" she said, tucking Emma into the bend of her arm.

"Phone, hon." Willow exchanged the baby for the phone. "I'll give her back when you're done," she said to the protesting woman. Christine growled but headed out into the hall, phone to her ear, steps creaking under her booted feet.

Willow hummed softly, gently dancing with little Emma. The baby had been fed and changed, and her eyes were getting heavier and heavier. Willow's voice got softer, lulling her to sleep. When finally Emma let out an adorable, little sigh, her mother placed her in her crib, making sure she was safe and warm. Kissing her softly on her head, Willow left the room, closing the door to a crack.

She jumped, heart pounding, when she heard a loud bang downstairs, then another, another, a crack, then more pounding.

Racing to the kitchen, she saw pieces of something flying, then realized it was the phone. Christine was pounding it on the counter in a frenzy, annihilating it.

"Christine!" she called out, trying to get the raging woman under control. She stepped toward the singer, reaching a tentative hand out to touch her arm, only to have Christine jump away from her, eyes ablaze.

Dropping what was left of the cordless onto the counter, Christine turned away, hiding her face. "Sorry about the phone," she whispered, voice thick. Willow reached out toward her again. "Don't touch me," Christine sobbed, hurrying out of the room. The front door slammed behind her.

Willow stood there, shaken to her core. Her frayed nerves were jolted again when she realized Emma was crying upstairs.

Taking several deep, shaky breaths, she ran a trembling hand through her hair and hurried back to her daughter's room, almost glad for the distraction of having to calm Emma.

Christine pushed her way out into the late April afternoon, a sob caught in her throat. She tried to swallow it, but it wasn't going anywhere. All she could hope for was to get far enough away, away from the house, from Willow and Emma, away.

She bunched her hands into fists, her vision beginning to blur, images and colors bleeding together, causing her to stumble over the new growth that was spreading across the flat land like wildfire. Catching her balance, she hurried on, only to stumble again. This time she fell to one knee.

"Doctor Weitz, calling on behalf of Alice..."

She let her other knee fall, hands touching the earth, fingers digging into the soft soil.

"...emergency appendectomy...complications..."

Tears fell to the ground making little round spots of mud, more, little spots joining, making bigger ones.

"...infection...immune system too weak..."

Christine threw herself back on her haunches, eyes squeezed shut, mouth falling open as a scream ripped from her throat.

"...so sorry..."

"No!"

Willow started, holding Emma close, eyes wide and frightened. "It's okay, my love," she whispered into the baby's ear. "It's okay."

Willow glanced over her reading glasses, hearing soft footsteps in the hall. She put her novel down and listened. Emma's door creaked open slightly, there were more soft footsteps, whispered words, then the door creaked again. The footsteps stopped in front of Willow's door, the floor creaking under the weight, then moved on down the hall, where a door clicked softly into place.

Pushing the covers aside, Willow got out of bed. She put both the novel and her reading glasses on the bedside table and hurried to the door. She flicked her light off before opening it, then tiptoed out into the hall, listening again.

There was a light under Christine's door, but as she watched, the crack under the door became dark.

Chewing on her lip, she tried to decide what to do. Remembering the look of absolute anguish on Christine's face earlier that day, she decided to check on her.

Standing in front of her door, she paused again, then finally raised her hand, knocking softly. Barely hearing the invitation, she slowly pushed the door open. The room was dark. Christine stood at the window, her form a silhouette against the moonlit night beyond.

Willow stepped inside, closing the door behind her so as not to wake Emma. She said nothing as she made her way across the room, stepping up beside her friend.

"I'm sorry," Christine whispered, staring out, unblinking. Willow took in her profile, her finger reaching out to catch the glistening tear that slowly rolled down her cheek.

"Oh, honey," she said, "what's going on?" Her heart broke as another tear made a lazy trail after the first, followed by another.

Christine turned, face crumpling as she grabbed Willow, releasing a soft sob into her hair. Willow held her close, eyes tightly shut as she felt the pain and sorrow radiating off her.

"Just hold me, Willow. Please, just hold me."

"Of course. Anything." Willow reached up and petted the thick dark hair, pulling Christine even closer, trying to give her every bit of strength and comfort that she had.

"Willow?" Christine said, her voice thick, raising her head from her shoulder. Willow said nothing, just looked up into that tortured face, brushing the continuous stream of tears away with her thumb. "Stay with me tonight? Please, please, be with me tonight?" Her whisper was almost filled with panic.

"Anything you need," Willow whispered back, her last word almost cut off by Christine's lips on her own. Her eyes popped open, stunned, feeling the persistence of the kiss, still feeling the wetness of Christine's tears against her own skin. She found her eyes fluttering closed, a tentative hand resting on the brunette's shoulder, Christine's arms wrapping around her, pulling her closer.

All thought was gone. All that was left was bare, naked need.

Christine's kiss became insistent, her breathing quickening with her heartbeat. Moving on instinct, she walked Willow backward until she hit the bed, falling back onto it, falling with her, on top of her.

Willow's mind was blown wide open, all thoughts flying. She kissed Christine back, her hands tangled in her thick dark hair, pulling her mouth further into hers, hearing Christine's desperate whimpers as their lips opened, the kiss deepening. Willow brought Christine's tongue into her mouth, her body relaxing under the comforting weight of Christine's body.

"Don't leave me," Christine begged, finding Willow's neck, licking and nipping, her hand moving up under Willow's t-shirt, fingers brushing against a bare breast, Willow gasping at the contact. "Stay with me."

"Yes, Christine, yes," Willow whimpered, her hands reaching down Christine's back, finding the hem of her shirt and tugging at it, feeling her frustration grow until Christine sat up on her knees just long enough to whip the shirt off and throw it into the darkness, falling back to find Willow's mouth again. Her hands desperately tried to remove Willow's own shirt, tugging it off, her hands immediately going to her breasts, filling her hands with them, hearing Willow's hiss as her nipples became rigid, tickling Christine's palms.

Willow arched her back, her mind exploding once again at the incredible sensations racing through her body. Not enough. Reaching down, she tore at Christine's jeans, shoving them as far down her hips as she could reach. Again, Christine was off her, this time standing, throwing her clothes off, a boot hitting the wall. She grabbed the ends of Willow's shorts, tugging roughly. Willow barely had a chance to lift her hips before the material was almost ripped off her. She shoved her own panties down, kicking them off, then grabbed Christine around the back of her neck, brusquely tugging her back onto the bed, back onto her.

Christine didn't feel any pain, just need. She ravaged Willow's mouth, right hand sliding down her body until she found the wet warmth between her thighs. She entered her, two fingers sliding right in, Willow gasping and crying out, her legs parting.

"I need you," Christine moaned, her mouth everywhere, kissing, licking, sucking. Willow couldn't keep up, having no idea where she was going next. She decided just to go with it, her hips bucking in time with Christine's thrusts, her body on fire, and climax not far away.

Grabbing Christine's arm with claw-like fingers, Willow bit her lip, trying not to scream as she so badly wanted to do. Realizing what was happening, Christine quickly found her mouth with her own, intercepting the cry.

They lay there, Christine's fingers still inside Willow, panting into each other's mouths, bodies covered with sweat and desire.

Willow shuddered as Christine slowly, carefully, removed her fingers, bringing her arms up, wrapping her in a cocoon of warmth, holding her close, burying her face in Willow's hair.

After a few moments, their bodies cooled and a chill settled over them. Christine helped Willow climb beneath the covers, then pulled her near, not daring to let go.

Willow lay there, shutting her mind off, raising herself when she felt Christine's body shaking anew with silent tears.

"Let me hold you, baby," she whispered, pulling the woman to her. Christine rested her head on Willow's chest, wetting the skin with her profound sorrow. Willow still had no idea what had happened, but she figured she would learn in time.

The morning sun was harsh. It woke Willow and there was no going back to sleep. Slowly opening her eyes, she blinked a few times, looking around and seeing Christine's room. She remembered the night, and she realized she was alone in the bed, but not in the room.

Christine sat in the chair in the corner, fully dressed, Emma asleep in her arms. Her eyes were half closed.

"Hi," Willow said softly, bringing the sheet up to cover her naked breasts.

"Hey." Christine's eyes opened a bit more, and her hand absently caressed Emma's tiny arm.

"How is she?"

"Good. She's changed and fed. Happy."

"Guess that breast pump came in handy, huh?" Willow said, feeling self-conscious in the light of day. Her eyes scanned the room, discreetly trying to look for her clothes. She blushed when she saw they were folded neatly and placed at the end of the bed. Reaching for them, she put her shirt on, then leaned back against the pillows. She was at a loss for words, not sure what to say to Christine when she had no idea what to say to herself.

"I'm going to have to go to New York for a few days, take care of some things," Christine said softly, breaking through Willow's muddled thoughts.

"New York?" Willow frowned.

"Alice is a mess, and she needs me right now." Christine looked at the baby, leaning down to lay a gentle kiss on the top of her head.

Willow's mind somersaulted over the information — *New York, Alice.* She gasped, and one hand flew to her mouth. "Adam."

Christine's eyes closed as she pressed her forehead to her tiny bundle. "Gonna miss you, little one," she whispered.

"Oh, Christine." Understanding flooded Willow, her eyes filling at her friend's deep loss. Throwing the blankets off her, she blushed deeply again, realizing she was naked below, too. She tugged her shorts on. Her feet hit the floor with a thud, and she hurried over to Christine's chair and fell to her knees beside it.

"I don't know what to say," she said lamely. Christine smiled, weak and heavy.

"There's nothing left to say."

"I'm sorry."

"Me, too."

"When are you leaving?"

"I have a flight this afternoon."

"How long will you be gone?" Willow turned her attention to her daughter. Looking into Christine's eyes was breaking her heart.

"A few days. Maybe a week."

Willow took in the information, her voice small when she spoke next. "Do you want me to come with you?" She looked into the blue eyes she'd grown to adore. It hurt to see them so far away. Christine shook her head.

"No. It would be too difficult to travel with Emma." Again she looked down at the baby, brushing the silky soft hair.

"Okay." Willow was silent, chewing on her lip, a question bouncing around in her head, refusing to go away. Without looking at Christine, she said quietly, "Are you coming back?"

"Do you want me to come back?" Christine asked, voice hard.

"Yes," Willow whispered.

"Please be safe," Willow murmured into Christine's ear as she hugged her tight. She wouldn't allow her mind to think about how that body had felt against hers the night before, naked, needing. She would have plenty of time to think about that over the next few days.

Christine held her, laying a kiss on Willow's head. "I will," she promised. Pulling gently away, she gave Willow the most reassuring smile she could, though she didn't feel it. She didn't feel anything. Numb. That was the only way she could describe her state. She would forever feel guilty about not going to see Adam at the end. She thought she had time. But then again, was it deeper than that? She couldn't deny that she hadn't wanted to see her friend like that. Was she a selfish bitch because of it? Christine shook herself from her morose thoughts. "See you soon."

With that, Christine climbed into her Jeep and turned the engine. A final wave, and she pulled out of the yard in a cloud of dust.

Willow watched, her heart in her throat. As the echo of the Jeep's engine died in the still day, she closed the front door, leaning against it. A feeling of dread was pulsing through her, and she hated it.

She walked through the rest of the day in a daze, doing what needed to be done around the house, only really coming alive when she had to attend to Emma, who was cranky. It was almost like she could sense something was amiss. Willow wished that Christine were there to sing the baby into calm.

Later that night, when Emma was fed, changed, and asleep, Willow sat in the huge, Roman tub in the main bathroom upstairs. Body reclined, eyes barely open, she stared up into the ceiling, the steam making her feel as though she were looking through gauze.

Her mind played back a series of memories from the night before: a look on Christine's face; the feel of her hand, her mouth. Willow pushed each one away, only to have another memory take its place.

What had happened? What force had taken them both over? Willow never would have done something like that on her own, and she trusted that

Christine wouldn't, either. Christine had needed her, that much was clear. Why had Willow willingly given all she had to give?

True, she'd do anything for Christine, give her anything she asked for. But not *that*.

"God, what did I do?" she asked the empty room, burying her face in her hands. Part of her wished she and Christine had talked about it, had cleared the air. How did Christine feel about it?

Willow knew it wasn't a gay/straight issue, nor did she see it as one. She never had. But why had she let the situation cross the boundaries of friendship, regardless of how close and deep that friendship was? What had possessed her?

She sighed, closing her eyes. She knew she could turn it every which way in her mind all night. What it boiled down to was it happened, and though she couldn't say she regretted it, she worried that they wouldn't be able to move past it. She worried it would become a hang-up, something forever between them.

Though all this surfed through her mind, somewhere inside Willow felt honored. She knew that what happened had been something that Christine wouldn't have shared with just anyone. She had trusted Willow enough to allow her inside. Even if Christine wouldn't talk to her, wouldn't let her inside her head, she'd let her inside her heart, and Willow cherished that realization.

When Christine came back, they would talk about it, perhaps. But no matter what, Willow wouldn't allow it to effect what they had built. Christine was part of Willow's family, part of her daily life, and she already felt lost and alone, just nine hours after the singer had driven away.

Willow allowed herself to relax fully, the bubbles in the water easing sore muscles, forgetting for the moment how amazingly wonderful it had felt to have Christine's hands on her, mouth on her, body on hers. Forgetting that though it had been a brief encounter, her body still burned from it and that never, in all her sexually active years, had she been made to feel so much like a woman.

Kevin often said she didn't like to deal with things.

"Yesss," Willow moaned, feeling fingers glide down between her breasts, over her abdomen, making the muscles there twitch, and finally moving lower. She gasped, back arching as those fingers slipped between the saturated folds of her sex, the wet heat gathering, overflowing. "Oh yes, baby," she moaned again, hips moving to find even more purchase to ease the ache.

Suddenly she was filled, head arching back, feeling hot lips on her skin, licking a trail up her throat as the pressure continued between her legs, a dull ache that was beginning to explode almost painfully into constant need.

"Kiss me," she begged, opening her eyes to see intense blue looking down at her.

Willow's eyes flew open with a gasp, the cool, night air grazing her half naked body, one breast exposed to the room, one covered by her own hand. The other hand was nestled between her own legs. Groaning, she slammed her eyes closed again, bringing her hands up to cover her face. She groaned again when she smelled herself on her fingers.

"This is insane," she whispered, her body still making its demand known, her sex throbbing with every beat of her heart.

The water rained down over her skin. Willow closed her eyes as she raised her face to the spray, the last of the soap vanishing into the drain at her feet. Slicking her hair back from her face, she blinked her eyes open, then turned off the shower. Sliding the frosted doors open, she stepped out onto the bathmat, reaching for her towel.

She was looking forward to the day. Rachel would be over soon, and they planned to get out of the house. Willow was in the last couple weeks of her maternity leave, and she hadn't been out much, enjoying her time at home with Christine and the baby. Christine was gone, so now it was time to introduce Emma to the outside world.

Wrapping the towel around herself, she padded into the dark bedroom, where the heavy curtains only allowed thin slivers of golden light from around the edges. Grabbing the bottom of the shade, she tugged until it snapped up. As it did, a bright flash startled a gasp out of her.

Looking into the tree not far from the window, she screamed when she saw a man clinging to a branch with one arm and holding a camera up to his eye with the other as he snapped off several more shots.

Getting her bearings, Willow quickly pulled the shade, running over to the side table to grab the cordless telephone. Seeing an empty base, she remembered the phone had been destroyed. She ran down the stairs, frantically digging through her purse until she found her cell phone.

She closed every shade she came to, freaked out of her mind. The surprise of seeing the man there, taking her picture, brought to mind someone breaking into the house. Somewhere inside she knew that was ridiculous, but thinking clearly was not on her agenda at that moment.

Struggling with the cell phone in one hand, the other holding her towel to her body, she managed to speed dial Christine's phone.

After two rings, the singer picked up.

"They're outside the house!" Willow exclaimed, hurrying from room to room, peeking out the window. She gasped when she saw someone running from the house, jumping into a dark blue mini van which sped away.

"What? Wait, what are you talking about?" Christine was concerned.

"A guy! He was in the tree, I got out of the shower, and he took my picture!"

"Fuck," she growled. "Those sons of bitches."

"Who was that?" Willow hurried up the stairs, into Emma's room to make sure the baby was okay. She was sound asleep in her crib.

"They must have found out I've been staying there," Christine said.

"What? Who?"

"The press. Listen, lay low, keep the shades drawn, and I'll handle it, alright? They're trespassing on private property. Are you okay?"

"God, Christine, I was half naked," Willow cried, shame filling her, making her feel nauseous.

"I'm sorry. God, I'm sorry," Christine whispered. "I promise I'll take care of it right now. Okay?"

"Okay." Willow took a deep, calming breath.

"Are you alright?"

"Yeah. He just really took me by surprise. I'm sorry to bother you..."

"No! Don't you dare apologize. It's my fault that bastard was there. Listen, I'll be home tomorrow, okay?"

"Christine, don't cut your trip short. I know you have things to do..."

"No. You need me there. I'll be home as soon as I can, okay?"

"Okay," Willow said, her voice quiet, relief flowing through her. God, she missed her. "How are you doing?"

Christine sighed heavily. "I'm okay. We went through Adam's papers last night, and today I'm settling some things for him. Alice isn't doing well."

"But how are *you*?" Willow gripped the phone tighter, wishing she could be there for Christine.

"It hurts. It hurts bad," she said softly. "I never thought I could hurt so much and yet not be bleeding somewhere." Her chuckle was humorless.

"You are bleeding, honey," Willow slid down one of the walls in the nursery, pulling her knees to her chest, "bleeding in your heart."

"Yeah. Guess so. Look, Willow, about the night before I left..."

"No, don't think about that now, Christine. You have too much else on your plate right now. We'll deal with that when we deal with it."

"Are you sure? I..." she sighed. Willow could almost imagine her running a nervous hand through her dark hair. "I feel like such an asshole."

"Don't. Please don't," Willow's voice had grown even softer. "I'm just," she swallowed, "I'm just glad I was able to be there for you." She waited. "Christine? Are you there?"

"Yeah. I'm here. Are you going to be home for a bit?"

Willow could tell the subject had been effectively changed. "I was planning to go out with Rachel, but now I don't know." She shivered, the memory and surprise still fresh.

"Please stay in today. For me? I'd feel so much better knowing you and Emma were safe inside the house. Not that you're not safe, but I don't know if those idiots will try and follow you or something. I don't want to put you through that. We don't need another Princess Diana situation."

"Okay. We'll stay here."

"Good. How is she? Emma?"

An instant smile lit Willow's features. "She's fine. She's been cranky. I think she misses you." Her heart softened at the soft chuckle she heard on the other end of the line.

"I miss her, too. I need to get going. You take care of yourself, and give her a great big hug and kiss for me, okay?"

"Will do."

"Okay. Talk to you soon."

"Christine?" Willow gripped the tiny phone with both hands.

"Yeah?"

"I...I miss you."

"I miss you, too, Willow. Be home soon."

The phone went dead, silence complete. Slowly flipping the phone shut, Willow rested her head against the wall behind her, sighing deeply.

Chapter 15

"So, I'm thinking we're going to enjoy our day with Aunt Rachel, not talk about anything but you and just have a good time. What do you think?" Emma blew raspberries as Willow carried her down the stairs, making the young mother laugh. "Well said, little one."

She carried the baby to the kitchen and fixed her a bottle. She knew she had to wean Emma from her breast for when her daughter had to go to, gulp, the babysitter.

Emma whined a bit, not sure about this whole bottle thing, but eventually her hunger outweighed the need to pout, and she began to suckle.

Sitting on the couch, Willow watched her daughter, who looked up at her with eyes the very same color as her own. Her heart warmed as Emma blindly grabbed Willow's pinky, all five fingers wrapping around it.

The doorbell chimed, and Willow carefully readjusted Emma in her arms so as not to disturb her eating, but still be able to unlock and open the door.

"I won't bring it up, won't bring it up. No reason to bring it up," she mumbled to herself, then pulled the door open. Rachel grinned from ear to ear, giving Willow a quick one-armed hug, then taking Emma from her arms. "Uh," Willow said, stunned, "nice to see you, too."

Closing the door behind them, and locking it, she followed Rachel into the kitchen.

"What's with the locks? Am I a captive here or what?" Sitting at the kitchen table, Rachel grinned down at the baby, running a single finger over impossibly soft skin, tiny fingers, and little button nose while holding the bottle with her other hand. Willow watched from the doorway, leaning in the arch, smiling.

"No, I just don't want some stupid reporter to do something...well...stupid," she explained softly.

"That really spooked you, huh?" Rachel asked, sparing a quick glance for her friend, who was walking over to the table, sat opposite her.

"I know it's silly, but yeah he did."

"It's not silly. Shoot, look at Princess Di. Those idiots have been known to do some crazy things. What is Christine going to do?"

Willow shrugged. "No idea. I'm sure she knows what to do, though. I mean, she's dealt with this crap for almost twenty years."

"I wonder what that's like," Rachel said absently, brushing her fingers over the silky soft hair. "Looks like her hair is going to be darker than both her mommy and daddy."

"Yeah. But then my dad has real dark hair."

"Hmm."

"So are you driving Connor nuts yet?"

"What, for a baby?" Rachel smiled. "No. It's not the right time and I know that. Yeah, I'd love to have one, but for now I'll just have to steal yours."

Willow laughed. "I don't know who you'd have a harder time getting past — me or Christine."

"Quite the little daddy, is she?" Rachel smirked.

"Nice. Hardly."

"No?"

Willow thought about it for a moment and could see where Rachel would get that. Daddy figure. She looked away, feeling a steady flush rise up her neck and cheeks. Ever the eagle-eyed friend, Rachel raised a brow.

"Are you blushing, Willow?"

"No."

"Liar." Rachel's humor died when she sensed just how serious Willow had become. She remained silent, not wanting to scare Willow away if she needed to talk.

Pretend it's nothing. It is nothing. You're fine, Christine's fine, the whole damn world is fine. Her inner turmoil came to a head when she felt a slight sting behind her eyes. Oh, no. She was not going to do that. Swallowing it down, she decided that she'd have to get it out one way or the other, via crying it out or talking it out. If she cried she knew she'd have to explain it anyway, so she prepared to speak.

"That night, the night Adam died, Christine was so devastated," she began softly, seeing the anguish in those beautiful blue eyes all over again.

"No doubt," Rachel agreed softly.

"She trashed the phone, then went outside. She was out there a long time. Eventually I put Emma in her crib and went to bed myself, reading, trying to get my mind off things, worrying, all that."

Willow stood, grabbing the bag of coffee from the cabinet, full strength, no more of the puny stuff. Filling the basket and carafe, she stood at the counter, needing some space between her and Rachel as she told her story. She could feel Rachel's eyes on her, and she ignored them.

"It got later, darker. I figured she'd gone somewhere, but her keys were still hanging by the door. I didn't know where she'd gone, but I knew I shouldn't follow. You have no idea how hard that was for me," she chuckled, stealing a glance at her friend.

"I can imagine," Rachel laughed, rocking Emma to sleep, the baby having had her fill of lunch.

"Anyway, so eventually she did come in. I listened. She checked on Emma, checked on me, then went to her own room. I followed."

Pushing off the counter, she sat back down, deciding that she needed to be as honest and open with Rachel as possible. By keeping her distance, it would seem as though she had something to hide or was perhaps ashamed.

"She was so upset," Willow whispered, again seeing Christine standing by the window, looking like such a lost child. "It was hard to watch. She's normally so stoic about things concerning herself. You know, she'll be so incredibly supportive of me, just like I know she would be of Emma, so perceptive that it's almost like it's her own pain." She looked off into space for a moment, thinking back over the months she'd spent with the singer.

"She's an incredible lady," Rachel said softly, eyeing her friend. She had a feeling that she was about to reveal something huge, but she had no idea what.

"Yes, she is." Willow's eyes met Rachel's for the first time since she had started the conversation. "She stood there, heartsick, though at that point I still had no idea what had happened." She rose again, hearing the coffee maker coming to life. She knew it would be a matter of moments before it was done.

Walking to the cabinet, she pulled out two mugs, got out the cream, sugar, anything to slow down time. Anything to forestall what she had to say.

Rachel was impatient, but she remained silent all the same. She was on pins and needles. It was almost like reading a book as someone wrote it, having to wait for that next chapter to be completed.

"Coffee?"

"Please."

Sighing heavily, Willow filled two mugs and brought them and all the stuff they needed to the table. Getting settled once again, she continued, her voice quiet, dreamy.

"She needed me that night. She begged me not to leave her." She watched almost in a trance as she stirred in French Vanilla creamer, the thick liquid swirling around the cup. "Sh..." Willow swallowed, "she needed someone to be there for her, to make her know it was okay, there was still life out there, I guess." Gently laying the spoon aside, she cupped her mug and blew across the hot surface of the liquid.

Rachel prepared her own cup with one hand, the other holding a sleeping Emma securely in her lap.

"I think she needed to reach out in the only way she could, the only way she knew how to at that moment of utter devastation to her universe." She searched Rachel's eyes, looking for understanding. The concerned blue eyes that looked back showed no judgment, no disgust, just attention. "I think she needed to speak with her heart that night, that she was unable to talk to me, unable to tell me where it hurt."

Confused, Rachel studied her friend, wondering where this was leading?

"She needed me to love her," Willow finally said, her voice just barely above a whisper.

The lightbulb flickered on, but Rachel did her best to not react. Looking her friend dead in the eye, she had to make sure they were on the same page. "You made love?" she asked softly.

Willow blinked at her, making Rachel wonder if she'd read it wrong, but then she nodded. "I guess you could say that, yes. Then I held her and let her cry herself to sleep."

"Wow," Rachel breathed.

"She left not long after I woke up," Willow finished, sipping her coffee. Rachel couldn't take her eyes off her friend, her mind somersaulting over what she'd just been told. She had no idea what her reaction was; her mind was a scramble of thoughts and emotions at the news. Later, it would shock her that her first instinct hadn't been that of a teenager, wanting to know how it was. It never even occurred to her in that moment.

"Say something," Willow whispered, terrified of what her friend was thinking.

"I'm not sure what to say."

Willow swallowed a sob, about to stand. Rachel's hand flew across the table, holding her friend in place.

"Don't you go running off. I'm not..." She paused, thinking of what exactly she was trying to say. "Willow, I don't think this is a gay issue or anything that base. You and Christine love each other. A blind man could see that. What you did that night was to honor that love, and you should be commended for it." She watched as her friend sat back down, eyes wary. "I mean, I'll be honest and say I'm not entirely sure how I feel, but that's not a bad thing. Considering I'm used to seeing you with Kevin, hugging, kissing, all that jazz. I mean, shit, you have a child by him."

Willow nodded, sipping her coffee, mainly to keep her hands busy.

"Do you regret it?"

Willow thought about this question for a moment, rolling it around in her mind. She shook her head. "No."

"What do you think will happen once she gets back?"

"I have no idea. She once told me she's never made love, that she looks at sex as a bad word, basically. So, that said, I have no clue how she feels. Maybe *she* regrets it. She flew out of here fast enough." Willow couldn't keep the bitterness out of her voice, even though she knew it was selfish.

"Hey," Rachel scolded lightly. "I don't think her actions that day are indicative of anything about Christine. Try and put yourself in the place she was. And if she said she feels that way about sex, then imagine the kind of trust it must have taken for her to ask that of you."

"You think so?"

"Absolutely! Considering the last time something like that happened, when she kissed you? You freaked out. Her coming to you was an act of desperation, Willow. No doubt she was trying to stay above water, clinging to you."

Willow studied her friend, stunned at what she had just heard.

"What?" Rachel asked, cup halfway to her mouth.

"When the hell did you get so insightful?"

Rachel chuckled into her mug. "I was a prophet in my past life. How are *you* feeling about all this?"

Willow shrugged. "Alright, I guess. I haven't really allowed myself to think about it much."

"Why not? You're just as entitled to your thoughts and feelings as Christine is. Sacrifices aren't made without consequences, my friend."

"I guess I've been afraid to think about it, to let myself."

"Why? You think you're gay or something?"

Willow said nothing.

"I told you, Willow — this isn't a gay issue."

"Then what is it? I mean, who the hell, after a sexual life with men that spans a decade, who suddenly has the most amazingly passionate sexual experience of her life — with a *woman*, no less — doesn't question that?" Willow looked incredulous.

"Willow," Rachel said very quietly, "I'm not trying to force anything on you or put you in a certain camp by any means. But I *am* saying that this isn't about gay, straight, or whatever. This was about *love*. Plain and simple. I mean, I'm no expert on the doings of lesbians, any more than you. But I know love when I see it, and I see it every single time I look at the two of you." She paused, waiting for the words to sink in. "For God's sake, you two are raising a child together!" She indicated the very child, asleep in her arms.

Willow could only look at her, having absolutely no idea how to respond to that. She hadn't given a second thought to what she and Christine were doing. They were just happy; that was all she knew.

"Bottom line," Rachel said at last. "I care about you, and I want to see you happy. If Christine is that happiness, who the hell cares?"

"It's not that easy, Rachel," Willow said, her insides in a turmoil, not sure where to go or where was safe.

"No, it's not. You're facing some pretty big decisions, my friend. The past year has been filled with huge changes for you, beginning on a cold night last February."

Willow grinned, looking up at her friend. "Did you realize that Emma was born one year exactly from the night I pulled the great Christine Gray out of Chandler River?"

Rachel sat back in her chair, her mouth hanging open. "You're kidding?" As her friend shook her head, Rachel shook her own in disbelief. "See? It's fate."

Willow rolled her eyes, getting up to refill her cup. Topping off Rachel's raised mug, she sat again.

"I don't know. Yes, Christine is a major, important part of my life, and I want her in it. I just don't honestly know what part I want her to play in it, what I can handle. I don't know that what happened the other night is a reason to decide to get into that kind of relationship with her."

"Well, something tells me it won't be a decision." Rachel stirred in some cream. "I think it'll just happen, Wills."

"Hmm." Willow sipped her brew, staring absently into space. "Maybe. I really don't know."

Not long after Rachel had left, the doorbell rang again. Wiping her hands on a dishrag, Willow unlocked the door and carefully pulled it open, peeking around it. She had not been expecting anyone else to call.

"Hello, ma'am. I'm Troy Leonard, head of Leonard Security."

Willow looked up at the small mountain that stood on her porch, his body almost blocking out any sunlight. A hand the size of a football was stretched out, waiting for her to take it. After enfolding her much, much smaller one gently in his, he produced a card from his inside pocket.

"Ms. Gray has filled me in on the situation, miss, so with your permission, my team will set up." He moved aside to reveal a black van sitting in front of the house, the back doors already open, and a man pulling equipment out, laying it in the dirt behind the vehicle.

"Oh, uh, okay." Willow stepped back, feeling like she was in a dream, and admitted the halfback-sized man, who was dressed in a black suit, hair slicked back to perfection. Two of his team members followed him inside, the man and the woman nodding politely at her. The three murmured amongst themselves as they moved around the house. Willow headed back into the kitchen where her macaroni and cheese was about to burn.

Three hours, five cameras, and a brand new electric gate, later, Willow was once again alone in her house, if not alone on the ranch. The team had assured her that none of the footage being monitored in the van came from inside the house itself, that all their lenses had been angled to view various locations around the property. Willow confirmed that on the monitor set up in her bedroom, flipping through the channels, seeing full color, live images of the ranch flicker into view. This must be costing Christine a small fortune, she thought, feeling bad that it had become necessary.

Willow pushed the button, once again changing the view. This time she was able to see the electric gate, a NO TRESPASSING: PRIVATE PROPERTY sign now attached to its face. A butterfly battered at her ribs when she noticed a very familiar Jeep pulling up to it. The driver unzipped her window, the plastic falling inside as Troy stepped up to the vehicle.

She watched as Christine and Troy talked, the huge man gesturing at things around the property.

Willow used the zoom feature, getting in close to see Christine's lips moving and her head nodding. Finally, a bright smile spread across her face, and her hand reached through the window, taking Troy's in a hearty handshake. He stepped aside, allowing the Jeep to continue.

Heart pounding, Willow stood up, taking a deep breath. She was so nervous; she hated that feeling. Quickly running her fingers through her hair, she made her way down the stairs.

Feeling like a stupid teenager, she tried to decide what to do. Look cool, act normal, sit down, and start reading a magazine. Maybe turn the TV on, like she'd been sitting there the entire time. What?

Standing in the middle of the entryway, trying to decide where to go, she realized it was too late when she heard the engine cut off just outside the door. Heart seizing, she heard a door slam, footfalls on the wooden steps, then finally the porch.

Stepping back toward the stairs, Willow raised herself to the first step, so at least she didn't look like she'd been standing there waiting for Christine to arrive. She already felt like an idiot.

Grabbing the balustrade in her sweating hand, she watched as the door slowly swung open, an overnight bag entering first and being set on the floor just inside. Christine materialized behind it, hair windblown and wild, eyes tired and red.

She closed the door behind her, then turned to see Willow slowly stepping off the stairs. She was about to say hello, but was too overwhelmed with relief that Willow was waiting there for her, was walking toward her.

Without a word, she grabbed her in a hug, eyes closing in relief.

Willow wrapped her arms around Christine's waist, resting her head against sagging shoulders. They held each other for a long time, each surprised at how much she'd missed the other, though it had only been a couple of days.

"You're home early," Willow finally said, stepping slightly back so she could look into Christine's tired features.

"Yeah. I came home tonight 'cause I'll be leaving again in a few days." Christine led the way into the living room where she flopped down on the couch.

"What? Why?" Willow sat next to her, tucking her legs in under her.

"I need to go to L.A., talk to my publicist. I need her to do some damage control now before things start to get out of hand," she explained quietly. Willow nodded sagely.

"I understand." She didn't like it, though. "How was it?"

"Long. Tiring. I've decided that was the longest two days of my life."

"I'm so sorry." Willow wanted so badly to reach out and take Christine's hand, but something stopped her, something in Christine's manner. Her arms were crossed over her chest, closing herself off. Willow gave her her space. As if on cue, short bursts of whining wafted down from upstairs, echoing in the baby monitor placed on the table next to Christine. Willow smiled. "She's calling you."

Christine grinned, ear to ear, and was out of her seat like a shot. Willow stayed where she was, uncertainty filling her. She'd never felt so unsure around her friend, not even when they first met. She sighed deeply, down to her soul.

"Shoot." She smiled through her sadness, listening as Christine talked quietly to Emma, gibberish as well as real speech, and Emma made her cute little noises in reply. It wasn't long before there were creaking footsteps on the stairs and Christine appeared around the corner, babe in arms. She reclaimed her seat on the couch, tucking Emma in the crook of her arm.

She glanced over at Willow. "I think she's grown."

"No doubt. She's growing like a weed." Willow reached out to gently tug down Emma's sleeve, which had gotten pushed up during the baby's journey downstairs.

"Yes, she is," Christine said absently, resting her head against the back of the couch. "Willow," she said, opening her eyes and glancing at her.

"Hmm?"

"I really am sorry."

Willow studied her for a moment, chewing on her lip. "You're sorry it happened, or you're sorry you initiated it?"

Christine's head flew off the back of the sofa, eyes wide in shock. Willow almost wanted to laugh at the way her mouth hung open.

"Careful, Christine," she said softly, "you'll catch flies."

Christine looked straight ahead, trying to get her thoughts and emotions under control. Interesting question, indeed.

"Listen," Willow continued, reaching out this time, in spite of what Christine's body language said. "It wasn't some night on a dark beach, getting caught up in the moment, Christine. You needed me, and I was there for you. I," she took a deep breath, "I don't regret it, and neither should you."

Looking back at her friend, Christine tried to mull everything she'd just been told, to find some meaning and sense in it.

"Willow, no, it wasn't a dark beach. You made your feelings quite clear on that dark beach, though, and I shouldn't have..."

"Honey, what happened the other night wasn't about sex. It wasn't about that. I know that. Believe me, I've thought a lot about this over the past couple of days, trying to decide if I should just let it go, never bring it up again, or what." She shook her head. "I care too much about you to sweep it under the rug like that. I'd say you feel the same way since you brought it up."

Christine nodded. "I do." Willow grabbed her hand, wrapping both her warm ones around it.

"Please don't let this come between us. Please. I'm not scared, and I love you just as much now as I did then." She knew she was jumping the gun on things that hadn't even happened, but she had to get it all out, make Christine aware of just how she felt, and what her fears were.

"Wow," Christine said quietly, looking down at Emma. "Okay."

Willow smiled, scooting closer to Christine and laying her head on her shoulder, both looking down at the baby. She heard the small chuckle as she released the sigh that just wouldn't stay in.

"What?"

Christine shook her head. "Nothing." Kissing Emma on her cheek, she stood. "I'm exhausted." Holding her hand out to Willow, she said, "Come on. Let's put her to bed."

The baby sighed sleepily, eyes never opening as she was put back into her crib and her blanket lovingly tucked under her chin. They both stood, looking down at her, watching her sleep.

"You know, part of me looks at her and thinks just how lucky she is. She has her entire life ahead of her, new things to see and do. All the potential she has, you know?" Christine sighed, then continued. "The other part of me feels sorry for her. All the things she'll have to do, all the things she'll have to live through — heartbreaks, disappointments."

"Yeah. I think about that a lot. I can't help but wonder what she'll be, *who* she'll be. Did I give birth to the first female President? Or did I give birth to the best second grade teacher who ever lived?"

"Either way, she'll be very loved," Christine said softly, resting her hands on the top rail of the white crib.

"Yes, she will." Willow looked up at her friend. "By both of us." Christine smiled. "You know, I can totally see you being the one she'll go to when her first boyfriend dumps her or she gets her first B on a test."

Christine laughed. "Why me?"

"Because you give such great hugs." Willow nudged her in the side, making her laugh again.

"Well, you two can do all that shopping nonsense. And girl talk." She wrinkled her nose.

"Oh, and we will," Willow assured her, leading the way out of the nursery, shutting the light off as she went and leaving the room dimly lit by the Care Bear nightlight. She closed the door to a crack.

Standing out in the hall, between Emma and Willow's doors, Christine gave her a quick hug.

"Good night."

"'Night, Christine. I'm so glad you're home, even if it is only for a couple days."

Christine smiled. "Me, too."

With that, they went their separate ways.

"Is it hard being famous?"

"What?"

"Is it hard being famous?" Willow asked again, laying her magazine face down in her lap, readjusting the pillows behind her and glancing over at her friend who sat with her back against the opposite arm of the couch, their socked feet tangling now and then.

Christine looked over her laptop, raising a brow.

"It's a simple question. Yes or no."

"It's a bizarre question."

"Perhaps, but I still want to know the answer to it."

Christine gently set her laptop aside, having a feeling that this was not going to be a quick question/answer session.

"What brought this on?" she asked.

"I was just reading about the Brad, Jennifer, Angelina saga, and it made me wonder what they were feeling, having the world's attention on their lives," Willow said, tossing the magazine to the coffee table.

"Ah, I see. Well," Christine blew out, "it's not always easy. Your privacy is thrown out the window, that's for sure. Everyone wants to know every single little itty bitty detail about your life." She scrunched up her face, bringing her thumb and forefinger together to emphasize her point.

"Have you ever gotten fan mail?"

"Of course. I have a lady who lives in this tiny little town in Oregon who goes through it all, sorting it, reading it, that sort of thing. She picks the letters she thinks I would like to read and sends them on to me."

"And the others?"

"She sends them a formatted letter that has my signature on the bottom." Christine shrugged, wiggling her toes.

"You're kidding? All those carnivorous fans out there, so excited that they got a response back from the great Christine Gray, are actually getting nothing but a form letter from some creepy mail lady?"

Christine laughed. "Don't make it sound so harsh. I don't have the time to go through all that mail myself. It would be impossible. I used to," she held up a finger, "I actually used to go through and read each and every one; personally answered most."

"Why did you stop?"

"Well, that was back in the very early days. Heck, I was so stunned that someone had taken the time to write me that I was overjoyed to respond, you know? But then as I got busier, my schedule crazier, and the fans got a bit nuttier and more numerous. It just wasn't possible anymore, and I hired Lindy."

"Do you miss it?"

"Miss what?"

"Having a bit more of a personal connection to your fans."

"Sometimes," Christine shrugged. "The sad part is, no matter how many letters I get, how many I answer or read, I'm still so far removed from them, you know? I feel like I can't be among them anymore. You see, my fans have put me up on such a ridiculously high pedestal over the years that there's no way I can live up to their expectations. If they knew the real me, I'd fall short."

"Oh, I doubt that," Willow said, chuckling softly.

"No, I would." Christine looked sad for a moment. "I read what's said about me, how I'm viewed. I'm expected to either be somebody's wet dream or sex kitten come to life or their role model. I'm none of the above. When it boils down to it, I'm just me. Not too interesting in the end. And *far* too human."

"Well, that's all in who you talk to." Christine rolled her eyes.

"Well, if you live out in the middle of nowhere with only a horse named Star to talk to, yeah, I'm sure I'm all that and a bag of gem doughnuts."

Willow laughed, swatting the singer. "You're such a shoot."

"A shoot? What on earth is a shoot?"

"You know what I mean!" Willow growled, swatting Christine again.

"You know, you keep hitting me like that and I'm going to have to file a domestic violence complaint." Christine raised a brow, and Willow blushed.

"Well, can't say I'm worried. After all, there are some requirements that have to be met in order for it to be called 'domestic violence'," Willow pointed out, proudly shooting down the comment. However, it backfired, as she blushed even deeper at Christine's rakish look. As soon as the look hit her face, however, it was gone, replaced by a look that Willow could only think of as...empty.

"Well," Christine said, closing the subject, "did I answer all your questions?" When her eyes met Willow's, they were the eyes of a stranger, remote and withdrawn.

"Uh, yeah. I suppose so." Willow was confused and slightly hurt. They had been playing, bantering, and just like that, Christine shut down. With a sad sigh, Willow took up her magazine again and pretended to read.

"Everything alright, ma'am?" Troy asked, his curiosity getting the better of him. Willow had been standing in front of the garage, rubbing her chin, for the past twenty-three and a half minutes.

"Mm, fine," she said absently. He nodded and turned to head back to his post. "Troy?"

"Yes, Ms. Bowman?" he asked, turning toward her again.

"How much do you think it would cost to convert this into a studio?" She glanced up at him, still rubbing her chin.

"A studio, ma'am?"

"Yeah. You know, like a music studio, somewhere where Christine could hide."

"Oh." Surprised, he looked at the two-and-a-half car garage, running numbers through his mind. "Thousands of dollars, ma'am. I'd say upwards of a couple hundred."

"Oh," Willow said, heart sinking.

"But that's with all the equipment, too, ma'am. I assume you'd want recording equipment?" he said quickly, not wanting to burst her bubble.

"Well, what about without all that? Maybe just sound-proofing, that kind of thing." She looked at him, hoping he'd have better news for her. He sighed, looking back at the building.

"Well, saying that nothing structural had to be done, that it was sound, that is," he shrugged, "fifteen, twenty thousand maybe."

She tugged the drawer open and began rummaging through the heaps of disorganized papers.

Willow murmured the names of each as she unfolded, uncrumpled, reattached.

"Bank receipt, receipt from Target, credit card statement," on and on she went, frowning in panicked concentration. She was a horrible bookkeeper, and it was at times such as this that she realized just how horrible. Tax season was murder.

Throwing out the last bit of paper, she sighed heavily, running a hand through her shaggy hair. Looking around the small home office, she searched her mind, desperately trying to remember where she'd put it.

Suddenly, light dawned. She raced out of the house praying that it was still there. Quickly opening the passenger-side door of the truck, she pulled herself up onto the seat and yanked open the glove compartment. She rummaged through the contents — maps, insurance papers, napkins from Baskin-Robins, and one last something, folded up, in the back.

Hoping against hope, Willow grabbed it, quickly unfolding it in shaking fingers.

"Yes!"

Christine hadn't bothered to call Millie in. She was only planning to be at the Beverly Hills house for two or three days. She walked its long, empty halls, seeing the beautiful, expensive things that filled its walls and rooms and realizing how meaningless it all really was.

She didn't want to be there. She knew where she longed to be, but the idea scared her half to death. She couldn't understand why Willow was taking things so well, considering how she'd freaked out over a simple kiss so many months earlier. It seemed like a lifetime since that had happened.

Despite everything Willow had said about what happened between them, which she wanted to believe, she was having a hard time with it. The thought had occurred to her more than once that perhaps Willow was just brushing it all under the rug out of pity for the mess Christine had been that night. What if inside Willow really hated her? What if she was just waiting for her to get over Adam's death, before letting on what her true feelings were?

Christine laughed at herself, not truly believing a word of her own paranoia. Another thought stopped her cold, however, as she looked out of the floor-to-ceiling french doors in her music room, hands tucked into the pockets of her jeans.

What if *she* were pulling away because she didn't want this closeness? What if *she* didn't want to open herself up so much to Willow and, in many ways, to Emma? What if *she* was feeling claustrophobic or smothered?

She sighed, running a hand through her hair. That wasn't it, either, and she knew she owed Willow more than that. She couldn't use that as an excuse or use it to justify her own fear.

Fear of what?

Christine turned from the doors, looking back into the room. The sun's rays were making a map across the wooden floor, leading up to the grand piano. She followed the path, brushing her fingers across the smooth surface of her beloved instrument.

That *was* something she was having a hard time with. No, she didn't miss the crowds and the craziness, even if it had followed her into a quiet life, but she *did* miss the music. Oh, she missed the music.

She pulled the bench out from underneath the keyboard and lovingly lifted the lid. She sat down, eyes automatically closing. The soul needed no vision.

Limbering her fingers and hands, she ran her scales, up and down, around, flat, sharp, back again. Flexing her knuckles and listening to them crack, she began to play for real.

Sighing deeply, she knew she was home.

"This is the mess you've gotten us into." The Enquirer skidded across the desk, stopping just short of falling off the edge and into Christine's lap. The headline blared: LOVE ON THE RANCH?

"Bastards," she muttered, seeing a picture of a half-naked and very surprised Willow. "And what do you mean I've gotten us into?"

"Why not you? You haven't given the children anything to play with. You know how they are — they get bored!" Roxanne Mills paced behind her desk, hands clasped behind her back. Flipping her long, curly black hair over her shoulder, she stopped, looking down at her long-time client. "You know how to play this game, Christine. Come on, I shouldn't have to lecture you on this shit."

"Don't start, Roxanne."

"Don't start what? Don't start this?" She poked her finger into the rag. "Don't stay single for so fucking long that the world wonders if you're a real live human? Is that what I shouldn't start?"

"I'm not going to lie and say I'm with someone when I'm not." Christine could feel her anger building. Roxanne stopped, her glare pinning her client.

"Your whole life is a fucking lie!" she barked, sitting down hard in the leather desk chair. "Jesus, you know this shit better than I do! What the hell were you thinking not giving them anything to play with? Jesus, you know they'll just keep digging, and this time, by God, they'll hit fucking pay dirt!"

"How did they find out? I was so careful to keep Willow out of this."

"Careful? You were careful?" Roxanne leaned forward, tapping a clawed finger on the shiny mahogany. "So careful that this woman has been in the news twice, both times linked to you. So careful that you had that fucking hospital locked down like Fort Knox while she gave birth to the kid, you at her side!" She pointed the claw at Christine as she spoke. "Yeah, that's how goddamn careful you've been."

She sat back in her chair, taking a deep breath and regaining her composure. "No doubt one of the hospital staff or another puppy pusher spilled the beans for a nice chunk of change. Bastards probably paid their kid's college tuition," she muttered absently.

"Fine. So I messed up. Now what? Can we fix this?" Christine looked so deeply into the impenetrable black eyes of her publicist that she made the woman squirm.

"I just don't know," Roxanne finally said. She crossed a leg over her knee, carefully tugging at her skirt, the picture of fashion perfection. She was so grateful Christine had introduced her to Sandra all those years ago. "Personally I think you should marry the girl and bring it all out into the open."

"It's not like that, Roxanne..."

"So make it like that, Christine!" the publicist almost yelled, sitting forward again. "You can't go back. Once the 'they're fucking' theory has surfaced on a story, there is no way to remove it. You two are playing house down there in Bumfuck, Oklahoma. Do you really think people are going to believe it's platonic? That the two of you have separate bedrooms, don't burp or fart around each other? Bullshit. I don't believe it," she planted her clawed hand on her chest, "and they sure as hell don't believe it."

Christine sighed, knowing full well that Roxanne was right. The publicist's voice softened.

"The way I see it is this — if you and the cute blonde can't make nice in domesticity, then you'll just have to ride it out, let the hubbub die down. It will eventually, as soon as some new asshole walks into the spotlight, someone who will actually talk to them and do something stupid, like turning into white trash after getting married to some loser with greasy hair and big shoes." She rolled her dark eyes. "Public nightmare."

"What if I moved back to L.A.?"

"So sorry to hear about your breakup. May we get a statement?" Roxanne said dryly, leaning on her hand.

"Shit."

"Stay with her, Christine. At least that way you can stop them from hounding her until all this blows over."

Christine felt a sense of dread fall over her as she played. Her eyes closed, and her head swayed with her hands as they raced across the keys. She felt so horrible for dragging so many innocent people into this — Willow, Emma, hell, even the people of Williamsburg, the tiny town by Willow's ranch. No doubt the bastards were staying there, grilling the unsuspecting citizens about both of them.

Images of Willow began to float before Christine's closed eyes. Her eyes, her smile, her body. The way it had looked as the moonlight caressed it through the large window that night. The way Willow's skin had felt, warm and smooth, so responsive. The little noises she'd made, the rapture in her eyes as she'd found ultimate pleasure.

Christine's fingers moved faster and faster over the piano keys as her heartbeat increased, feeling every sigh, every kiss, every whispered encouragement, all over again.

Was that what it was like with someone you loved? Was that what it was like to feel loved? Is that how it felt to be *in* love?

Shaking that last thought off as quickly as possible, Christine stilled her fingers. Her eyes opened to see the darkness beyond the glass panes of the large doors. *No, no. Can't go there. Can never go there.*

Willow paced restlessly, her hands fidgeting nonstop. Glancing out the window again, she saw the truck still parked directly in front and heard the muffled voices of the movers shouting out orders. Her hand reached for the doorknob, but then she saw Howard from Troy's team looking in at her. He had been assigned to keep her in the house and out of the way, by her own orders. She began to pace again.

It was close, so terribly close. Sneaking a peek at the grandfather clock in the corner, she hissed in worry.

A knock on the front door sent her running toward it, pulling it open so fast she startled the head mover guy. What did he say his name was?

"It's all done, ma'am," he said proudly. "Gotta say, that was one helluva tight space."

"Is it okay? How does it look? Did the trailer work out alright?" she asked, speaking of the climate-controlled trailer the piano had been shipped in, trying to peer around him, as if that would do any good.

"Well, in my opinion, it looks real good." He beamed, his face ruddy from the exertion.

"Thank you so much." Reaching into her back pocket, she pulled out the bank envelope and glanced at him questioningly.

"Oh, ah..." Looking at his order paper, he pulled a small calculator out of the breast pocket of his work shirt and began to punch numbers in with a pudgy finger. He gave her a figure, and she happily dug the amount out of the envelope, plus a hefty tip. That was just about the last of the money, but she didn't care. It was all worth it.

"Thank you, ma'am." He tipped his sweaty hat, handed her the handwritten receipt, and turned away, gathering all his men into the truck, heading out.

Willow hurried up the stairs, bolting into the bedroom at top speed, shucking clothing as she went. The fastest shower in female history later, she was dressed and taking care of Emma, getting the baby ready.

Exactly thirteen minutes after the movers had left, the front door opened, and Christine walked in, carry-on in her hand. She was surprised to see Willow waiting for her, beaming like the Cheshire cat.

"Welcome back!" Willow gushed, hurrying over to her. For a moment, Christine's heart soared, her happiness almost overwhelming. But as Willow got closer, she began to freak, thinking back to the vow she'd made to herself in L.A.

"Hey, uh..." She breezed past her. "Hands are full. Let me get rid of this stuff." Smiling sheepishly, Christine hurried up the stairs. Willow watched her go, shock and hurt in her eyes.

Chapter 16

"Wow. Okay. Bad flight, I guess," Willow mumbled to herself, unsure what to do. Should she follow and ask? Leave her alone? The decision was made for her, as within minutes, Christine was on her way back down the stairs, carrying Emma. She was kissing the baby and making crazy faces and voices at her.

"I think she gained another five pounds since I've been gone," she said as she reached the bottom of the stairs. "Haven't you, you big goober?" Emma squealed and gurgled.

Though touched by the scene before her, it was hard for Willow to respond, the hurt still stinging. When she got no response, Christine looked at her friend, smiling.

"How has your week been?" She passed Willow, heading into the kitchen.

"Uh," Willow said, shaking herself out of her shock of absolutely being avoided, "fine. It was fine. Good, I guess."

"Good." Christine handed Emma off with a kiss to the baby's forehead, then began to dig through the fridge, famished from a long day of traveling.

"And how was your trip? Anything productive happen? Anything you can do?" Willow sat on a barstool with the baby in her arms, watching her friend getting out the ingredients for a sandwich.

"No," Christine sighed, spinning the lid off the jar of Miracle Whip. She licked her thumb as some of the tangy spread smeared on it. "Looks like we're stuck. We'll just have to weather the storm." She finally looked at Willow for the first time since she'd arrived. Willow was looking down and away, focused on some tile or other. As Christine watched, she nodded slowly.

"Sorry to hear that."

"Yeah. Me, too." Turning back to her snack, she angrily flopped a couple pieces of turkey onto the Miracle Whip- and mustard-slathered bread. She was angry, all right, but angry at herself. She could tell Willow was hurt. She wasn't dumb, and Christine had been stupid to think this would work. She'd been home for less than twenty minutes, and already she felt like a schmuck. There was no way in hell she could keep her distance from Willow; it wasn't possible. The woman just had a way of finding the tiniest cracks in the strongest suit of armor and wheedling her way inside.

Damn it!

Slapping the two pieces of bread together, she shoved the plate aside and began to tidy her mess.

"Christine?" Willow's voice, though soft, was filled with such uncertainty. "Are you okay? Did something happen?"

Sighing, Christine leaned against the counter for a moment, head hanging. Finally she pushed off, turning to her confused friend. She shook her head.

"No." Walking over to where Willow sat with Emma, she carefully gathered the two in a warm, all-encompassing hug, feeling a relieved sigh escape her friend. "No," she repeated, inhaling the smells — Herbal Essence and Johnson & Johnson baby shampoo and powder.

Pulling away, she smiled down at Willow, who looked overwhelmingly happy. Christine couldn't help but smile in return. Yeah, how could she *ever* have thought she could push this one out?

Willow listened quietly as Christine ate her dinner and explained what Roxanne had said. "I've screwed myself, basically," she said, around a bite of sandwich. Swallowing quickly, she continued, "It's not going to stop, Willow, until they've found someone else to harass. I hope you understand that I never wanted this to happen."

"I know that," Willow said softly, though a wrinkle had formed between her eyes.

"What are you thinking about?"

"Nothing, really." She sighed, glancing over at Emma, who lay on a blanket on the floor. "It is hard, Christine. I won't lie to you. Sometimes, when I open my front door, see the van, or see Troy or Howard out there talking, walking the perimeter of the place, I feel like I'm a prisoner in my own house."

Christine listened, nodding her understanding. "I know. I'm so sorry." She wanted to reach across the table and take her hand, but she resisted. No, she might not be able to push Willow out, but she wasn't going to torture herself, either. "The only other thing I can do is to leave." She studied Willow's face, looking for any sort of silent answer.

"No." Willow's answer was stern, one word.

"Or not." Christine grinned, secretly relieved.

"We'll face these a-holes together," Willow continued, her jaw set, body tense.

"Okay. So be it."

"And in the meantime..." Willow stood, walking over to the sleeping Emma and gathering her into her arms. "Let me put her down; I have something I want to show you."

Christine shivered at the mischievous grin that accompanied these words, then mentally slapped herself.

"Uh, Willow, you do realize we're outside, right?" Christine said, her words dripping with sarcasm.

"Very good." Willow replied, patting her arm, unfazed. She led her over to the garage, her heart pounding. Producing the key to its brand new, extremely sturdy lock, she carefully slid it into the hole, turning it until the tumblers hit home. Her hand on the doorknob, she turned to look at a very confused Christine. "I hope you won't be mad at me," she said quietly before pushing the door open with her hip.

Wondering what on earth Willow could have done to make her mad, Christine followed her into the garage. It smelled different. Gone were the smells of gasoline, cut grass, and oil. Now there was the smell of polish and paint.

Willow flicked a switch and can lights, sunken into the brand new ceiling, shone down on polished wood flooring and reflected on the white walls, covered in soundproofing material. And they illuminated the greatest gift of all — Christine's grand piano.

She sucked in a breath, taking it all in, stunned, touched deeply, and wanting to cry. "You did all this?" she breathed, stepping further into the transformed garage. She ran her hand over a very familiar piano lid.

"There was just no way for me to afford a new one, or even a used one, for that matter, so uh," Willow explained quickly, trying to get the words out before Christine could get mad, "Joey helped me to get yours shipped here."

"How did you? I was there. I played it until the night I left..." Christine was just amazed by it all.

"I know," Willow rolled her eyes. "It was a nightmare. Joey's girlfriend was spying on you, letting us know when you came and went," she grinned, proud that they'd pulled it off. "Please tell me you're not mad."

Turning her focus to her friend, Christine slowly shook her head. "I can't believe you did all this," she murmured, then remembered there was a question on the table. "No, no, I'm not mad."

She grabbed Willow in a hug so tight, so profound, that Willow almost couldn't breathe from relief and happiness.

"I can't believe you did this," Christine whispered to the top of her head. She gently pulled back, frowning slightly. "*How* did you do this? This isn't cheap. How did you pay for it? Please tell me you didn't hurt yourself..."

"Shh." Willow gently covered Christine's lips with her fingers. "In all honesty, *you* kind of paid for it all."

"Me?" She was totally baffled now.

"Well," Willow blushed, "let's just say I got super lucky at the bank, considering that hush-money check was more than a year old."

Throwing her head back, Christine released a deep, full-bodied laugh as she pulled Willow in for another hug. Willow chuckled along with her, her uncertainty from earlier melting away.

"I can't believe you did this," Christine said again. Stepping out of the hug, she walked around the large room, trailing her fingers across everything, in awe that Willow had managed to pull everything together in a few days. "I almost feel like I'm in an episode of 'While You Were Out'," she joked, tapping a few keys before moving on.

"It basically was that crazy and chaotic, too. The movers with your piano left literally less than fifteen minutes before you got here." Willow leaned against the wall, a soft smile on her lips, delighted that Christine was happy and also pretty damn proud of herself.

"That would explain why your hair's still sort of wet," Christine chuckled, making a full circuit around the room and coming to stand next to her friend.

"Play something for me. That is, if you're not too tired after a long day of traveling."

"Too tired to play?" Christine asked, brow raised. "Never." Grinning, she sauntered over to the piano, easing herself down on the bench, her mind checking through the huge list of titles she knew, including the ones she had written herself.

Willow walked over to her, leaning against the beautiful instrument. She'd never seen a grand piano up close before. When the guys had first taken it off the truck, she had been struck almost breathless by its beauty and grace. Much like its maestro.

The music began slowly, a few keys at a time high up the scale. Soon the momentum built, and Christine's voice joined, soft and sweet.

Willow slowly made her way toward the bench, seating herself next to the singer, drawn, almost hypnotized, by the music and the soft, soothing voice. In that moment she knew she'd done the right thing. To keep this beautiful, talented creature from her music would be a crime.

The song slowly came to an end, and Willow sighed. "It's been settled," she said, voice dreamy. "You can never leave this room."

"Oh yeah?" Christine chuckled, playing randomly, her heart filling with joy, knowing that this was hers, that any time she wanted, she could come out here, play, compose, be alone, create. For her, a day without creating was a day not worth living. Somehow Willow had known that. What an amazing gift.

Deciding to give something back, she began a different song. Willow listened to the words, and suddenly she let out a small gasp.

Her eyes filled as she looked over at Christine, who was already looking at her, singing about a little girl, so filled with life and joy, a joy that made her feel whole. A little girl who had come into her life, giving her a whole new reason to live and love.

"You wrote a song about Emma?" Willow whispered. Christine nodded, continuing the song. Tears freely running down her cheeks, Willow continued to listen, hearing just exactly what the baby meant to the singer.

Christine was worried at first, unsure whether Willow would think she was nuts for writing the song or would be angry for some reason. Seeing the expression on her beautiful face and the tears in her green eyes, she felt her heart swell. Again. What she didn't reveal was that the song was for Emma *and* Willow.

"There she is! Oh, give me some sugar," Mary Washington took Emma gently away from a grinning Willow, rushing the baby down the hall to show to every single staff member on the floor.

"You know you will *never* see Emma again, don't you?" Dr. Benjamin Keele laughed.

"Eh, I know where Mary works," Willow grinned at him.

"How are you feeling? Ready to come back Monday?" he asked, leaning against the nurses' station counter.

"Yes, actually, I am. I mean, don't get me wrong, I'm going to miss my daughter like crazy, but I'll be glad to get back into the swing of things, you know?" She watched as a group of nurses and orderlies oohed and ahhed further down the hall, Mary in the middle of it all, holding on to the three-month-old for dear life. "I was glad to get the extended leave, though."

"My wife would have loved to have a twelve-week leave with Brian, our first. But by the second and third, she was ready to go back to work by the next day." They both laughed, Willow only now understanding the truth behind those words. She absolutely loved staying home with Emma, and with Christine for that matter, but she was starting to feel unproductive, as though she wasn't bringing anything into the household, and that bothered her.

"How old are your kids now, Ben?"

"Oh, let's see," he stared up at the ceiling, mentally calculating. "Brian will be twenty-two this year, Kathryn fifteen, and Kelsey will be twelve."

"Twenty-two," she whispered absently, watching her baby being passed into another set of arms as more staff gathered. "Wow. I can't imagine that."

"It goes fast. Trust me." Ben looked down at his pager, which was vibrating against his hip. "Got to run. It was great seeing the baby again, Willow. See you Monday."

"Bye, Ben."

"Did she like it?" Rachel asked, stuffing her mouth with salad drowned in Italian dressing.

"She loved it," Willow grinned, eyes sparkling. "You should have seen her. She was like a kid in a candy store. So adorable. And, oh! I haven't even told you the best part yet."

"What's that?" Rachel popped a crouton into her mouth, crunching it loudly.

"She wrote a song for Emma."

"No!"

"Yes. It's so beautiful. It's called 'My Angel'. I started to cry. I don't know," she put a hand to her chest, trying to find the words. "Nothing has ever touched me like that. She really loves my baby, and that makes me so happy and so relieved, you know? Like if something ever happened to me, I know Christine would take care of Emma."

"Wow." Rachel whistled. "That's a whole ton of trust."

"I know and from someone who doesn't trust easily." Willow sipped her water, smiling at a nurse who passed by their table in the hospital's cafeteria.

"What about the other stuff?"

"What other stuff?"

"You know, the-night-before-she-left-for-New-York other stuff."

"Oh." Willow put her bottle down, swallowing before she answered that loaded question. "We've talked about it. I flat told her that I was just being a friend for her, that there were no worries or reasons to be afraid. I didn't hate her, didn't judge her. I told her it was beautiful and we should leave it at that."

"What did she say?"

Willow shrugged. "Not much." Leaning her chin on her hand, she watched as Rachel mixed her salad around some more, then stabbed a forkful and put it into her mouth. "I sense something's off, still. I don't know. I can't really put my finger on it." Her face scrunched up as she thought about it.

"Like what?"

"Well, she's been back from California for a few weeks, and things are great. I mean, we get along as wonderfully as we always did, and she adores Emma, plays with her, offers to feed her, change her, you name it. She plays a lot, out in her little music room. She's so cute," her smile returned. Rachel watched her carefully. Something was missing from Willow, and she couldn't quite figure out what it was.

"Trouble in paradise, huh?" She put her fork down, wiping her mouth with the cheap paper napkin.

"I don't know." Willow looked down, glancing over to see Mary and another nurse holding Emma, chatting quietly. It had taken a great deal of coercion for her to allow the two other women to keep hold of her daughter.

"Sure you do. Out with it."

"She's so distant," Willow said, a rushed almost whisper which fell out of her mouth before she even had time to think about it.

"What do you mean, 'distant'?" Rachel pushed her bowl away and took up her wrapped cookie dessert.

"Well, physically. Christine is actually a very affectionate person, very physical. Hugs, playful nudges, a quick squeeze in passing. Things like that, you know?"

"But not so much lately?"

"Not so much, no. It seems that even if I *look* like I want a hug or am getting too physically close to her, she either steps away or magically has something already in her arms. Often times it's Emma." She nodded toward the other table.

"Interesting. And this started when she got back from New York?"

"No, more when she got back from Los Angeles. I don't know. That first night was really bad. I mean, I wanted to cry, but it was almost like something clicked in her head, and she was basically normal. I figured maybe she'd had a bad visit with her publicist. I mean the news wasn't good."

"Right."

"She was so wonderful when I showed her the music room, full of hugs." She smiled at the memory. "God, that woman can hug."

"Among other things," Rachel snickered, earning herself a glare.

"But, after that night, again it was like something flickered inside her, flickering off this time. She keeps her distance now. Hugs are few and far between. She'll sit on the couch with me, but curled up against the opposite arm."

"When she does that, do you curl up against *her*?"

"I did once, and she let me, didn't move away, dangled her arm over my shoulder. But I don't do that anymore."

"Why not?" Rachel offered her a piece of her gooey cookie. Willow studied the treat, finger poking at a particularly large chocolate chip.

"Because I'm not about to force her. If she needs her space, wants her space, whatever, who am I to take it?"

"Hmm." Rachel sighed, staring at her own cookie for a moment, thinking. "Wills, I don't want to hurt you with this question, but I have to ask it."

"Okay." Willow felt her heart stop.

"Do you think maybe she doesn't want to be there? Maybe she wants to leave but doesn't know how to tell you?"

"No, I don't. I've thought about that, too. A lot. But I watch her, see how she is with the baby, with the ranch, Star. Heck, even with *me*. I honestly don't think that's it. I just don't know. It's like it deals with me specifically."

"Ah hah."

"Do you think it's me? Did I do something wrong?"

"Well." Rachel thought about it for a moment, going over any and all information she had about Christine and any and all events that had happened between them.

Willow turned her attention back to her chunk of cookie, unable to look at Rachel for fear of what she might see.

"I think she wants you."

"What?" Willow choked on the bite she'd taken, spitting it out into the palm of her hand. Rachel grimaced.

"Yuck."

"You're nuts."

"No. I really think that's it. I think she wants you, and it scares her to death."

"I just don't know, Rach."

"What's to know? Think about it, Wills. I want you to watch her, catch her looking at you. Watch as she watches you walk away, stares at your breasts. Whatever."

"I don't think that's it," Willow insisted. Rachel shrugged.

"Then I'm at a loss. We'll just have to agree to disagree on this, 'cause I know I'm right." Rachel began to gather her trash, piling it all on the orange plastic tray. "You done?" she asked, tapping Willow's water bottle. At the nod she got, she tossed it on top of the heap. "I have to get back to work. Man, getting used to these days is kicking my butt."

Standing with her friend, Willow nodded absently, only partially hearing what Rachel said. Her mind was focused primarily on Rachel's words and Christine's actions.

"Huh?" she said, realizing she'd missed something.

"I said, how do *you* feel? What do you want for this happy, albeit strange, little family you've got going?"

"I don't know," Willow said miserably, walking next to her friend as they headed back to the ER. "To be perfectly honest, I'm very confused." She pulled her to the side, ducking inside a cavernous doorway. "It's like I think about that night sometimes, Rachel. I know it was under extremely painful and stressful circumstances for her, but I have never felt so loved during sex in all my life. It was like, yes, my body was loved, it felt good, all that stuff. But," she paused again trying to find the words that so often eluded her where Christine was concerned, "it was all of me, like she reached inside my chest, grabbed my heart, and squeezed as hard as she could until it almost hurt. Somehow I don't think my heart has ever been the same."

Rachel studied Willow for a long time, looking deeply into her eyes, into her soul even, Willow thought.

"Willow, I want you to think about this, and I want you to think about it long and hard. In my personal, professional, medical opinion, your heart hurts because you're in love with her, and you're afraid, unwilling, or unable to tell her how you feel. I don't even know if *you* fully understand it. Also in my personal, professional, and medical opinion, I think you two belong together." She paused, waiting for the reaction, mentally trying to remember how many bandages and bottle of aspirin she had at her station were she to need them. When Willow said nothing and no body parts began to fly, she continued. "I think if anything is to come of this, if anything is to happen, it's going to have to be because *you* start it. I don't know what that *it* is; that's for you to figure out and decide. But she's afraid, and I don't think she'll *ever* fully admit what you mean to her."

"You're serious, aren't you?"

"Completely."

Willow sighed, nodding. "I heard you, everything you said. I just don't know. It's nothing I can think about or decide right now."

"I know," Rachel gave her a quick hug. "I know whatever you do, it'll be the right thing for you both. Now," she stepped back into the hallway, "I have to get going. Go find your baby." With a quick smile, she was gone.

Willow used the few minutes she had alone to think, walking down the halls with her hands stuffed into her pockets. Rachel's words rattled around her brain, and she tried to catch one now and then, like a Venus flytrap snapping for a morsel of truth. She thought about Christine's behavior and, trying to be as objective and unemotionally connected as possible, she wondered if just maybe Rachel were right.

Christine seemed to walk on eggshells around her, though she didn't treat her any differently in any other way. They still joked, talked endlessly. She still felt that bond and connection with her, but she also felt that Christine was very obviously limiting physical contact between them. She honestly didn't think it was Christine's fear anymore of having hurt Willow or overstepped her bounds that night. She felt they had discussed that as openly and honestly as possible and felt good about it.

And how did she feel about Christine? She loved her, of course. That was easy enough. Could she imagine herself and Christine living the way they were now? Basically as best friends who happened to be roommates? And who just happened to be raising a baby together? Somehow Willow couldn't see Christine moving out any time soon, if at all. The singer was happy, that much she knew.

Okay, so they had the cohabitation thing down. They got along completely, rarely disagreed, and if they did, they always managed to find some way to get around or through it.

That left physicality.

Willow by nature was an extremely affectionate person. She couldn't live without that kind of contact, and she knew it. Okay, so say Christine started acting like her old self the next day, and Willow got her daily dose of hugs, squeezes, and pats. Would that be enough to sustain her?

This was a niggling question. No, it wouldn't, but at the same time, she absolutely could *not* see herself going out and finding some random guy to fool around with and get her kicks with. Did that have to do with Kevin? Perhaps she wasn't totally over him?

Willow grimaced with a small growl.

Okay, moving on. Making love with Christine. Willow smiled, her arms crossed over her chest, almost as if she were hugging herself. She didn't feel ashamed at the thought or the memory, but curiously excited, curious, anticipatory. Willow's instinct was to shake that thought off in revolt or dismiss it as just plain lunacy, desperation, and loneliness.

But somehow that didn't seem right. In fact, it seemed dead wrong. She cleared her throat, which helped to clear her mind.

Okay. Can you imagine yourself having sex with Christine again?

Willow waited for the answer to come to her.

No. What I can see is my making love to her. Bringing her the peace that I did last time.

She was surprisingly calm at this revelation. She also now realized that the idea had slowly been growing within her for some time now. Everything that she had taken as one thing had in actuality been something entirely different. What she'd taken for her nervousness at this famous woman visiting was actually nervousness at *Christine* visiting. When her heart rate increased and her mouth went dry, which happened so often, it wasn't the flu, or a cold, or hot flashes, or any other crazy explanation she had managed to come up with. It was because Christine was near, was next to her, or was due to arrive. It was all about Christine.

Okay, so the physical was taken care of. What about the rest of it? Was that something she could handle? What people thought of her? She was no dummy and knew how cruel people could be. Yes, she was afraid of what people might think of her. She'd worked long and hard to be a liked, respected member of the community and hospital. Would that change?

Looking around as she walked, passing fellow staff, some of whom she knew, most whom she didn't, she couldn't help but wonder. She had been very pleasantly surprised after the article had broke about her in Texas with Christine and when the picture of her half-naked body had appeared on the cover of that magazine. Most of the people who asked about it did so out of genuine curiosity. She had not been judged or whispered about. Well, not that she knew of, anyway.

Was it worth it?

Willow sighed, her head hurting from so much thought. She gathered up her daughter and escaped into the mid-May afternoon. It was beautiful out. She wished Christine was with her, so they could take Emma to the park.

She contemplated calling the house, but she didn't want to attract attention after the recent mess in the press. So she just went home.

Christine rested her hands on her thighs, her head hanging in defeat. The music wasn't coming to her tonight. No, it wasn't just that; the music was *tormenting* her, coming within inches of her creative fingers and then laughing evilly as it receded into the darkness. She growled and got to her feet, the piano bench screeching as she shoved it back.

"Damn it!" she yelled to the empty room, throwing her pencil, watching it hit a wall and "tink" to the floor. She paced like a wild animal. Glancing out the window, she saw that night had fallen. She'd been at it all day, every day, for the past week. It wasn't coming to her. It was really pissing her off.

She was also hiding. She didn't like to admit that part to herself. She was scared. How could one woman, all one hundred and twenty pounds of her, scare her so badly? But she did.

She was getting short tempered and fidgety. She was unable to concentrate on her music. It was as if her muse had gone on vacation. She was frustrated, damn it!

"I can do this!" she growled, seating herself at the keyboard once more. She gritted it out again. "I *can* do this."

Willow looked down at her daughter, bundled into the baby seat in the back of Rachel's car.

"You know, we can do this another time," Rachel suggested.

"No." Taking a deep breath, Willow took a step back, the cool night air caressing her face. "I can do this."

"She'll be fine."

"Of course she'll be fine." Willow smiled, although she didn't believe it for a moment. "You have all the bottles? Prepared? Remember, test them on your wrist, don't make it too hot..."

"Willow!" Rachel took her friend by the shoulders, shaking her lightly. "She'll be fine, okay? For God's sake, I'm a nurse. And I do have nieces and nephews, you know. I know what I'm doing."

"Okay." Willow nervously ran her hands through her hair. "I can do this, and Emma will be fine." Rachel smiled, taking her friend into a hug. Willow clung to her for a moment, shivering. Rachel wasn't sure if it was from the chill night air or not.

"I support you," she said into her friend's ear before giving her a soft kiss on the cheek.

"Thank you." Willow's smile was genuine for the first time that evening. "Now go before I change my mind."

"You got it." Rachel closed the back passenger door, then walked around the car to the driver's side. Willow waved at her sleeping daughter through the window. Slipping behind the wheel, Rachel called quietly out to her friend. Willow looked at her. "I want a full report!" she hissed. Willow rolled her eyes and waved them off.

Christine reached up and drew some notes on the score, flipping the pencil around to erase a mistake, then flipped it back around to make more marks.

Clenching the pencil between her teeth, she played everything she had written all in one shot. Stopping midway, she applied eraser to paper once more, rubbing out a really bad chord choice. As she did so, she heard the baby monitor that rested next to her sheet music crackle to life.

"Christine?"

She pushed the button for hands-free walkie-talkie mode. "Yeah?" she asked, penciling in a quarter note.

"Could you come upstairs for a minute? I'm having a wee bit of trouble in the main bathroom."

"'Kay. Be there in a minute," she muttered, slightly irritated; the song was finally starting to come together. Finally with a sigh, she headed out. Figuring she was probably finished for the night, she flicked the switch, shrouding the music room in darkness.

The night was surprisingly chilly for May, and Christine felt goose bumps erupt across her arms. She mounted the stairs to the porch, her shoes making hollow thuds, echoing in the quiet night.

"Willow?" she called out, closing and locking the front door behind her.

"I'm up here."

"Who was here earlier?"

"Rachel stopped by for a couple minutes."

Nodding in acknowledgement, Christine made her way up the creaky stairs. She wondered if there were some way to fix the noise without rebuilding half the house. But then again, it would come in handy as Emma got older.

"What's up?" she asked, pushing open the bathroom door. The question died on her lips when she saw the flicker of candlelight. The room was filled with candles, all aflame, the only light in the room. She also smelled roses, the smell drawing her attention to the Roman tub. It was filled with steaming water and had hundreds of rose petals floating in it.

The door softly clicked closed behind her. Turning, she saw Willow holding a fluffy white towel in her arms, a smile on her face.

"Alright, you," she said, laying the towels on the toilet lid, and walking over to a stunned Christine. "I want you to get in that tub, close your eyes, and relax." She took the pencil out of Christine's limp hand, gently laying it on the counter next to the sink. "Come on," she encouraged when Christine didn't move. She gently nudged her to the edge of the tub, pushing on her shoulders. Christine sat, looking up at Willow as if she were nuts.

"I don't want to see you for at least an hour. You understand me?"

Christine nodded dumbly, watching as Willow made a silent exit from the room, closing the door behind her. Feeling as though she'd just been hit over the head, she looked around the room, noting all that Willow had done. She smiled when she saw the disc player in the corner, next to the tub, a stack of her favorite CDs on top. Next to that was a small pile of magazines and the novel she had been reading.

A long, slow sigh escaped from between Christine's lips as her body slipped into the water, which was just the right side of too hot. Her entire body in, water reaching to the tops of her breasts, she knotted her hair back and rested her head against the inflatable pillow Willow had suctioned to the porcelain.

The music of Delirium filled the room. "Lamentation" began its more than eight-minute run, sinking into her bones. The sensuous tones brought chills to her flesh, making her grateful for the hot water.

The tension between Christine's shoulders slowly began to release, her muscles relaxing, her hands floating limply atop the water, toes curling and uncurling as pleasure rippled through her. A rose petal tickled her breast as it lazily floated by, drawing a smile.

As the music began to build, its incredibly sexy beat took Christine with it. She closed her eyes, sighing deeply as she imagined Willow before her closed lids, her body moving sensuously in time with the music, her hands slowly running down her own body, and her eyes locked onto Christine's, beckoning her, daring her, *wanting* her.

Christine's body was on fire; the mere thought of the gorgeous woman nearly wiped her out. The images were so real, so raw, that if she had not known any better, she would have thought Willow was in the room with her, sliding her hands down over Christine's wet skin, dragging her nails back up.

She shivered, whimpering quietly as the frustration she had begun to lose slowly began to build once more, right dead center between her legs. She had been fighting the attraction to Willow for...well, in truth, for months now, but consciously, for weeks. She had always felt a connection to Willow, a bond, but she'd always been more than fine with the physical aspects. Yes, Willow was a very beautiful woman, but other than that one indiscretion on the beach, Christine had been fine with it. Really.

Until *that* night.

That night, everything had changed. Everything. Now she couldn't get Willow out of her mind. She had no idea what to do about these feelings. They were new to her, and she was trying to run from them.

But God, the way Willow's body had felt against hers... Shaking herself out of her lustful daze, she reached down and grabbed her novel, doing her best to distract herself and ignore her body's pleading for some release. She was in there to relax, not get more keyed up.

Over an hour later, Christine wrapped herself in one of the huge, soft towels Willow had left for her. She blew out the candles, filling the small room with smoke, and opened the bathroom door. Feeling something soft and cool under her bare foot, she looked down and saw more rose petals.

After a moment, she realized they were in the shape of an arrow, an arrow that was pointing toward Willow's bedroom. Curious, she followed it and found the bedroom door slightly ajar. Inside, she could see, was more flickering.

"Come on in," Willow said, her voice soft on the other side of the door. Swallowing hard and fighting the very strong urge to run, Christine pushed the door open the rest of the way.

At first Willow was nowhere to be seen, so Christine concentrated on the scattered candles, the bed, turned down to the fitted sheet, and a tray resting near the pillows with various bottles on it.

"Come on, don't be shy," Willow said, suddenly appearing from around the door. Christine's eyes widened, taking in the silky gown she wore, reaching to not quite mid-thigh. The spaghetti straps showed off her strong shoulders as the candlelight played across them. She tried not to stare at Willow's full breasts, hugged by the satin.

"Uh, what's going on?" she finally asked, meeting Willow's eyes.

"Come on." Willow took her hand, ignoring her question. She pulled Christine to the bed, where she was instructed to lie down on her stomach. Doing as asked, she felt the soft sheets beneath her overheated skin. Glancing at the tray of bottles not far from her head, she saw that they were all types of massage oil. "Relax," said a gentle voice, and a hand on the back of her head gently pushed it toward the pillow.

Christine tried to do just that, but it was proving quite difficult. She felt the mattress give under Willow's weight as she kneeled next to her.

"Lift just a bit."

Christine did, panicking for a moment when she felt the towel wrapped around her very naked body being pulled out from under her. When Willow just brought the terry cloth down a bit to reveal her back, she relaxed again, but just a little.

Strong hands gently pulled her hair out from around her neck, making her shiver again. She closed her eyes and tried to "see" with her ears. She heard the silky material of Willow's gown whispering as she reached over her to pick up one of the bottles. There was a squirting sound and then the sound of the palms of Willow's hands being rubbed together to warm the oil.

Christine's mind wanted to scream for her to end this, to run far, hide, and not have to face this, but she couldn't move. She was unable to do anything but lie there, feeling those warm hands moving on her back, smoothing the slick oil into her skin.

"You've been so tense lately," Willow said softly, a softness at odds with the strength in her hands which coaxed a small moan out of the singer with their expert touch.

"Hmm," Christine said in response, making Willow smile. "You're good at this."

"Well, luckily for you one of my instructors in nursing school was a strong believer in us getting certified in massage therapy. It helps with patients who are bedridden or too sick to get up and walk around. You see," she explained, rubbing more oil into Christine's skin, "keeping the blood flowing helps to maintain muscle tone, as well as the use of limbs. Things don't cramp up."

"Mmm," Christine purred as Willow hit a particularly tense spot. "Smart move," she groaned.

Willow looked down at the gorgeous skin beneath her hands and the muscles of Christine's upper back, her hands wandering over them, feeling them, caressing them. Her eyes and her hands wandered a bit, to the lower back, nudging the towel until it rested just above the singer's beautiful backside.

"God, that feels good," Christine whispered into the pillow, her fingers relaxing from the fists she'd had clenched at her sides.

"I'm glad," Willow whispered, her hands moving back up Christine's sides, fingertips barely grazing the skin, gently pushing her arms up and out. Her eyes roamed unabashedly down her spine. "Relax," she breathed, blowing the words across Christine's skin and making her shiver again.

Willow's hands, which had been kneading the skin of Christine's shoulders and upper arms, now traveled down, over the upper back, her nails dragging down the spine, then slowly worked their way back up to her shoulders and across. She smiled when she heard another soft moan breathed out.

Taking this as a good sign, she shifted her nails to fingers, gliding over the slick skin, daring to dip down, brushing ever so lightly against the rounded curve of the outside of Christine's breasts, making her gasp quietly.

Willow moved down the bed, her fingers massaging their way down, gliding over Christine's covered backside, down to the backs of her thighs, her hands finally coming in contact with naked skin again at the backs of the knees. Rubbing more oil into her hands, Willow brought them to Christine's calves, feeling the muscles there flexing under the skin as her body tensed and released, tensed and released.

"Relax. I'm not going to hurt you," she whispered, smoothing the tension out of the calves with a stroke of her hands. Moving off the bed completely, Willow concentrated her effort on Christine's feet, lifting one off the bed, watching the hamstring flex with the movement. She rubbed her thumbs into the balls of Christine's foot, making her groan louder and flinch slightly at the bit of tickle she felt.

Willow looked up the length of Christine's body, amazed once again at what a truly beautiful woman she really was. A perfect specimen.

"You are such a beautiful woman, Christine," she said softly, moving to the other foot, her movements slowly turning more into caresses than massage.

"Thank you," Christine whispered, her eyes never opening.

"I remember that first concert of yours I went to, the one that Rachel went to with me." Her hands slid up the right calf, fingers pressing here and there, thumb caressing in their wake. "Looking up at you on that stage, seeing how crazy all the women went. Wow," she breathed. "Amazing. I understood why they screamed hysterically." Willow smiled slightly, her nails tracing the backs of Christine's knees. The singer whimpered softly, eyes opening just a bit. "So beautiful. So sexy."

Willow's hands found the backs of the singer's thighs, tracing the strength beneath the softness, running further up, brushing under the towel, to where the rise of a beautiful backside met her exploring fingers. Finally they were filled with the flesh of Christine's buttocks, squeezing, kneading, cupping. She watched the movements under the towel, mesmerized.

Christine let out a long breath, doing her best to not open her thighs. She realized, suddenly, that the towel was gone, that the cool air in the room was washing the entirety of the back of her naked body.

Willow climbed back onto the bed, slowly, deliberately, one thigh stretching across Christine's. She slowly lowered herself until she was sitting astride Christine's backside.

Christine groaned when naked wetness grazed her own skin; Willow wasn't wearing panties, she realized.

"So lovely," Willow whispered, her hands caressing the skin of the singer's hips, trailing back up her sides, fingernails blazing a trail across the sides of her breasts again. She leaned down, her own, satin-covered breasts grazing Christine's back, nipples hardening at the contact. "Turn over, baby," she whispered into Christine's ear, laying a gentle kiss on the back of her neck.

Willow lifted herself slightly as she felt the body beneath her turn. Lying on her back, Christine looked up at the goddess straddling her, at *Willow*, her breasts heaving with every excited breath she took.

She gazed down that satin-covered body, seeing bare thighs, resting her warm hands upon them.

"You're the beautiful one," she whispered, knowing now that she had lost the battle, the war, everything. There was nothing she could refuse Willow, and she was tired of trying.

Willow smiled, her hands resting on Christine's stomach, feeling the muscles contract under her touch. Her hands moved up over soft, supple, and beautiful skin. Her fingers found the full breasts with rigid nipples.

Christine hissed, eyes closing as Willow palmed her. The blonde was fascinated by the other woman's reactions to her. She watched as Christine arched up into her hands, a small whimper escaping as Willow held the nipples between her forefinger and thumb, squeezing, twisting, testing.

Strong hands glided slowly up Willow's thighs, under her negligee, up to her hips, which had started a very slow rocking movement, matching that below her. She closed her eyes, feeling her sex come alive as it slowly pressed against Christine.

Those hands didn't stay on her hips long. Soon they were gliding up her stomach, then up over her breasts. Willow's head fell back; her nipples so sensitive. Christine's lips were suddenly on her exposed throat, and Willow wasn't going to miss a chance.

Bringing her head down, she caught Christine's mouth, wanting to devour it, but stopping herself. She wanted this to be special, something they'd both remember for as long as they lived, no matter what happened tomorrow.

She held her forehead against Christine's, their lips a hair's width apart.

"I love you, Christine," she said. "I'm *in* love with you."

"Oh, Willow," Christine breathed, her hands caressing the side of Willow's face. "I've tried to fight it, to push you away, but I can't anymore."

"Don't."

"No. I love you, too."

Willow smiled against her lips, feeling the gesture returned, then gently brushed her lips across Christine's, feeling them respond and move against her own. Slow open sweeps of their mouths, brought their breasts together.

Christine grasped Willow's hips and pulled them further into her own, making her gasp.

"I'm scared," Christine whispered, flicking her tongue against Willow's upper lip.

"Oh," Willow sighed, "I am, too. But you're worth it." She deepened the kiss, sighing into Christine's mouth as their tongues met. She was lost, heart, body, and soul.

The cool night air kissed her skin as her negligee was lifted up and over her arms and her naked breasts pressed fully against Christine's. She still couldn't get over how soft she was — her breasts, her skin, her lips. Everything a man wasn't. The difference was intoxicating.

Christine fell back onto the bed, pulling Willow with her, their kiss never breaking. Rolling them over, she lay between Willow's legs, which wrapped around her.

Bringing a hand up, Christine cupped one of Willow's breasts, making her moan into her mouth. Moving her hips a bit, she moaned again. Christine reached down, gently nudging her legs far apart, then reached between their bodies and gently stroked Willow's sex with her fingers, which were instantly wet. Opening herself up, she shifted until her own swollen clit moved against Willow's.

Willow gasped, clutching Christine to her. She had never felt anything like this; pleasure ripped through her, intense and wet.

Bringing her hand back up, Christine painted Willow's nipple with her fingers. Hips moving slowly, she bent down, snaking her tongue out, swiping across the pebbled flesh, making Willow cry out. She took care not to suckle, since Willow was still nursing, but she licked away every drop of the woman's desire.

Willow's back arched, her body on overload.

Hips moving faster, Christine returned to Willow's mouth. The kiss was deep and passionate, and they both panted as their pleasure grew, so close to the breaking point. Eyes opening and pulling back a bit, Christine looked down at Willow, seeing her face flushed, lips glistening, mouth open.

Willow's green eyes slowly slid open and looked so deeply into Christine's that she felt their connection to her core. Willow's breath came in short bursts as she felt her body become engulfed in pleasure, then explode. She cried out, clinging to her lover, unable to catch her breath.

Christine buried her face in Willow's neck as she, too, was lost.

Her hips stilled, and Willow wrapped her arms and legs around Christine, raining tiny kisses along the side of her head and face, her body still pulsing.

Finally finding her way back to the land of the living, Christine lifted herself and placed a gentle kiss on Willow's lips, then began to kiss a trail down her neck, licking the hollow of her throat.

Willow's eyes closed, losing herself in sensation as she felt Christine's hands and mouth everywhere. She was amazed she could still go on. Typically one orgasm wiped her out, but tonight she couldn't have stopped the singer if she wanted to. She just wanted to lose herself in Christine.

Her eyes popped open as she felt her legs being gently placed over Christine's shoulders. She looked down the length of her body and saw Christine's head delivering soft kisses to the insides of her thighs.

She waited in nervous anticipation as she felt those lips nearing her sex, still overheated from a few moments ago. She gasped loudly, and her head fell back into the pillows as a tongue glided its way through her wetness, ending up at her clit, which was sucked into a hot mouth.

"Oh my God," she moaned, her hands finding their way into Christine's hair. She was lost, her body feeling things she'd never known it was possible to feel. It was so intense, almost painfully so. She cried out as Christine's fingers entered her, her tongue still working through her wetness.

Christine murmured happily as she gave Willow as much pleasure as possible, fighting to keep Willow's bucking hips and squirming body under control. She was close, so close. Christine decided to let her have it.

Concentrating completely on Willow's clit, she used both hands to hold her down.

"Christine, oh God, baby." Willow felt as though her mind was becoming separated from her body. It drifted, useless, as the rest of her being began to pulse, building, building, until she cried out, slamming her head back as she exploded once again.

Christine held on for dear life, milking Willow's body for all it was worth, making her convulse a second time, then a third. Only when Willow begged her did she stop, climbing up her lover's body and taking her into her arms.

Willow buried her face in Christine's chest, her breathing still erratic and gaspy. She calmed, hearing the soft words Christine spoke to her, telling her how beautiful she was, how amazing and wonderful.

She pulled back slightly, looking into Christine's face, so beautiful and peaceful. Caressing her cheek, she smiled.

"Thank you," she said, softly kissing Christine's lips and tasting herself there.

"For what?" Christine asked, laying a kiss of her own on Willow's forehead.

"For not running away again." Willow looked deeply into Christine's eyes, wanting her to know that there was no reason to run, no reason to hide. Christine smiled, shaking her head.

"No more. I'm terrified, and I hope you'll be patient with me, but I don't want to run any more." She moved onto her side, holding her head up on her hand, her other hand tracing lazy patterns on Willow's stomach.

"What do you want?" Willow asked, teasing a few tendrils of Christine's dark hair.

"I want to be with you and Emma," she said simply.

"What about the life you've known? The fans, the adoration, the big city? Won't you miss your normal life?"

"Sweetie, this, being here with you, has been the most normal life I've ever had. You give me such peace. I'd be a fool to give that up," she whispered, and they kissed again.

Willow slowly pushed Christine onto her back, situating herself atop her. As their kiss continued, slow and languorous, her fingers moved to once again cup one of Christine's breasts.

"You have such beautiful breasts," she whispered into Christine's mouth. "So soft."

Christine's eyes closed, a soft moan escaping as Willow left her mouth, lips tasting her throat, tongue blazing a fiery trail down between her breasts.

Willow contemplated those marvelous mounds, wondering at their texture and feel. She weighed their heft in her hands, then slowly brought her head down, eyes slipping shut as she sampled the nipple with her tongue. Encouraged by the soft sigh released above her, she tongued the nipple again. Exalting in Christine's response to her touch, she took the entire thing into her mouth.

"Oh, Willow," Christine sighed, her hand gently running through the shaggy blonde strands. Pleasure coursed through her body, gathering smack dab between her legs. She gasped in surprise as she felt a hand insinuate itself between her legs, fingers playing with the hair they found there.

Willow was in tactile heaven as she explored Christine's body — the textures, the nuances, the similarities to her own, and the differences. Feeling hot wetness meet her fingers, she ran them down the entire length of Christine's seam, finding her opening and tucking a finger shyly inside.

"Yes, baby. Go inside, please," Christine moaned, holding her breath as she waited to see what would happen next.

Willow moaned, too, feeling her finger being sucked inside, relishing the tight heat that engulfed it.

Lifting her head from Christine's breast, she looked down at her hand, mouth open in wonder, and watched as her finger slid out, then back in again, slicing through the wetness.

"Incredible," she whispered, slowly pushing back in and adding a second finger. Christine gasped again, her hips bucking as she was filled, her hand reaching down to caress any part of Willow she could reach.

Spurred on, her own heart beginning to race, Willow returned to Christine's breast, experimenting, seeing how her mouth could pleasure this woman she loved so deeply, wanting to swallow all her pain.

Christine felt like she was flying and her body no longer was attached to her spirit. Her hips bucked, and she begged Willow to move faster, arching her back and offering herself up to her, giving her everything she had to give.

When she couldn't take anymore, her world and Willow's collided, and both were blown apart, Christine's cry heralding the blast. Her mind, body, and spirit flew apart, coming back together as a stronger, more whole person.

She lay there, her hand across her eyes as she tried to get herself back together. She felt Willow climb up beside her, hold her, and rain small kisses on her face, lips, neck, back, and lips, wrapping her in safe warmth.

Willow held her, rocking her slowly. She was afraid, for a moment, when she felt wetness where Christine's face was buried against her own neck. Worried at first that she'd hurt her somehow, she knew somewhere inside that that wasn't it. That wasn't it, at all. She held her in silent understanding, vowing to never let her go again. Ever.

Chapter 17

"The sun's coming up," Christine said, glancing out the window. Reaching down to where Willow's head was resting on her stomach, she ran her hand absently through the blonde's hair.

"Mm," Willow responded with a contented sigh from her position between Christine's legs. "Are you tired?" She turned her head, resting her chin on the singer's flat stomach. Christine looked down at her, other hand tucked behind her head.

Christine shook her head. "Interestingly enough, no."

"Me, either."

Christine groaned and growled as she stretched, taking Willow with her as her body arched.

"How *do* you feel?" Willow asked, getting herself settled again.

"Hmm." Christine sighed, thinking, hand still playing. "Happy, content, satisfied. Sore." Willow chuckled at that last one, totally able to sympathize.

"Who knew?" she whispered, climbing up to lie beside Christine and resting her head on her shoulder. "I feel like running out to the streets right now and telling the world how much I love you." She raised her head, smiling down at the beautiful woman smiling up at her.

"I know what you mean. Not entirely sure how wise that would be, but I do understand. Come 'ere." She pulled Willow even closer, wrapping her arms around her, slowly pulling her body onto hers and tucking her head under her chin. Christine smiled, unable to stop it. She felt like a different person, reborn. She felt like writing one of those corny love songs people loved to listen to, finally able to understand the lyrics behind them.

"What are you smiling about?"

Willow was looking at her, a smirk curling up one side of her mouth. Christine shook her head, embarrassed.

"No. It's nothing."

"Bull honkey. After everything we've been doing all night, I see no reason why you'd be suddenly shy." Just to prove her point, she playfully nipped one of Christine's nipples, making her yelp in surprise.

"Alright. I was just thinking that finally all those stupid songs make sense. And all those Meg Ryan movies I hated to watch. I feel like popping 'When Harry Met Sally' into the DVD player."

Willow chuckled, completely charmed. "God, I love you."

"I love you, too."

"We are saps, aren't we?"

"'Fraid so."

"Ah, well," Willow laid her head back down, sighing in utter happiness. "The world will just have to get used to us."

They were quiet, both lost in their own heads, mainly replaying the incredible turn of events over the past twelve hours.

Willow kept seeing pivotal moments in the night — a sigh, a kiss, or a look of rapture on Christine's face. Her body was too sore to repeat any of it, but it still burned at the thought. Nothing could have prepared her for what it was actually like to make love to the woman beneath her.

Yes, their first night together after Adam's death had been amazing. But it paled vastly in comparison to the night and morning they'd just shared. She had never experienced anything like it. Not even with Kevin.

"When is Rachel bringing Emma back?" Christine asked, inadvertently breaking Willow's train of thought.

Willow smiled. "How did you know she was with Rachel?"

"A simple matter of deduction. You wouldn't trust her with anyone else, plus you mentioned Rachel had *stopped by* for a few." Christine's chuckle reverberated through Willow's body.

"Yes, well, I couldn't very well say, Rachel came by to pick Emma so we could be alone when I seduced you, now could I?"

"Might have been fun." Christine pulled her in for another kiss which quickly deepened into something more passionate. However, though the spirit was certainly willing, the flesh was sore and chafed.

Pulling away after some minutes, Willow smiled. "What do you want for breakfast?"

"What?" Willow finally asked, holding the charts she'd just grabbed to her chest. She eyed the doctor suspiciously.

"Well, I'm just trying to figure out who put some Tinkerbell dust in your Wheaties, because, honey, you've been practically floating for the past week," Maureen Halston said with a wide smile.

"Oh." Willow grinned.

"See? There it is again." The doctor leaned against the nurses' station counter, genuinely curious and happy for the sweet woman with the even sweeter baby girl.

"Well, it's...it's just that I'm happy, I guess," Willow said, beaming.

"That's obvious. I think you could power all of Oklahoma City with that megawatt smile you've got going. Come on, tell me your secret."

Willow looked around, making sure no one was listening, then turned back to the older woman who had helped her through so many things, both personal and professional.

"Okay, but you can't tell anyone, Maureen, okay? It's still kind of under wraps."

"Alright." Her face becoming serious, the pediatrician waited.

"I'm in love." Willow beamed.

"Oh, honey! That's wonderful!" She gathered Willow into a quick hug. "Who? Kevin isn't back in the picture is he?"

"Oh, no," Willow waved that idea off. "That ship has sailed. No, it's with someone who is the most wonderful, kind, generous person I've ever met." She couldn't keep the smile from her lips. The mere thought of Christine made her all warm and fuzzy inside.

"That's hard to find."

"Certainly all in one person. Plus, she loves Emma. Heck, I think she almost spends more time with my daughter than *I* do!"

The smile froze on the Maureen's face. "She?"

"Yeah," Willow gushed. "Remember Christine Gray, that friend of mine who was here when Emma was born?"

"The singer."

"Right."

Maureen nodded her understanding. "Well, uh, Willow, I must say I'm happy for you." She gave her another quick hug, then hurried away as her beeper vibrated against her leg.

"Thanks." Willow grinned, almost skipping as she headed to the room of Alex, the seven-year-old boy she had been looking after for the past few days. Even seeing the sick little man, so tiny in a big bed, couldn't dampen her spirits. Nope, she'd found not the fountain of youth, but the fountain of eternal happiness — and oh didn't that constant stream taste good!

She giggled silently at her own naughtiness.

"I can't believe you're doing this, Christine," Rachel said, holding up a ratty old t-shirt. Scrunching her nose, she tossed it to the trash pile.

"Why? It's just a bunch of old shirts and pictures," Christine said, rifling through her file cabinet.

"Well, that may be true to you, but to some fan out there, not so much."

Christine shrugged, about to reply when Willow chuckled, grabbing Christine and Rachel's attention.

"Honey, tell me why when I look at this I see Tiffany singing 'I Think We're Alone Now' in a mall somewhere?" she asked, holding up the old denim jacket with holes in it.

Christine laughed, turning back to the folders of pictures — publicity shots and old music. "That's probably because you did."

"What?" Rachel asked, walking over to her friend, taking the jacket from her hands and examining it. "Tell me you didn't know Tiffany," she said dryly.

"When you're in the business for a long time..." Christine let the sentence die off, a grin on her face. Willow rolled her eyes.

"Don't tell me you knew NKOTB, too?" asked Rachel.

"Who?" Willow asked with wrinkled brow.

"Nice group of boys, actually," Christine said, nodding. It was Rachel's turn to roll her eyes in exasperation.

"Who the heck is NKOTB?" Willow asked, looking from one woman to the other.

"New Kids," Christine said absently, tugging a particularly thick stack of pictures onto her lap and beginning to sort through them.

"Oh."

"I had the *biggest* crush on Jordan Knight," Rachel said, her voice wistful as she hugged the jacket to her chest.

"Who didn't?" Christine mumbled.

"And you actually will admit that, Rach?" Willow grinned.

"Oh, I wouldn't talk, blondie. Which one were you more into — Gunner or Matthew?" Rachel asked.

"I don't know what you're talking about," Willow said, quickly turning away. Christine snickered.

"So do you plan to sign everything?" Rachel asked, turning the conversation back. She started to toss the jacket into the donation pile when Willow tugged it out of her hands and tossed it to the trash pile.

"Wait! Hold the phone!" Christine snatched it back, holding it protectively against her, glaring. "This is *not* leaving this house," she growled.

"Christine," Willow said, her hand back on her hip, "the thing is disgusting. It's worn, halfway ripped to shreds, and you are *not* wearing it in public."

Rachel watched, utterly amused, her head swiveling back and forth between the two women.

"Yeah huh. It stays with me. I have a lot of memories in this jacket." She caressed it lovingly.

"What, of bubble gum angst? Honey, that thing is ancient."

"Then so am I," Christine said, eyes boring into Willow's, daring her to try and take it from her again. Willow sighed, throwing her hands up.

"Fine. Keep it. Whatever."

"Thank you." And just to tick off Willow a bit more, Christine put it on. Willow rolled her eyes but turned back to the pile of clothing she had been going through.

"It's funny," Christine said, moving back to her pile of pictures, "you don't realize how much shit, I mean *crap*, you have until you have it all shipped to you." She chuckled, looking at the boxes scattered around the music room and the clothing draped over her piano.

"Well, that's what happens when you've got a castle to fill," Rachel grumbled, breaking down the box she'd just emptied and tugging her box cutter out of her back pocket to start on another one.

"Castle." Christine snorted.

"Well, I still think it's wonderful that you're willing to donate all this stuff to the hospital's auction, honey." Willow walked over to her, moving the photos off her lap and sitting in their place. Christine wrapped her arms around her.

"Thanks, babe," she said against Willow's lips before taking them in a soft kiss. Rachel rolled her eyes.

"You know, at first it was cute, but now you two just piss me off," she said, opening the flaps of her new box. Christine and Willow looked over at her.

"Why?" Willow asked, absently fingering the neckline of Christine's shirt.

"Because Connor isn't that way with me! Do you really think he and I make out all the time? Hell, even when we were first together we didn't do it as often as the two of you do."

Christine eyed Willow, seeing a very curious blush sweeping her features. The trio grew quiet when they heard a car pull up just outside the building.

Willow jumped from Christine's lap after a quick kiss and walked over to the window.

"Who is it?" Christine asked, taking up her pile of pictures for a third time.

"Not sure. I'll be right back." She made her way outside, knowing that Troy and his agents wouldn't have let this guy in the Cadillac through if he were not important.

"Good afternoon," the man said, slamming the heavy car door closed and shielding his eyes from the bright June sun.

"Hi there. What can I do for you?"

"You know these guys, too?" Rachel whined, holding up a snapshot of Christine with the Rolling Stones.

She chuckled, shaking her head. "No, not really. I just happened to bump into them when I was in London doing a show about ten years ago."

"Wow," Rachel breathed, looking at the picture, her mouth watering as she looked at Mick Jagger, smiling hugely next to the beautiful singer. "Can I have this?"

Christine chuckled again. "Sure."

"Oh, thank you!"

About to run over to Christine and give her a big wet one, Rachel stopped in her tracks as the door of the music room was flung open and a *very* angry Willow came flying in.

"That bastard!" she yelled, her voice muffled by the soundproofing. She threw some papers onto the floor, her face red and tears of anger beginning to fall.

"What is it? Sweetie, what's wrong?" Christine was immediately on her feet, rushing over to her upset lover and taking her in her arms.

"I hate him," Willow cried, clutching Christine.

"Oh, Wills," Rachel sighed, frowning as she read over the papers she'd picked up. "I can't believe he's doing this."

"Who's doing what?" Christine asked, looking at Rachel over Willow's head.

"Kevin's going to try and take Emma."

"What?" Christine's eyes flared, making even Rachel shudder.

"How can he do this?" Willow cried, taking the papers from Rachel's hands and rereading them.

"He's not. We *will* fight this," Christine said, ensuring Willow saw her determination.

"I can't believe this," Willow whispered, tears brimming in her eyes. "He's citing me as an unfit mother — on moral grounds."

"What?" Rachel flew over to her friend, reading over her shoulder. "That's crazy."

"I don't understand," Willow said, shaking her head, looking with pleading eyes at Christine's somber ones.

"I have some calls to make," she said, her voice cold, and sharp. She walked over to one of the boxes and quickly dug through it, bringing out a small, black book, then she was gone.

Willow turned to her friend. "How can he do this to me, Rachel? He didn't even want this baby."

"I know, honey. I'm stunned. Truly, I am. I never figured Kevin to sink this low. And on moral grounds." Confusion filled Rachel's eyes. "I don't get it."

"I honestly don't, either." Willow set the papers on the piano bench, not wanting to look at them another moment. "Come on," she said, taking a deep breath. "Let's get all this cleaned up."

Willow felt her palms sweating and wiped them on her jeans. She swallowed, glancing at her watch. It was eleven-thirteen, and the plane was due in at a quarter after. Soon.

She walked around the baggage claim area, trying not to pace, but failing. Finally, at twenty after, as arranged, she raised the sign she'd made the night before.

She looked nervously at the crowd of people gathering in the baggage claim area, the buzz of voices getting louder with greetings and concerns.

"Hello," said a voice behind her, curt and to the point. Willow's turned around to see a beautiful woman standing before her. Her dark hair was long, naturally curly, and swept over her shoulders. Her large, brown eyes were capped by finely arched brows, and her face had a no-nonsense expression. Her white, open-collared button-up was partially hidden underneath a form-fitting dark gray blazer.

Christine got me Bette Porter for a lawyer.

"Hello. I'm Willow Bowman." She held out her hand, which was quickly taken in a cool, well-manicured one.

"Jennifer Barnes."

Willow hid her smirk, tossing the sign with the woman's name on it in a nearby trashcan. The lawyer looked her up and down, sizing her up.

"A perfectly innocent angel. This could work," she said, her voice hard-edged, very confident. With that, she walked over to the luggage carousel, grabbed her rolling suitcase, and breezed past Willow, her head held high and her perfume wafting in the air behind her.

"Okay," Willow breathed, hurrying to catch up.

"Here's the deal, ladies," Jennifer said, leaning over the table where myriad papers were scattered. She stared into the eyes of the three other women at the table in turn. "Nicole will be the 'official' counsel, as I have no license to practice in this God-forsaken state, but it will be me that you all listen to." Her gaze pinned Nicole Martinez to the spot. The other lawyer had already been briefed on this and after some discussion had agreed to be the mouthpiece.

"Agreed," she said, leaning back in her chair.

"Good. Kevin sounds like a real prince. He's going to take the lesbian angle on this and use that to try and take Emma. But," she held up a manicured finger, a grin spreading across her features, "he wasn't counting on me."

Willow gave Christine a worried look, receiving a calming squeeze of the hand in return.

Jennifer turned her doe eyes, which belied an interior as hard as nails, to Willow. "I want you to tell me *everything* about this guy. And I mean everything. I want to know what he was like in the sack. I want to know how many times a day he takes a shit on average. Arguments you had and their running themes. I want his background, family ties, all of it."

"Okay," Willow agreed, blowing out a breath.

"Good. Nicole talked to his attorney this afternoon, and it looks like they're wanting to hit court by the end of the month. That gives us three weeks to prepare for the fate and future of your daughter, ladies." Jennifer stood, tossing her hair out of her face. A very slow, sly smile crept across her lips. "One other thing, ladies." She looked at both Willow and Christine, making sure she had their full attention. "I need to know every little skeleton you have in your closets. No surprises from this asshole, got me?"

"What are you thinking?" Christine asked, after driving for fifteen minutes in complete silence. She glanced across the Jeep at Willow before returning her eyes to the road.

Willow sighed, looking out the passenger window, watching the hot June day pass by. She shook her head, chewing on her lower lip. "I don't know. I just don't know."

"She's good, I promise you that. Only the best, Willow."

"I know." She sighed. "Why does it have to be this way? How is it that I now hate someone I used to love so much?" It wasn't really a question so much as a spoken thought. She felt so sad, her heart so heavy. And angry.

"I don't know, baby. I really don't. It's selfishness on Kevin's part. Perhaps even a way of getting back at you." Christine shrugged, reaching over to take Willow's hand. "I'm so sorry he's doing this to you."

"Me, too. What if he wins? Then what? He knows nothing about babies." She laughed bitterly. "Emma will be four months old on the twenty-second of this month, and he's never even seen her! His damn mother sent me a birth congratulations card, but do you think he could? *No,* that would have been too much goddamn trouble!" Her words got louder with each thought that came into her troubled mind. "He doesn't want to be Emma's father, he wants to control me! Well, fuck him!"

It was a moment before Willow even noticed they weren't moving anymore and that Christine had pulled off the side of the road.

"Hey, hey," she said, pulling Willow into her arms. As soon as she realized she was in Christine's embrace, Willow broke. The tears fell hard and heavy, her entire body shaking almost out of control. She was devastated and so scared. "Shh, baby, I know." Christine squeezed her eyes shut, her own fears rearing their ugly heads. She knew deep down that Kevin didn't stand a chance of taking the baby completely, though...what if?

She couldn't think of that now. She had to be there for Willow and stay strong. She caressed the soft blonde hair, waiting for the tears to abate.

"I swear to you, Willow, I will *not* let him take her from you. I'll do anything in my power, anything at all." Christine pulled back slightly from her, wiping at Willow's tears with her thumbs, ducking a bit so she could look into her face. "Anything. I don't care how much it costs, what it takes, you understand? I love her, too," she whispered, laying a soft, gentle kiss on Willow's tear-streaked lips. She could taste Willow's salty pain. "Anything."

Willow's heart swelled with love and gratitude. Finally she nodded. "Okay."

"I love you."

"I love you, too." Willow hugged her close, taking all the strength that was offered her, holding it close to her heart. "I can't lose her, Christine. I can't."

"I know. I know."

Jennifer looked from Willow to Christine and back again.

"Is there a problem?" she asked, hand on hip, other hand resting on Nicole's desk.

"I can't do that," Willow said, her voice quiet. "Kevin's father's drinking hurt him badly. I can't throw that in his face, Jennifer," she shook her head. "I can't."

Jennifer studied her for a long moment, making Willow feel like she was a lab rat, waiting for either the cheese or the shock.

"I see," the attorney said, her eyes never leaving Willow as she slowly made her way around the desk. "You don't feel right about dragging Kevin's family through the mud and bringing up painful memories for him, is this correct?"

"Well, yeah," Willow said, though she felt like she'd given the wrong answer to a test. She really was not fond of Jennifer Barnes.

"Hmm, well, let me tell you something." Jennifer stood inches in front of her. "While your conscience is eating at you for bringing up a bit of dirty laundry about your ex-husband's father, your ex-husband is trying to ruin your name and question your character and lifestyle. Yes, Ms. Bowman, that's what his case is based on," she said, seeing the shock in her client's eyes. "He's heard of your relationship with Christine, and he's pissed. He's pissed because that's an affront to his manhood, and now he wants revenge. Did I mention he's pissed?" She raised a brow. "How pissed?" She leaned in close. "Pissed enough to take your daughter from you."

Willow gasped, her stomach roiling with revulsion, though she wasn't sure who it was aimed at more — Kevin or Jennifer Barnes.

"He's pissed enough to not give a damn about your feelings. He's not thinking about what this will do to you, Ms. Bowman. No, he's thinking with that thing between his legs. Thinking about his perceived zing." She paused, letting her words sink in. She knew Willow didn't like her, and that was fine. But when it came down to it, she was going to win the case and keep that baby where she belonged.

"I need some fresh air," Willow said, her voice thick with nausea. She made her way out of the small office, sucking in lungfuls of fresh air.

"Honey, what's wrong? What happened in there?" Christine said, hot on her heels. "What's the matter?"

"I don't like her, Christine," Willow almost yelled, turning on her lover. "She's so, so...*mean.*" It sounded childish, but it was the only word that came to mind.

"But she's right, Willow," Christine said softly, resting her hand on Willow's shoulder, She shrugged it off.

"Don't *do* that. My *morals* might be called further into question," she seethed. Christine, stung, looked as though she'd just been slapped.

"What did I do?" she asked, hurt.

"It's because of those goddamn magazine articles!" Willow hissed. "He saw those. He confronted me on the one about Texas, and then no doubt he saw the one of me half naked!"

Christine was stunned, taking a step back, unsure what to do or say. "That wasn't my fault," she murmured, in a daze.

"Wasn't it?" Their eyes locked in a battle of wills until finally Christine slowly shook her head, heartsick.

"And you say Jennifer is mean." With that, she turned and walked away, headed toward the parking lot, digging her keys out as she went. Willow was frozen in a spell of anger, fear, and self-loathing. She couldn't speak the words she badly needed to say, nor could she move to stop Christine from leaving.

So she sat, right there on the stone planter outside Nicole's office building. Still unable to move, she watched the Jeep roar out of the parking lot.

She wasn't sure how long she'd been there when she felt, rather than heard, someone sit down next to her.

"Lovers' quarrel?" Jennifer asked dryly. Willow whirled on the attorney, her eyes blazing.

"Haven't you said enough for one day?" she seethed, her blood boiling at the unaffected expression on the other woman's face. Jennifer looked steadily at her.

"We need to talk, Willow," she said finally, her voice quiet.

"I have nothing to say to you, Ms. Barnes. You're here to do a job, and I know that. Beyond that, I have *nothing* to say." Willow stood, stunned when a hand reached out and tugged her back to the planter.

"Sit down and shut the hell up for a minute."

She was too stunned to do anything else. Once the attorney saw she had her full attention, she continued.

"Listen, you don't care for me, I get it. But what you have to understand is that your best interests are my priority, and if that means playing dirty, I will. Kevin isn't going to hold back, Willow." She looked into her eyes, realizing what a lovely color they were. "He's going to pull every trick out of his sleeve that he can in order to win." She turned slightly on the planter so she was facing Willow directly. "For him it's about winning; it's not about Emma. Understand?"

Willow stared out over the parking lot, sighing. She nodded. "I understand."

"I'm not trying to make you angry, either, Willow. I just need for you to understand the severity of this."

Willow met her eyes, nodded her understanding. "Is he going to take her from me, Jennifer?" The question was very soft and filled with fear. Jennifer smiled a white and brilliant smile that turned her face from beautiful to stunning.

"No," she said simply, but with the utmost conviction.

"God, I hope you're right," Willow blew out, standing up.

"You and Christine really need to stay strong in this. It's going to be hard. I've seen it tons of times."

"Yeah, we will." Willow looked down at her shoes, scuffing at the sidewalk. Jennifer of course didn't miss this.

"Ride skip out on you?" she asked, her voice back to its usual dry tone.

"Something like that." Willow sighed.

"Well, I don't know her. I only met her a time or two at various parties and such. Come on." Jennifer picked up her briefcase and headed toward the parking lot, not even bothering to see if Willow was following. Unlocking her rental car, she noted Willow slowly ambling up to the Taurus. Their gaze met over the top of the car. "Stay strong," Jennifer said, then ducked her head inside.

The open-top Jeep left clouds of dust down the side streets of the outskirts of town. Her flying hair whipping her in the face, Christine plowed down the dirt roads, the Jeep shimmying over the large rocks embedded in them. Her hands gripped the wheel with fists of iron.

She had shut her mind down and was acting on pure instinct — which told her to drive like a mad woman, taking turns at dangerous speeds, two of the Jeep's wheels trying to leave the ground at one point. That had gotten her attention, and she'd taken the next turn slightly slower — but only slightly.

It wasn't working. The harder she pushed at the memory, trying to lose it, the harder it pushed back. The look on Willow's face, her eyes so angry and cruel.

Had it been just Willow's fear talking? Whether or not, the words had ripped into Christine like nothing else. She had no idea what to think. She was doing everything in her power to be there for Willow, hiring the best attorney possible and helping her through this. All for what? To have her entire life thrown back in her face?

Christine bared her teeth, swinging around another curve as the Jeep screeched in protest.

Yes, Willow was angry and frightened, she thought again, but yes, there may have been some damage done.

"She didn't even stop me from leaving," Christine growled, jerking the wheel again, the Jeep shuddering in the new direction. Her leaving hadn't been an act of manipulation, but...if only Willow had done something, *anything*. Surely she didn't really blame her for this?

It was well after dark when the Jeep pulled up in front of the lit farmhouse. Christine cut the engine, then just sat behind the wheel, chewing on her lower lip, her thumb tapping a beat. She glanced up at the house, wondering if Emma was asleep yet. Probably. Then she wondered what Willow was doing.

Guilt flooded her as she remembered driving away from Nicole Martinez's office, stranding her lover. She'd obviously gotten home okay, but still...

With a tired sigh, she hopped down from the Jeep's open cab, taking a step toward the house, then stopping, glancing over at her music room. Needing more time, she headed that direction instead. Unlocking the door, she pushed through, clicking on the light as she did and closing the door softly behind her.

Willow leaned her head against the window seat upstairs, pulling her knees closer into her body. She watched as the woman she loved stepped away from the Jeep, then disappeared into her music room.

She wasn't terribly surprised, but it still hurt — mainly because she knew she was responsible.

She had no clue what to do, whether to go to Christine, leave her alone, go to bed. No, that wasn't an option. She knew that the large bed would be horribly empty that night. Sighing again, she unfolded herself, stood up, and headed out of the bedroom door. She heard quiet noises coming from Emma's room, so she pushed the bedroom door open further, widening the sliver of light on the opposite wall.

"Hey, sweetie," she cooed, looking down at her very alert daughter, laying on her tummy, holding her head and shoulders off the mattress and trying her best to hold herself up on her arms. "Look at you!" Willow gushed, awed and inspired all over again, for about the billionth time that day. "Momma's strong girl."

Chuckling, she wiped away the string of drool that ran from Emma's mouth to the bed, picked her up out of the crib, and headed out of the room toward her own bedroom. She needed Emma close as loneliness closed in around her.

The last notes fading into the darkness beyond, Christine gently closed the piano lid over the keys, running a hand across its polished surface, then standing. Her back creaked as she stretched, making her gasp as a sharp pain settled between her shoulder blades from hours of playing.

Stepping outside, she saw that it was a beautiful night, with stars glittering like diamonds on black velvet. A night for lovers.

Sighing heavily, she opened the front door, closing and locking it, then made the slow trek up the stairs.

She had managed to achieve what she'd strived for — to play until she was too exhausted to think or see straight. Her body wavered, threatening to fall over. The house was quiet. It was past three in the morning. No doubt Willow had gone to bed hours ago, and Emma was sleeping through the night now.

Thinking of the baby, whom she hadn't seen all day, she eagerly tiptoed over to the bedroom, surprised to see her bedroom door fully open and her crib empty. It was not hard to figure out where the baby was. Christine leaned against the door frame that led to the bedroom she now shared with Willow.

Willow lay on her back, head to the side, chest rising and falling in even, peaceful breaths. On that chest was Emma, lying on her stomach, mouth open. A single arm was wrapped protectively around the baby, and Christine felt her heart melt. It was so beautiful to see, so endearing, charming, and painful.

The woman she'd fallen in love with looked so sweet, but her harsh words came back all over again.

Shaking her head, Christine took a deep breath and one last look at the two most important people in her life. Then she slowly turned and headed for the guest bedroom.

Chapter 18

Willow opened her eyes groggily, squinting at the bright moonlight coming into the bedroom. Feeling a warm body curled up within her own, she looked at Emma sleeping peacefully, her cute little baby breaths steady and even.

Looking around, she realized they were the only two in the large bed and felt panicked for a moment. Then she remembered.

"Oh, Christine," she whispered, flopping her head back on the pillow and squeezing her eyes shut again for a moment.

Creeping down the hall, she gently laid the still-sleeping baby back in her crib, tucking the blanket around her and kissing her lightly on the forehead.

"Sleep well, my little one," she whispered, caressing the thickening brown hair. Pulling the door closed to an inch, Willow made her way further down the hall to the door of the guest room.

She remembered a previous night when she had stood in this very spot, wondering, as now, if she should go inside. Knowing she had to, she quietly pushed the door open, clicking it shut behind her.

Christine lay on her stomach, facing away from the door, her breathing even, obviously asleep. Willow wondered how long she'd been there. Padding silently over to the bed, she pushed the covers aside just enough to allow her body to slide under them. She scooted over to the sleeping woman, the welcome body heat surrounding her.

She lay on her side, looking at the mass of dark hair splayed out over the pillow. Within moments, Christine took a deep breath, releasing it noisily as she turned over to face Willow. As if by instinct, she scooted closer, taking the smaller body into her warm arms.

Willow closed her eyes, allowing Christine's nearness to envelope her. She snuggled in, her head tucked under Christine's chin.

"How's Emma?" Christine asked quietly, startling Willow, who hadn't realized she was awake.

"She's fine." Willow snuggled in closer, her hand caressing Christine's t-shirt-clad back. "I'm so sorry," she whispered. "It's not an excuse, but I'm so afraid, and I lashed out at you. I hope so much that you can forgive me for what I said, what I implied."

Christine was quiet for long moments, making Willow think she'd fallen asleep again.

"You really hurt me," she finally said, fingers playing in Willow's hair.

"I know. God, I know, and I hate myself for it." She pulled back, just enough to be able to look into Christine's face, brows drawn. "I was so worried when you weren't here after Jennifer dropped me off. I even ran to check if your clothes were still here."

Christine smiled softly, shaking her head. "No. Still here. I thought about going, to be honest—" she brought a hand up to still Willow's words, seeing tears begin to fill her eyes, "not because I want to. I thought that maybe all this would be easier if I weren't here, and, well," she sighed, "it *is* because of me that he's doing this. Maybe I'm bad for you and Emma." It broke Christine's heart to say all that, but deep down she knew it was true.

"Don't you ever say that again," Willow said, her voice growing in strength, her heart beginning to beat again after stopping cold at what she thought Christine was going to say. "You're the best thing that's ever happened to me, to *us,* and don't you ever forget that. Okay? Okay?" she said again, louder, when there was no response.

"Okay."

Willow gently traced Christine's features with her fingers. "You truly are the most beautiful woman I've ever seen." She leaned in, placing a soft kiss on those full lips she loved so much. "I love you, and I really am sorry," she said against them, feeling Christine's nod.

"Okay. And thank you." She rolled onto her back, pulling Willow on top of her. She looked up into the face of the woman who'd saved her life and then her heart. "You know," she said, seriously, "we need to work together on this, Willow. We have to stay strong to get through this."

Willow snorted ruefully. "Jennifer said the same thing."

"She's just trying to help, babe. She's not the enemy—"

"I know." Willow cut her off, running a finger lazily down Christine's jaw. "She and I had a talk today, in the car. We came to an understanding of sorts. No matter what I may think of her, ultimately she and I have the same goal, so I won't get in the way again."

"Good. I'm glad to hear it."

"So was she." They both grinned, sharing another small kiss. Willow pulled away slowly, only to lean back in for another. Christine met her, bringing a hand up to the back of Willow's head, holding her in place as the kiss deepened.

"Willow?" Christine whispered into the kiss.

"Hmm?"

"Make me forget this ever happened. I need to know we're really okay."

The pleading in her voice broke Willow's heart, knowing that she had put that doubt there. They had only been together for a few short weeks, certainly not long enough to cement the kind of bond that could easily withstand such an argument. Willow's actions had shaken them both to the core, and she was eager to feel that security again.

Without a word, she moved the hand that had been on Christine's face, burrowing it into the dark hair, deepening the kiss all the more. Christine whimpered softly, her body beginning to ignite.

"We're very much okay," Willow whispered, her mouth moving down Christine's jaw, finding her neck. "Very, very okay."

"I love you."

"I love you, too." Willow gently nudged Christine's shirt aside, kissing and licking the skin she found. "I'm going to show you how much."

Christine's eyes fell closed as she felt her shirt being lifted and hands running over the heated skin of her stomach, then her breasts, making her hiss.

She helped by lifting her upper body, as the shirt flew off into the darkness. Immediately a hot mouth was on her breast. Her hands found Willow's head, holding it to her, needing to feel the connection between the two of them.

It had been utter torture, spending the day feeling so alone and lonely. Most of her life had been spent alone, though she had constantly been surrounded by people.

Christine helped again, lifting her hips as her panties were pushed down her legs. She raised her legs, feeling Willow nestle herself there.

Christine's heart had been so heavy, her mood so dark. It was the worst kind of torture to have been given such happiness, then suddenly have it taken away with a few cruel words.

"Baby," she breathed as she felt herself being opened up by seeking fingers and tongue. "Yes."

She knew it would not be easy for Willow to love her. Trust was such a huge issue in relationships, and Christine had very little of that to go around. She balked and ran at the slightest tarnishing of that bond, though somewhere deep inside she knew it would happen again, as it was human nature.

Christine moaned, feeling Willow moving inside her, a slow, steady rhythm that made her boil.

Sometimes she couldn't help but wonder if maybe she was indeed bad for Willow. How fair was it to expect her to walk on eggshells so often, Christine not trusting her and waiting to be hurt?

"Did I hurt you?" Willow asked, concern lacing her words as she made her way up her lover's body. "Baby, what's wrong?" She petted Christine's hair, looking into her face, the wet trails that were slowly sliding down into Christine's dark hair and ears making her shiver.

Christine was herself shocked, having no idea what was making her emotions rise to the surface and seep from her eyes.

"I'm so sorry." Willow wasn't sure what she'd done, but she had a bad feeling that Christine's emotions stemmed from what had happened outside Nicole's office. She cradled her head, kissing her face, and tried to figure out some way to make it all better.

Christine allowed herself to be held, feeling the dam of her emotions break, and she began to cry, *really* cry.

Yes, part of it was her hurt showing itself, the hurt from the day's events that she hadn't dealt with, but part of it were fears she hadn't let herself entertain. She was offering herself to be a partner and co-parent, and she realized that she was terrified! Yes, she loved Willow and Emma more than anyone or anything she'd ever loved before, but it was such a huge responsibility. What if she failed? What — and this is what tore her up — if she failed either of them? Let Emma down? Or hurt Willow?

The tears continued to come with a vengeance, worrying Willow more and more with each passing minute. She had no idea what to do. She didn't know what was happening.

Feeling like an idiot, Christine finally got herself under control, sniffing like a child, and smiling shyly, deeply embarrassed.

"Sorry," she said, wiping her eyes with the sheet.

"What happened? What's wrong, baby?" Willow asked, so afraid of the answer.

"I don't know. Guess I just got overwhelmed." She tried to pull away a bit, but Willow wouldn't let her.

"Uh uh. You're not going anywhere until you tell me what's going on." Willow looked into her eyes, beseeching. "Please talk to me, Christine."

Christine took several deep breaths, then nodded. Both women moved onto their sides, facing each other. "What if I'm no good at any of this, Willow? I'm so afraid. I'm so afraid that I won't be good for you and Emma. What if I'm no better than my own mother was and no better than my father was to his wife?"

Willow could hear the fear in her voice, and it made her so sad. How could she take that kind of fear away?

"Oh, baby," she said, caressing Christine's cheek. She was relieved when her lover leaned into the touch. "You're nothing like them. You're so loving toward us both. Your parents were the way they were because they were selfish and weak. You're nothing like that. I've never seen anyone so strong, making it through all that you have with flying colors." She smiled with wonder. "You amaze me." She chuckled. "I see the doubt in your eyes, and you can doubt all you want, but when it comes down to it, you're the most amazing person I've ever known. I've learned so much from you."

"From me?"

"Yep. And I think you'll have some pretty profound lessons for Emma, too. You've been there, done that, and you're so wise for it." She cupped Christine's face. "I'm in this for the long haul, baby, but if you're not sure," Willow had to swallow several times in order to keep her own emotions down, "you're not a prisoner here. You can, well, you can go at any time. I won't stop you."

"You'd let me go? Just like that?" Christine was amazed; part of her wanted to pout like a child.

"I'd have to, Christine. If you were going to be happier away from us, then I'd have to say goodbye."

"Wow," she said quietly, stunned. "I think you have us mixed up, because I gotta tell you, I don't know if I could be that generous."

"Well, you know that cheesy old saying? If you love something, set it free, if it comes back, it was meant to be, or something like that. You're the rhymey one, not me."

"I love you," Christine said, leaning in, "and I'm in this for the long haul, too. I just get scared sometimes."

"So do I. Just please talk to me, baby. Don't let it build, please." Willow felt their foreheads touch.

"Can we try again?" Christine whispered.

"Try what again?"

"This..."

Willow felt her world settle in its axis at the extremely passionate kiss that she was caught up in. It didn't take long for her to find where she'd left off.

Willow tapped the steering wheel impatiently as she glanced at the dash clock again.

"Crap," she murmured, finding she had three minutes to complete a twelve-minute drive. For the first time in six years, she was going to be late for work. A mischievous smile swept across her features, as she remembered the reason for it.

How on earth was she supposed to resist Christine's gorgeous body, lying there on the bed, spread out like an offering? Willow had got out of the shower, a towel wrapped around her body, and couldn't resist. The towel had hit the floor with a flop, and she had basically attacked the singer.

Sighing with happiness, she flicked her turn signal, passing the slow dump truck, and then speeding on. She glanced over at her cell phone, sitting with a stack of CDs on the passenger seat of her truck, and contemplated calling ahead, but decided against it.

Glad she'd followed Christine's advice and dressed in her scrubs before she left, Willow was able to pull into staff parking and run toward the building, straight up to her ward.

Willow breezed into the nurses' lounge, jug of water in her hand.

"Linda! Vicki, morning, ladies," she gushed, bending over to shove some things aside, making room for the gallon jug. When she heard no response, she glanced over her shoulder, see her fellow nurses looking anywhere but at her. Frowning, she looked around the small room. Two of the four-seater tables were being used. Orderlies Richard and Terrance sat in the back corner, both looking at her, a grin on Richard's face. Terrance leaned over, to say something, his voice very quiet. Richard's grin grew bigger. His eyes never left Willow.

She looked over to the two women, noting that Linda was looking at her but that Vicki seemed engrossed in the news program that murmured on the ceiling-anchored television.

Something was wrong here. Glancing back at the boys again, she saw both their heads dropping and heard quiet laughter filling the small room.

"Okay," she breathed, a feeling of dread swirling in her gut. She turned back to the counter next to the fridge, grabbing the backpack that she'd set there.

Willow walked down the hall in a daze. She'd been working at Mercy for six years. She'd received awards for excellence every year but one and was a highly respected colleague. Never had she had any trouble making friends or getting along with her co-workers.

She flashed back to her childhood, when her parents moved around every six months to a year, tearing her out of one school to place her in the next. It had been difficult, even painful at times, never being able to make good friends before they were a thing of the past. Willow had often felt the outcast, always the "new girl". It was a feeling she hated and was loathe to relive the way she just had in the break room.

Her day got worse as it wore on, as she overheard whispered words, "left him for a woman" ... "they're living in sin!" ... "that poor baby"...

Willow was hurt more than she could say. She had worked with all those people for so long, they knew her, and she *thought* they were all friends.

Wanting to cry, she hid in the bathroom for a few moments before lunch. She looked at her reflection and saw the stress on her face. Her mind raced, trying to figure out where the information had come from, why were they being so vicious.

"Maureen," she said to her reflection, disappointment gripping her insides. "No."

"I'm sorry," Christine murmured, holding her tighter. "God, I'm sorry." She felt she was to blame for this. If she hadn't been there, Willow wouldn't have to face the ostracism and whispers.

"I thought they were my friends," Willow cried, feeling like a child as she was rocked gently in Christine's lap.

"One thing I've learned, baby, is that you can't rely on most people. They're cruel and petty. And," she continued, kissing the top of Willow's head, "they'll do anything for a good story."

"I feel so stupid." Willow pulled away, sniffling as she swiped her hand across her nose. She laughed bitterly. "I was so excited to tell someone about us, about how happy I am. I really thought I could count on Maureen to be happy for me. So stupid." She shook her head in utter dismay.

"I know. There are some people in the world who will judge you no matter what, Willow." Christine gently brushed some hair away from her tear-streaked face before caressing her cheek. She knew how sensitive Willow was and knew this had to be eating her alive.

She wanted to march down to that hospital and beat the shit out of the staff of the children's ward. Bastards. How could they be so cruel to one of the kindest souls in the world? They weren't deserving of Willow.

"It was so awful, Christine. I felt like wherever I went I was being watched, laughed at. I mean, granted not everyone was involved. But enough were." She felt the tears sting again, as she laid her head against Christine's shoulder. "I feel betrayed. I know it's stupid, but I really do."

"It's not stupid, baby. It's not. But you have to know that this will make you stronger. You can't let them win. I know you," she smiled, "you're stronger than that." Christine watched as Willow pulled away again, looking into her eyes. "When it comes to stuff like this, it may be crude and pessimistic, but you just gotta say fuck 'em."

"Fuck 'em," Willow repeated, nodding. "You're right." She swiped at her eyes, then took the Kleenex that was offered and blew her nose. Tossing the balled-up tissue to the coffee table to join all the others, she nodded again, feeling her resolve strengthen. "Fuck 'em."

"It won't be easy, but in the end, it's worth it. If you let those kind of people get to you, it'll drive you insane."

Willow studied the singer, looking into her eyes and seeing truth there, as well as deep understanding.

"You're so strong," she whispered, cupping Christine's face.

Christine smiled ruefully. "Nah. Just a survivor."

"Same difference." Willow kissed her lightly. "I love you for it."

Christine grinned, holding Willow tighter to her, grateful to have her. The bliss was interrupted by the chirping of her cell phone. One last kiss and Willow headed into the kitchen and Christine answered her phone.

"Hello?" she asked, flipping the phone open.

"So, the domestic diva answers her own phone now, I see," a deep baritone said dryly.

"Who is this?" She sat up from her place on the couch, brows drawn in alarm.

"Come on, Gray, tell me you haven't forgotten me already!"

Her eyes widened in pleasurable surprise. "Larry? Larry Tippen?"

"How you doing, kid?" he said, a smile shining through in his voice.

"I'm great! My God, it's been forever." She stood up, as a host of memories flooded back to her.

"Try twelve years."

"Wow. Has it been that long?" She paced around the room, glancing out of a window before turning and walking the circuit all over again.

"Ain't seen hide nor hair of you since you worked for me. So what's all this I hear about you playing daddy with a cute little blonde in hick country?" he asked. Christine smiled, almost able to see her producer friend lounging back in his oversized leather office chair. His booted feet would be propped up on the massive desk, silver tips catching the Tiffany lamp light. Though it was after eight o'clock his time, his dark glasses would be on, and a turtleneck, gray or black, would be tucked into his Levis.

"I'm happy, Larry," she said simply.

"Glad to hear it, Gray. That's not so easy to do in this business. Speaking of which, what's this B.S. I hear about you retiring?" Anger laced his words now.

"I had enough, man. I couldn't do it anymore. I gave all I had to give, did my time, I'm finished," Christine said, waiting for the tirade that would surely follow her simple explanation.

"Hmm. Well, I have to admit I'm glad to see you get away from that rock and roll shit you used to do. It wasn't you, never was. Why, after what you composed for that short of mine, I never understood why you didn't go where it was obvious your heart was. Hell, you helped me win at Sundance, for Christ's sake."

"I know, Larry. I know." She smiled at the memory, seeing her friend's face as he took home the prestigious honor.

"Listen, kid, I'm calling because I want you for a project I'm working on."

"Oh, Larry, I don't know." Christine shook her head, running a hand through her hair.

"Sure you do. You can work from your little love nest there and actually create something with some meaning."

"Larry, I'm retired..."

"Bullshit, Christine!"

She was taken aback by the vehemence in his voice. She stood there, stunned.

"You are too goddamn talented to let it die. You got tired of what you were doing, who wouldn't? Now let your real creative genius come out. I wanted you to work for me for years, but that prick Knowles never would allow it. He's dead, so now I'm asking. Compose for me, Christine. Please. I've got a large budget to work with here and some major players in this project. I want you, and only you, and I *won't* take no for an answer," he paused, allowing his anger, which had surprised him as well Christine, subside. Finally the musician spoke.

"Can I think about it?"

"Don't take too long. I've got the green light on this, and I need to move. Call me and we'll discuss contracts."

Christine pulled the phone away from her ear, flipping it closed. She'd always hated that Larry never said goodbye. When he was finished talking, the conversation was over.

Tossing the tiny phone to the couch, she sighed, staring out into the night. She had a big decision to make, though she already knew what her heart wanted the answer to be. She would give herself a few days to think. This work would be good for her, she knew, but also it meant putting herself out there in a new way. She felt vulnerable just thinking about it.

"Damn, it, Larry," she whispered. "Do you have any idea what you're asking?"

Willow felt almost sick as she sat at the long, polished table. Nicole sat to her right, as the acting attorney, and Jennifer to her left, as her assistant. Feeling her palms sweating, she rubbed them against her skirt-clad thighs. She absently brushed a shaggy strand of hair aside, then clasped her hands on the table before her.

"Are you ready?" Jennifer whispered, leaning into her. Willow nodded, swallowing nervously. "Good. Kevin and his attorney are coming in now."

Willow fought the urge to shoot visual daggers at her ex-husband as he made his way down the aisle of the near-empty courtroom. Christine sat next to Myra in the gallery, one row behind the wooden partition. Kevin stared at her angrily. Christine didn't flinch, giving as good as she got.

Knowing Willow would be a mess, she leaned forward and placed a hand on her lover's shoulder. Her hand was covered by a smaller, sweaty one and squeezed in acknowledgement. Sitting back, Christine crossed one leg over the other and settled in.

Willow watched Kevin sit down at the other table, smoothing his tie as he did so. He looked past his attorney, meeting her gaze. Raw hatred burned in eyes that had once only looked at her in love.

She held his gaze, proud that it was Kevin who looked away first. It was a small victory, but one she needed.

"All rise, the honorable Judge Malcolm Howard presiding," the bailiff said dryly. The seven people in the court room stood as a heavy-set man, robed in black, stepped up behind his desk, motioning for everyone to sit as he did so himself.

Willow swallowed as she sat, wincing as her chair scraped noisily against the polished wood flooring beneath her feet. She felt a hand on her arm. Glancing over, she saw Jennifer's brown eyes, silently communicating that everything would be okay. She nodded, wishing she had the same confidence.

"Alright, let's see what we've got here," the judge said, using one hand to tug half-shelled glasses onto his bulbous nose and the other to flip open the case file before him. "Kevin Bowman versus Willow Bowman for the custody of Emma Christine Bowman, aged four and a half months." He glanced up. "Are both parties currently in attendance?"

"Yes, your honor," Nicole said, rising just long enough to speak.

"We are, your honor," Kevin's attorney echoed, smoothing her skirt before she sat, clearing her throat, which sounded like a firecracker in the quiet room.

"Good, good. Let's proceed," the judge said, removing the glasses. "Mrs. Jamison, why don't you start," he said, indicating Kevin's attorney with a flick of his wrist.

"Yes, your honor." Kevin's attorney stood, glancing down at the laptop that was open on the table before her. "Your honor, my client is asking for full custody of his daughter, Emma Bowman. He feels he is a much more stable parent and can provide a nurturing, loving, more *moral* environment for the child."

Willow again felt the hand on her arm as her blood began to boil. *How could he?*

"Continue," the judge encouraged. There was a dramatic pause, the only sound being the court reporter finishing her last few clicks before her hands rested, poised millimeters above her keyboard.

"It has come to my client's attention that his ex-wife, Willow Bowman, has been sharing her residence with a woman who had a drug habit, lived on the streets, and prostituted her own body when she was barely out of childhood herself." Carol Jamison waited for this information to sink in before continuing. "Kevin Bowman feels it is in the best interest of his child to remove her from such an environment."

"Thank you, Mrs. Jamison. Ms. Martinez?" The judge's eyes moved to Willow's table, looking expectantly at her "lead counsel".

"Thank you, your honor." Nicole stood, looking sophisticated and confident in a charcoal gray pantsuit with an open-collared silk blouse. "Your honor, my client, Willow Bowman, has been a loving mother to little Emma since the day of conception. The baby weighed in at a healthy seven pounds, fourteen ounces, proving that Willow was diligent during her pregnancy, eating healthily and living a healthy lifestyle, leading to the uneventful birth of her first child. I might add, your honor, that it was during this time that the marriage was dissolved, largely as a result of Kevin Bowman's refusal to accept and support the pregnancy or even acknowledge his responsibilities to his unborn child."

Willow felt herself trembling, fear, anger, and hurt coursing through her veins and turning her blood cold. She clutched the gold, heart-shaped locket Christine had given her the night before with Emma's picture tucked inside.

"Yes, your honor, it is public record that Christine Gray, loving and contributing member of the Bowman household, has had problems in her past. It is also public knowledge that Ms. Gray managed to remove herself from a destructive life on the streets and become a world-renowned recording artist. She is not only emotionally capable and willing to help parent baby Emma, but financially capable, too. More importantly—"

"It's wrong!" Kevin exclaimed, trying to stand, but his attorney stopped him with a warning hand on his arm.

"Your attorney had her chance to speak, Mr. Bowman," Judge Howard warned, his voice booming in the large space.

"As I was saying your honor," Nicole said dryly, sparing a fleeting glance for Kevin's attorney, "more importantly...Willow Bowman is fully capable of performing her duties as Emma's mother even without the emotional or financial support of Ms. Gray. She has an established career in pediatric nursing, and she owns her own home." Nicole paused, looking the judge in the eye. "She kept this child, your honor, despite Mr. Bowman's encouragement for her to have an abortion. Willow has *always* wanted this child, and she chose to walk away from her marriage rather than lose her. She has raised Emma to the best of her considerable ability and will continue to do so."

As Nicole sat down, Willow breathed a small sigh of relief, feeling for perhaps the first time that maybe she had a chance. Heck, Nicole had convinced *her*.

Judge Howard looked to Kevin. "Mr. Bowman, would you like to add anything, sir?"

"Yes, your honor, I would." Kevin buttoned the bottom two buttons of his suit jacket as he stood, clearing his throat. "I made mistakes in the past, your honor, acting childishly when I found out about Willow's pregnancy. I admit that, and I can never take it back, no matter what I might say. I know that. But, your honor," his voice softened, filled with wistful words, "since the morning in March when my daughter was born," he took a deep breath, shaking his head, "I've thought of nothing else but holding her in my arms and being the father that I was too stupid to realize I wanted to be."

Kevin looked at the judge with big, puppy-dog eyes. "Please, your honor. I want my daughter raised right, in a good Christian home, with a father and a mother. I'm getting married in a couple months, and I'll be able to provide that. Willow won't. Thank you, sir."

Willow just about flew out of her seat at Kevin's pitiful excuse of a plea. It took both Jennifer and Nicole's hands on her thighs to keep her in her seat.

"Ms. Bowman? You may speak, now."

"Thank you, your honor." Willow took several deep breaths, trying to keep her calm. "It's pretty simple what I have to say, sir. I love my daughter more than I can tell you. I'm sure you're a father, sir, so you know what it's like, waking up each day to see the miracle."

She smiled, thinking of Emma, her smile, the cute little noises she made as she tried to stick her toes in her mouth.

"I will do anything for this child. Heck, I even gave up coffee for her during my pregnancy, and that, your honor, was quite a sacrifice, trust me." She grinned, then turned serious. "All kidding aside, sir, I wanted Emma from the moment I discovered I was pregnant. And Ms. Gray has been there for me every step of the way. Yes, Christine Gray has had some problems in her past, sir, but she's overcome them. She helped me save my house when I was about to lose everything after the divorce and she has been a constant in both mine and Emma's lives."

Willow swallowed, feeling the weight of the situation on her shoulders. It was hard to stand up straight, let alone hold her head high as she pleaded for the court to not take her daughter away from her.

"Your honor," she continued softly. "I've been with that beautiful little girl since the moment she was born. I was there for her first cry, her first breath, her first smile. Kevin has not only NOT changed a single poopy diaper, but he hasn't bothered to try to see Emma or to provide for her in any other way. Please don't take her from me for no good reason, sir. That would be a crime. Thank you."

As Willow sat, Jennifer stood. "Your honor, if I may, I'd like to add for the record that Emma was born on the afternoon of February 22 and not some 'morning in March'."

It was the longest wait of her life, each second that ticked away on the clock seeming as long as a full day. Willow paced, heels clicking on the highly polished linoleum of the outer chamber, while Kevin stayed near the elevators with his camp, avoiding eye contact with her. Finally, the large, double doors opened, and the bailiff appeared.

"Please come back inside," he said, prompting a race for the doors before he disappeared into the courtroom.

Taking her seat again, hearing the others take theirs, Willow clutched her locket, her heart pounding in time with the throb in her head. Breathlessly, she waited for the judge to take his seat again.

"I have come to a decision involving the care and custody of Emma Christine Bowman," he said, his voice somber as he looked over his glasses at both parties. "You both having given truly moving testimony today, and both have valid claims to this child. However," he tossed the glasses aside, his bushy brows drawing together, "a decision has to be made. Someone will walk out of this courtroom today happy. And someone will not."

The court waited, holding its breath, as the judge paused.

"Mr. Bowman," he turned his attention to Kevin. Willow felt Christine's presence behind her as she waited to hear what the judge had to say. "You bring up some valid points here today. This court has had an opportunity to look over the records and claims you have presented, however, and — while I personally may not agree with the lifestyle that Ms. Bowman and Ms. Gray have chosen to pursue, it is not the purpose of this court to pass judgment on that. Therefore, this court finds no moral wrongdoing in the raising of Emma."

Willow felt her breath stop with her heart, afraid to hope that the judge was saying what she thought he was saying.

"In fact, upon inspecting records from Emma's physician, a Doctor Brenda McHale, it is clear that Emma is doing well in all aspects. She has been very well taken care of. She is happy and healthy.

"You are the biological father of this child, however, and that means you have a legal right to spend time with her." The judge picked up his gavel. Willow was about to break into pieces, waiting for his decision.

"This court awards full custody of Emma Christine Bowman, aged four and a half months, to Willow Bowman, the child's legal mother and guardian. Kevin Bowman, said child's father, will have visitation rights, to be worked out with a court-certified mediator. In addition to those rights, he also has responsibilities. It is my finding that Willow Bowman is entitled to child support payments, the amount of which will also be determined at a later date."

Willow cried out as the gavel cracked, finalizing the decision. She was stunned, tears of utter joy and gratitude stinging her eyes.

"And Mr. Bowman — a word of advice," the judge continued. "For God's sake, man, learn the birth date of your daughter. Court adjourned."

Willow was in a daze as she was gathered into a tight embrace, her head coming to rest against the shoulder she knew belonged to Christine.

"You did it, baby," was whispered into her ear, as soft lips brushed against her forehead.

"Oh, God," Willow breathed, realization dawning. Her arms wrapped around Christine's waist, pulling her tight against her. The stress and fear of the past month finally oozed out of her, to be replaced by hope and a sharp excitement for the future.

"Nice job, ladies," Jennifer said, pride evident in her voice. Willow pulled away from Christine and turned to the attorney.

"I can't thank you enough, Jennifer," she said, taking Jennifer's hands in her own. The attorney smirked.

"You don't have to. Just pay my bill." She winked, squeezed Willow's hands, and pulled away, gathering her briefcase. "Back to civilization I go." She turned to Christine. "Tell Sandra hello for me, won't you?"

"You got it." Christine watched her go, then turned back to Willow, who was hugging and thanking Nicole. For the first time in her life, Christine felt complete. No matter what the world had to throw at her and Willow, they'd be able to handle it. She had a family, a real, honest-to-God family, and there was no way in hell she was going to let it go.

She had something to fight for again.

Epilogue

"Christine! Over here! Christine, who are you wearing? This way, please!"

Christine squinted slightly. The vast number of flashes going off at once was almost a welcome sight. At least this time the photographers were supposed to be there. It was nice to know she was still wanted.

"You okay?" she asked quietly, glancing down at her date.

"Oh, yeah," Willow breathed, "peachy."

Christine smiled again, taking in the absolute beauty that was on her arm. The Vera Wang creation, made especially for Willow, hugged her incredible body and its classic lines perfectly — while providing a hint of cleavage to make it sexy. The green velvet brought out her eyes to perfection.

"Well, you said you wanted us to come out with a bang," Christine smirked.

"Yeah, but at the Oscars?" Willow hissed in response. Christine chuckled, seeing the reporter from Entertainment Tonight in their path. They were led toward her, beginning their rounds of all the major networks and shows covering the event outside the Kodak.

"Christine! You look absolutely gorgeous, tonight!" Melissa Haggerty gushed, holding her microphone up for comment.

"Thank you, Melissa. You look beautiful, yourself," Christine said, turning on the charm.

"Oh, thank you!" The reporter got down to business. "So this must be a bit surreal for you. From the Grammys to an Oscar nomination for best score in a film. How do you feel about all this?" The reporter waved her arm toward the screaming fans and the other celebrities making their way down the red carpet.

"Well, you know, just another day in the office," Christine said with a grin. Melissa chuckled.

"Indeed. Good luck tonight."

"Thank you."

Willow watched in awe as Christine handled the press and fans with grace and aplomb. She was breathtaking in her fitted black floor-length halter dress. When she had stepped into that dress in their hotel suite and asked Willow to zip it for her, Willow's mouth had gone dry. She had never been truly speechless before that moment.

Now, walking hand in hand with her, Willow was overcome with pride and love.

The inside of the huge theater was beautiful. Willow wanted so badly to look around, but decided it might not look that cool to gawk like some yokel — especially when you were sitting next to Michael Douglas and Catherine Zeta-Jones.

"Out of your league" — tonight the phrase was hitting home as never before for Willow. She felt like a hick from the sticks, while Christine was putting on the charm and talking to people, the likes of whom Willow had only seen on a movie screen. She swallowed hard and sat still, watching Billy Crystal in his hilarious opening.

Christine hadn't felt nervous at an awards ceremony since her first win at the Grammys, more than a decade ago. For the most part, she thought they were pompous and ostentatious. But tonight, for some reason she was filled with a nervous energy and nausea. She wasn't sure why. It was as if she didn't so much want to win as she wanted Willow to be proud of her.

She glanced over at her partner sitting in the next seat, beautiful and utterly enthralled with the performance on stage. Christine smiled, feeling silly, but smiling all the same. Willow turned to her and smiled back, squeezing Christine's hand as the presenters began to read the nominees.

"Here we go," Willow whispered, nervous enough for both of them. Christine nodded, turning back to the stage. She heard her name called. A round of applause deafened the house, and the cameras focused on her. Her smiling face appeared on the huge screen off to the side of the stage, her name and the name of the film underneath it.

"And the winner is," the presenter said, his co-presenter fumbling with the envelope. They both looked at the results, and together read, "Christine Gray, 'Twilight'!"

The crowd was on its feet, and Willow was openly crying. Christine looked at her, and her world slowed down. She felt the pressure of Willow's hand in hers, squeezing, as she rose and headed to the aisle. Around her people smiled and cheered their approval and congratulations. She was sure she nodded, or smiled, or acknowledged them in some way as she made her way up the aisle, her heart pounding in her ears, a journey that seemed to take forever.

Time didn't fully return to normal until she felt the weight of the statue in her hand. Then all of her senses returned, full blast — the brilliance of colored lights gleaming on its golden surface, the roar of applause, the softness of a congratulatory kiss on her cheek from the presenters, and then the sound of her own voice.

"Wow," she breathed quietly, though it erupted from the microphone before her, filling the theater. Polite chuckles followed. "Um, I know that everyone usually gets up here with a list as long as my arm of people to thank." This prompted more chuckles. "I don't have that, I'm afraid. The people who helped make this possible already know I'm grateful — because they're still alive!" She leaned in close to the microphone, "Larry."

Larry Tippen laughed loudly, his smile about to split his face wide open.

"It's been an interesting road, my life, and I'm grateful to have traveled it." She looked at the statue again, thinking how much she wanted to give it to Emma when she grew up. "The songs I wrote came from my deep love for my art, from a deep belief in my passion — music. They wouldn't have been possible, though, without Willow."

Willow found it impossible to see through her tears. She could feel Christine's eyes on her, however. She brought her fingers to her lips, kissing them, then threw that kiss to the stage. Christine smiled at the gesture.

"Willow Bowman and our daughter Emma, that's what life is all about. They've given me a reason to love music again. This is dedicated to them." She lifted the Oscar in victory. "Thank you."

Kim Pritekel is a Colorado native, and has been writing since the age of 9. She is currently working on other books, as well as projects as co-owner of ASP Films, LLC. She can be reached at either XenaNut@hotmail.com or kpritekel@officialaspfilms.com

Other works by Kim Pritekel:

First

ISBN: 978 - 1 - 933720 - 00 - 5 (1-933720-00-X)

Emily Thomas is a successful New York attorney who has left her childhood back in Pueblo, Colorado behind her. She lives well and is happy with her partner, Rebecca. All of that changes with a simple phone call from her brother.

Beth Sayers was Emily's best friend from the time they were children until the day Beth left Emily stunned, confused, and alone in a college dorm room ten years later.

Emily must delve back into her past and into a friendship that had fallen apart, taking her love and trust with it

Lessons

ISBN: 978 - 1 - 933720 - 08 - 1 (1-933720-08-5)

Chase Marin is an 18 year old girl filled with more confusion than common sense. Daughter of successful parents, and equally successful big sister, Chase is expected to go to college at the University of Arizona and prove herself. How can she do that when she doesn't even know herself?

Dagny Robertson is everything that the Marin's would want in a daughter- too bad Dagny's own parents don't even know their one and only child, born from their intense love, exists. Now, Dagny works on her graduate degree while acting as TA in Psych 101.

Can this older woman, once worshipped babysitter of a lost eight year old girl, help her find herself?

Available at your favorite bookstore.